YOUR LIFE
HAS BEEN
DELAYED

YOUR LIFE
HAS BEEN
DELAYED

MICHELLE I. MASON

BLOOMSBURY

NEW YORK   LONDON   OXFORD   NEW DELHI   SYDNEY

BLOOMSBURY YA
Bloomsbury Publishing Inc., part of Bloomsbury Publishing Plc
1385 Broadway, New York, NY 10018

BLOOMSBURY and the Diana logo are trademarks of Bloomsbury Publishing Plc

First published in the United States of America in August 2021 by Bloomsbury YA

Bloomsbury books may be purchased for business or promotional use.
For information on bulk purchases please contact Macmillan Corporate and
Premium Sales Department at specialmarkets@macmillan.com

Library of Congress Cataloging-in-Publication Data
Names: Mason, Michelle I., author.
Title: Your life has been delayed / by Michelle I. Mason.
Description: New York : Bloomsbury, 2021.
Summary: Jenny takes off on a flight in 1995 but lands twenty-five years later, leaving her to
grapple with a whole new world: one where family and friends have moved on without her.
Identifiers: LCCN 2020056066 (print) | LCCN 2020056067 (e-book)
ISBN 978-1-5476-0408-1 (hardcover) • ISBN 978-1-5476-0409-8 (e-book)
Subjects: CYAC: Time travel—Fiction.
Classification: LCC PZ7.1.M3762 Yo 2021 (print) | LCC PZ7.1.M3762 (e-book) |
DDC [Fic]—dc23
LC record available at https://lccn.loc.gov/2020056066
LC ebook record available at https://lccn.loc.gov/2020056067

Book design by Jeanette Levy
Typeset by Westchester Publishing Services
Printed and bound in the U.S.A.
2 4 6 8 10 9 7 5 3 1

To find out more about our authors and books visit
www.bloomsbury.com and sign up for our newsletters.

For Greg. All the best things in this century have happened with you.

YOUR LIFE
HAS BEEN
DELAYED

CHAPTER ONE

I check my watch for the seventh time, willing the white-haired man with the crisp tie to finish hogging the pay phone so I can return Steve's call before my flight boards. Three minutes and fourteen seconds later, he hangs up and wastes precious seconds hoisting his briefcase onto his rolling suitcase before finally striding away. I dump my backpack and purse on the floor, my phone card ready. I punch in the 800 number, wait for the second dial tone, then put in Steve's number.

After four rings that take forever, a woman answers. "Graham residence."

"Hi, Mrs. Graham. It's Jenny. Is Steve home?"

Please be home. Please be near the phone.

"He's right here, Jenny."

I tap my toe, picturing Steve ambling into the kitchen, a baseball cap covering most of his dark blond hair, which always curls at his collar.

"Hey, Jenny!"

My heart tip-taps at his familiar voice. "Grandpa said you called last night? I'm sorry I didn't call you back sooner. He forgot to mention it until we were on the way to the airport."

"Yeah . . . you're at the airport now?" He sounds surprised, like it's weird I called him from here.

"Uh-huh. I'll be in St. Louis in a little over three hours."

"You have one minute remaining," an electronic voice interrupts.

Already? I thought I had several minutes left on this card. "So what did you call about?"

"Huh?"

He's wasting our minute. "Last night. What did you call about?"

"Oh. Just, you know, it'd been a couple days, so I missed talking to you."

I sag against the wall, my muscles turning liquid as a grin takes over my face. "I miss you too."

"And I was thinking, when you get back tonight, maybe we can finally—"

A persistent beep cuts Steve off.

"Noooo!" I stare at the black receiver in my hand, as if it might finish Steve's sentence. Maybe we can finally what? *Kiss?* Because the sad truth is we've been dating for two months, but the closest his lips have gotten to mine was the night before I left, when he leaned in, a panicked look crossing his face, and sideswiped to my cheek.

Why, stupid phone card, did you cut Steve off? Not that I really thought he'd announce plans to kiss me over the phone, but then I wouldn't be left agonizing over that unfinished sentence for the next three and a half hours.

The airport intercom signals a message. "We are now boarding

Mid-States Airways Flight 237 from New York to St. Louis at Gate D2."

I replace the evil phone on its hook, gather my stuff, and trudge toward my gate. Standing in the waiting area, I'm envious of the passengers hugging and chatting with family members before they board. I wish Grandma and Grandpa Waters had come inside with me, but Grandpa had a doctor's appointment, so they dropped me off at the door with instructions like "Don't talk to strangers!" and "Don't lose your luggage claim tag." Maybe I should have used my couple of minutes on the phone with Steve to ask *him* to pick me up when I land. Then I could run into his arms and lay one on him like in a movie.

I snort. As if I'd have the guts to do that. My best friend, Angie, on the other hand . . . She says Steve is so shy it's amazing he even asked me out in the first place, and it's up to me to make the first move. But I'm not like her. Anytime I think about leaning in and kissing *him*, I'm overwhelmed by a deluge of thoughts about *why* Steve hasn't kissed *me* yet. What if it's more than him being shy? What if he likes hanging out with me but has realized he doesn't like me *that way* and doesn't know how to say it? What if I do kiss him and he's embarrassed because I rushed him? Or I'm horrible at it and he's so disgusted he never calls me again? The whole sum of my pre-Steve kissing experience is my freshman homecoming date missing and landing awkwardly on the corner of my mouth for a millisecond. We never went out again.

I barely register moving through the line, showing the flight attendant my boarding pass, and making my way onto the plane.

3

As I maneuver into seat 12B, my overloaded backpack makes me stumble toward the college-age guy in the window seat, giving him an up-close view of the "I Heart NY" logo plastered across my chest.

"Nice shirt," he says.

I'm glad his smirk is more *you're lame* than *I'm a creepy guy staring at your boobs*, but like he has any room to comment. His T-shirt features a giant hand, palm out, saying, "Talk to the hand."

I smile tightly, answering, "I love New York."

I'm not ashamed to be wearing a T-shirt available in every corner souvenir shop—well, really, even on the street, if you don't mind the letters peeling off the first time you wash it, as happened to my younger brother, Bradley, after our last visit. It's part of my three-phase strategy to convince my parents Columbia is the best choice for my future. Grandma Waters took me to visit the campus, and despite its location in what my parents consider the most dangerous city in the world (news flash, Mom and Dad: St. Louis has a higher crime rate than New York), I swear my eyes turned into cartoon hearts. So I don't care if my shirt is cheesy; it's Phase One of Operation Columbia.

I retrieve my spiral notebook from my backpack, dislodging a large bottle of hair spray, which falls out and starts rolling away. I catch it, stuff it back in with everything else, and jam the bag under the seat in front of me.

"It doesn't look like anyone's sitting in the aisle seat," window guy says. "You could move over."

The flight attendant approaches, checking to ensure we're all buckled up and our carry-on items are tucked safely away. She's

4

young, her chestnut hair in a neat French twist and her uniform all pressed. She's probably fresh out of flight attendant school.

"What if she checks our tickets?"

"Really?" Window guy gestures at the flight attendant, who is now holding up the laminated card with emergency information. "She doesn't care where you sit."

I mean, I don't *want* to be right next to your-cheesy-shirt's-worse-than-mine guy, and it's probably silly to be so worried about it, but the idea of defying the directions printed on my official boarding pass causes my eye to twitch. Ignoring him, I listen to the flight attendant give the safety instructions, and, like my parents always do before we take off, I send up a brief prayer for the pilots; I can them see through the open door to the cockpit, making final preparations. It's more out of habit than an actual fear our flight will crash midair, but you never know what will happen when you're thirty thousand feet above the ground. Returning to my notebook, I click my pen. Out. In. Out. In.

Okay. Phase Two.

Usually I write the headline last, but I already know this one:

COLUMBIA UNIVERSITY BEST PREPARES STUDENTS FOR JOURNALISM CAREERS
By Jenny Waters

Even in my own notebook, writing an editorial for my parents, it gives me a thrill to see my byline.

NEW YORK, Aug. 2, 1995—Students across the country are flocking to Columbia University's journalism program

5

"Hey, did you know if you have headphones you can listen to the pilots talk to air traffic control during the whole flight?"

Sighing, I click my pen again and set it pointedly on my notebook before turning toward window guy. His pale, pockmarked face is lit up like Bradley's when he rents a new Super Nintendo game from Blockbuster.

I just want to write my persuasive article, but clearly that's not happening. "Is that so?"

"Yeah." He nods enthusiastically, moppy hair flopping in his eyes. "It's the bomb!"

Should he use that phrase on a plane?

"You plug your headphones into this port here"—he demonstrates—"and switch the dial to channel five."

Since I can tell he won't shut up anytime soon, I widen my eyes and lean in slightly, a technique I use when interviewing people for my school paper, the *Parkwood Press*. It never fails to make them feel important and interesting. "What sort of information do you hear?"

He puffs up. "Oh, you know. Like what runway to go down and where we are in line to take off. Dude, it's awesome."

"Sounds like it." *Not.*

I wonder if he gives this spiel to whoever's sitting next to him on every flight. I didn't know plane groupies even existed.

"And sometimes they talk about changing weather!"

Um, no thanks.

He taps my notebook. "You should write about that instead."

I scrunch my nose, irritated he was reading over my shoulder. "I'll think about it."

Phase Two will have to wait. I can't write with an audience;

it'll totally screw with my mind. "I'm going to read. But you enjoy your"—I wave at the headphone port—"pilot chatter."

The side of his mouth quirks up, but before he can give me additional plane facts, I'm hunched over, stuffing my notebook away and pulling out a romance novel. Thankfully, the plane is taxiing away from the gate, so he puts on his headphones, the big red foam stark against his pale skin, blissfully closing his eyes.

Whatever floats your boat—or, I guess, flies your plane.

Three hours later, the pilot announces we're approaching St. Louis. The lights flicker, sort of like when there's a storm outside at home; only when I glance out the window, the sun is shining. Weird.

"What's going on?" Plane groupie guy stares at the headphone port, then peers outside too.

I poke his shoulder. He jumps and turns toward me, uncovering his right ear. "What?"

I motion toward his headphone. "Is something happening?"

He inhales, and for a moment I think he plans to brush me off, but then he bends toward me and words spill out faster than I can process them. "St. Louis air control doesn't have our squawk. They've asked the pilot for our call sign. The tower doesn't have our flight plan. They want our IFR clearance."

It's like he's speaking a different language. At least I know what a flight plan is. Well, sort of. "Translation, please?"

He sighs loudly.

Excuse my lack of plane knowledge. I bet he has a room full of model airplanes back home.

7

"Every time a plane takes off, it's given a four-digit code called a squawk," he says. "It tells the air controllers on the ground everything about the plane—its navigation equipment, landing requirements, yada, yada, yada—and it's all recorded on a strip of paper. It doesn't make sense that the St. Louis controllers don't have our strip. How'd they lose it between New York and here?"

He can't expect *me* to answer, so I shrug. "What about the other stuff you mentioned?"

"The clearance has to do with being cleared to fly, including at certain altitudes. They don't just let any planes up in that airspace." He holds up a hand to indicate he's listening. "They're asking the pilots to contact a flight service station."

"Is that uncommon?" I glance around the cabin. Nobody else seems concerned. The elderly white couple across the aisle are dozing, the woman curved toward the man with her cheek against his shoulder like it's fit there perfectly for decades. A businessman is studying a file. A woman in a long, flowered dress a couple of rows behind me is reading *People* magazine.

"I've never been on a flight where this has happened before." Plane groupie sounds equal parts excited and nervous. His gaze darts toward the cockpit, where two flight attendants stand outside the door that's now closed. They have their heads bent together; the younger one is gnawing on her fingernails. I suddenly feel a distinct urge to do the same.

"If they can't identify our plane, they won't, like, shoot us out of the sky or anything, right?" I lean over plane groupie to peer out the window, scanning the clouds for fighter jets.

"I don't think so. We are on a commuter airline."

"You don't *think* so?"

He purses his lips and tilts his head as if listening. "It's weird. They really can't find our plane. They—"

When he stops abruptly, I sit back. "What?"

He rubs his chin. "The air controller just cut off the feed and told the pilot to hold. Now the original air controller is back. He's giving instructions . . ."

I curl my hands into fists. If he's playing a joke on me, I will whack him with my overstuffed backpack.

"He says they've identified us but don't have a gate, so once we land, we're being instructed to taxi to a side runway and they'll pull up airstairs."

The pilot comes on and explains there's been a mix-up with our gate and we'll be disembarking in the sunny ninety-degree weather. His explanation doesn't sound ominous at all.

But two minutes later, plane groupie gasps. "They turned off channel five!"

He reaches up and jabs the call button, but even I know it's too late for that. The nose of the plane is angled sharply downward, indicating our final descent.

Plane groupie swears, and I don't bother asking him additional questions. I'm relieved when the wheels touch the runway. No matter the drama with the air controllers, we're here. We're home.

My seatmate, obviously not as reassured, presses his nose against the window. "Alaska Airlines? What's a plane from Alaska Airlines doing here?"

This guy just won't stop. "Maybe you can ask when we get off."

Which will happen very soon, thank God.

"But where's TWA? The airport should be full of TWA planes. And more Mid-States Airways planes."

I don't care about TWA planes. All I want is to get off this plane and away from this guy, who I'm starting to believe is on a mission to turn what's probably a minor misunderstanding into a huge conspiracy. I mean, I didn't actually hear any of this stuff he claims happened over the radio. Maybe he made it all up. The flight attendants could've been talking about running low on peanuts for the next flight.

I imagine walking into the terminal, my parents and Bradley waiting for me at the gate. Then once we get home, I can call Steve and find out what he meant to say. Hopefully something along the lines of *When you get back tonight, maybe we can finally lock lips in a dramatic, choir-of-angels-singing kiss.*

Conspiracy guy continues to mutter beside me, pointing out inconsistencies in our landing procedure, but I ignore him. I bet he's majoring in aviation science or something and he's just all in a twist because we aren't following expected protocols. The plane glides to a stop, and the pilot instructs us to wait while they attach the airstairs.

I crane my neck to see what they're doing outside. There are a *lot* of people running around on the tarmac. A pale guy holds up a small rectangular device, a little smaller than the graphing calculator I had to buy for my math class last year, but flatter. It's almost like he's aiming it at the plane, but for the life of me I can't figure out why, and a tingle of unease starts at the base of my spine. A Hispanic man in a suit rushes over and grabs the device from the other man.

By now, other passengers are starting to murmur around us.

I'm unable to distinguish specific words or phrases; it's all an indistinct buzz. I'm too focused on the action outside and the sense that something isn't right about what I'm seeing. I can't pinpoint what it is, but the people attaching the airstairs and milling around the plane just look *wrong*.

A bus pulls up at the base of the stairs, and the pilot announces it's time for us to disembark. His voice sounds off too. The tingle trickles up my spine.

We're twelve rows back, so it doesn't take long for us to reach the front of the plane. I've only flown a few times, but usually the pilot stands at the front and wishes you a good day as you exit. Not today. He and the copilot are whispering furiously. The pilot has taken off his hat, and his gray-flecked brown hair is sticking up in crazy clumps as if he's been yanking it. As I pass the cockpit, he points out the window and says loud and clear, "That terminal wasn't there yesterday!"

CHAPTER TWO

Something is very, very wrong.

I whip around, my pulse skipping erratically, but I can't see what the pilot's pointing toward.

Someone bumps me from behind. "Excuse me, honey."

I stumble. "Did you hear that?"

The elderly lady stares blankly, focused on clutching her purse close. Her skin is so paper-thin and pale her veins shine through. "Hear what?"

Obviously not.

We exit the plane into blinding sunlight. The metal railing of the airstairs is scorching hot. The people on the ground—who still look wrong—stare at me with wide, unblinking eyes as if *I'm* a freak.

Many of the people wear uniforms like I'd expect to see on ground crews, sort of like jumpsuits, bright yellow. But others are in black pants and blue button-down shirts with gold badges. I don't think they're police officers, so they must be airport security. I can't make out the letters on the shoulders of their uniforms before I'm herded onto a bus, the sort you use to get to long-term parking. I search for plane groupie so I can ask him more about what exactly he overheard on the radio, but he's not on this shuttle.

I move to the back and sit beside a window, removing my backpack and stuffing it between my feet. The bus is stiflingly hot, a sharp contrast to the plane. I dig in my purse for a scrunchy and pull my hair into a ponytail. I'm sure my cheeks are flushed. My fingers itch to pull out my notebook and start writing everything down, to record it all. Facts aren't real to me when they're only in my head. I need them on paper, etched onto those pale blue lines with my ballpoint pen, but it's crowded here, and by the time I get it out I'd be packing it back up.

The passengers seated to my right murmur about how odd it is they didn't take us to a jetway. I glance out the window and see the pilot and copilot talking to the man who confiscated the calculator-looking thing, as well as one of the uniformed security men. The bus pulls away without the pilots. Too bad. They're the key primary sources. I could have gotten some additional facts and written about it for the *Press*. But I guess this is all about to be over anyway. Soon we'll be in the terminal, and I can go home.

Except instead of taking us to a gate or baggage claim, the bus stops in front of a door that says "Authorized Personnel Only." We all get off and line up at the door, murmuring amongst ourselves. The second bus unloads behind us, and then the door opens. A blond woman and a hulking Mr. T–looking security guard usher us inside, and I can finally read the letters on the guard's shoulder: TSA. I'm about to ask what that is, but the woman's unnerving gaze stops me. She opens her mouth like she intends to single me out. I pause, but her eyes slide past me, and I move into a large meeting room with everyone else. A dry-erase board covers a whole wall, and a projector hangs from the ceiling. Blinds are closed over the windows, shutting out the light.

The door clicks shut behind us, and the woman leans against it. She's dressed quite casually for someone I assume works in the airport, in clingy knit pants and a loose top that hangs almost to her knees. It looks like an outfit you'd wear to kick back on the couch and watch soaps.

"What are we doing here?" says the businessman I saw reading files on the plane. He glances at his watch. "I have a meeting in one hour."

The woman bites her lip. She steps away from the door. I can't tell if she's intimidated or worried.

"I'm sorry, sir," she says. "Mr. Fernandez, the airport director, will be here shortly to explain."

The businessman looks around the room. "Do you have a phone I can use to call and let them know I'll be late?"

She pales. "Not in here, sir. If you can please be patient."

"No phone in a conference room?" He bends down, peering under the table. He reaches underneath and pulls out a wire with an empty phone plug at the end. "What are you trying to pull?"

He's a domino, toppling the other passengers into action.

"Why are we being held in this room?"

"Who were those TSA guys? Some sort of private security?"

Private security? Maybe there's a dignitary visiting the airport. I eye the door. My parents must be out there somewhere, waiting for me.

"Where's our luggage?" demands a man behind me.

"Why aren't we at our gate?" asks another.

Every question is spot-on. The airport woman shakes her head, silent, her hands clasped tightly in front of her.

I feel sorry for her, but I want answers too, and they're not in this room. So instead of standing around making noise like everyone else, I look for a way out.

I'm close to the door, and I reach it in about three seconds. I push down on the handle and swing it open. There's a collective gasp behind me, as if to say, *Why didn't we think of that?*

But my victory is short-lived. As soon as I edge the door open, a muscled wall of chest blocks my path. I forgot about Mr. T.

"Miss, you're gonna have to stay in the room for now, please." He's a foot taller than me, and there's a long stick hanging from his waist, so I back up. So do the couple of dozen people who've crowded behind me.

We're not getting out of this room.

I whirl back to the woman. "Where are my parents? This is, like, kidnapping or something."

"I assure you, Miss Waters," a new voice says, "we do not intend to hold you here much longer."

I jolt at my name and turn; the man who took the calculator from the other guy out on the tarmac has entered the room behind me, along with the uniformed man and the pilots and flight attendants. The crew all look as if they've been run over by their own plane. Strands of hair hang loose from the flight attendants' twisted chignons, and the pilots' ties and jackets have been discarded. Their faces are shell-shocked. I retreat farther into the room, scenarios running through my mind:

They couldn't find our plane because the pilot took a wrong turn and we landed at the wrong airport.

They couldn't find our plane because our pilots are criminals and changed the squawk thingy.

They couldn't find our plane because it's part of a secret govern-ment experiment.

"I demand to know why you're detaining us in this room," the businessman says. "I have an important meeting. If I don't make it, you could cost me millions of dollars."

The guy who knows my name—and seems to be in charge—nods. "I understand your concern. We are making every effort to expedite your departure from the airport. But there are some"—he glances at the uniformed man—"security concerns we must address."

"Security concerns?" Oh, joy. It's plane groupie.

"Does this have anything to do with air traffic control not recognizing our plane?" he presses eagerly.

The man purses his lips. The pilots exchange a loaded glance, and the younger flight attendant appears ready to burst into tears. If they're that flustered, it can't be good for us.

The man clears his throat. "My name is Antonio Fernandez, and I'm the airport director. If everyone could please have a seat—"

The businessman charges toward the door and the hulking guard. I take a half step forward, to do what I'm not sure. The guard raises a weapon and points it at the man. His back is to me, so I don't see clearly what the guard hits him with, but I see him fall. A coiled wire stretches from the guard to the man, and there's a *tick-tick-tick-tick-tick-tick-tick* noise. He jerks on the ground, crying out. Ohmygosh, what *is* that thing? If I hadn't backed off, would he have used it on me?

I retreat until the backs of my knees hit a chair.

People are yelling out curses, and I just want to hide. I don't need answers if it means more of whatever they're doing to that man. I tuck my feet up and curl into a ball. *"Makeitstop, makeitstop."*

Someone rubs my back. "It's over, honey."

I peek up; it's the old lady who was behind me exiting the plane. She pulls up a chair beside me. "I'm Agnes Spring. What's your name?"

I wipe a tear off my cheek. "Jenny Waters."

She hugs me, and her lily-scented perfume reminds me of Grandma Waters back in New York. "Thank you."

"Of course, honey. Whatever's happening here, we'll get through it together."

She gestures for an older gentleman to join us. He has a crazy mess of white hair that reminds me of Albert Einstein, and large square glasses. "This is Mr. Spring."

"Hi." I know they're trying to distract me, but I can still see the paramedics taking the businessman away and hear other passengers shouting about what the guard did to him.

"Why did they hurt him?" I ask in a small voice. I'll be eighteen in a few months, and I usually don't like it when adults speak to me like I'm a child, but right now, I just want my parents beside me, telling me everything will be all right.

Mr. Spring glances toward the door and presses his lips together in a noncommittal hum.

I tell them what my seatmate heard over the radio and what the pilot said about the terminal. "What do you think it means?"

"It's a mystery to me, honey," Mrs. Spring says, "but Mr. Fernandez looks like a man with answers."

He does. He's wearing a smart suit, not a wrinkle in sight. His shoes are so shiny I could probably see my reflection if I looked close enough.

"I need my notebook."

Mrs. Spring crinkles her eyebrows. "Your notebook?"

I plant my feet on the floor to steady myself and swipe a hand across my cheeks. "It helps me process."

Mrs. Spring moves closer to her husband as I dig through my backpack. I'm reporting every word Mr. Fernandez says. And I need to record what they've already done here. I flip to a blank page.

ST. LOUIS, Aug. 2, 1995—Air traffic control was unable to identify Mid-States Airways (MSA) Flight 237 when the pilot radioed in for landing clearance this afternoon.

I continue to document the experience, Mr. and Mrs. Spring a comforting presence beside me. I already feel more in control.

I continue to write.

After unloading passengers on a remote runway, airport personnel guided them to a conference room and refused to let them leave.

Man, that sounds creepy. My palms start to sweat. I rub them against my shorts and refocus. When I glance up to gather details about the room (the markers for the whiteboard look different too), I notice Mr. Fernandez attaching a headset to his ear. Fancy.

"I'm so sorry for what just happened with Mr. Kostro," he says, his voice now amplified over speakers throughout the room.

How does he know the man's name? I turn the page in my notebook and jot down this question.

"As I stated, for security reasons, we cannot allow you to leave."

"For how long?" someone shouts.

"Why?" another voice demands.

Both excellent questions.

"This is a delicate situation . . ." Mr. Fernandez looks toward the pilots, who are standing against the wall, staring at nothing. Whatever is going on here, they already know.

I click my pen, waiting for the bomb to drop.

A guy decked out in Mets gear steps forward. "Is there a fugitive aboard our plane?" He peers suspiciously at the crew. "Were the pilots running drugs?"

That would make an interesting story! Maybe I could get a byline for the *St. Louis Post-Dispatch*, an insider's perspective.

"No." Mr. Fernandez shuts that down with a sharp jerk of his chin. "Nothing so simple."

Fugitives and drugs are simple? I straighten.

"There's no easy way to tell you this." He starts to touch his hair and puts his hand back down, but it's shaking, not so in control. "I'm not even sure I'm the right person for this conversation. MSA . . . maybe a priest or rabbi . . . or the governor . . ."

My palms get sticky again. If Mr. Fernandez is so afraid to talk he needs to bring in spiritual backup, this mess is beyond anything I can imagine.

The pilot pushes away from the wall. "Mr. Fernandez, either say what you need to say or release these people and let them discover it for themselves."

Mr. Fernandez blinks and shakes his head, like he's pulling himself together. "You're right. Of course, you're right."

We hold our breaths for his next words.

Mr. Fernandez exhales. "Your plane disappeared between Kansas City Center and St. Louis Approach. Twenty-five years ago."

CHAPTER THREE

I ignore the part about twenty-five years ago because he probably meant twenty-five minutes. I raise my hand.

"Yes, Miss Waters?"

"Could you please explain what Kansas City Center has to do with our situation?" Kansas City is on the western side of Missouri. We flew in from the east.

Mr. Fernandez nods. "Kansas City Center is the name of the high-altitude controller. Incoming planes are transferred to St. Louis Approach, then St. Louis Tower. Your plane, MSA Flight 237, disappeared between Kansas City Center and St. Louis Approach."

"What do you mean 'disappeared'? How can a plane disappear?" I blurt out my question without raising my hand this time, and I'm not the only one.

Mr. Fernandez holds up his palms until the clamor dies down. "We have no idea. It's been a mystery—for twenty-five years."

Wait. He really meant that earlier? TWENTY-FIVE YEARS?

The number is an echo in my mind, and other passengers must be experiencing the same thing. People start shouting all sorts of questions.

"What do you mean twenty-five years?"

"We were only in the air for three hours!"

"Is this some sort of joke?"

"I don't believe you!"

The businessman who sat in my row on the shuttle bus elbows his way forward. "What are you trying to pull here? I want to talk to whoever's in charge!"

Mrs. Spring is on the same wavelength, but her tone is more mystified. "You can't be serious."

Mr. Fernandez stands with his hands clasped, waiting. The pilots are statues. The flight attendants huddle together, the younger one softly crying on the older one's shoulder.

I jump to my feet, my pen and notebook falling to the floor. I charge toward Mr. Fernandez, squeezing through the throng of passengers until I'm right in front of him.

"Are you saying that our plane *traveled* through *time*?"

The idea is so preposterous I can't believe he even went there. Seriously. Time travel?

"This is awesome!" Only plane groupie would immediately accept this information as truth and also think it's good news. "Our plane is a TARDIS!"

I have no idea what a tardis is and don't care. Like every other sane person in the room, I'm sure Mr. Fernandez must be playing an elaborate joke on us. The air control tower was in on it too, for some reason.

I poke Mr. Fernandez's chest, forgetting every lesson my parents taught me about respecting adults. "Why are you doing this? Is it some sort of social experiment? To see how we'll react?"

"I'm afraid not, Miss Waters."

It takes a moment for me to identify the expression on his face, the sad smile coupled with furrowed eyebrows. Pity. I'm sure it's fake, and I'll expose him as the liar he is. I'll write about what he's done and publish it in the most respected newspaper in the country. The *New York Times*! Yes, they'll be dying for my byline on this egregious abuse of airport power.

"Ask the pilots," Mr. Fernandez continues. "They saw proof."

Dread pools in my gut as I recall what I overheard. But they must be in on it too. I shake the thought out of my head. "I won't believe them either. You're all part of this . . . whatever this is you're doing to all of us innocent people. What is it? *Candid Camera* or something?"

I scan the room with narrowed eyes, searching for hidden cameras.

"Jenny." Mrs. Spring grips my elbow gently. "Let's hear them out."

Mr. Fernandez pulls a rectangular device out of his pocket. "This is my phone. An iPhone Ten." He chuckles awkwardly. "It's actually a few years old."

"That's a *phone*?" The Mets fan reaches for it. "How does it work?"

My heart is thumping so hard I fear it will jump out of my chest. Mr. Fernandez turns the "phone" toward us. It's the same thing I saw the guy holding on the tarmac.

"There's no way that's a phone." I point at the device. "It doesn't have any buttons."

"Technology has advanced beyond your imagination," Mr. Fernandez says. Then he holds the thing up and touches the surface, which lights up. A few seconds later, it plays a movie. A *movie* on that small screen.

I stumble backward.

"He can't be telling the truth," I say to Mrs. Spring, even though that device seems like something out of a movie. "It's a trick."

She clings to Mr. Spring. Her eyes are welling up. "I don't know, Jenny."

If it's true, I'm not sure what it means. For me. For my family.

I swing toward Mr. Fernandez. I'm not buying it. His handheld movie is not proof enough. It's probably a special effect they whipped up in the prop department.

"What about our families?" I shout.

And there's silence. Just for a beat. Then the voices rise again, and I see a brief moment of panic on Mr. Fernandez's face. This is why he brought out that "phone"—to distract us. Because once we see our families, it will be obvious this is all a big hoax.

CHAPTER FOUR

Mr. Fernandez stuffs the "phone" into his pocket. "I have a team of people working. We've mobilized the Flight 237 Support Network, and we're trying to get your next of kin here as quickly as possible."

Next of kin. Like we're the victims of a tragedy. Like we're *dead*.

He's really laying it on thick, suggesting there's a support network. As if Mom, Dad, and Bradley have believed I was dead for the past twenty-five years.

"This can't possibly be real." I look up at Mrs. Spring skeptically, but I find only confusion and despair in her slack expression.

Plane groupie bounds over to us. "Sure it can. There's all sorts of support for time travel being possible—"

"Young man," Mr. Spring says, "now is not the time. What's your name?"

"Art Ross."

"I'm Ted Spring." He holds out his hand, and Art shakes it.

"Art, I understand your enthusiasm, but most of us are reeling from this revelation, so it'd be great if you could tone it down for now."

Huh. It sounds like Mr. Spring might believe Mr. Fernandez.

"Oh." Art scrunches his eyebrows together. "I didn't notice."

Clearly. He's ready to burst out of the airport and start shouting that he's the world's first time traveler.

"Aren't you concerned about your family?" Mrs. Spring asks. Art shrugs. "We're not close."

"I want to call my parents," I say. "Do you think Mr. Fernandez will let me call my parents?"

They'll straighten this mess out. Mom ran the PTO for three years while working forty hours a week. She will have Mr. Fernandez quaking in his shiny shoes.

"Let's go see." Mrs. Spring stays close as we approach Mr. Fernandez. She taps his arm. "Mr. Fernandez, may Jenny please call her parents directly? Seeing as she's the only minor here?"

I scan the room and realize she's right. There were no other kids on the flight with us. The closest person to my age is Art, who I'm guessing is around nineteen or twenty, so technically not a minor even if he acts like one.

Mr. Fernandez looks up and frowns. "Actually, I've just received an update on your parents, Miss Waters. They're unavailable."

"Unavailable? What does that mean?" My voice hitches up. They were supposed to meet me here. Did he do something to them as part of this prank? "Are they okay?"

His face smooths. "Oh, yes. Completely fine. Your brother will explain. He's here already. Saw the news online"—he grimaces—"and raced over here. We've confirmed his identity, and I've conferred with TSA. They've agreed you can speak with him."

News online? And how did they get a story out so fast? Maybe he means a radio show. And why would I need permission to talk to my brother anyway?

But wait. Bradley is twelve. He can't drive here.

"Did my grandparents bring him? How can Bradley be here without my parents?"

Mr. Fernandez wears that pitying look again. "Miss Waters, your brother is thirty-seven years old. He's an adult."

Thirty-seven.

When I left St. Louis a week ago to visit Grandma and Grandpa Waters in New York, my mom was forty-one and my dad was forty-three. Mr. Fernandez is telling me that my brother, who *just last week* was playing video games all day and agonizing over whether he should walk next door and ask Cara Statten to go to the snow cone shop with him, is only four years younger than my mom. That my little brother is now twenty years older than me.

I burst out laughing. I can't help myself. They are taking this way too far.

"Honey, are you okay?" Mrs. Spring holds my gaze, her eyes both kind and concerned.

"It's not real. It can't be. It's all an elaborate prank. You see that, right?"

She glances at Mr. Fernandez. He shakes his head, once.

"Your brother is waiting in another room," he says.

Sure. My brother. Some actor they've hired. There better be some sort of prize at the end of this prank. Like an all-expenses-paid trip to the Bahamas for my whole family. Or my college tuition!

"Do you want me to come with you?" Mrs. Spring asks.

Maybe. I scan the room, wondering what they have planned for everyone else. I'm a minor. They can't keep this up for long without getting my parents. It has to be against the law.

I lift my chin. "I'll be okay."

"If you're sure. I'll get your things." Mrs. Spring shuffles over to the chair where I left my backpack and purse; she stuffs my notebook and pen inside.

After she returns, I adjust my purse over my right shoulder and swing my backpack on, then hug her. "Thank you."

Her eyebrows crinkle over her faded blue eyes. "Good luck, honey."

I don't know her well, but if it turns out she's in on this joke, too, my faith in humanity will be severely tested.

I nod to Mr. Fernandez that I'm ready to go. He motions for Mr. T to open the door.

"Hey, where's she going?" someone shouts. There's more, though the sound dims as we slip out and the guard shuts the door decisively behind us.

But not for long. "Jenny Waters!"

I plaster myself against the door, my heart thumping. People are gathered down the hall; they appear to be airport workers. "How do they know my name?"

Mr. Fernandez eases between me and the group. "They know the names of every person on that plane."

I shiver, refusing to accept it. But they sure have thought through this scenario really well.

"Come along, Miss Waters." He leads me down the opposite hallway, and their stares follow until we turn another

28

corner. He stops at a double door. "Your brother is in here. He's alone."

I can't fathom this statement. Bradley is a preteen boy with freckles sprinkled over his pale nose and cheeks and a shock of red hair he never bothers to comb. A slob whose room stinks of sweaty socks mixed with the hay and vegetables he feeds his guinea pig. He can't be here, alone.

"Are you ready to go in?" Mr. Fernandez asks.

I'm so sure this is a lie I'd bet my position as editor in chief of the school newspaper on it. Except—all the air whooshes out of my lungs—if it isn't a lie, there's no position for me to give up. It's someone else's paper now.

No. Freaking. Way. I'm poking holes in this phony story right now.

I square my shoulders. "I'm good to go."

Mr. Fernandez opens the door. At first I don't see anyone, and I deflate a bit. Then a man pops up from beneath a table, turning toward us. "Sorry. I dropped my phone. When will you have an up—"

He stops, his mouth hanging wide open enough for a bird to swoop in. He stumbles backward and smacks into the table.

"I've brought your sister, Mr. Waters," Mr. Fernandez says.

Mr. Waters. Nope. Absolutely not. That name belongs to my dad, not this . . . man. Mr. Fernandez expects me to believe this is Bradley?

"Jenny!" the man chokes out. He blinks rapidly, like he can't believe his eyes and the next blink might transform me into something more conceivable. "Impossible. You're exactly the same. You're—"

"No." I retreat toward the door. Ice spreads through my veins. "You're making this all up. Or I'm trapped in a horrible dream or something. But that"—I point at the man—"is not my brother."

He's a man-boy really, in straight, dark wash jeans and a T-shirt for a band I've never heard of. His hair is a darker red than Bradley's is, and he has a *beard* with gray streaks in it. *Gray.* Strangely, the gray doesn't make him look older. He has one of those boyish faces, probably thanks to the sprinkle of faded freckles.

The man-boy curses, one quick word, and puts his palms on the sides of his head, pressing hard. "Sorry. I don't usually . . . you . . . you're . . . still a teenager! I didn't believe the tweet. Or even when Lilli . . . Today of all days! I was sure it was a stunt. It's been so long . . ."

His hands drop from his head, leaving his hair sticking up crazily, and he steps tentatively away from the table. He reaches for me, and I flinch. No way is this stranger claiming to be my little brother touching me.

"I'm sorry." He fiddles with the hem of his T-shirt and glances at Mr. Fernandez, like he wants him to leave. "You look exactly the same. And wearing the 'I Heart New York' T-shirt Grandma"—his voice breaks—"Grandma told us you were wearing when you took off."

This entire exchange is too creepy for words. "I want my mom and dad."

He raises his hands helplessly. "They're in Guatemala. On a mission trip. For the first time in twenty-five years, I finally convinced them to get on a plane, and . . ."

He laughs nervously, then snorts with a sort of hiccup.

I gasp. I know that laugh. That annoying, snort-hiccup laugh. It's Bradley's laugh. But that's impossible. How did they get an actor who could do that?

"Do that again," I demand.

"Do what again?"

I move forward. "Laugh."

He chuckles awkwardly. "I can't laugh on command."

I need proof. "You can't be Bradley."

His face scrunches up like someone's pinched him. "Nobody's called me Bradley in years. Just Brad."

Mr. Fernandez clears his throat. "Do you still need me here? Because I have a number of other details to attend to."

Even though I'd momentarily forgotten him, I'm tempted to beg him to stay. Because at least he's become familiar over the past fifteen minutes, unlike this man-boy who shares my little brother's laugh.

"I think we'll be okay," can't-possibly-be-Bradley says. "Right, Jenny-san?"

I freeze again. Ohmygosh, ohmygosh, ohmygosh. My hand flies to my chest, as if I can calm the rapid beat of my heart. Bradley's nickname for me. Because we both love *The Karate Kid*. We called each other Jenny-san and Bradley-san for months after we first watched the movie. He hasn't done it in a while, but I can't imagine how a stranger would know about it.

Mr. Fernandez takes my silence as permission and scuttles out the door.

"I still don't believe any of this. It doesn't make sense." A laugh and a nickname aren't enough to convince me this guy's the same brother who stood a head shorter than me a week ago.

He rubs his beard. "You're right. It doesn't. But here we are. How old are you?"

"Seventeen," I say in a small voice.

He inhales shakily. "Yeah. And what day is it?"

"August 2, 1995," I say, except I'm not so certain anymore.

"The August second part is right. But the nineties are a distant memory." Alleged-Bradley looks wrecked. "Jenny, an hour ago I thought you were dead. I've thought you were dead for twenty-five years! And then a tweet came up saying Flight 237 had popped into the air the same way it popped out. I figured the picture was Photoshopped, especially since it's the anniversary. It wouldn't be the first time someone pulled a prank on this date. There's always a stray reporter or two who call us up and ask Mom and Dad how they're feeling . . ."

I guess if our plane really had disappeared in the sky, even with no wreckage, the obvious conclusion would be that we'd died.

"But then I remembered a girl I went to college with worked here," he continues, "so I messaged her, and she confirmed she'd actually seen you, so I dropped everything and drove over here, and now here you are and you're—well, exactly the same. So, yeah, I get why you don't believe it. It shouldn't be possible, but somehow it is. All I can do is assure you that I am Brad Waters, your brother. Here."

He pulls a wallet from his pocket and flips it to his ID. I don't want to take it from him. I'm afraid it will change everything. But I do.

Bradley James Waters
Date of birth: April 5, 1983

The letters and numbers blur before me. It's like my brain can't handle the information. It's all starting to add up to a truth I just can't process.

"That's my brother's name," I say, closing my eyes. "His birthday."

He brushes my bangs back, like my dad would. "That's *me*, Jenny. Look at me."

He keeps saying my name, over and over, like if I hear it enough I'll believe him. I look at him, and when my eyes catch on his, I see the hint of green in his blue eyes that always made me jealous when we were younger. But the point is I *recognize* them despite the grown-up face they're sitting in.

"It's me, Jenny-san. There's no trick." He's looking down at me. My little brother is looking down at me. Now I do tear up.

"It's me, Jenny-san."

"I want Mom and Dad." I'm practically whimpering, but I can't handle this. Because if I accept that he's my brother, it means everything Mr. Fernandez told us in the other room is true. I just lost twenty-five years of my life. Everyone I love—not just Bradley—is twenty-five years older. It's not right. It's not *fair*. It shouldn't be possible.

He nods reflexively. "Yeah. Yeah. We'll call them." He pulls out his phone, his hands shaking as he taps at it, and holds it up to his ear. "The site they're working at . . . Dad's helping build a school, and Mom is doing English classes with kids."

That's so my parents. We're at church every Sunday, and they've talked about going on mission trips. But this is the worst timing in the history of ever. I feel incredibly selfish resenting the children they're helping while I'm in a crisis, but I want my parents *now*.

"No one's answering, and they don't have their cell phones there, only a landline," Bradley says. "I'll just leave a message."

He walks off, his voice a low murmur.

"Okay." I hiccup, holding in a sob, but he doesn't hear me anyway.

Then the door swings open, and the woman who herded us into the conference room sticks her head in. "The FBI is here."

CHAPTER FIVE

"The FBI?" I echo. "What do they want?"

"I figured they'd show. Thanks for the heads-up, Lilli." Bradley returns to my side, wrapping an arm around my shoulder.

It's a little weird, since I still don't know this version of Bradley and we weren't very touchy-feely before, but I don't push away. "You know her?"

He nods. "Like I told you, we went to college together."

I'm not sure when he mentioned that, but I guess it explains the strange moment earlier when she zeroed in on me.

Lilli smiles tightly. "Welcome back."

She makes it sound like I've just returned from summer camp. In which case, I want my money back. "Um . . . thanks?"

"Nice one, Lilli." Bradley rolls his eyes.

"Well, what am I supposed to say?" Lilli throws up her hands. "Are the aliens friendly, and will they treat us well when they invade?"

Is that what I can expect everyone to think? Although, she has a point. If everyone else kept moving along for the past twenty-five years, where *were* we during that time? I can't begin to process it right now. "'Welcome back' is fine. Really."

Lilli smooths her shirt over her hips. "Well, the FBI is here.

They're kind of annoyed we even let everyone off the plane, but it's not like the TSA had a protocol for the plane poofing out of nowhere, and it's ninety-five degrees on that runway! Anyway, they want to talk to all the passengers, so you can either try to leave before someone blabs that Jenny's not in there, or get it over with."

I shrink against Bradley. He smells like deodorant and, oddly, ink. "Get *what* over with?"

"Your official interview," she says, as if talking with the FBI is an experience I should have expected.

"Why would they want to interview *me*?"

Lilli's tucked chin indicates I'm missing a very important point. "Because your plane disappeared for twenty-five years?"

"I don't know anything about that!" My voice hitches up. I sound almost hysterical. But I didn't break any rules. I didn't even move to the aisle seat when that plane groupie guy, Art, suggested it. "Will they put me in one of those rooms with a mirror on one side and a window on the other? Will they lock me up?"

"Of course not." Bradley ushers me toward the door. "How about we just pretend we left before the FBI arrived? Then Jenny will have time to adjust before she talks to them."

Lilli stares at the ceiling. "I didn't see a thing."

Bradley tugs me behind him. I don't love the idea of ticking off the authorities, but a big part of me wants him to lead me away from the terrifying prospect of an FBI interrogation.

"Should we leave?" I ask. "I mean, I don't want to break the law or anything."

Bradley pauses to shake his head at me. "You are definitely my sister. Ever the rule follower."

You are definitely my sister? I can understand why I doubted him—he's a completely different person since I saw him—but I'm me.

"Come on." He opens the door and pulls me through.

Lilli follows us. "If anyone asks, I'll say you're still in there. Good luck."

Bradley grins at her. "Thanks."

I'm frozen for a moment, watching Lilli stride away. What is the FBI doing to the other passengers?

But Bradley jerks me in the opposite direction. "Let's go."

My feet obey him, my well of courage empty. For once, I have zero inclination to seek out all the details and write them down. I just want to get as far as possible from that room where they have the other passengers clustered like a herd of cattle and pretend this day never happened. "What about my luggage?"

Bradley scans the area, I guess searching for anyone who may stop us. "I think you can consider your luggage lost for now."

"But I bought souvenirs for everyone!" Not to mention my clothes and makeup and stuff. I realize this is a ridiculous thing to say considering the circumstances, but my brain is so overloaded with everything that's happening I can't seem to focus on what's most important. What *is* most important when everyone's telling you it's a completely different century?

"Aw." Bradley bumps my shoulder, even as he checks the next hallway for security or FBI or who knows what. "What'd you get me?"

I appreciate his attempt to lighten the situation. "A snow globe with King Kong climbing the Empire State Building."

"I'd have loved that. The thing is, Jenny-san, we have to assume they'll be going over everything in that plane under high-resolution microscopes to try and figure out how this happened." He pats my backpack. "If we weren't leaving, they'd probably take that too."

I grip my backpack straps tightly. My notebook is in there! "Whatever caused this isn't in my stuff!"

"I'm sure you're right." Bradley motions me through the automatic door that leads to the parking garage. "But, Jenny, I think your luggage is the least important thing you lost on that flight."

Bradley walks swiftly to a silver sedan and removes something from his pocket; a loud beep sounds, making me jump.

"What was that?"

Bradley glances at me. "I unlocked the car."

"Oh." I peer into Bradley's backseat and do a double take. "What are those?"

Bradley's eyes flicker down and then up to meet my gaze. "A car seat and a booster," he says calmly.

My pulse thumps. "For *whom*?"

He laughs, and once again that awful snort-hiccup reassures me my brother's inside this stranger's body. "I'd forgotten how you talk. They're for my kids."

"Kids?" I squeak. The idea of my little brother, who couldn't get up the courage to walk next door to visit his crush, with *kids* . . . I gasp. "Are you married?"

"Yes to both. Eli's eight. Kira's four. They're gonna love you."

I brace my hand against the car. "I'm an aunt."

A knot forms in my throat. This is not real life, to get on a plane and three hours later disembark to find your twelve-year-old brother is married with two children.

"You are," he says and gets in the car. "And we need to go."

I slide into the passenger seat, still trying to digest this new information even as I observe that he doesn't use a key to start the car. He pulls out, and the car barely makes a sound. I notice that even though Bradley seems pretty calm, his hands are gripped so tightly on the steering wheel his knuckles are white.

As we exit the parking garage, he hisses, "Get down!"

When I don't immediately obey, he pushes my face into my knees. "What's going on?" I mutter into the floorboard.

"Media. They're everywhere."

"Like the *Post-Dispatch*?" I try to sit up, but Bradley presses me back down, even while he turns the car.

Bradley snorts. It's not that I want to be interviewed right now, particularly when the FBI may have noticed that I'm missing, but newspapers are my oxygen. Any chance to meet a real-life newspaper reporter is golden.

"If they see you, we're done," Bradley says.

That sounds disturbingly final, so I relax into my knees. Sensing my compliance, Bradley takes his hand off my neck.

I'm not at all sure we made the right decision leaving.

CHAPTER SIX

The car picks up speed, a sure sign we've escaped the airport. "Can I get up now?" I ask, my voice muffled.

After a long pause, Bradley finally says, "Yes."

I sit up, rolling my shoulders. Bradley is focused on the road ahead, though he keeps glancing at the rearview mirror, like he expects the FBI to zoom up behind us.

"Where are we going? Your . . . house?" I hesitate, because the thought of Bradley owning a house is so weird.

"Not yet."

Well, that's super informative. I have a million questions, but as soon as I look out the window, I'm riveted. If I weren't already convinced I'd traveled to another century, this would do it. The cars are so different, much sleeker and somehow shinier, like there are specks of gold or silver in the paint jobs. An Acura Integra passes us, the exact model I drooled over every time we drove past the dealership, but it looks boxy and faded compared to the other cars. I notice the cars all have wheels, so *Back to the Future* was wrong about us using flying cars by now. Many of the billboards are different too. I'm amazed when I see one that's like blinds, turning vertically in dozens of strips from one scene to another. Then that's completely eclipsed by the next billboard, an actual movie screen right out on the side of the highway, like at a drive-in but without a projector.

I press my nose against the window. "How do they do that?"

Bradley follows my pointing finger as we whiz past the movie billboard. "Uh . . . I don't know? The magic of technology."

I sink into my seat with a smirk. It's good to know that even as an adult, my little brother doesn't have the answers. My world isn't entirely screwed up.

"Where are we going?" I ask again.

His brow furrows. "I'd rather wait till we get there. Let her explain."

Thump-thump goes my heart. "Let *who* explain?"

He casts me a quick glance I'm unable to decipher. "We'll be there soon."

With our parents out of town, I can't imagine who's so important he'd take me there immediately, and he said "her." "Is it Angie?"

Besides my parents or Steve, my best friend seems like a logical person to go see. Maybe she'd be able to help me make sense of this jumbled-up satire my life has become.

He shakes his head. "Not Angie."

I'm so exhausted from this whole experience I just want to curl into a ball and hide, but I have a feeling that will be very hard to do.

My brain won't let me rest, continuing to observe and catalog details about my surroundings. Houses don't look that much different, but the few people I see outside do. Like the man running along the road with wires running from his ears to a device strapped to his arm. And the older woman walking her dog in skin-tight leggings with see-through panels on the sides. I realize now that what struck me about the people when I was getting off the plane was their hairstyles. Clothes-wise, except for Lilli with her lounge outfit, they were in uniforms or suits, so that wasn't too different.

Bradley slows the car and switches on his blinker. We're not turning onto a residential street. We're turning in to Riverside Retirement Community. Underneath the main header, it advertises "with Assisted Living Units."

Oh. *Oh.*

Grandma and Grandpa Waters live in New York. It must be Grandma Elaine. It makes the most sense; she already lived in St. Louis.

Bradley said "her," not "them." I'm afraid I already know what's coming next. "Grandpa Boyd's dead, isn't he?"

The air thickens in the car as I wait for his answer. I welcome it. I don't want to be comfortable receiving this sort of news.

Bradley turns toward me. "Last year. He made it to ninety-two and then . . ." He shrugs as if this explains it. But it doesn't explain anything. Because Grandpa Boyd should be sixty-eight, out tinkering with his tomato plants, not buried in a cemetery. This reality sucks, and my feet itch to run as far from it as I possibly can. I'm afraid there are many more truths I don't want to hear.

I feel wetness on my face. I didn't notice the tears burning my eyes, but they're coursing down my cheeks. Dear, sweet, gruff Grandpa Boyd, who taught me how to play checkers and took me out for ice cream.

"Did it hurt?"

Bradley opens his mouth and closes it, as if he's rethinking what to say next. "He went in his sleep."

There is more to this story, but it will not help me to know the who, what, where, when, and why of Grandpa's death. He will still be gone.

Bradley's gaze flicks toward the building outside my window. "Grandma's waiting for you. Saw everything on the news. She called me while I was waiting at the airport and said if it was true to bring you here straightaway and she'd talk to you about everything."

Suddenly he doesn't seem so adult, bringing me to Grandma when Mom and Dad aren't available. It helps to see he isn't handling it all as well as he appears, but it's also another reminder that he's so much better at masking his emotions than he used to be.

"Let's go in," he says.

He's out of the car before I can interrogate him further. Besides, seeing Grandma Elaine is more important. I gulp as I stare up at the two-story brick building. There's a fancy overhang where cars can drive up to let out residents, but this doesn't reassure me. All it does is reinforce the fact that Grandma Elaine is old enough she needs to be sheltered from the weather. Can she still walk, or does she have to use a wheelchair?

"Hey." Bradley waves to get my attention. "Grandma's in good shape for her age. Uses a walker, but that's not unusual. Goes down to play bridge every day and gossip with her friends."

I nod and wipe my cheeks.

When we enter, I'm pleasantly surprised by the lobby, which is nothing like the nursing homes I've been in before. There's a nice floral arrangement on a pedestal. I go over to sniff it, only to discover the flowers are fake, but at least they aren't dusty. Maybe old people can't be around real flowers.

Bradley greets several residents as we walk through.

"You come here a lot?" I'm taking everything in, relieved it looks cheerful. It's nothing like the sterile, impersonal environment of a nursing home, where you feel like it's a holding place on the way to death. Riverside radiates more warmth. Most of the people we pass are smiling, and my shoulders relax, just a bit.

"We try to bring the kids every couple weeks. They like to visit." He grins back at me as we enter a stairwell and start up. "She keeps a bowl of butterscotch candies on her end table."

I huff a small laugh. Same old Grandma. Loves her butterscotch.

We exit on the second floor and wind down another hallway.

"Here we are." He stops at a door and knocks twice. I look up and jump.

"She lives in apartment two thirty-seven?" I ask incredulously. That can't be a coincidence. "Did she ask for that?"

"Yeah, I for—"

"Come in!" Grandma's muffled voice calls, and she doesn't sound like she's about to keel over.

I don't wait for Bradley. I jerk the door open so hard it slams against the wall. I don't notice anything about the apartment. I just see Grandma standing fifteen feet ahead of me, leaning one hand on a walker. "Jenny!"

She reaches her free hand toward me, and that's all the invitation I need. I rush forward, careful not to throw my weight on her when I wrap my arms around her. She's not as soft as when I left, and in fact she seems a little shorter, but she smells the same, like butterscotch and hairspray. I rest my cheek against her hair, relieved it feels as firm as ever, proof she still has it styled and set every week.

Bradley is a stranger, a man instead of the boy I left behind. But Grandma is Grandma. She's older but not transformed into a person I no longer recognize. Her hug provides the comfort I've been seeking since I got off the plane.

"Oh, Jenny girl, I knew you'd return to us someday. It's why I picked this apartment, to always keep you top of mind." Grandma steps back so she can scan me, her green eyes glistening. She smirks. "Although, your method of return is unexpected. You still know how to write a good story."

So Grandma. When I'm too serious, she finds a way to lighten the mood. And yet I can't ignore the absence in this room. Tears well up again. "I'm sorry about Grandpa."

She tilts her head. "It was his time. I'm only sorry you missed him."

She makes it sound as if he went out for coffee with his friends. I want to know more, to ask how he died and how she ended up here and, most importantly, how much time I have left with *her*, but she's so happy and I don't want to ruin that now.

"Grandma, maybe you should sit," Bradley says.

"Bradley James," she says, turning with her finger wagging in his direction, "I am perfectly capable of deciding when to stand and when to sit."

I curl my lips in to hide my smile. Bradley stuffs his hands in his pockets. "Yes, ma'am. Can I get you anything?"

Grandma nods. "A glass of milk for me." She pats her hip.

"Gotta keep these bones strong. And a Coke for Jenny. Plus whatever you'd like."

She moves to her chair, a recliner that looks much more comfortable than the chairs in the lobby. I don't dare comment on the fact she took Bradley's suggestion. She gestures toward the couch, and I comply. Grandma is clearly the queen of this castle. Once Bradley returns and passes out the drinks, he sits beside me.

Grandma takes a sip of her milk and sets the glass carefully on the end table. "Now, dear. Your brain must be exploding with questions. Brad was right to bring you here. Some truths aren't mine to tell—" She holds up a hand at the protest she must see forming on my lips. "Patience, Jenny. I wish I could wave a magic wand and take us all back to 1995." She pats her hair, which bears a striking resemblance to the cartoon fairy godmother's. "Since I can't, we have to figure out how to play with a pinochle deck no matter how much we want to play bridge."

"So you're saying there's no use trying to figure out how to go back." If hitting rewind were an option, I'd pick it over staying in this alternate reality where Grandma's so old I could lose her any day.

She leans forward. "We can ask some questions, but I doubt it will lead anywhere. For twenty-five years they've been trying to figure out where you disappeared to. If they couldn't make sense of it before, I doubt they will now."

"They didn't have the plane before." Or my luggage. (Like they're going to find a time machine packed with my disposable razor?)

"True," she says thoughtfully. "But in the meantime, you

need to move forward. And that's gonna come with some bumps and bruises on your heart."

The organ in question clenches. "What do you mean?"

She reaches for my hand, and I scoot to the edge of the couch so she doesn't strain. "Jenny, I think you might already suspect."

I do. God help me, I do. I know what she's going to say. I've suspected it since Bradley's breath caught over my T-shirt. My eyes are already burning again. "Grandma and Grandpa Waters?"

I picture them waving to me from the car as I walked into the airport. *This morning.*

"About ten years ago for your Grandpa Waters. He had a heart attack."

Oh, no. That sounds horribly painful.

She squeezes my hand until I meet her eyes. "It was quick."

Bradley scoots closer to me. "I didn't know how to tell you." His voice is choked, like he's reliving the news with me.

"And your grandma," Grandma continues, "three years ago. Pneumonia, unfortunately."

Pneumonia. Isn't that a bad sort of flu? And yet it took my grandma. My grandma who days ago walked the Columbia campus with me and made plans for Saturday morning meetups at a local diner.

"It doesn't seem possible." No more tears fall; maybe I'm all cried out. Or in shock.

"I love you so much, Jenny."

And I'm undone. I crawl over to Grandma and bury my face in her lap.

She strokes my hair and hums a melody that seems familiar, but I can't put a name to it. "Remember, Jenny, we're here for

47

you, no matter what else you discover that seems too much to handle."

A voice inside urges me to ask her to explain, that voice that always demands answers, but her hand and her familiar scent are so soothing. Besides, if she's going to tell me more people are dead, I don't want to know.

CHAPTER SEVEN

We stay at Grandma's for a couple of hours, but it gets late, and she doesn't have a place for me to sleep, so we have to leave. As we drive toward Bradley's home and his *family*, a family that's separate from what I think of as *our* family, I hesitantly touch his arm.

"Thank you for taking me to Grandma. It was"—my voice hitches—"hard, but I needed her."

He stays focused on the road. "I figured you'd feel more comfortable there."

I pull my hand back into my lap and watch the lights whizzing by. "You were right."

We wind through a few more streets, and Bradley pulls into the driveway of a modest house with a one-car garage. A light clicks on over the open garage; a lawn mower and bikes of varying sizes barely fit alongside a large vehicle. There's a bumper sticker on the back that says "Trust Me, I'm an Engineer." I peer at the saying, trying to decipher the drawings around it—a wind turbine, space shuttle, calculator, pi sign.

I now know more about Bradley's wife and what she does than I do about Bradley. We've been together for hours, and I haven't asked him anything about who he is now. I don't know if he's an accountant or a construction worker or a drummer for a rock band (as his T-shirt perhaps implies). He's dressed very casually on what's obviously a workday, so he probably doesn't work in an office, unless people don't dress up for work anymore.

The passenger door opens; Bradley's waiting. "You coming inside?"

"Yes." I grab my backpack and purse. I hope his wife and kids like me. He probably told me their names, but I can't remember. I hop out and turn to face the brick-front house, more afraid of what awaits me inside than what's happening back at the airport with the FBI.

Bradley takes my hand like we're little kids and leads me through the garage. This comforts me actually, that he's guiding me into the house like a family member. Which I am. I know I am, but still, this small gesture causes a tightness in my throat.

We walk through a laundry room. He releases me because we have to walk single file to maneuver around a basket overflowing with brightly colored clothes. *Miniature* clothes. Proof his children exist as well. My hands tremble at my sides, and I stuff them in my pockets to still them.

After the laundry room, we pass down a hallway, and it's weird. Because there are nails on the wall but no pictures, like they've taken them down.

Bradley notices what's caught my attention. "We're getting ready to paint."

"Oh." It's a plausible explanation, but the way he looks quickly away is suspicious. Why would they remove the pictures from the walls? I can't imagine what they wouldn't want me to see.

Finally the interminable hallway ends, and we enter a living room. The first thing I see is a massive screen. I resist the urge to rush toward it. "What is *that*?"

Bradley glances swiftly to the right before he notices what I'm locked onto. "The TV. Didn't you notice the one at Grandma's?"

"That's a *TV*?" It's completely flat, balanced above a stand instead of enclosed in a box. And no, I didn't see anything like this at Grandma's, but I was pretty focused on her. "It's huge! Are you rich?"

Bradley's awkward snort-hiccup again, easing the knot in my gut.

"Definitely not," an amused new voice says.

I whirl to the right, where Bradley's eyes had gone before, and I stumble as I catch my first glance of his wife.

"You're Black!"

Oh no, oh no, oh no. I did not just say that to Bradley's wife. I cover my face with my hands. I wish for a hole to open up in the floor and swallow me. Better yet, for the plane to swoop in and carry me back to 1995. "I'm so sorry. I'm an idiot."

A hand lands on my shoulder, and based on the lavender scent that accompanies it, it's not Bradley's. "You've had a super-long flight today and just learned about your grandparents. Let's sit down."

Bradley's wife guides me to a sofa, but I still can't look at her after the abysmal way I just greeted her. There's nothing I can say now to redo her first impression of me. Why, oh why, did my horrible habit of blurting my thoughts before I think have to show up right now?

"Jenny, it's okay." Her hand squeezes my knee. "Let's blame Brad. That's what I like to do anyway. He obviously didn't tell you anything about his gorgeous wife."

I peek through my fingers. She's smiling, and even though she's joking, it's true. Bradley seriously leveled up. With amazing curly hair and deep brown eyes, his wife *is* gorgeous. "I'm sorry. Again."

"Already forgotten." She raises an eyebrow at Bradley. "As for you . . . what's with walking her in here and introducing the TV before me?"

Bradley rubs his beard. "Yeah. I'm a little rusty on sibling etiquette."

"Actually," I say, "I think this is about how we always treat each other."

We've never been the closest siblings in the world, with a five-year age gap. Last week he stood at the gate mouthing, *Don't come back*, over Mom's shoulder. He was angry I told Mom about his crush, which was a bit of a sister fail. Now our dynamic will be screwed up even more.

"I'm Kelly, by the way, since Brad *still* hasn't introduced me."

Brad. Not Bradley. It's weird to hear her call him that, like he's a real adult. Now that I think about it, Grandma did, too, after that initial scolding.

I smile tentatively. "Nice to meet you."

"Now." She pats my knee, and despite the fact I only met her a few minutes ago, it's easier to focus on Kelly than my time-warped brother. "What do you need?"

Honestly, that question is so huge I don't know where to start. I need to rewind this day to before I got on the plane, when I was in New York with my *living* grandparents, having breakfast in a diner, chatting about the possibility of attending Columbia next fall and meeting up on a regular basis. Or maybe even further, to last week, when I was here in St. Louis with my family—including twelve-year-old, no-idea-Kelly-exists-yet *Brad*—and Angie and Steve.

But since neither of those are feasible, I opt for the next-best option. "I need my parents."

I'm a little surprised my voice breaks. Again.

"Oh, sweetheart." Kelly hugs me close, enveloping me in her lavender scent and silky blouse.

"Hopefully they'll call back soon," Bradley says.

Kelly rubs my back. It's soothing. She knows what she's doing. But I guess she would; she's a mom. I shudder, the reality of it all hitting me again. Kelly is the mother of my *brother's* children.

I pull back. "Where are the . . . kids?" I can't help my hesitation. It's just too weird.

She smiles gently. "With my parents. I thought they might be a bit much for you to handle tonight."

Considering I've traveled through time, evaded the FBI, been reintroduced to my little brother as an adult, hit with the news most of my grandparents are dead, and am now sitting with my apparently not-so-new sister-in-law . . . "Good call."

Music begins playing, and I search the room for a stereo, wondering how it came on without Bradley or Kelly moving. Bradley holds up his phone. "It's my ringtone."

"Your phone plays music to ring?" I'm momentarily distracted by this concept. Then, "Is it Mom?"

He shields the phone from me. "No. Give me a sec."

I feel like our roles are reversed. There are so many instances I've hidden things from Bradley to protect him, and I'm sure that's what he's doing now. He leaves the room and shuts a door so I can't hear what he's saying to whoever's on the other end of the call. I'm tempted to press my ear to the door, but Kelly's watching me.

"Who do you think it is?" I turn to her with a raised eyebrow. "Why are they calling now? Is it about me? What do they want? Why did Bradley go into another room?"

"Wow." She holds up a hand. "Brad told me about how you used to go into interrogation mode, but it's something to actually experience it."

I narrow my eyes. "Nice deflection."

She holds up fingers to tick off her answers. "I don't know who it is. It might have to do with you, or it could be completely random timing. Maybe it's even a work call, but considering you're all over the news, it probably is about you."

I nod. "Thanks for being honest."

"I'll try to always tell you the truth, Jenny."

Shouldn't it just be "I'll always tell you the truth"? I'm about to call her on it, no matter how nice she is, when Bradley returns.

"Who was that?"

They exchange the sort of loaded glance I've often seen between Mom and Dad, like they're having a telepathic conversation. "I'm right here!"

Bradley finally breaks their weird staring contest and looks at me. "Work call."

He's so lying, but just when I start to say so, his phone blasts more music and he leaves the room again. Kelly shrugs, as if that's any sort of answer. We sit in awkward silence until Bradley comes back a few minutes later.

"I have Mom on the phone," he says. "Dad's still out at the worksite but should return any minute. I explained about you being, well, the same, but I'm not sure she totally gets it."

My pulse accelerates. Finally!

Bradley passes me the phone. I'm not sure how to hold it. It's flat, with no clear spot for my ear. "Here." He pushes a button on the screen. "Mom, you there? I've got you on speaker."

"Brad? Jenny?" Mom's voice is frenzied. "Jenny, are you really there?"

I gulp, trying to form words around the knot in my throat. Because it's my mom. It really is her on the other end of this odd phone. Unlike Bradley, Mom sounds the same.

"I'm here, Mom." Tears course down my face. I'm just so grateful to hear her voice. She sounds so familiar in the midst of everything else that's completely foreign.

"Oh, thank God! Jenny—" She breaks off, and I hear her sobbing. It's heart-wrenching. She sounds like her guts have been ripped from her body and stomped into the ground. I glance at Bradley, unsure what to say. I asked for this, to call her, for me, and it's hurting her.

"Mom, I'm okay." I'm not. I'm nowhere near okay, but it seems like the right thing to say.

Bradley grimace-smiles in approval.

"Carol? What's wrong?" Dad's voice is muffled. Mom clearly doesn't have the phone she's using on speaker, but I still recognize Dad in the background, and I slide off the couch onto my knees. He's the same too. No matter what has happened, my parents are still my parents. I close my eyes and thank God for that.

"Jenny's alive!" Mom says. "But Brad says she's still somehow seventeen. It's . . . I don't . . ."

Bradley leans over the phone. "She's wearing the 'I Heart NY' T-shirt, and her bangs are curled like she always had them."

I raise a hand to my bangs, wondering why that's relevant.

"Jenny, you're really there?" Dad says.

Just like Mom. And once again I confirm, "Yes, Dad. I'm here."

"It is her," he says, his voice full of wonder. "How? When? Why?"

I got my inquisitive nature from Dad. "I don't know." I have a feeling I'll be repeating this story for the rest of my life. "I left Grandma and Grandpa in New York this morning, and I landed here this afternoon, and everything was different."

Dad inhales. It must hurt for him to think about me seeing his parents so recently.

"Incredible," he finally says. "I believe you. I know you and Brad wouldn't lie to us, but it's just so . . . I'm at a loss for words."

"I don't think there are words for this, Dad. It's unprecedented."

He chuckles shakily. "That one works."

"Let me talk to her!" Mom's voice is calmer. "Jenny. It will take us a few days to get home. God works in mysterious ways, but we will figure this out together. No matter what, I want you to know how much we love you. We'll be there for you. And Brad and Kelly too."

"Of course." Bradley nods.

"Absolutely," Kelly says behind me. I'd forgotten her.

Mom swallows audibly, her tears gone, which doesn't surprise me. She's a rock. "It's a miracle you're all alive. Bradley said it's not just you, but the rest of the passengers on the plane too?"

I murmur agreement, but internally I beg to differ. Not that I'm ungrateful to be alive. And from Mom's perspective, I suppose a time-delayed daughter is better than no daughter. But if this is a miracle, then God has the most warped sense of humor in the universe, and I'd like to schedule a one-on-one interview so we can discuss why He put my family through twenty-five years of anguish and delayed my life.

"I can't wait to see you and hold you, Jenny."

Yes, that's what I really need. There's nothing like a Mom hug. "Me too."

"Now Dad needs to speak with Brad about some details."

"Okay." My voice hitches up in a question. Dad and Bradley are going to discuss me like they are two adults and I am a child. I'm a seventeen-year-old about to start my senior year of high school. Bradley is my little brother. But he's not anymore. I can't wrap my mind around this concept.

He moves away, and I watch him nodding into the phone. When he finishes, I expect Bradley to hand the phone to me so I can continue my conversation with Mom and Dad, but he pockets it.

"Hey! I wasn't finished talking to them."

There's so much more to say, so much more to catch up on.

He presses his lips together apologetically. "They want to talk to you more too, Jenny-san, but they have a lot of arrangements to make."

Kelly stands and holds out her hand to help me up. "You should rest. We don't have a guest room, but you can stay in Kira's room." Kira. That's my niece's name.

It takes all my energy to get to my feet. The day has taken a toll on me. I follow Kelly down a hallway to a purple-walled bedroom. I'm about to flop onto the twin-size mattress when the doorbell rings. The bed is so tempting. But when Bradley clearly shouts, "No!" I'm instantly alert.

I rush out of Kira's room toward the living room, where I find Kelly physically restraining him. The focus of his chin-jutted gaze is a deeply tanned woman in a sharp black pantsuit. The jacket fits her like a glove, tailored in at her waist. There's another person standing behind her, but I can't see anything more than a pale blue pant leg and white tennis shoe.

"My sister's been through a lot today," Bradley says. "She needs to sleep. I won't let you bother her."

Sharp suit tilts her head at me. "Looks like she's awake to me. Good evening, Miss Waters. We missed you at the airport."

Of course. She's FBI.

Her reproving tone zings me right in the gut. If you ask Angie, it's a weakness, but I've always considered it a strength that I'm so tuned into authority figures. The downside is that when they level that I'm-so-disappointed-in-you look in my direction, it hits me hard. Still, I can't regret skipping out earlier to see Grandma. Despite the awful news she laid on me, her presence grounded me in a way Bradley couldn't. I don't think I could have held it together, stuck in a room with a bunch of strangers, *plus* the FBI.

I cross my arms over my chest and mimic Bradley's chin jut, squashing down the urge to cower and beg forgiveness. All I did was leave the airport, which is what any normal passenger would do after a flight. "What do you want?"

The woman steps forward. "I'm Agent Willa Klein with the FBI." She pulls out a badge and holds it up for my inspection. "I have a few questions for you, and then we would like to get a fingerprint and a sample of your blood."

"What?" My voice comes out high-pitched, and I recoil.

Bradley shakes off Kelly. "Her blood? Why do you want her blood?"

Agent Klein exhales through her nose. "This would have been much easier if you'd remained at the airport with the others for a full explanation."

When we continue to stare at her, waiting for *her* to explain, she shifts aside, revealing her companion, a twentyish guy in scrubs holding a soft-sided bag. "Micah here is with our forensics team. They'll be comparing your fingerprints and blood samples with information already on file to confirm your identity."

I tighten my arms around my torso. "How can you have that stuff on file?"

Bradley's brows lower. "I don't think they can. Not for you."

Agent Klein purses her lips. "A fair point, Mr. Waters. As a minor without any sort of record, we don't have her fingerprints. However, we can at least verify her blood type against her medical records. It's a start toward investigating this situation."

Bradley strides over and wraps an arm around my shoulders. "You don't have to, Jenny."

I burrow into him, drawing strength from his presence. I peer out at Agent Klein. "What will you do with it? My blood? Besides check my blood type?"

After a brief pause, Agent Klein smiles slightly. "Smart question, Jenny. There are some additional tests to verify your age within a range, that your DNA hasn't been altered in any way."

Bradley's hand tightens on my shoulder, and I shiver. "You mean you want to make sure I'm not an alien or something."

Agent Klein holds out her hands. "We don't mean you any harm, Jenny. We just want to figure out where you've been."

"I want to know that too," I say quietly. I really do. It doesn't make any sense. If a blood test might help answer that question . . . "Okay."

Bradley twists me to face him, blocking me from Agent Klein. "Are you sure? Because I don't think they can make you. You're a minor. Mom and Dad probably have to approve it."

He may be right, but if I don't get this over with, they'll just keep coming back. I step around him. "Do you need my parents to sign a waiver or something?"

"Not in these circumstances," Agent Klein says.

I swallow. "Then let's do it."

Agent Klein inclines her head. "Where can Micah set up?"

Kelly sweeps her hand out. "The kitchen?"

She leads our odd procession. Bradley leans in. "It's gonna be fine, Jenny-san."

"Easy for you to say," I mutter. "Nobody's about to stick a needle in you to make sure you aren't harboring alien DNA."

"Jenny." He stops me outside the kitchen and meets my eyes without wavering. "You will ace this test the way you ace every other test you're given. No studying necessary."

He sounds like such an *adult*. Like my dad. It's just so wrong. But I also hear his underlying message, that he doesn't believe they'll discover I'm anyone other than who I say I am. "Thank you."

"Ready, Miss Waters?" Agent Klein says.

"Yes, ma'am." I march into the kitchen and sit at the table, holding out my arm for Micah.

Seated across from me, Agent Klein pulls out her phone. "I'm going to record this, if that's all right."

"Okay." I eye the phone, wondering what else it will do. Micah ties an elastic band around my bicep.

Agent Klein taps at her phone and says, "Interview with Jennifer Waters, age seventeen, passenger on Mid-States Airways Flight 237."

Bradley and Kelly sit together at the end of the table, holding hands and showing support with encouraging expressions.

"Did you notice anything out of the ordinary during your flight?" Agent Klein asks.

I wince as the needle pinches into my vein. I glance over, watching Micah collect my blood. "Uh . . . not really. It was a smooth flight. I mean, until Art started telling me all that stuff about the air control tower."

"The air control tower?" Agent Klein repeats like she doesn't already know. "Tell me about that."

So I do, distracted by Micah filling three vials with my blood before finally removing the needle and covering the pinprick with a small cotton ball and Band-Aid. Kelly hands me a juice, which I gratefully sip.

Micah gets out a fingerprint kit.

"What about outside?" Agent Klein asks. "Did it suddenly change from cloudy to sunny?"

My gaze snaps to her face. "What? I don't think so. Did that happen?"

Agent Klein remains impassive. "It was quite cloudy in St. Louis on August 2, 1995. It was sunny today. We're just trying to ascertain exactly where the . . . inconsistency occurred."

Huh. I did notice some wispy clouds when I was searching for fighter planes, but I'm assuming that was after we jumped forward. "Well, I wasn't looking outside until after Art started freaking out, but *he* definitely was. He would've noticed something like that."

Really, it seems like the pilots are the best witnesses for that sort of information. Micah takes my finger, presses it into the cool ink and then onto a paper. Once he wipes it clean, I pull my hand into my lap.

Wait. "Why does it matter what I saw? Didn't everyone say the same thing?"

She tilts her head. "That's the point of these interviews. To confirm you all had the same experience."

"Did we?"

She smiles, giving nothing away, and stands. "We're finished, Miss Waters. Thank you for your cooperation."

"That's it?" Bradley says, standing as well.

I understand his hesitation. I'm uncomfortable with her presence, but she didn't tell us anything. "When will you have the results from the tests?"

Agent Klein motions for Micah to follow. "Very soon. This investigation is of utmost priority. I expect once we conclude these initial tests we'll do others. We'll be in touch if we have further questions for you."

I trail her to the front door. "What if I have questions for you? Can I get your card or something?"

I didn't care much about answers earlier, but I do now. I have an inside track on this story.

She turns back with another frustrating, noncommittal smile. "That's not how this works, Miss Waters. I'll follow up with your parents when they return. One more thing: don't talk to the media until we've completed our investigation. The situation could easily spiral out of control if the passengers start speaking out individually."

The door closes in my face.

No media! I can't write my story for the *New York Times?* I mean, I guess she has a point, but still. It would've been the most amazing scoop.

I swivel around; Bradley and Kelly are waiting behind me. "I feel strangely violated. They came, they took my blood, but there wasn't a single hot vampire."

Kelly stifles a laugh. "Yeah, Ian Somerhalder would've definitely improved that whole visit."

"Is he in the *Interview with the Vampire* sequel? I heard Tom Cruise was going to do a Lestat movie." I rub my finger against my shorts. It feels like there's still ink on it.

Kelly opens her mouth, then shakes her head. "Let's get you to bed."

I don't protest as she leads me back to Kira's room. I dimly notice the stars and hearts lining the walls as I finally flop onto the twin-size mattress. It's so comfy I snuggle in and, despite the questions bombarding my brain, am asleep in seconds.

CHAPTER EIGHT

I cuddle into Steve's unusually soft shoulder. There's a hint of stubble on his neck and a small spot where he nicked himself shaving. He smells like fabric softener, as if his shirt just came out of the dryer. I nuzzle in, and then—*whap!*—I ricochet off his shoulder. My entire body bounces.

Wait. My eyes snap open. What I thought was Steve's shoulder is actually a pillow. I'm bouncing because there's a small body jumping beside me.

"Auntie Jenny, Auntie Jenny!" A little girl with light brown skin and Bradley's blue-green eyes leans in until her nose nearly touches mine. "I've been waiting to meet you your whole life. You're an unsolved mystery!"

Well, that's one way to wake up in the morning. At least I assume it's morning based on the sun streaming through the partially open blinds. And does she mean she's been waiting to meet me *her* whole life?

"This is my room," she says. "Wanna see my Barbies? I have nine. My birthday's next month, and I'll be five."

I run a hand over my face. I think kids are okay, although I'm not like some of my friends who choose to babysit for extra cash.

This girl's adorable, though, and she's my *niece*. I attempt a smile, but I'm never fully alert when I first wake up.

"Hi, Kira." My voice is scratchy. I clear my throat, hoping I remembered her name correctly. She doesn't stick her tongue out at me or anything, so I must be okay.

"Mama's making breakfast. She took the day off work. Nana and Papa brought us home this morning, but they didn't stay 'cause Mama said you needed time before you meet strangers. But I'm not a stranger. I'm family. And—"

"Kira! There you are." Bradley swoops into the room, his face flushed. "Sorry, Jenny. I thought she was on her tablet. I turned my back for a second, and she was outta there."

He shakes his head, but there's affection under his frustration. I'm sure "tablet" has some other definition here, since I can't imagine he means that she was sitting on a stone slab, unless that's some sort of new parenting thing.

Another head peeks out behind Bradley—obviously his son and my nephew. Despite being older than Kira, he's clearly not as outgoing. I sit all the way up, grateful I'm still wearing my T-shirt and shorts from yesterday, because at least I'm decent for all the introductions.

"It's all right." I redo my ponytail, which is a tangled mess, and swing my legs over the side of the bed.

Kira snuggles up beside me and points toward the door. "That's my brother, Eli."

I press my lips together, hiding a smile. "I figured." I wave. "Hi, Eli. It's nice to meet you."

He steps out from behind Bradley but keeps a hand wrapped

around his dad's leg. His expression is super serious, as though he's contemplating a heavy philosophical question. "Did you really travel through time?"

I wish I could cram my face back into Kira's pillow and return to my dream, where I was back in 1995 with Steve. Unfortunately, I have Kira, Bradley, and Eli here to prove that everything I experienced yesterday was the truth and five minutes ago was make-believe. In actual reality, Steve is *old*, five years older than Bradley. The thought makes me squirm. I'd rather keep him tucked in my memory as the boy on the other end of the phone at the airport. "It appears so."

Eli shifts forward. "That. Is. Spacetacular."

"Uh-huh," I say noncommittally. I'm not quite on board with Mom's assessment it's a miracle or Eli's creative description either. If nothing else, I guess I'm the coolest aunt ever. Or maybe not. Kelly might have three awesome sisters who take the kids out for ice cream and the zoo once a week.

At a muffled call from outside the room, Bradley tilts his head toward the door before facing us again. "Kelly says breakfast is ready."

I suddenly realize I have an urgent need for a bathroom. I haven't gone since Grandma's yesterday.

"Bathroom?" I say.

Kira grabs my hand. "I'll show you."

She leads me down the hall and about follows me in. I hear Bradley dragging her away on the other side. Living with kids will take some getting used to, but hopefully I won't have to do it for long. Mom and Dad should return soon.

Ten minutes later I'm seated at the breakfast table with my brother's family, and I'm on sensory overload. Thankfully the food is normal. I suspect Bradley told Kelly what I like because she made ham-and-cheese omelets, and they're delicious. The kids eat from plastic plates while we use nicer ones. Their milk cups feature cartoon characters I don't recognize.

What's weird is that Bradley and Kelly both have their phones sitting next to their plates. Two minutes into the meal, Kelly's trills out a two-tone signal and lights up. She sets down her fork and taps on the screen, murmuring something to Bradley about a person I don't know. A few minutes later the same thing happens with Bradley's phone. He casts a look at me before tapping on it.

"What are you guys doing on your phones?" I ask.

Bradley sets his phone facedown on the table, grimacing guiltily. "Texting. Sorry, it's rude. We shouldn't do it at the table."

Kira scoops omelet onto her fork with her fingers and shoves it into her mouth, then speaks around it. "Daddy does it all the time."

It's cute how she throws her dad under the bus, although it doesn't explain anything. "What's texting?"

"Uh . . ."

And there's the Bradley I know and love.

Kelly explains that you can instantaneously send written messages through phones. She shows me a conversation between herself and her mother, arranging to bring the kids back this morning.

While I'm holding the phone, a box pops up on the screen. There's an outline of a blue bird in the corner. "What's this thing with the bird?"

"Bird?" Kelly frowns at her phone. "Oh. Twitter. It's a social media site where—"

"*Social* media?" Anything that has to do with media has my attention. "Is it like a newspaper?"

"What's a newspaper?" Kira asks, and for a moment my heart stops. Because if I've traveled to a time where newspapers don't exist, God doesn't just have a wicked sense of humor; He's playing the cruelest trick of all on me.

Eli points his fork at Kira. "It's those gray papers Nico puts in his hamster cage."

The pressure in my chest releases. I'm both relieved Eli at least knows what a newspaper is and disappointed his only point of reference is as a pet hamster's cage liner. Although, Bradley used to do the same thing.

"It's sort of hard to explain social media out of nowhere." Kelly bites the corner of her bottom lip. "It's all online, and it connects people. There are several different social media sites, and you can access them on your computer or phone. Twitter uses a short format, like headlines, but you can also link to web pages with more information or add photos or videos."

"Why wouldn't you read the paper and get the whole story?" Just adding that word "social" in front of "media" makes it sound sketchy to me, like it's a club to join instead of real news.

"You can." Bradley's no better than his four-year-old, talking around a mouth full of food. "But it's faster online. Like yesterday they posted a picture of the plane right after it landed. It had twenty thousand retweets within five minutes."

This Twitter thing reminds me of those chat rooms my lifestyle editor is so into. She keeps trying to get me to sign on because "nobody knows who you are and you can say anything you want." But I'm not interested in wasting hours gossiping with random strangers on a computer when I can call my friends and get together in person. Besides, we don't even have internet access at home, so I'd have to go somewhere else to do it, although I guess in this time you can chat on your phone.

I remember the man outside the plane holding up what I now realize was a phone. "Do phones take pictures?"

"Duh," Kira says.

So that guy outside the plane was photographing us before Mr. Fernandez confiscated his phone. Wow. There must not be any secrets in this time.

"I went shopping yesterday while you were at your grandma's," Kelly says.

Um, random. I'm not sure how to respond. "Fun?"

"For you, I mean. Since you don't have any clothes."

No clothes. The airport kept my luggage yesterday, but I sort of figured I'd go home and—my shoulders hunch. Of course Mom and Dad didn't save my clothes for twenty-five years. But still, I want to know for sure. "Mom and Dad got rid of my clothes?"

Bradley clears his throat. "They held on to them for a long time. Like ten years. But then they were convinced to give them away."

I wonder who convinced them. Some well-meaning people, I'm sure. *You have to move on, Carol. She's never coming back.*

"There might be a few things they set aside," Bradley says. "Packed away somewhere. But you'd have to wash them since it's been so long . . ."

So long. I was gone for a week. I talked to them the night before, called them from Grandma and Grandpa's house. It's just too much.

"We can go over there if you want," he says. "I have a key."

I exhale. Everything is different. It makes sense the house will be different. "Not without Mom and Dad."

Kelly leans in with a broad smile, clearly trying to lighten the mood. "If you're done eating, let me show you what I bought," she says cheerfully. She's trying so hard.

"I wanna see!" Kira climbs out of her chair. She might be the best thing in this whole place, excluding the following-me-into-the-bathroom incident.

We leave Bradley to clean up breakfast (he never did that before!) and head into the living room. The TV still looms like a giant specter in the space. I can't get over its size. I turn my back to it so it won't distract me, and I settle into a chair.

Kelly fingers the bags she has lined up on the couch. "Brad told me your favorite store, but it went out of business." She grimaces. "And styles are a lot different now, so I just sort of guessed."

She pulls out a bright pink top with "j'adore" scrawled across the front. I try to mask my grimace, but I'm unsuccessful based on the way her face falls.

"No problem." She sets the shirt aside. "Maybe this one."

Her next choice is a striped halter top. I'm more of a basic T-shirt and shorts girl.

"Can I have it?" Kira dances forward and grabs the shirt, pulling it over her head like a dress.

Kelly's next few top options are all too flashy for me, with sequins that change color when Kira runs her hand across them and sayings across the front. The simplest is a blue V-neck shirt with sequins on the shoulders.

Kelly's own shoulders are slumped by the end of the unveiling. "Sorry. I'm used to shopping for a four-year-old girl."

Yeah. A four-year-old girl who likes to sparkle. "No, I really appreciate it."

"I like it, Mama," Kira pipes up.

Kelly ruffles Kira's springy hair and gazes down at her fondly. "She's still young enough I can pick out her clothes."

Kelly would've been better off choosing something like her own outfit, a pair of jeans and a cap-sleeved button-down shirt. I'm not so sure about the paisley pattern, which seems a bit seventies to me, but it's better than sequins.

I look awkwardly at the TV because that monstrosity continues to distract me. "Mom stopped buying clothes for me about seven or eight years ago. I always shop with . . ."

Oh, no.

Kira bounces before me. "Who, Auntie Jenny?"

Tears prick my eyes. All the activity in the room this morning kept me from thinking about everything else I've lost. "My friends," I say softly. "Especially Angie."

Kelly inhales in a way that makes me think there's something I should know about Angie. I whip my face up and catch a glimpse of Kelly's consternation before she can mask it. "Is Angie okay?"

She glances toward the door. "Brad?" she calls, an odd note in her voice.

He bounds into the room, Eli on his heels. "Yeah?"

She nods toward me. "Jenny's asking about Angie."

My pulse kicks up. I'm sure now that she's dead or lost her legs in a car accident or some other horrible incident they're too afraid to tell me. I leap to my feet. "What? What happened to Angie?"

Bradley throws up his hands, a dish towel in one. "She's fine. Great. She wants to see you. She's texted and called me multiple times."

I exhale, sinking back onto the chair. "Man. You had me worried."

Although even if Angie's perfectly fine, she's—I quickly calculate—forty-two. She should be partner in a law firm by now. Maybe she's married, possibly with kids, although I doubt it if she stuck with her goals. I want to see her, but like Bradley, she will be a different Angie. It's on the tip of my tongue to ask them about Steve too, but it's hard enough to fathom Angie as an adult.

Maybe I'll ask Angie about him. Maybe after I see her I'll be able to consider Steve as someone other than the boy who loved chess and baseball and maybe would have loved *me* with more time.

Kira crawls into my lap, startling me from my thoughts.

"Are you okay, Auntie Jenny?" She blinks up at me, her eyes full of worry.

Even though I'm nowhere near okay, I nod. Eli, Bradley, and Kelly are all staring at me like they're afraid I will shatter into a million pieces on their living room floor.

"I'd like to see Angie." She'll be different, but there must be some of my best friend in there.

Bradley slaps the dish towel against his thigh. "All right."

My stomach clenches. Because even though he agreed, he couldn't hide his dread.

CHAPTER NINE

I choose the shoulder-sequined V-neck shirt and a pair of jean shorts with lace on the pockets for my visit to Angie. At least I'm out of the "I Heart NY" shirt.

"Do you want to listen to some music?" Bradley asks as we pull out of the driveway.

"Sure." I reach for the tuner.

He swats my hand. "Not the radio."

"Why not?" I rub my knuckles.

He glances at me quickly and then refocuses on the road. "There's nothing good on the radio anymore. You wouldn't know any of the stations or the music."

Well, that's a nice reminder I'm clueless in this century. Although, I also find his behavior suspicious, like there's a reason he doesn't want me listening to the news.

"We'll listen to the playlist on my phone," he says. "I have a lot of eighties and nineties stuff you'll recognize."

I'm tempted to ignore him and flip on the radio, but I don't know the controls in this car. Like, what are HDD and XM? I pick up his phone. "So in addition to being a phone and a camera, this is also like a mixed CD?"

He laughs, snort-hiccup. "Sort of."

"Why would you want to listen off that? I'm sure your car has better speakers than this thing."

He shakes his head. "It sends a signal to the car so we *are* listening through the car's speakers."

Wow. "Like your phone is the radio signal?"

"Uh . . . sure."

"Just tell me what to do." I follow his instructions to turn on the playlist. "It's so weird I just touch the screen to use this thing."

"Yeah. A lot different from what we had as kids."

Technically I still *am* a kid for a few months. But I don't say it because I can see from how his mouth tugs at the corner he's already realized his mistake.

He clears his throat. "If you see a song you want to listen to, touch it."

I scan through the songs, and I recognize several but none I particularly want to hear right now. I startle at a name I *don't* expect to see. "Justin Timberlake? That kid from the *Mickey Mouse Club*?"

Bradley smirks. "Um, he's a lot older than you now. And he's definitely not singing M-I-C-K-E-Y anymore. He's good, though."

"Huh." Maybe later. I keep scrolling. "Ooh, I love Prince."

I tap a song I recognize, "1999," and it blasts out of the speakers. "Yikes!"

I cover my ears while Bradley turns down the volume. "Sorry."

I chuckle. "You always listen to your music too loud." I'm constantly pounding on his wall because I want to sleep and he has his stereo up high. Although, I guess that's all in the past for him. "This sounds different. Is it a new version?"

"Yeah, he updated it in 1999."

And I bet people bought it all over again. But I still can't wrap my mind around the fact that's more than twenty years ago. "Does he have new music?"

He winces. "No. Prince died, like, four or five years ago."

It's nowhere near as personal as my grandparents' deaths, and yet the news is still shocking. Prince is an icon! He's singing about partying like it's 1999, and I'd do anything for it to be true—to at least be in my own century. I turn to the road, my enjoyment in the music dimmed.

Bradley drums his fingers on the steering wheel, the way he used to drum them on the table waiting for Mom to serve dinner. "Are you sure you want to see Angie now? Maybe we should wait until after Mom and Dad—"

"No." I straighten in my seat. "I want to see her today."

Bradley and Kelly acted weird when I brought up Angie. And Grandma made all sorts of cryptic comments. I need to know if Angie's messed up in this future reality. I may not be able to face the thought of Steve as an adult, but Angie's my best friend. The girl who faithfully watches episodes of *90210* with me every week, discussing developments during commercial breaks. Who goes to Six Flags with me and every single town fair, even though half the rides make her sick. Who trades romance novels and stands in line with me for whatever new chick flick is coming out at the theater. When I get too stuck on the rules, she argues her case until I'm going along with some outrageous scheme—without ever making me cross a line she knows is too far for me. Our history goes back so far I feel like the age difference won't matter as much.

I need it not to matter as much.

I'm surprised when Bradley heads west instead of east on the highway. "We're not going to Clayton?"

He frowns. "Why would we?"

"Because Angie's a lawyer, right? So she should live in one of those swanky apartments close to the courthouse."

Bradley inhales. I'm beginning to hate inhales. Exhales too. And sighs. Anything that involves people using their breath to avoid saying something they're afraid will freak me out. Bradley already assured me Angie is alive, so this one must mean she's not a lawyer.

"So she decided to do something else?" It's hard for me to picture her anywhere but in a courtroom, dressed in a stylish suit, probably in a powerful color like red. She was so set on this plan she coerced me into participating in mock trial last year. I didn't mind it that much—after all, I like to ask questions—but once I got to the bottom of the story I was content. Angie was determined to win.

"Just . . ." He taps the steering wheel. "I realize this is like trying to jam the crescent rolls back in the can after you've already opened it, but can you save all your questions for Angie?"

I snort. "I can't believe you even know how those work."

He sits tall. "I help with dinner all the time. Ask Kelly."

He *was* washing dishes this morning. I remember my intention from last night to get to know Bradley. "What's *your* job?"

"Oh." He glances at me. "I'm an illustrator. For children's books."

"Seriously?" That's so not what I expected to come out of his mouth. "But you hate books."

He shrugs. "Not anymore. And I love to draw."

"Yeah, all over the walls." But also, admittedly, on random pieces of paper scattered throughout the house. Huh. Who'd have thought? "That's sweet."

He glances at me with his right eyebrow raised. "If you mean 'sweet' in the sense of 'cool,' then yes."

I didn't, but whatever works for him. I'm silent the rest of the drive, pondering this new side of Bradley. My brother, an illustrator. I'm not sure what I thought he'd become. At twelve, he hated school and had to be forced to do his homework. He spent most of his time at friends' houses.

The exit we take is familiar. "Are we going to Mom and Dad's?"

"No, but Angie lives close to them. Visits a lot."

"That's nice." I'm glad she's taken care of my parents. I would've done the same if our places were reversed.

Bradley doesn't respond as he navigates the road. The area is both familiar and unfamiliar at the same time. Some of the roads have been rerouted, which is disorienting. We turn into a new development wedged in between two older neighborhoods. "They sure crammed a bunch of houses in here."

"Yep." He laughs awkwardly, snort-hiccup.

They're nice houses, though. Two stories with pretty lawns. So maybe Angie *is* a lawyer and she commutes.

The neighborhood seems to wind back forever. I bounce in my seat. "Are we ever going to get there?"

"Jenny . . ." Bradley trails off, his knuckles white on the steering wheel. He pulls over.

I glance at the house we've stopped in front of, white with blue shutters and a blue door. "Is this it?"

"No." His Adam's apple bobs. "Before we go in, I just want to remind you we're all here for you. And Angie loves you too. She was so devastated."

He keeps talking, but his voice is like the Charlie Brown teacher's in my head—*wah, wah, wah, wah*—because a boy has just walked past my car window, and his gait is so achingly familiar I zone in like I'm writing a cover story. My heart lifts as I reach for the door handle. "Why didn't you tell me?" I cry.

Because this makes it all better. That God left me this one thing in the midst of everything else taken from me.

"What?" Bradley says behind me. "Jenny, no!" His fingertips brush my back as he tries to grab my shirt, but I'm out of there.

I slam the door behind me and bolt after the boy. "Steve!"

He doesn't turn at my call, but I'm undeterred. He's two doors down when I reach him, and I tackle-hug him from behind.

"Oof," he says, turning in my arms.

"Steve, I can't believe you're here," I say into his soft T-shirt. "I thought I lost everything, but you're here. You're really here."

He's silent and rigid in my embrace. Why isn't he wrapping his arms around me? I could really use a comforting hug from my boyfriend right now.

"Jenny." Bradley pries me away. "That's not Steve."

"Yes, it is." It's Steve. Same walk. Same shoulders. Same lean, toned build. Same dark blond hair. Same . . .

Actually, not the exact same face. A face that's shaking left and right with a pained expression. He waves a hand awkwardly. "Steve's my dad."

CHAPTER TEN

Oh. *Oh.* Before I can collapse onto the sidewalk, Bradley's there, holding me up. God or the aliens or whoever didn't save Steve for me. He moved on, found someone else to love, and produced a copycat Steve. Almost. From the back, they're almost the same, but from the front, there are more differences. This boy's nose is slimmer. His eyes are brown instead of blue, and his hair doesn't curl at the nape of his neck. He's wearing ratty cargo shorts paired with flip-flops and a dark gray T-shirt with a faded sunset on it, unlike Steve's regular uniform of colorful polos and jean shorts.

"This is Dylan," Bradley says.

"You know him?" I ask incredulously.

Because it makes sense for Angie to stay in touch with Bradley. We've been friends since grade school. But for Steve to maintain a connection with my family . . . My heart aches at the thought he must have cared for me even more than I realized. Maybe he was the one, and I missed my opportunity at true love. Maybe what he meant to say on the phone was that we could finally profess our love for each other. I mean, I didn't think we were there yet, but maybe he was.

Dylan shifts awkwardly. He looks over my shoulder at

Bradley, opens and closes his mouth several times. Finally, he says, "I'm sorry about what happened to you, Jenny."

His voice startles me, both because it reinforces how different he sounds from Steve—more self-assured somehow—and because of the way he addresses me as if he knows me. Both Mr. Fernandez and Lilli acted like they knew me too. It's unsettling, but at least in Dylan's case it's probably due to his dad reminiscing about his long-lost girlfriend.

I detach myself from Bradley, strong enough to stand on my own now. "I'm sorry I attacked you. From the back, you look a lot like your dad, and for a moment I thought maybe not everything in my life had been totally screwed up."

Dylan tugs on a band around his wrist. The face is the shape of a watch, but it doesn't show anything. "About that. My parents—"

"Dylan, don't." Bradley steps up beside me. "Why are you even home?"

He holds Bradley's gaze for a long moment, then lets out a frustrated huff, as if they just had a silent battle of wills and Bradley won.

"Mom sent me on an errand," Dylan says, "but *somebody* drove the car and didn't refill it with gas, so I didn't even make it out of the neighborhood."

I wonder who merits "somebody" loaded with so much disdain.

Bradley sighs heavily. "This is going to make everything harder."

I don't understand anything that's happening here. "*What* are you guys talking about?"

"Follow us." Bradley purses his lips, then grips Dylan's arm and marches him away from me down the sidewalk. Dylan casts me a clenched half smile before bending close to whisper with Bradley. I have so many questions, but since they've shut me out for the moment I ponder them internally. As I stare at Dylan's back, which has the baffling words "Watch more sunsets than Netflix" printed on it, mortification begins to set in. I *attacked* him, this total stranger. Steve's *son*.

Bradley and Dylan turn up a driveway toward another two-story house, this one cream with gray shutters and a wooden sign that says "The Grahams" over the door, and I balk. "Why are we going inside with Dylan? What about Angie?"

Dylan casts me such a pitying look I don't ask another question. I follow them through the garage, into a mudroom, and then a hallway, my brain swimming. We're in Steve's house. Is Steve home? Am I about to encounter my ex? *Is* he my ex since we never technically broke up? I don't want to see Steve. In my imagination, Steve is still seventeen, not old enough to father this boy who resembles him. Or am I about to meet Steve's *wife*? Why would Bradley do that to me?

By the time we stop at the entrance to a family room, I've twisted my shirt hem into a crinkled mess and I want to murder Bradley for dragging me inside this house when we're supposed to be visiting Angie. A woman I assume must be Dylan's mom stands with her back to us, but my gaze is immediately drawn to the girl facing her. Her hair is purple, starting with lavender at the crown of her head and deepening to violet at the tips, like a comic book character. Her eyes are ringed in bright eyeliner as well, making their light color pop even from across the room.

She's wearing a magenta tank top, cuffed black shorts, and gold sandals with straps that crisscross up her calves. I assume she's Dylan's sister, even though I don't see much resemblance.

"Jennifer Olivia Graham!" the woman says in that universal mom-voice, and I snap to attention even though only the first name belongs to me.

Wait. Steve named his daughter after me? And his wife was okay with that?

The woman wags her finger at Jennifer Olivia. "You were supposed to be out of this house thirty minutes ago. You know how important today is. Why couldn't you do this one small thing for me?"

There's something familiar in the woman's voice, something about her commanding tone and how she owns the room. I shift forward, and my tennis shoe squeaks against the wood floor.

The girl spots us, and her eyes widen, making them even more striking. Her mouth drops open gleefully. "Oh, this is going to be so epic."

"What are you—" The woman turns. "Jenny?"

She rushes toward me and envelops me in her arms. In the split second before she tackles me, I take in dark layered hair, glasses, and a flowy shirt tucked into shorts.

"Mom, you're suffocating her," Dylan says.

Dylan, son of Steve.

"Jenny, Jenny," she says. "You're here. I've missed you so much."

My shoulder is wet. She's crying. She's crying because she's so happy to see me. Steve's wife is hugging me like I am her long-lost daughter.

My heart is pounding. I won't. I won't. I won't make this connection.

"JoJo, why do you always have to make everything worse? Draining the gas in my car was a jerk move," Dylan says. "She didn't have to find out this way."

Find out this way.

Jennifer. Ohmygosh, there's another reason Steve's wife would name her daughter after me.

She's hugging me like a long-lost *best friend.*

No. Nonononononono. I shove her off me. "NO!"

When I really look, I *see* her. The deep brown eyes behind the glasses. The tiny freckles still sprinkled over her nose. She's older, but she's there. My best friend. My best friend who apparently married my boyfriend. "Angie?"

CHAPTER ELEVEN

Angie wipes her eyes with one hand and reaches for me with the other. "Jenny, I—"

I can't. I can't listen to excuses. I wrench away and run back down the hall.

"Jenny!" A chorus of voices calls after me. Bradley. Angie. Even Dylan.

Not my namesake, though, I notice.

I'm out the garage door and running down the driveway in seconds.

That whole vague discussion between Bradley and Dylan before—it was about Angie trying to conceal the fact that she used my disappearance to steal my boyfriend. How could she? There's a girl code. Your best friend's guy is off-limits, like, forever.

"Jenny!"

Crap. Angie's chasing me. And there's a stitch in my side because I'm no runner. I can't keep this up.

"Jenny! Wait!" Angie pulls even with me, and I give up, bending over to catch my breath.

"Hey," she says. She plops onto the grass and sits cross-legged so she can look up at me, breathing heavily in the middle of the sidewalk. She's a little out of breath, although it's sad a forty-two-year-old woman caught up to me. But then, Angie ran track. She probably still jogs. I bet it's why she's in good shape.

I collapse across from her, pulling my knees up in front of me, and study her more closely. It's easy to see why I didn't recognize her, despite the dozens of clues. I mean, we came here to see her. It should've been obvious. But my Angie streaked her hair with lemon juice to lighten it every summer; she kept it in a ponytail most days. This older version has uniformly dark chestnut hair, layered and full around her shoulders. She's fit but more . . . womanly, I guess? And the glasses totally threw me off. Angie hates glasses!

She plucks a piece of grass. "I'm sorry you found out that way. I tried to get the kids out of the house."

The kids. I glare at her. "You think that makes it okay? He's my boyfriend! Or he was when I left last week." I rub my temples with the pads of my fingers. "It's so confusing. Everything's so recent for me. I went to New York a week ago. You came over in the morning to help me with last-minute packing and waved from the driveway when my dad took me to the airport." She was standing there in a U2 T-shirt and shorts, shielding her eyes (in contacts, not glasses) as she waved goodbye. "And I talked to Steve on the phone *yesterday.*"

"I know."

I whip up my head.

"But . . . it's not like you disappeared and I jumped Steve five minutes later," she says.

I remember a conversation Angie and I had the day before I left. *If you're so worried about kissing him, just grab him and lay one on him. Chocolate milkshakes on me for a month if he pushes you away.*

I can't help but wonder if at some point she took her own advice. With my boyfriend.

I tug my knees closer. "Thanks for that image."

"I'm sorry. Seriously. I don't even know where to start. I never thought you would come back and—"

"Gee, thanks. That makes it all better." I release my knees and start to stand.

"No!" She tugs me back down. "That's not what I meant at all. It's amazing you're back. The best news in the world. It's just . . . sort of freaky too."

I jerk away from her. "Freaky that you moved in on my *boyfriend*? And named a kid after me?"

"Because we love you!"

I huff. "Strange way of showing it!"

"Everything is about how much we missed you. My whole life changed after you left." She rubs her forehead between her eyebrows, and I see another glimpse of my Angie. She always does that when she's tense. "I don't even know where to start."

"You?" I widen my eyes. "At a loss for words? Shocking."

I'm being sarcastic, but she seems to take my words as a sign of softening because her shoulders loosen.

I mimic her cross-legged position, plant my hands on my knees, and stare down my former best friend. Because news flash, Angie: the "forever" in best friends forever expired when you stole my boyfriend. "Why don't we start with how you stabbed me in the back?"

Angie jolts. She takes a deep breath. "I don't think that's the best place to start."

I raise an eyebrow. "Where then?"

She purses her lips. "With you, Jenny. And August 2, 1995. The day I was sitting at home, watching a movie, waiting until you returned and called to tell me all about New York. I expected you to fill me in on whatever phased plan you'd concocted to convince your parents to let you go to Columbia, since you had your heart set on it."

I wince at the reminder that she knows me so well.

"Instead, my mom ran in and told me to pause the movie because there was breaking news. A plane approaching St. Louis had disappeared. A plane arriving from New York. *Your* plane." I harden myself, trying *not* to imagine myself in her place. "I needed to know what was happening. I tried calling your parents, but they were already at the airport, waiting for you. Brad too."

Wait. Where is Bradley? I twist in the direction of Angie's house. The traitor. Although, once again it hits me how I've neglected to think of him in all of this. What it was like for him. I've been so focused on me and how my life has been upended. But Bradley was there at the airport with my parents, waiting for me to land.

"I would've called your grandparents too if I'd had their numbers, but I didn't." Angie's continuation of the story causes me to swivel back toward her.

"So I called Steve," she adds.

Ah. So that's where it started.

"He hadn't heard anything about it, but as soon as I explained the situation, he was frantic too. He picked me up, and we went to your house. We camped out on your front porch steps until your family came home, hours later. They had nothing to tell us.

The airline, the FAA, even NASA didn't know where your plane had gone.

"Steve went home and left me there. Your mom hugged me so tight." Angie wraps her arms around herself as if she can still feel the embrace. The lump in my throat is huge, but I refuse to cry again. I've cried more in the last twenty-four hours than in the past year.

"Since they hadn't found any wreckage, I kept hoping you'd be found safe somewhere, that maybe the plane's communications were damaged. I was over at your house all the time. Steve came a lot too. Other friends as well. Eventually the copilot's mother formed an official support group. Your parents got really involved, and they weren't home as much, so that's when Steve and I started hanging out together."

"And when you screwed me over," I say bitterly.

"No!" she says emphatically. "It wasn't like that. You were missing, Jenny." Then, in a softer voice, she adds, "Pretty much it was like you were dead."

The words hit me like a punch to the gut. *It was like you were dead.*

"We were grieving." Angie plucks at her shorts. "At first all we talked about was you, but then we started talking about ourselves and getting to know each other outside of you, going for jogs and sitting together at lunch, and, well . . ."

She shrugs as if that's all the explanation that's necessary. I realize that to a certain extent it is. I can see shy Steve being attracted to driven, go-getter Angie. We actually share a lot of the same qualities. We both like to plan. We're both stubborn. And apparently we have the same taste in boys.

"How long?" I ask.

She hesitates, and I'm not sure what answer will satisfy me. I mean, how long is long enough for me to be dead before my best friend and boyfriend get over it and get it on?

"I guess our first official date was the prom." She winces slightly as she says it.

I do a quick mental calculation. August to May. Eight months. But the length of time isn't why she winced.

"The *prom*?" From the first time we watched *Footloose*, then every other prom movie we could get our hands on, we'd planned to double-date to prom. I always envisioned our dates as arm candy there to enhance our prom experience. "That's when you decided to take the plunge with Steve? On *our* night?"

Angie holds out her arms in a sign of surrender. "I'm sorry. I couldn't say no. They dedicated the prom to you."

"What?" I sputter. If there was a poster of me smiling down at Angie and Steve while they slow-danced to "The Way You Look Tonight," I might vomit all over her neighbor's freshly mown lawn.

"Sarah Pritchard thought it'd be a nice gesture," Angie adds. "At least that's what she said. I'm pretty sure she thought if she dedicated it to you, reporters would show up to cover the prom and she'd get to make a statement on TV."

"Reporters?" I echo.

"Yeah. You were one of the most popular stories, since you were the youngest passenger. You and the Springs, who went to New York to celebrate their sixtieth anniversary."

The Springs. For the first time since we left the airport, I'm jolted out of my own messed-up world. What must they be going

89

through? I lost grandparents. The Springs probably lost all their friends. Their kids must be the same age as them, or worse . . . I can't even finish that thought.

"Anyway," Angie continues, bringing me back to my *current* mess. "It didn't work. Or at least not the way Sarah hoped. They might have come if the school hadn't forbidden it. But Steve and I had to be there with you being honored. It wouldn't have been right to stay home."

"But did you have to go *together*?" This is an important distinction. She didn't have to stay home, but she could've gone with a different boy or even with a group of girls.

She folds her hands together and gazes at me seriously. "At the time I thought we were just going as friends to remember you, but looking back . . . I wanted to be with him."

Oh.

There's such simplicity in the statement. Angie's always been prone to arguing her point, with a list of facts to back up why she's right, but this basic declaration, putting her emotions out there, is more powerful than a three-minute closing statement. It's also yet another reminder she isn't the Angie I remember. She's more mature. An honest-to-goodness adult.

Despite my resolve to stay strong, tears prick my eyes again. "It's not fair."

She reaches for my hand. "It's not. I can't change the choices Steve and I made, but I'm happy you're back. I want you in my life. I've missed you so much, Jenny, and I don't want to lose you again. Can you at least try to forgive me?"

I stare at our interlocked hands. Her nails are painted, just like she always had them before. But on the fourth finger of her left hand, a princess-cut diamond rests beside a gold wedding band. Angie's twenty-five years older than me. She's married. Her *kids* are my age. And what she did feels like a betrayal, even if she acted on the belief I was never coming back.

I scoot backward, withdrawing my hand. "I really don't know. I need time."

She clears her throat. "Of course."

I stand and brush off my lacy shorts. "I'm going back to the car. Can you tell Bradley I'll be waiting?"

She flutters her hands, like she doesn't know what to do with them. "Sure."

Good. She should be uncomfortable. "Goodbye, Angie."

I don't necessarily mean it as goodbye forever, but if it sounds that way to Angie, I'm okay with that for now.

CHAPTER TWELVE

On day three in the twenty-first century, I sleep in until eleven o'clock. Either I'm catching up on twenty-five years or my brain has set up a protest against the revelations that happen when I'm awake. I suspect it might be the latter. I'm a generally optimistic person, but this whole situation sucks.

Kelly's at work, but Bradley stays home with me and the kids, explaining, "My schedule is flexible."

As I walk around the house, I notice something odd. "Why don't you have any phones on the wall?"

For a moment he looks confused, but he quickly masks it and pats his pocket. "Most people don't have house phones anymore. Mom and Dad do, I guess 'cause they always have, but we don't really need them."

"Oh." It's weird to think you don't need to be in your house to call someone. Even though cell phones existed in 1995, I didn't know anyone who had one. They were more like this advanced, unattainable technology spies and rich people used in movies. But here, in this house, it's frustrating that Brad and Kelly have a monopoly on my only means of contacting the outside world.

"Is there someone you want to call?" he asks, obviously noticing I'm staring at his pocket.

I refocus on Bradley's face. "Actually, I'd like to talk to Agent Klein."

His eyes flick to the side before meeting my gaze. "I've been in touch with her. What do you want to know?"

I resist the urge to stomp my foot. "What's going on? Do they have the results from the tests yet? Are they going to do more?"

"Curious as always." He scratches his ear. "They confirmed everyone's identities based on the initial tests and are holding off on more for now. There's no need for you to talk to her directly."

"What if I want to?"

Bradley sighs. "You heard her. She's a busy person. I know you want answers, but she can't do her job if everyone's calling her constantly."

Ouch. He makes me sound like an annoying little kid.

Bradley's eyebrows pinch together. "Jenny. I'm sorry."

"Never mind. Go draw. I'll bother the kids."

Eli and Kira are playing with their tablets, which look like big versions of Bradley's phone. I ask them to show me how they work, but all they're set up for are learning games and kids' shows. It still amazes me that everything operates by touch instead of using a controller or keyboard.

After lunch (which Bradley makes!), we play board games. I'm relieved Sorry, Chutes and Ladders, and Memory still exist, even if I don't recognize the cartoon characters on the Memory game. Grandma calls on Bradley's phone to talk to all of us. It's obvious the kids adore her. In the afternoon, Bradley turns on the mammoth TV in the living room to watch stuff they've recorded *on the TV*, no VCR required. Bradley takes the remote with him.

I suspect it's *not* to prevent Eli or Kira from changing the channel.

To be sure, at dinner I ask Kelly, "Why don't you guys watch the news?"

"Boring!" Kira says in a singsong voice.

Kelly meets my eyes without flinching, so much stronger than Bradley. "There's so much violence on the news. It's not appropriate for the kids."

I'm not a kid—well, not a little one. "I want to see what they're saying about our flight."

"We don't watch the news here," Kelly says in such a final tone I realize it's pointless to argue.

That night, alone once again in Kira's room thanks to her extended "sleepover" with Eli, I write, filling my notebook with stories about what I've experienced since my return. Admittedly, most of my potential headlines look like they've jumped off the front page of the *National Enquirer*:

TEEN GIRL RETURNS FROM TRIP TO DISCOVER BEST FRIEND MARRIED BOYFRIEND

NEW YORK–ST. LOUIS FLIGHT JUMPS TWENTY-FIVE YEARS

TWENTY-FIRST-CENTURY FAMILIES ADDICTED TO DEVICES CLAIMING TO BE PHONES

WORLD AGES TWENTY-FIVE YEARS WHILE FLIGHT 237 REMAINS SAME

Maybe if I put the words on paper in a different order or find exactly the right phrase, I'll make sense of it. Grandma said there wasn't any point in trying to find a way back to 1995, but that's what I want more than anything.

When I wake up on the fourth day, I'm more energized. Because today Mom and Dad come home. It's taken this long for them to get a ride to the airport from the remote area in Guatemala where they were working. A part of me believes seeing my parents will make all of this magically go away.

Bradley appears in Kira's doorway. "Are you ready?"

I stuff my notebook in my backpack. "We really can't go to the airport and wait for them at the gate?"

He rubs the back of his neck. "It's still crazy there. Besides, since 9/11 you can't go to the gate anyway."

My gut clenches. "What's nine eleven?" He said it matter-of-factly, and yet if it changed access to airports, it must be more world-rocking news.

He opens his mouth, then closes it with a snap. "A really horrible thing that happened while you were away."

While you were away. Is that how we're labeling my time jump? I lean toward him, my fingers splayed against the small of my back. "I want to know about it—and everything else that's happened in the past twenty-five years. I'm not a four-year-old like Kira that you have to shield from the mean old world."

"I know, Jenny-san, but it's not up to me. Take it up with Mom and Dad."

So this no-news edict came from Mom and Dad. Probably part of that conversation where Bradley went off to talk with Dad alone. "I will. But can you at least tell me why they're so bent on keeping me from it?"

"Because . . ." He tightens his hand on his neck. "Some of it's not nice."

"What do you mean?"

He tucks his chin so he's now cupping his beard. "Some people think Flight 237 is a hoax. That somehow there's a trick being played."

"What?" I laugh but stop when I realize he's serious. Plus, Agent Klein did say they wanted to be sure everyone saw the same thing. "How could a whole plane full of people be a hoax?"

He shrugs. "They have a bunch of theories. But the important thing is *we* know you aren't a hoax."

It's nice to know he believes in me, but still. I don't like the idea of people out in the world thinking I'm part of an elaborate plot to . . . do what exactly?

"What about the FBI's tests?" I massage the spot where they drew my blood. "You said they proved we aren't a hoax."

Bradley releases his chin and nods. "The problem is a lot of people don't trust the FBI."

"Seriously?" I mean, I understand there are conspiracy theorists out there, but what has happened in the past twenty-five years to make it so people don't believe the government when they lay out scientific proof? Granted, thanks to Bradley I haven't seen how they presented the proof, but still.

"Plus, they aren't letting any of the passengers make statements," he adds.

Fair point. "It would probably help their case to let people hear from us."

"Maybe. But there are seventy-two of you. That's a lot of people who could be wildcards."

Also a fair point. "Yeah, who knows what that Art guy would say. Even if it's the truth, he does *not* come across as trustworthy."

"Come on." Bradley turns down the hallway. "We need to get you home."

Home. Yes. I want to be home.

Thirty minutes later, we pull into our driveway, and the tension in my shoulders eases slightly. Same faded brick halfway up the house. Same not-quite-gleaming white siding above. Same fire-engine-red door. I'm not naïve. I expect changes. But after all the revelations I've been hit with, these small familiarities are like the comfort of being wrapped in my favorite Grandma Elaine–crocheted blanket—which had also better be waiting for me inside.

Bradley gets out and I follow. He jangles his keys as he walks to the front door.

This is different: entering through the front door instead of the garage.

But what's the same: the smell. I inhale deeply as I walk through the door into the split foyer. A hint of coffee because Mom brews multiple pots each day, the lemon cleaner used on the tile entry floors, and another indefinable scent that's just the Waters house.

It's stuffy inside. They probably left the thermostat up for their trip; Dad's thrifty that way. I jog up the stairs into the hallway but am stymied by the control pad. It's a touch screen like the phones. I figure it out and turn the temperature to seventy-six, as low as Dad is willing to pay for.

I glance behind me into what was Bradley's room and do a double take.

Different: Bradley's room is a sewing room.

"Wow." I step inside. I knew Mom could sew. She made costumes for me a couple of times in grade school, but I had no idea she was this into it.

Bradley comes up behind me. "Yeah, she makes a lot of clothes for the kids, especially dresses for Kira."

A hook over the closet door holds a full-skirted, sleeveless dress covered in brightly colored circles, with a wide green ribbon as a belt. "I can totally picture that on Kira."

"It keeps her busy since she retired," he adds.

Retired. Of course. *Different.*

I turn to face him. I'm afraid of the answer, but I have to ask. I don't want to go in there and be shocked. "What's in my room?"

I brace myself for him to say it's an office or storage or a playroom for Kira and Eli.

He smiles gently. "They say it's a guest room, but except for taking down the Jason Priestley and Chris O'Donnell posters, it's pretty much still yours."

Considering the lack of anything being still mine up to this point, I'm afraid to believe him, but I stride out of the sewing room and down the hall with hope. When I walk inside, my heart balloons. Because . . .

Same: My bed is still there, covered with the quilt Grandma

Waters made for me. Folded at the foot is my precious afghan, crocheted by Grandma Elaine.

I sink onto the bed and sweep the afghan into my arms, burying my face in it to inhale. It's a bit stale but still familiar. I scan the rest of the room.

Same: my bookshelf. I'd have to do a complete inventory to be sure, but it appears many of my books are still there, plus some others shoved in. My desk remains, though it's clear of the notebooks I stacked carefully on it before I left for New York. I cringe a bit, thinking of some of the diary-like stories I wrote inside. For sure Mom read through them, if she thought I was dead.

Different: my closet holds unfamiliar sweaters and long-sleeved shirts, probably Mom's winter clothes. Her closet isn't big enough to keep all seasons, so she usually switches them out and stores the off-season in the basement. Since Bradley thinks they got rid of my clothes, it makes sense she'd use my closet instead of tramping up and down the stairs.

Same: my corkboard, except it isn't hanging on the wall; it's leaning against the closet wall.

I retrieve it and sit cross-legged on the floor with my back against the bed.

Bradley crouches beside me. "I forgot about that," he says softly.

I point at a photo strip of me and Angie, making a range of goofy faces at the camera. "We took these at the mall." I turn my face up to him. "A month ago."

"I'm sorry, Jenny." He strokes my head, as if I'm Kira. It's comforting but yet another reminder of how much he's changed.

The corkboard is covered in pictures of me and Angie, from second grade to last month. In complementary princess dresses for Halloween. Both smiling huge with braces on our teeth. On a float trip. At my church's youth camp last summer, when she came along. On loungers at the pool. Dressed up for a mock trial competition. So many memories—recent for me and distant for her. An open wound instead of a faded scar.

I study another photo of me and Angie, our arms looped around each other at the county fair, where we volunteered at a booth to raise money for Ronald McDonald House. There's one of her in glasses, back in grade school, before she switched to contacts. But I can see her in the woman I met the other day too.

Her plea for forgiveness has been on my mind constantly, but I don't even know how to process what she's done.

I only have one photo with Steve. It's from the last day of junior year. We're leaning against a lab table in our chemistry class, our arms touching but not looped together or anything because we weren't dating yet. It's not even just us; Steve's best friend, Matt, is hamming it up in the background behind us, his arms spread wide. Steve stopped me on the way out of school later that afternoon to ask me out. It was the best last day of school ever.

Maybe if we'd started dating during the school year, I'd have more photos documenting our relationship, but it's not like you carry a camera around with you to the movies or Six Flags. We hung out nearly every week this summer, but informally. Angie must have photo albums full of important events with Steve. My heart clenches at the sad fact this is all I have left of him.

Below me, the garage door rumbles.

"They're here!" I scramble to my feet, the corkboard falling to the floor as I dart for the hallway.

Moments later, Mom calls from the door into the garage. "Jenny?"

We're both running to meet each other. I know she will make everything better. She'll fix this as only she can. A sob catches in my throat. I reach the top of the steps. She's on the landing by the front door. I practically slide down the steps to collapse in her arms.

"Mom." I bury my face in the hollow space between her neck and shoulder. She's damp from the heat, but even mixed with sweat, she smells like cinnamon gum and rose perfume.

She grips me tighter, and there's an extra squishiness to her middle. *Different.*

"Jenny," Dad says before his arms wrap around us too, adding Old Spice to the mix.

This. This is what I've needed since I got off that misdirected plane and encountered my misdirected life.

"I missed you so much," I say, my eyes tightly shut as I savor the moment.

"Oh, Jenny." Mom chokes. "You can't even imagine how much we missed you."

And I feel selfish. Because I missed them for a week and three days, while they've been missing me for twenty-five years.

Dad lets go first but keeps a hand on my back, as if afraid I'll disappear. Mom takes hold of my arms and pushes me back, but I don't open my eyes. I'm afraid to see the changes in my parents.

Mom gasps. "It's true. Brad said, and the news reports, but . . . Mark, look at her."

Dad rubs my back. "She's not a sideshow, Carol. She's our daughter."

He says it so firmly I feel like he's talking to more than Mom.

"Aren't you going to look at us, sweetheart?" Mom says gently. Dad finally lets his hand drop, and I hear him move.

I breathe deeply, open my eyes, and there are my parents. They're *old*.

CHAPTER THIRTEEN

I try to disguise my panic, but I've already lost three grandparents, and my parents look like grandparents. They both have more wrinkles around their eyes and mouths, plus a few age spots. Dad's hair is iron gray, and it's not all there. It's receding along the temples. He appears to be in decent shape, but he's . . . sixty-eight. Nearly seventy years old! There's a slight slump to his shoulders where he always stood tall before.

And Mom . . . her hair's not strawberry blond like mine anymore. It's light brown and clearly dyed because I can see roots at the part. It's cut in a short bob that curves around her face, which is significantly more rounded, as is the rest of her body. She used to wear tailored pants and blouses, even on her days off. Now, her knit pants and shirt just scream "grandma."

But I won't say it. I won't mention how old they look or that I'm internally calculating how long it will be before they join Grandma Elaine at the assisted living facility. I think I understand now why all the photos are missing from the walls at Bradley's house. He—or more likely Kelly—didn't want me to freak out over how Mom and Dad have aged.

I stretch my face in a smile, ignoring the tightness in my

chest and the mental slideshow that's rapidly aging them to seventy-five, eighty-five, ninety-five. "I'm so glad you're here."

Mom squeezes my hand. "Let's go upstairs. Brad can get our luggage."

Even after days with Kelly calling his name, I still don't think of him as Brad, but I might have to start if even my parents no longer call him Bradley.

"On it." He jogs down the steps. Although he is younger than my parents were when I left, he is closer to what I expect them to be.

I start up, Mom behind me.

"Give me a sec," Dad says. "Bad knee."

He holds the railing and takes the steps slowly, one foot up, then the other on the same step.

"Is he okay?" I ask Mom, my voice rising.

Mom hugs me against her side. "Eventually he'll get a knee replacement. It wasn't too bad, but he stepped off a ladder wrong the other day at the site and it flared up again. Part of getting older."

"But you're not supposed to be this old!" I burst out, ruining my resolve.

Dad pauses on the top step. Mom stares at me, her expression full of regret. "I know, sweetheart. But this is the hand God dealt us."

My parents raised us as a family of faith, so I get where she's coming from. My faith has always been pretty comfortable; I like rules, after all, and God provides a book full of them, giving me a set of life guidelines to follow. But if God dealt me this hand, I want to scream at Him. To drive over to the church, march up to the altar, and yell at Him to deal me a new one. Because this time jump is so outside any set of guidelines I can grasp. Where's the Bible story about time travel? *That* would be super helpful to me now.

Mom's still watching me, waiting for me to be strong, but now that she and Dad are here, I just want to let go. "How am I supposed to live here? I don't understand how things work in this world anymore. Everything passed me by, including my friends."

Dad cups my cheek. "We may be older, but we're still your parents. We're the same people. We love you more than anything on this earth, and we will get through this. Together."

I close my eyes. At least that's the same.

Our first evening together is full of tears and many stories. We are a family unit, as Bradley runs out to pick up Grandma (she's offended at my surprise that she can leave the retirement home). We eat pizza in the living room off paper plates since Mom hasn't grocery shopped in a week. Thankfully my favorite pizza hasn't changed.

Mom, Dad, and Bradley tell me their version of my disappearance. Hours in the airport, waiting with other families at the gate and then in a conference room. Finally coming home without answers, only the barest hope that my plane was lost somewhere and might someday be found. Endless months and then decades of unanswered questions. Pressure from the world to declare the passengers and crew of Flight 237 dead, and how the family members of others left behind helped them through. Grandma adds in her anguish, sitting with Grandpa at their house when the news came through, trying to support Mom while she was grieving herself. It's like having my heart ripped out all over again, but I listen because they need to tell it. By the end, my limbs are all heavy, as if full of the words they've spoken. I will write them down with my other stories.

After they finish, they ask to hear every detail of my experience, even though it's not that exciting except for when we tried to land and they couldn't find our plane. They have so much more time to cover. They tell me more about the grandparents I lost. Bradley tells me how he met Kelly, about the wedding. It's like they feel the need to cram twenty-five years into one night.

I tense as I consider why they might be taking me on this emotional roller coaster of all the highs and lows I missed. Is it because they're afraid I'll disappear again? I've been here for days, so I feel pretty safe, but their uncertainty plants seeds of doubt. After all, nobody knows where we were. Considering I am exactly the same, I tend to think we weren't anywhere, that instead of flying from one location to another, we flew from one time to another. But how? That's the question I can't possibly answer.

When I awake the next morning in my own bed, I am still in the same-different room. Moving back home didn't reset the space–time continuum. I'm not sure if I'm relieved or not. I want to be in 1995, where everything is familiar, but in 1995, there's no Kira or Eli. If I somehow returned and lived my life as planned, would Bradley's story with Kelly still play out the way he told it last night? Or would I mess it up somehow? It's confusing—and not a question I'm equipped to tackle before I'm fully alert. I smell coffee and bacon, so Mom must have made an early-morning run to the store.

The aroma draws me down the hall. I'm about to go in, but the tone of her voice stops me. "She's going to find out eventually, Mark, whether we keep her holed up in the house or not."

Find out what? I plaster myself against the wall, trying to blend in.

"But school?" Dad protests. "Those kids will eat her alive! It's bad enough what people are saying in the media. Imagine what her classmates would subject her to."

I've been so focused on the now and what happened on the plane I haven't considered my future, but school is a part of that. I can't go to college without finishing high school. Also, I really want to know what they're saying in the news! This media ban is ridiculous.

Dad's next words catch my attention. "And Angie still needs to talk to her about—"

"Jenny!" Mom pops around the corner, wielding a greasy spatula. "You're up!"

I slap my hand over my heart. "Geez, Mom, way to Norman Bates me!"

She waves the spatula. "No knife. Come on in. Sit."

I eye Dad suspiciously, but his mouth is sealed tight now that he knows I was listening. I zero in on his ratty blue robe. "Is that the robe I gave you last year?"

I realize my mistake, that my last year is twenty-six years ago, but Dad smiles. "Couldn't give it up."

I lean over to pat his chest. "I think it might be about time." "Maybe."

A timer beeps. Mom places the bacon on a plate covered with a paper towel. "Mark, could you get those biscuits?"

"I'll do it." I move to open the second drawer down; thankfully the pot holders are still there. The enticing aroma of fresh biscuits mingles with the bacon as I open the oven and set the pan out to cool. I pour my coffee—one part milk, two parts coffee—and sit in my usual spot.

"No eggs?" There's a distinct whine to Dad's voice.

Mom points at Dad. "You're lucky I'm letting you eat bacon."

I don't ask because I'm afraid this is a topic related to aging. It sounds like the sort of thing Grandma Waters used to say to Grandpa Waters. I swallow around a lump in my throat.

Dad slumps into his seat at the table while Mom plates the food and brings it to us. The table is also the same, nicks and dings carved into it from banging our silverware or setting a plate down too hard.

I wait for Dad to bless our food and then dig in. By my second piece of bacon, I'm ready to address what I overheard. "What's this about school?"

Dad glances at Mom before he answers. "It starts in a couple of weeks—"

"What? It's still the first week of August!" With no newspaper or TV, I've lost track of the days, but school doesn't start until September. "Have they moved Labor Day?"

Dad chuckles briefly. "No, just the first day of school, but we were thinking it's probably better for you to do school online this year."

I hold the bacon in front of my mouth. "*Online?*" I don't understand how that would work. Like here, at the house? On a computer or something? We use computers for typing and stuff at school, even to lay out the *Press*, but I can't imagine how I could do all my classes that way. "And miss my senior year?"

Mom scrunches up her face. "Sweetheart, it's not really *your* senior year."

I let the bacon drop to my plate. "I *know*." As if I need a reminder my most important high school year happened for Angie and everyone else without me. "But what does that even mean? No other students? All my classes some sort of independent study? How does that look for college?"

I may be out of the loop, but missing my final year of high school can't be a plus sign on my transcript.

"We'd work all of it out," Dad says.

I love Mom and Dad, but I don't think I can stand to be stuck in this house with them forever, with no other people my age. I place both palms on the table. "I want to go."

"Jenny . . ." Mom looks helplessly at Dad.

"Why are you even arguing, Mom? I heard you talking to Dad. It was your idea."

She butters her biscuit. "In theory it sounded like a good idea, but it's so soon since you returned, and some of the classes you already took are obsolete—"

"Obsolete?" I flinch. The word makes me sound irrelevant in this century. It's a nice way of saying, *You're a dinosaur, Jenny.*

"Well . . ." Mom shrugs. "That computer programming class you took sophomore year. Computers are much more advanced these days. They don't even really look the same . . ."

Dad jumps in. "Our phones are basically minicomputers."

Now that I think of it, I didn't see a computer at Bradley's house. He always closed the door when I went near his office. "My phone will be my computer?" Based on what I've seen in this century, I need one of those.

Dad shakes his head. "That's not what I meant."

"When can I get one?" I need a crash course in technology if I'm going to survive here.

Dad and Mom share another glance. "We'll talk about it."

"The phone?"

"School," Mom says. She taps my plate, as if I'm a small child. "Your bacon's getting cold, Jenny."

Obediently, I shove the bacon into my mouth, but I'm not finished with this conversation. My senior year will not be spent within these four walls. There's a whole new world out there for me to explore, answers to track down. I'm pursuing this story whether they want me to or not.

CHAPTER FOURTEEN

After breakfast, Mom and Dad seclude themselves in their room, I guess to discuss my school demand. I am starving for news of the outside world. I get dressed in one of the outfits Kelly bought me—since Bradley was right about Mom donating all my clothes and it feels weird to wear my "I Heart NY" shirt again—and find myself creeping into the living room, even though nobody's told me I can't be there. They've updated since I disappeared, with new couches and a giant flat-screen TV like the one in Bradley's house. At least the framed Thomas Kincaid bridge print behind the love seat is the same. The wall adjacent to the windows still has family photos, although Bradley and Kelly's wedding picture, as well as photos of Eli and Kira, have been added to the collection. I take in all the changes as I head for the familiar end table beside Dad's recliner, where he keeps the remote control.

It's not on top, where it used to be. I kneel beside the end table and check the shelf, but it's not there either. After several minutes searching the floor, the seat of his armchair, the other end tables, every inch of the room it seems possible to set the remote control, I conclude Mom and Dad have resorted to Bradley's tactic: they've hidden it.

Standing, I survey the room and consider my options. I could confront them, although at this very moment I'd rather focus on the school issue with them than the news issue. I could give up, or I can come up with a new plan. Since I can't *watch* the news, maybe I can steal a paper from a neighbor? Or just go borrow one.

Or I could go to a direct source. I've already confirmed Mom and Dad do, indeed, have a normal phone like I'm used to. It's on the wall in the kitchen.

Glancing down the hallway, I verify their door is still closed and then head for the kitchen. My target is the bottom drawer on the left-hand side of the oven, where we keep the phone book. My hand on the knob, I send a quick prayer upward that, like the pot holders, the phone book will still be in its usual place, then jerk open the drawer.

I push aside a mess of papers and breathe a sigh of relief when I spot the phone company logo, although when I pull out the book, it's super light. Do people not list their numbers anymore? That could screw up my plan. I take the book to the kitchen table. The date on the cover is 2012, so they've had it for a while. I hope whoever I find in here still has the same number. And that's the question: Who should I call?

Even if the FBI is listed, I doubt they'd connect me to Agent Klein. Besides, Agent Klein is "busy" and probably wouldn't tell me anything anyway.

I briefly consider calling a news station for answers, but that would be a direct violation of Agent Klein's orders. Even though I don't believe "no comment" is the best strategy, I won't openly defy the FBI.

That leaves the other passengers. It seems likely that anyone else who was on the plane would be staying with family, like me, even if they are adults. Maybe some of them don't have the same last names, but maybe they do. As annoying as he is, plane groupie would probably be the best source. I expect Art's thoroughly researched what happened with the plane by now, but I don't remember his last name. I know he said it when he came over and talked to me and the Springs, but I was still trying to ignore him at that point. Which brings me to my last shot.

I open the phone book to S for Spring. His name is Ted, and there's actually a Ted and two Theodores. Maybe his son? It's worth a try.

I retrieve the cordless phone from the wall and take it along with the phone book to the basement for privacy. A woman answers on the third ring. "Hello?"

"Hi. I'm looking for Ted and Agnes Spring."

She laughs. "You and everyone else. They're all over the news! But the Springs who used to have this number aren't even related."

"Oh." I deflate. "Sorry."

"No problem."

All three variations of Ted/Theodore are a bust, so I start at the top, with Andrew Spring. Nobody knows Agnes and Ted, or if they do, they're not talking to me.

When I get to Connor Spring, I know immediately that I've found the right house, because I recognize the voice that answers.

"Mrs. Spring?" I say, my own voice full of hope.

"Yes?" She sounds hesitant, like she might hang up if I don't talk fast.

"It's Jenny Waters. I've been calling every Spring in the phone book, trying to find you."

"Jenny!" There's a smile in her voice now. "Oh, honey, how are you?"

Tears clog my throat. I thought I was done with them, but her simple question hits me in a way I can't explain. "Um. You know. Trying to find out what's going on."

"Aren't we all," she says, only not like a question. "Honey, do you know about the meeting tomorrow?"

"Meeting?" I straighten.

"Yes, I think Captain McCoy, the pilot, talked to your brother about it. Those of us from the flight are meeting tomorrow night, to share our stories and support each other."

"Bradley knows about this?" If the pilot talked to Bradley, surely he told Mom and Dad. We were all together last night. Why didn't anyone mention it to me? Add it to the things-we-won't-tell-Jenny list. "Hold on."

"Sure, honey."

Cradling the phone to my ear, I march upstairs and knock on Mom and Dad's door. After a moment, Mom opens it. Her eyes widen at the sight of the phone. "Who are you talking to?"

"Mrs. Spring. She asked if I'm coming to a meeting tonight with the other people from the plane."

"Did the phone ring?" Mom's still focused on my ear.

"No. I called her."

Dad joins her at the door. "We know about the meeting. Captain McCoy called us."

So he talked to Bradley *and* my parents. They don't tell me anything! But blasting them about it right now won't get me out of this house.

"So can I go?" I put on my best puppy-dog look. "You said your group helped you."

Mom looks at Dad; he shrugs. They're doing their silent communication thing. I've never been able to interpret it, and they've had even more years together to perfect it. Mom finally turns back to me, resigned.

"Okay, we'll take you," she says.

Yes! I'm not so sure about the sharing part, but I'm all about getting answers.

"I'll see you tomorrow," I tell Mrs. Spring.

CHAPTER FIFTEEN

The following evening, Mom and Dad drive me twenty-five minutes north, up near the airport, to a small church. When they direct me to the basement, I feel like I'm joining AA (or how AA is portrayed in movies, anyway), but I guess this is what I signed up for.

Mom rubs my back. "They're inside. Are you sure you'll be okay in there alone?"

"Jenny!" a familiar voice calls.

"I won't be alone." I turn to greet Mrs. Spring; Mr. Spring is, of course, at her side. "Mr. and Mrs. Spring!"

I introduce them to my parents, who visibly relax in their comforting presence.

"All right, if you're sure," Mom says. "Brad only lives ten minutes away, so if you need us, you can call us."

"With what?"

Mom digs in her purse. "I'll leave my phone with you. The passcode is your birthday—011578." She hands me the phone and shows me how to navigate to Dad's phone number.

I pocket the phone. "Thanks. I'll see you at eight thirty."

Mom and Dad both hug me, casting several glances back as they walk to their car.

Mrs. Spring keeps a hand on my shoulder as we walk in. "We didn't get to chat very long yesterday. So how *are* you doing, honey?"

I shrug, only realizing afterward that doing so dislodges her hand, and it was nice having the support.

She sighs. "I'm glad you came. We've been worried about you."

I pause to really look at them. They took care of me in that horrible room at the airport, and they were still stuck there for who knows how long. It probably took hours for the FBI to interview everyone and take samples. I'm glad Bradley got me out of there, but I'm sorry no one came to rescue them. "Thank you."

We descend the stairs to a fellowship hall with accordion-style partitions that slide along tracks to separate the larger room into smaller meeting rooms. My tennis shoes squeak on the linoleum floor. It smells like coffee—a pot is brewing on a table by the wall—and, strangely, paint. The walls do look pristinely cream. Beside the coffee is a pitcher of water and a plate of brownies that are calling my name.

"Do you want a brownie?" I ask the Springs.

Mrs. Spring shakes her head, but Mr. Spring starts toward the table with me. "I never say no to a coffee."

A man approaches the table from another direction at the same time. I don't recognize him at first without his uniform. It's the pilot.

"Jenny, I'm glad you came," Captain McCoy says.

I wonder if this is a standard phrase you say at support groups.

"Thanks," I reply. He looks different in jeans and a short-sleeved button-down shirt that hangs loose. I'd guess he's somewhere between the age my parents were when we got on the plane and now.

"We'll start in a few minutes." He gestures at the brownies. "Please enjoy the refreshments."

Since it seems weird to say thanks again, I nod and stuff a brownie in my mouth. It's delicious and clearly not from a mix. Although, who am I to judge? They might've really improved brownie mixes while we were gone.

Mrs. Spring motions for us to join the circle of chairs set up in the middle of the room. The fluorescent lights are harsh overhead. I settle into my seat and scan the others. It's not the whole roster of passengers. I mean, obviously some of them don't live in St. Louis. For example, I don't see the poor businessman who got Tasered by the security guard. (Bradley explained those things to me, and it sounds even more awful now that I know what they are.) Or the lady who was reading *People*. Or a lot of others for that matter. There are about twenty people here, though, including the other copilot and the younger flight attendant, so I guess most of the crew was St. Louis–based.

Captain McCoy glances at a clock above the coffee table and claps his hands. "I think most everyone is here, so why don't we all take a seat and get started?"

Captain McCoy leaves a seat between himself and me, and nobody sits in it. I'm grateful for the breathing room and anxious to get this conversation started. There's so much I want to know.

Captain McCoy leans forward with his elbows on his knees. "Our flight's unexpected detour through time has caused quite a stir."

I snigger. I can't help myself. I mean, "unexpected detour through time"?

Captain McCoy sits back and grins at me. "Like that, do you?"

My cheeks grow warm as everyone focuses on me. "Well, it's just . . . the way you said it. Like we'd encountered a delay or something. But our whole lives have been upended."

His grin slips. "That's why we're here. Most of you"—he sweeps a hand around the circle—"are strangers to each other. Walter, Tracey, Stephanie, and I at least knew each other." He points at the copilot and young flight attendant. I assume the other woman he mentioned is the absent flight attendant. "We've been able to talk about adjusting to life here, how to respond to incessant requests from the media, etcetera, and we realized it might be beneficial to expand that support to the passengers."

"It's definitely helpful to have someone else going through this with you," Mrs. Spring says, gripping Mr. Spring's hand. Tears sparkle in her blue eyes. Poor Mrs. Spring. She's probably lost more people than I have. "I don't know what I'd do without—"

"Did you start yet?" a voice echoes down the stairs.

It's plane groupie.

"I'm here!" Art declares as he bursts into the room. His shirt says, "Eat. Sleep. Time Travel. Repeat." If he's here for support, I'll chug the entire pot of coffee, black. If Agent Klein hadn't put a gag order on us, I bet he'd be granting interviews left and right, telling reporters how awesome it is we've jumped ahead to a new century.

"Welcome, Mr. Ross," Captain McCoy says.

Ross! That's it.

Art waves a hand. "Dude. I'm not formal like that. Y'all can call me Art. Some of my friends even call me Artie. But they're all, like, *old* now." He laughs, but it goes on so long I wonder if maybe he does feel a twinge of discomfort about our situation. Maybe there's more to Art than the obnoxious front he puts on.

There are several chairs open in the circle, but of course he makes a beeline for the open spot beside me. He plops down and leans in. "Hey there, Jenny, what's the 4-1-1?"

I'm tempted to scoot my chair closer to Mrs. Spring, but not only will the metal folding chair make an awful screech and draw even more attention; I don't want to show Art he's bothering me. Also, did I tell him my name on the plane? Although, this doesn't matter, since according to Angie, everyone knows who I am. She said it was because I was the youngest on the plane, though, and Art isn't *that* much older than me—maybe nineteen or twenty?

"We were just getting started," I say, nodding toward Captain McCoy to indicate Art should give him his attention.

"Ooh," Art says. "I have so many theories about how we got here. Like—"

"Perhaps we can discuss that another time," Captain McCoy says. "The purpose of this meeting is to share our stories. It's a support group, Art."

Art leans back and stretches his legs out before him. "Gotcha."

"Excuse me." I raise my hand. "Is that the *only* reason we're here? Because I'd really like to talk about what's going on with the FBI and these people who think we're a hoax."

"We have a limited amount of time tonight, Jenny," Captain McCoy says. "We'll dig into that another day, okay?"

Not really. That's why I came! I open my mouth to protest, but he's already moving on.

"So why don't we go around the room," he says, "introduce ourselves, and share a bit about what's happened since we returned. Walter will start."

As the copilot clears his throat, Art grabs my hand and leans close to my ear. "I'll talk to you about that stuff after, Jenny."

He writes a phone number across my palm, and it's sort of weird, like when I blushingly wrote my number on this guy's hand at a youth rally last year (he called once, and it was awkward, so we never talked again). But also I really do want to talk more about the plane and the FBI, and Art sounds serious for once, so I nod and curl my fingers closed.

I missed part of the copilot's introduction, something about living with his mom. "Anyway, she's gone. Ten years ago, I guess. All by herself because I don't have any brothers or sisters. Our airline doesn't exist anymore, so I'm applying elsewhere. And I have to retrain for my job because planes are different now."

People murmur condolences for Walter's mother and ask questions about the job. My own questions about what the world is saying about us, whether the FBI has discovered why we jumped ahead in time, fade into the background in the face of Walter's despair. Poor guy. He's so dull, with his grayish skin and stubbled cheeks. And now he has no one.

Tracey the flight attendant is next. She tugs on the chestnut braid hanging over her shoulder. A diamond ring flashes on her ring finger. "Well. It's weird. Everyone's older. I'm twenty-five, and when I left, my fiancé was twenty-seven."

Oh, man. I'm afraid to hear where this is going.

"He's fifty-two now, but . . . Keith waited for me." Her lips tremble. "He waited twenty-five years, said there was never anyone else, and how can I turn that down, even if he is so much older?"

"Wow," I breathe. What if Steve had waited for me? I haven't seen him yet, and I honestly don't know how I'll feel when I do, but I can't imagine dating a forty-two-year-old man. It seems gross—and possibly illegal?—but then, Tracey's story is different. They were engaged. She's an adult.

The testimonies continue. Parents who have died. Pretty much everyone has to start over job-wise. Being a student, I haven't considered how the time jump would affect someone with a career, but it makes sense. I've seen how much technology has changed, just with the things around our house. Some jobs don't exist anymore, like poor Miss Klaffke's—she was a computer operator. Apparently everything she used to do is automatic now.

"I'm Valerie Wen," the next woman says. I remember her from the conference room at the airport. She's attractive, younger than Angie but older than Tracey. "I teach grade school—third grade. A lot's changed, but the school district will let me teach again if I get up to speed and recertify, assuming the FBI clears us." She casts a glance at Captain McCoy. "So I do care about what's happening with the investigation. And I'd really like answers too. Imagine standing in front of a class full of kids. They'll have a million questions about where I was!"

"Of course," Captain McCoy says. "We all want to know what happened. There just aren't any answers yet."

Valerie exhales through her nose. "I know! It's just so frustrating. Because while I can probably get my job back, my personal life is a mess, and it'd be nice to understand why. My husband had me declared dead and remarried five years after we disappeared. He's very happy. Has three teenagers. *We* were very happy before Flight 237, so it's awkward. He feels guilty, but he loves his new wife. Basically he's a bigamist." She shrugs as if there's nothing to do, and I guess there isn't, but it's awful. I feel so sorry for both of them. "And to top it all off, this really cute guy came up to me in Starbucks the other day and asked me out. Took me a while to place him. He was one of my students." She holds up her hand. "Like, one of my students when I disappeared."

"So he was"—Tracey scrunches up her nose, calculating—"ten the last time you saw him?"

Valerie tips her head to the side. "Nine. Cute kid." She pauses. "*Surprisingly* attractive man. Who I used to scold in class for his inability to sit still."

By now, half the circle is chuckling.

"So?" Mrs. Spring leans forward. "Did you say yes?"

Valerie throws up her hands helplessly. "I told him I'd think about it. But I'm not really over my husband, you know? It's been years for him, but for me it's been barely a week."

Exactly! I can't help but identify with Valerie's situation. I mean, I wasn't married, but with how it feels like yesterday and everyone expects me to just accept that it happened forever ago.

"We're all going to be feature stories in *People* magazine," I say. "Or someone's gonna write a book."

Art gasps. "Try books, plural. Haven't you seen—"

"Excuse me, son. I'm Ted Spring, and I'm going to take the floor for a moment," Mr. Spring interrupts.

I swallow a laugh. Guess I'm not the only one Art annoys.

"And this is my wife, Agnes," Mr. Spring continues. "I wish we had a story about long-lost love like Tracey or even a student harboring a crush. Unfortunately, we've mostly encountered sadness since our return." He chokes up, and my lingering amusement vanishes.

Mrs. Spring takes over. "Yes. We went to New York for our sixtieth anniversary, so as you can imagine, most of our friends were in their later years already in 1995. So now, so many years later, all of our friends are gone. Our son is gone. He had a heart attack at seventy. Our oldest daughter lives in an assisted living facility. She's a year older than me. Our younger daughter lives in California near her kids. Our house was sold not too long after we disappeared, our belongings distributed among our children. We're currently living with our son's son and his wife. They're still working, so we mostly have the house to ourselves, but I know it's odd for him to have grandparents living with him who are the same age as his mother."

I knew the Springs would have it tough, but I didn't imagine this. News flash, Jenny: other people on Flight 237 came back to much more devastating situations than you.

Mr. Spring already has his arm around Mrs. Spring, but I reach out and hug her from the other side. "I'm so sorry."

Mr. Spring smiles tremulously. "It's not all bad. We have grown great-grandchildren, so we have great-great-grandchildren too. Not many people have the opportunity to know so many generations. We will get to teach them about our family."

"You have such an amazing attitude, Ted," says Captain McCoy. "Thank you for sharing with us." He turns to me. "Jenny? What's going on with you?"

My concerns seem petty after what the Springs just shared. "Um. You know. Friend stuff."

Mrs. Spring squeezes my knee. "That can't be all, Jenny."

She furrows her brow, staring into my eyes, not allowing me to hide.

I crinkle the napkin that held my brownie. "All but one of my grandparents died. My best friend married my boyfriend. My parents and my brother are so much *older*. Plus, I'm basically grounded. It's amazing they let me out of the house to come here. They won't even let me read a *newspaper*."

I'm surprised to feel tears welling up, in this room full of relative strangers who are now nodding at me, but I know they empathize. Because they understand—these random people who just happened to book the same flight as me. It changed us all in ways we never could have imagined, and now we're in this together.

CHAPTER SIXTEEN

The next morning, I'm in my room writing out a list of reasons Mom and Dad should let me attend school, when the doorbell rings. A peek out my window reveals an unfamiliar car in the driveway, but then, the only familiar cars at this point are Bradley and Kelly's. I leave my notebook on my bed and set out to investigate. Mom is shut in their room on the phone—also curious—so it's Dad who answers the door. I peer around the corner down the steps.

Dad wedges himself into the door. "I've told you—all of you—no interviews."

"Mr. Waters"—the voice is female, crisp and persuasive—"we just want to know how your daughter is doing. A human-interest story. We—"

"No. That's my final answer. And if you or any other reporters show up on my doorstep again, I'll call the cops. Spread the word." Dad shuts the door and splays both hands and his forehead against it.

I step fully into view. "Reporters want to interview you?"

Wait. Of *course* they do. Assuming the passengers and crew are following the FBI's orders, our family and friends are the next best thing. The FBI can't possibly muzzle all of them—although I bet they're trying.

Dad lets his hands fall to his sides and turns. He appears more resigned than surprised I overheard. Then again, it's the second time in two days. Mom and Dad are obviously out of practice with the whole parenting gig. "They've been calling Brad ever since they learned you left the airport with him. Now that they know we're home . . ." He shrugs and starts up the stairs.

"Angie said I was sort of famous." I can't help the bit of delight that slips into my voice. I haven't really aspired to fame, but maybe it'd be nice to be noticed.

Dad stops. "*Angie* mentioned that?" His knuckles turn white on the railing, and his emphasis on her name doesn't escape my notice.

My own reporter instincts are heightened. "Why was it weird for her to mention it?"

School was top of mind in our breakfast conversation yesterday, but now I remember Dad brought up Angie before he knew I was listening in.

Dad doesn't answer until he reaches the top of the stairs. "Believe me, it's better to stay out of the limelight. Your mom and brother and I discovered that years ago. In time Angie will have something to share with you about that too."

"Well, that's not at all cryptic."

He chuckles.

I lift my chin. "Besides, I'm not speaking to Angie right now."

He tugs me in for a hug. "You will. You girls always get through your spats."

"Spats!" I sputter. "Dad, she married my boyfriend!"

"Yes, well . . . she's been hurt by you, too, even if it isn't your fault. She missed you terribly."

My face burns. "It's not the same at all. I didn't *choose* to disappear."

"It's not, but consider that Angie lost her best friend. I know what she's done seems catastrophic, but when you left last week"—he stumbles over referring to my timeline as *last week*—"did you believe you'd one day marry Steve?"

"I . . ." What were my expectations for my relationship with Steve? When I got on the plane, I was hoping he'd finally kiss me. I was barely thinking about homecoming yet, much less prom or the rest of our lives. Obviously Angie stole all that too. I cross my arms. "That's not the point, Dad."

"I think it is, Jenny. Because you seem to care a lot more about Angie than Steve in this scenario. Your mom and I had each other when you disappeared. And Brad. Is it any surprise they turned to each other?"

I don't want to look at the situation from Angie's viewpoint. I hate that he's making me consider they might belong together.

Mom and Dad's bedroom door bursts open, banging against the wall.

"It's all settled," Mom declares as she marches toward us.

I glance up at Dad before facing her again. "What's settled?"

She clasps her hands together. "I've registered you for school."

I retreat a step. "That was quick."

I really thought I'd have to work on them more. I already had fourteen reasons they should let me attend school.

Mom smiles gently. "Your resourcefulness tracking down

Mrs. Spring the other day proved we can't expect you to sit around in this house with us for the next year. So your dad and I talked more and decided you're right—you deserve a senior year. The school board agreed to accept all your existing credits based on your special circumstances."

"Well, that's . . . that's great." My voice squeaks. It's what I wanted, but now that it's happening—and fast—it's a terrifying prospect.

"It'll be fine, Jenny," Mom says, obviously sensing my nerves. "English is still English. History is still history." She frowns slightly. "Well, there's an extra twenty-five years in there to learn, but the rest is the same. Math is math."

Of course it is. I can do this. "Is my school different?"

Mom and Dad exchange a look. "Not that much actually," Dad says. "A few updates, obviously. Different teachers. New technology. Some extra security."

"Why? Is high school more dangerous these days?" I picture fights breaking out in the hallways, metal detectors at the entrances.

Mom and Dad exchange another loaded look.

"I'd rather not get into it," Mom says.

They make me want to scream, the way they keep doing this, hiding the truth. "You know I'll eventually learn whatever it is you're hiding about what I missed."

"We just don't want to pile everything on at once," Dad says.

"What, like my brain will explode?" When their gazes remain steady, no give at all, I throw my hands up. "Fine. Can you take me to the library?"

"Why?" Mom recoils in a suspicious overreaction to such a simple request.

"So I can do some research on the last twenty-five years and get up to speed before school starts." And read an actual newspaper. I am dying to hold the *Post-Dispatch* in my hands, to inhale its crisp scent.

Mom clears her throat and smooths her expression. "I'll get you whatever resources you'd like."

Sure she will. As long as it doesn't include whatever information she doesn't think I should see. It's too bad Art didn't answer when I called earlier. I didn't leave a message, because who knows if Mom and Dad would give me the phone if he calls back?

Fortunately there's one other person I can lean on, no matter how much it galls me to do it. "You know what? I'm going to need new clothes for school."

Mom brightens. "I can take you."

Ugh. Shopping with Mom was torture before. It'll probably be even worse now that Mom wears an all-knit wardrobe. Besides, new clothes are only one goal of this shopping trip. I have an ulterior motive: information.

With what I hope is a sheepish smile rather than a grimace, I say, "I think I'd like to call Angie."

"You would?" Dad's eyebrows crinkle into his forehead. Understandable, considering our conversation five minutes ago.

"Yeah." I nod solemnly. "You're right, Dad. We need to work things out."

Mom beams. "I think that's an excellent idea."

CHAPTER SEVENTEEN

Angie isn't available over the weekend, so we arrange to meet up on Monday. Mom and Dad aren't comfortable with me driving myself to Angie's, even though I've had my license for a year and a half—or twenty-six and a half years, depending on how you calculate it. I'm not even sure it's valid now. It's a weird fluke of time travel, I suppose. The expiration date on the license is 1997, but I would argue that it's a technicality and the license is really supposed to be good until I turn nineteen, which will now be the year 2022. Regardless, my parents argue that the roads have changed since I left, and I don't have a phone yet to call them if my car breaks down or I get lost. What a ridiculous reason, the phone thing. I never had a phone before. I mentally add driving to the list of reasons I obviously need one. Plus, that recording feature will be super useful for interviews.

When we arrive at Angie's house, Mom turns to me with a nervous smile. "Do you want me to come in?"

A few weeks ago I might have rolled my eyes at her for hovering like it's my first day of kindergarten, but after listening to her story our first night back together, I understand the weight of our lost years. I wonder how long this imbalance will skew our dynamic, if I will forever feel like I have to tiptoe around her. "No, thanks."

"All right." She touches my wrist. "Before you go, Jenny, I want you to know we heard you the other day. I found a couple of miniseries for you to watch—one about the nineties and another about the 2000s—so you can catch up on current events. We'll have to improvise a bit for the past ten years since there isn't one about the 2010s yet, but at least you'll have a better idea of what's happened in the world."

I purse my lips. Is she trying to keep me informed, or are these documentaries another way to prevent me from doing my own research? It's not exactly the information I want, but it *is* a start, and I still intend to work on Angie.

"Thanks, Mom. Love you." I kiss her cheek before getting out and run up to knock on the door.

Dylan answers, an instant reminder of how I humiliated myself at our first meeting.

"Hey, Jenny. How's it going?"

"Uhh . . ." I stare at his bare feet, afraid to face him after I made such a fool of myself before. But that wasn't his fault, and it's rude for me to ignore him, so I drag my gaze over his knee-length basketball shorts and land on his T-shirt. It says "Run like the Hunger Games just started"; that seems like the perfect conversation starter. "Do you run track?"

He shifts, and I realize it's also sort of creepy to stare at his chest, so I reluctantly meet his eyes.

"No, I'm a baseball guy like my . . ."

My dad. I cast a quick glance around, but there's no sign of Steve. Thank you, God.

"Why'd you ask?"

At his question, I jerk my attention back to him and gesture at his shirt. "That. It looks like it's from a meet you participated in or something."

Dylan stumbles backward with his hand over his heart and widens his brown eyes dramatically. "Jenny. You have so much to learn."

True, and while it's a sore point, his exaggerated reaction eases my embarrassment about tackling him. He's actually sort of adorable. I can't help the grin that ticks up one side of my mouth. "I assume this has to do with something I missed while I was away."

Now *I'm* using euphemisms for my disappearance, but I can't help smiling.

Dylan moves back toward me. "Only one of the best book series in history."

I raise my eyebrows. "In *history?*" I rack my brain for a comparison. "Like, better than Shakespeare?"

He shakes his head sadly, his lips quirked teasingly. "Weak, Waters, weak."

I knew it was lame as soon as it came out of my mouth, naming a writer we had to read for school. But now that I put it out there, I have to own it. "Shakespeare is legendary. Everyone knows who he is."

"You'd be surprised how many people know who Katniss Everdeen is." He purses his lips in thought. "She's epic, surviving unimaginable trials. So epic she deserves her own theme park. Actually . . . I've heard there are already a couple of *Hunger Games* rides at a park in Dubai."

"A theme park for a *book*?" That doesn't seem possible. "Wait. Who's Katniss Everdeen?"

"The girl on fire!" He pumps his fist in the air. "We must educate you. But yes, a theme park, since the movies were so successful."

I'm so confused right now. I guess Katniss Everdeen is the main character in the hunger books? If they made movies out of them, they must be decent, even though this girl-on-fire stuff sounds pretty violent. "Maybe I should read these books."

"You can borrow mine if you want." He smiles fully, and I realize that after that first mention of baseball, I wasn't thinking about him being Steve's son. Maybe because he doesn't dress at all like Steve. Or because Steve and I never once had a book conversation. Huh. That's strange considering how much I love to read. It's still weird that Dylan resembles him, but it's quickly becoming evident how different he is.

I grin. "I'd like that."

Dylan is surprisingly easy to talk to.

"Jenny!" Angie strides toward me, her arms outstretched.

My grin slips. When I make no move to reach for Angie, she drops her arms. "I'm so glad you're here."

She stands there, waiting. She has her hair in a ponytail today. I wonder if it's an attempt to channel her younger self or a style she wears often. Now that I'm here, I don't know what to say. I planned out how I'll interrogate her on all the issues Mom and Dad refuse to discuss, but I failed to consider this I-haven't-forgiven-you-but-I'm-standing-in-your-entryway moment. Finally I say, "Yep. I'm here."

Dylan's gaze darts between us, but he remains silent, as if Angie's presence muzzled him.

A mean-natured chuckle sounds from outside our circle. "This isn't awkward."

Oh, great. Now JoJo's here. I didn't miss the interaction that first day. I heard what Dylan said about JoJo draining his gas tank so I'd find out about Angie and Steve in the most humiliating way possible.

"JoJo!" Angie says brightly. "I'm taking Jenny shopping for school. Wanna come with us?"

No! That'll completely derail my plans. Besides, I don't see JoJo becoming my twenty-first-century style guru. Her shirt declares that "Zombies have feelings too," and she doesn't even have a skirt or anything over her shiny, skin-tight leggings. It's like wearing workout clothes in public, some weird goth/Jane Fonda mashup.

"Like I want to hang out with you two." JoJo loops a lavender lock of hair around her finger. "Swapping stories about your crushes on Dad. Ew."

"JoJo!"

Angie's tone makes *me* want to duck into the coat closet, but JoJo doesn't budge.

Angie continues, "When I get home we're having a serious discussion. In the meantime, I'll take your phone."

JoJo's mouth drops open. "No way."

I may be new here, but I already understand confiscating JoJo's phone is a major punishment.

"I might return it after our discussion." Angie wiggles her fingers.

JoJo sulkily gives Angie the phone and stomps out of the room. Angie stuffs the phone in her purse and turns to Dylan with a grimace-smile. "Thank you for welcoming Jenny the way I'd expect."

"Sure, Mom." He blushes a bit. It's sweet.

"I'll be back in a couple hours." Angie pushes up on her tiptoes to kiss his temple. I hadn't really noticed his height before, but he has several inches on her.

"'Bye," he says, waving.

"See ya," I reply.

I'm determined to keep the conversation away from a rehashing of the Angie-Steve situation, so as soon as we climb in Angie's gigantic car, I pick an easier topic. Because if I jump to the big stuff too quickly, she'll be onto me. "So where are we going? Chesterfield Mall?"

Angie peers at the rearview mirror, then bites her lip. "I wish. I miss that place."

Miss it? "What do you mean?"

"It's empty. Probably will get turned into something else soon."

"Empty?" Chesterfield Mall had more than a hundred stores plus a food court. We used to spend hours walking its two floors, pausing for lunch, sometimes catching a movie. "How is that possible?"

"Too much retail on the market," she says. "They kept building more around it; plus people buy so much online these days, and the mall died."

I recognize the words she's saying, but they're the words of an adult, not my Angie, who would never talk about "retail" or "the market" unless she was giving a school report. It emphasizes the gulf between us, and I'm suddenly less sure of my ability to put pressure on this version of my friend.

I weave my fingers into my hair. "I feel like I'm in some sort of alternate universe."

Angie glances at me. "You sort of are."

Yeah. Guess I am.

"Anyway," Angie says, "I'll take you to the outlet mall."

I perk up. "We have an outlet mall?"

She nods. "Two. They're pretty good—but also helped kill the regular mall."

"Oh." I waver between excitement at the prospect of outlets and longing for *my* mall. I mean, I know twenty-five years is a lot, but a mall is, like, an institution.

"They have good stores, though," Angie adds.

I make a noncommittal sound. I don't know what to say to her. We've been friends for ten years, but I'm at a disadvantage. She knows everything about my life, but from my viewpoint, hers changed in the blink of an eye. I have to completely relearn my best friend, and I'm not even sure I want to. To forgive or not to forgive . . . it's a big question. Mom and Dad think it's so easy, but their best friends didn't morph from talking about SAT results and the cute guy at work to "the market" and driving a car meant to haul around a baseball team.

I flip the air vent toward me. "So why aren't you at work on a Monday?"

Angie brushes a wisp of hair behind her ear. "I don't work."

"Whaaat?"

Angie jumps at my overly loud response. But this news shocks me nearly as much as Bradley being married with kids.

"What about law school? Making partner by thirty-five?"

I don't give her time to answer. "I thought it was weird you lived out in the suburbs and had kids. What happened to you?"

"What *happened* to me?" She glares, and I catch a glimpse of my Angie, the Angie who led the mock trial team to a state championship by reducing the other team's star witness to a stuttering mess. "My best friend disappeared, and Flight 237 became as legendary as the *Challenger* explosion. I didn't know how to deal with it, so I . . . well, my priorities changed."

"So you what?" I know that pursed-lip, refuse-to-look-me-in-the-eye expression. There's more to that statement.

She shrugs. "When I took the prelaw classes, my heart wasn't in it anymore."

"So what did you do instead?"

She doesn't answer until after she maneuvers the car off a looping exit. "I did some writing."

"You? Writing?" That's *my* thing.

She pauses at a stop sign. "It made me feel closer to you."

"Oh." Her answer shuts down all the questions I was about to ask, about what sort of writing and for whom. It also makes me feel like the gum on the bottom of a shoe for orchestrating this outing to grill her.

I wonder what I might have done if our roles were reversed, how I might have tried to feel closer to Angie. Dad asked if I'd envisioned myself married to Steve, and I honestly don't know. We could have ended up on different sides of the country for college, with my goal being Columbia, and deep down, I know I would have picked school over Steve. Perhaps we would've kept in touch, or perhaps we would've met up at a reunion someday. I don't know, and the fact that all these possibilities have been snatched from me still rubs me raw. I see Angie's point about holding a part of me close, but it also seems like she stole parts of my life I didn't give her permission to take over.

She turns into the outlet mall, and I'm distracted by the stores. "Where do we even start?"

She smiles. "I have a plan."

Five minutes after we park, my shirt is sticking to my chest and I'm wiping beads of sweat off my forehead. I never considered the discomfort of outdoor shopping during August. It's only ten thirty a.m., but it's already eighty-five degrees, and the storefronts offer little respite from the harsh sun.

"JoJo likes this one," Angie says, opening a door. "I'm not sure you will, but it's worth checking out."

I'm so relieved to be inside with the air-conditioning I take a moment to bask in the coolness before walking toward the first display. "Um, where are the shoulders?"

Angie smirks at the crochet-trimmed rose top. "It's a style. I think they call it cold shoulder—so you can wear off-the-shoulder but it won't fall off because you have straps."

"Oookay. I mean, it's cute, but does the school still keep the air set at sixty-five degrees?" I shiver and move on to the next display. "And this one? It's missing the sides." The shirt I point at has the sides cut out and Xs crisscrossing to hold it together. "If I came home with this, Dad would either order me to return it or go find a sweater."

"He so would." Angie snorts. "Do you remember that all-white outfit you got with the super-short skirt? It looked so great on you! And when you came out, your dad went into the kitchen and came back with a ruler. He held it up to your leg"—she deepens her voice—"'Here is the appropriate length for a skirt. That's a good six inches below the length of this skirt. So you either need to find a way to lengthen the hem or change, but you're not leaving this house.'"

I'm giggling by the end of Angie's impression. It's so spot-on. But also . . . that was, like, three months ago for me. It was an outfit I bought special for the end-of-school-year awards banquet. It's like my Angie is stuck inside this older body. I keep catching glimpses of her.

"It's because of your dad I don't get in the middle of JoJo's wardrobe choices," Angie adds. "I remember how mad you'd get when he'd make you go change."

Her comment stops my laughter. I mean, yeah, my dad's strict about what I wear, but it's only because he cares. It's weird, though. A week ago I would have been commiserating with her. I was really ticked when he wouldn't let me wear that outfit. I loved it. I bought it with money I saved up from my job at Frosty's. But now I don't like the way she's ragging on my dad, even if it's out of shared memories. I can't joke about my parents with Angie because I feel empathy for them. Like after what they've been through, they deserve extra respect. Plus, there's a part of me that feels like Angie's lost the right to side with me against them. Our dynamic is so off. *All* my dynamics are off.

I'm not ready to figure that out, so I focus on another point that interests me.

"What's the deal with JoJo anyway?" I finger a silky tassel hanging from a sleeve. "She seems to really have it out for me."

Angie gazes out the window. "We shouldn't have named her after you." She heads for the door. "*I* shouldn't have done a lot of things."

I follow her. "What does *that* mean?"

A swirling in my gut says she isn't talking about Steve.

Angie holds the door for me. "New store?"

I nod, eyes narrowed. Apparently she's ignoring my question, as she turns out into the concourse. Giving up—for now—I scan the shops and spy a familiar store. "Finally something I remember!"

I'm surprised Angie didn't mention this one. But when I reach the door, I deflate. The clothes are similar to what we saw in the other place—cropped tops and shirts with holes strategically cut out of the sides and back.

"What's with all the holes?" I ask dejectedly. "I'm not a holey person."

Angie snickers. "Actually, I'd say 'holy' is a rather apt description for you."

"Ha ha, a church girl joke." I roll my eyes, but I actually don't like it when she turns my faith into a joke. "Where can I get some clothes with no holes and no sparkles?" I pat my shoulders; I'm wearing the navy shirt Kelly got me again.

"I can think of a couple places." Angie hooks her arm through mine, as if she didn't make a cryptic comment about her mistakes that left me hanging. "Come on. We'll find a compromise between your comfort zone and the twenty-first century."

This feels more like old times, walking arm in arm through the, er, mall. As long as I don't look at Angie and the crinkles around her eyes. Or think about how we're way past trying on the same shirts in different colors so we can almost match or giggling over inappropriate items in Spencer's. The trickle of sweat running between my shoulder blades is unfamiliar too, but I can deal. I have a goal for today after all.

The next store is Tommy Hilfiger. I dig in my heels outside the door. "I can't afford Tommy Hilfiger."

Also, it feels pretentious to me, like only private school kids shop there.

Angie sighs. "It's an outlet. Besides, you don't have to worry about money."

I'm so startled by this statement I allow her to pull me inside. "I don't?"

I wonder if my parents won the lottery while I was gone. Their living conditions don't seem any different.

"Nope. Your parents never closed your savings account while you were missing. Didn't they tell you?"

I'm sure I resemble a gaping fish by now. "No. But even if they did, I'm saving my money for college."

"That's covered too," she says brightly. "I guess you guys have had other things to talk about."

"I didn't even ask them for money for this shopping trip. I don't know what I was thinking." I completely forgot the practicalities of shopping.

Angie laughs. "Don't worry about it. We're good."

We're good. There have been moments today where I've experienced small glimpses of the Angie I know, but mostly she's a stranger. She hasn't become the person I expected her to be, and that baffles me as much as the person she's turned into. Not to mention this odd imbalance where she's trying to pick up where we left off when she was still seventeen.

No, we're not good, but maybe we'll be okay—if she's straight with me.

It's time to ask my questions. "So ever since I got back, my family's been keeping me in a bubble. They won't let me watch the news or even take me to the library."

Angie fingers a T-shirt. "They're a bit paranoid after what they dealt with before. When you disappeared."

I narrow my eyes. "You remember what high school's like, right? I can't stand the thought of people whispering about me and having no clue what they're saying."

Angie bites her lip. She's silent for several moments, as if she's fighting an internal battle, but she still doesn't face me when she asks, "What do you want to know?"

"Bradley said some people called us a hoax. What's that about?"

Angie shifts back and forth, then exhales. "It's just a bunch of wackos making noise. A couple scientists and politicians and such."

"But why? Bradley said Agent Klein made some sort of statement about our blood tests."

She shakes her head, making her ponytail swing. "She did, but they're not releasing the test results to the public."

"What do you mean they're not releasing the results?"

She tips her head sideways. "Do you *want* the FBI handing your medical records to the media?"

"Well, no." That would be creepy, if everybody watching the

news knew my blood type or could make a copy of my fingerprint. "What about the plane? Did they do tests on that too?"

Angie nods. "The FBI and a team of forensic specialists examined it thoroughly as soon as you landed. Everything lines up with the age of the plane at the time it took off—the paint, the fuel, the equipment."

I throw up my hands. "Why won't Mom and Dad just let me see this stuff for myself?"

"Because they got mercilessly hounded by the media when you disappeared." There's a grim twist to her mouth. "You're lucky the FBI is taking the heat this time."

I cross my arms. "For now. But is that really working? Is everyone keeping quiet? What about family and friends? Does it extend to them? Because a reporter showed up at our house trying to talk to Dad."

"They've shown up at my house too." Angie grimaces. "But at least as concerns you, we're all agreed not to talk to anyone. Other passengers, well"—she shakes her head—"some of their family members haven't helped the situation, and that's part of why those conspiracy theorists are out there."

"I don't blame them!" I pace between two racks of clothes. "*I* want to know what happened! I'm sure to them their wacko theory that we're a hoax makes more sense than the truth, but meanwhile, I still don't understand what the truth *is*. There has to be somebody who does."

Angie sighs. "The FBI is working on it."

"Are they?" I stop and look at her.

She starts gathering clothes. "They must be. They haven't told you to go ahead and tell your story yet, have they?"

A good question. I'm not sure my parents would tell me if they had. "You're sure you haven't seen any of the other passengers talk?"

"Not even when they try and ambush them."

Then at least that's one thing my parents aren't keeping from me. "Is there anything else? Because Mom and Dad keep acting weird, like there's more they're hiding."

Angie presses a stack of tops and shorts into my arms and turns me toward a changing room. "I'm sure they're just being protective. I can't think of anything else you need to know."

CHAPTER EIGHTEEN

As anxious as I am to get out into the world, the first day of school arrives more quickly than I'm quite ready for. I cope the only way I can—by writing.

ST. LOUIS, Aug. 20—Seventeen-year-old Jennifer Waters, a survivor of Mid-States Airways Flight 237, will attend her first day of senior year—twenty-five years after she finished her junior year.

"Jenny! Breakfast is ready," Mom calls, and I set down my pen.

I wonder if some newspaper somewhere is writing this story, if an enterprising reporter has dug enough to discover I'm returning to school today. At least now I can find out myself. At the first opportunity, I'm heading to the library for a newspaper.

I place my notebook in my desk drawer and grab my backpack, then pause at the mirror on the back of the door. I'm happy with the clothes I picked on our shopping trip—a simple, hunter green V-neck T-shirt without any sparkly embellishments, and khaki shorts that will pass Dad's ruler test. He's more lenient with shorts than skirts anyway. My strawberry blond hair hangs straight to just below my shoulders. I haven't done anything to style it differently for this new century, except to let my bangs lie flat instead of curling them. Angie gave me that tip.

Satisfied I won't embarrass myself, I head toward the kitchen and the enticing aroma of waffles. Mom always makes waffles on the first day of school. I rush to hug her waist. "You remembered."

She sets my plate on the counter and twists to return my embrace. "Of course."

Dad strolls in and grabs my plate. "Yum, waffles!"

"Hey!" I playfully wrestle it back from him, careful not to tip it and lose my precious first-day breakfast. "Mine."

He tweaks my nose. "You sound like one of those seagulls from *Finding Nemo*."

"Huh?"

"Oh." Dad tilts his head. "It's a movie."

More to catch up on. I expect I'll be overwhelmed with unfamiliar pop culture references at school. Books, movies, celebrity scandals. I started watching the 2000s miniseries since I already experienced half of the nineties, and I only made it partway through the third episode before I had to stop. The footage of 9/11 broke me. I can't imagine living through that. What must it have been like for Grandma and Grandpa Waters in New York? They didn't live or work downtown, but surely they had friends who did. In any case, the little I watched of the documentaries didn't really bring me up to speed on the type of information I might encounter at school.

Like those books Dylan mentioned the other day. "Dad, do you know about Katnip?"

He sits with his own plate of waffles. His brow furrows for a moment. "Huh?"

"Katnip Ever-something? She catches on fire?"

His brow clears. "Oh! You mean Katniss Everdeen. In *The Hunger Games!*"

I groan. Scratch my earlier thought; I am *definitely* going to look like a complete moron. I should've insisted on going to the library instead of taking Mom up on the offer to "binge-watch" the rest of *90210*. I could've read through *People* or *Teen Beat* to catch up on this year's Jason Priestley. Oh, man. It's probably his *son*. They're going to crucify me.

Mom joins us at the table. "I can get you a list of the most popular TV shows, movies, and books for the past five or ten years."

I bite my lip. It's not a bad idea.

She blows on her coffee. "Young adult novels are very mainstream these days. I've even read a few."

Huh. "Guess I'd better check those out then."

I drag my last bite of waffle through the syrup and pop it in my mouth. At least Mom hasn't changed her recipe. Considering there seems to be some concern about Dad's cholesterol, that wasn't a guarantee. I scoot my chair back and kiss her cheek. "Thanks for my first-day waffles. I'm gonna go brush my teeth, and then I'll be ready to go."

It's a hint for them to move along. I don't know which of them is taking me to school, but Dad's in his robe, and Mom has on a caftan thing that I guess is her own version of one.

The doorbell rings while I'm doing a final check for zits—thankfully only a tiny one on my jawline. If it's another reporter,

Dad will go ballistic. I rush down the hallway to make sure he doesn't cause a scene, but Mom's at the top of the stairs, smiling.

"Your ride is here," she says.

"My ride?" I echo dumbly. "You're not taking me?"

I sound a bit like a lost eight-year-old, but considering what I've been through, I fully expected my parents to drive me to my first day of school.

Her smile falters. "We haven't driven you to school since freshman year. You said it wasn't cool."

I don't remember saying that, but I probably did. I close the distance between us and hug her tight, inhaling her coffee scent. "I'm sorry, Mom."

Someone clears a throat. "Um. We should probably get going."

I close my eyes and exhale, giving myself a moment before I look down at the landing. "Dylan. You're my ride?"

He grins. "Yep. Don't worry. I passed every part of the driving test except parallel parking, and we won't have to do that at school."

"How reassuring." But I smile.

Angie didn't give me a heads-up during our shopping trip that Dylan and JoJo go to my school, but I should've guessed based on where they live.

"All right. Let's do this." I grab my backpack and kiss Mom on the cheek. "See ya."

"Have a good day, honey!" she calls as I walk down the stairs.

Dylan opens the door for me. He's wearing a *Star Wars* shirt today. At least, it says "Star Wars," but I don't recognize the characters' faces.

"You look confused," Dylan says as we walk down the concrete steps to the driveway.

I don't even want to go there because this is high on my list of concerns about school. It looks like even *Star Wars* has changed during my absence. "Your shirt. Just something else I missed."

Dylan pokes me so I look up at him. He wiggles his eyebrows. "You spend a lot of time staring at my chest."

My cheeks warm. Is he *flirting* with me? Or just kidding? I mean, Dylan's cute, seriously cute, but he's also Angie and Steve's son, and that's . . . weird. Still, it seems like flirting, and I have no intelligent response, but it doesn't matter because he's already moving toward the driver's side of the car. *Get yourself together, Jenny!* I shake it off and head for the passenger side, but when I reach for the door, I realize the front's already occupied. JoJo glares at me from the other side of the window, and I quickly shift to the back and get in.

Of course JoJo's riding to school with us too. I'm such an idiot.

"Hi, JoJo." I may not understand where she's coming from, but I'd like to start over with her.

She grunts and stuffs a small white thing in her ear. So the effort's obviously going to be one-sided.

I lean forward. "What is that?"

Dylan glances toward JoJo as he backs out of the driveway. "Earbud. It's like a really small headphone."

"So she's basically taking ignoring me to the next level."

Dylan twists his lips to the side. "She might thaw. By, like, graduation."

He makes it sound like we'll all be doing that together. "Wait. Are you two twins?"

He flattens his hand on his chest. "You couldn't tell by our strikingly similar looks and behavior?"

I laugh and lean back in the seat, relieved he's not sending any more potentially flirty signals. I'm not sure how I'd handle it if Dylan were interested in me. I mean, family connections aside, I sort of just got dumped. And I've got more important stuff to focus on.

"We just turned eighteen, the week before you came back," he adds.

"Well, happy belated birthday." It's strange that Dylan and JoJo are technically older than me.

"Thanks."

"It's so quiet in here," I say as I observe new neighborhoods and businesses that have popped up along the way.

"Yeah? What's your usual ride like?"

"Well, last y—" I stop, because it's weird to say "last year," and I'd better not do it at school or it will require all sorts of clarifications. "Before, on the way to school, Ang—my friends and I would sing along to the radio with the windows rolled down."

He smirks at me in the rearview mirror. "You weren't afraid it would mess up your hair?"

That is such a boy thing to say. And also so uninformed. "That's what hairspray's for. Or a scrunchy."

He laughs. "If we weren't almost there, I'd find something for you to sing along with."

My lips curl. "It's only fun if you do it too."

"Noted." Dylan pulls into the senior parking lot of Parkwood High School. "Does it look the same?"

I exit the car and stare up at the two-story building, with its pebbled walls and sad handful of windows. An extra twenty-five years haven't made it any more inviting.

"Pretty much," I answer. "Still looks like a prison from the outside. I mean, would it hurt them to let some sunlight in?"

I swing my backpack over my shoulder and join the wave of students. I expect JoJo to race ahead of us across the drop-off lane, but she stops at the curb and turns to me, tugging the earbud out and tossing her purple hair. She opens her mouth, clears her throat, and I wait, expecting some sort of declaration. But she seems to think I'm not worth it. Instead, she just says, "Never mind."

Before I can reply, she turns and darts across the street in front of a minivan; a harried mom slams on the brakes and lays on the horn.

Dylan frowns down at me. "I'm sorry she's such a jerk."

"Yeah. I totally hold you responsible. Except . . . what is her deal?"

I've heard Angie's take, but I'm curious to get his too.

His mouth softens. "It's just . . . you've been sort of a phantom person in our family."

It's close to a hundred degrees out here, but his words cause a shiver to skate down my spine. The straps of my backpack suddenly feel too tight. It's easier to think Angie and Steve discarded me than that I was a constant presence. It's not really fair to me or JoJo that they named her after me.

"Anyway, it's different now that you're here." Dylan gestures for me to follow, and we wait for a break in the carpool line. "Like that singing-in-the-car thing. Mom's told lots of stories, but I never heard that one before."

Several students call out to Dylan, and most of the interactions seem normal. I receive a lot of curious glances, but he doesn't introduce me. I wonder if he doesn't know how.

This is Jenny. She transferred here from the nineties.

Or, even worse: *This is Jenny. She's my mom's best friend.*

Awkward.

For both of us. I mean, our connection is sort of ever present in my mind, but now that we're here, at school, it's amplified. He's the son of my best friend and ex-boyfriend. I should be, like, Auntie Jenny or something. But thanks to the crazy twist my life has taken, we're the same age, I'm on shaky terms with his mom, and I met him for the first time two weeks ago. We're basically strangers in bizarre circumstances.

Either way, I'm not addressing it here and now.

People are standing in front of the school, holding out their phones. I've learned enough to understand they're taking pictures of themselves. Kira and Eli took about a hundred photos and videos of themselves with their tablet while I was at Bradley's house.

"Aren't you going to take a picture?" I ask Dylan.

"A first-day selfie?" he scoffs. "I don't need to insta every moment like JoJo."

I mentally note these phrases so I can write them in my notebook for future reference.

A bulky guy comes up to us, his fist moving toward Dylan. I flinch, about to call a warning, when Dylan raises his own fist and bumps the other guy's knuckles with his own. I relax, realizing it's a greeting. Like a high five, I guess.

The guy smiles, but it's more like a leer. "Hi, Jenny."

"Hi." I leave a question mark at the end, waiting for him to introduce himself.

When he makes no move to do so, Dylan says, "This is Drew." I nod.

"So, Jenny," Drew says like we're already in the middle of a conversation, "we're having a back-to-school party tonight. My brother's hooking us up with a keg. Wanna come?"

My gut reaction is "not in a million years," but I do my best to hide it.

"On a school night?" When I was a freshman, I read an article in the local paper about a party in the next county where the police handed out citations to everyone there under twenty-one, regardless of whether they were drinking. That was enough to convince me to avoid Drew's type of party. I'm not taking any chances when college scholarships are on the line. "Thanks, but I don't think my parents will let me."

Drew purses his lips as if holding in a laugh. "*Let* you?"

I've obviously just failed some sort of test. Maybe I shouldn't have brought up my parents, but it seemed like the easiest out. "They're sort of overprotective, what with me being missing for so long."

Drew's eyes gleam. "So you're, like, grounded?"

"Lay off, Drew." Dylan nudges me away. "His parties always get busted. You wouldn't want to go even if it was your thing."

I stop, causing him to stumble since he's so close. "How do you know it's not my thing?"

154

Uneasiness flickers across his face, like he's torn, and then he laughs. "Your expression, Jenny, when he mentioned the keg. Your nose sort of scrunched up."

"Guess I didn't hide that very well." I fiddle with the end of my backpack strap. He says I was a haunting presence in their house, but I wonder how Angie and Steve made me sound. Based on his reaction back there, he already thinks I'm a killjoy. Parties were one of the few things Angie and I argued about.

"You know, Angie"—I really can't bring myself to call her "your mom"—"probably would've gone. She was a lot more adventurous than me."

Dylan grunts, not meeting my eyes. It's so different from how he was earlier, teasing me and apologizing for JoJo. I take this as a signal he doesn't want to hear about Angie's high school years. I can't blame him. I wouldn't want to think about my parents in high school.

Once we're inside, Dylan stops. "You know where the office is?"

"Is it still at the bottom of those steps?" I point at the curving staircase before us.

"Yep."

"Then I do."

"Okay. Good luck!" He waves as he walks off.

Guess I'm on my own.

CHAPTER NINETEEN

Parkwood High School might look essentially the same as before, but my place in it has clearly changed, as I discover the first time my name is announced during roll.

"Jennifer Waters?" Mrs. Sims, my calculus teacher, calls, and every head in the room whips toward me.

"Jenny Waters? *The* Jenny Waters?" the girl in front of me says, like I'm Julia Roberts. "I can't believe you're here, at school. And you look so *young*."

Desk chairs creak as other students lean in around me, maybe to check my face for hidden wrinkles.

"Class!" Mrs. Sims taps the whiteboard with a marker. "As fascinating as Miss Waters's situation is, we're here to learn calculus, and that's what we'll be doing. So please rotate your torsos to the front of the room and give me your attention."

I sigh internally as the class follows her instructions, but it doesn't stop people from casting me sly glances throughout the remaining hour.

Based on that first girl's reaction, I expect them to mob me with questions after class, but instead they stare with a combination of fascination and fear. Here I was worried about not fitting in because I don't understand twenty-first-century pop culture, and I don't even have the chance to be embarrassed by my ignorance. The fascination I expected; the fear, though . . . Maybe there's more to those people stirring up trouble than Angie thinks.

When lunchtime arrives, I'm torn between an almost physical need to hold a newspaper and a desire to talk to some people my own age. As much as I love my parents and Grandma and even Bradley, I need to make friends. I decide the newspaper can wait. I enter the cafeteria cautiously, holding my insulated lunch bag with its reusable water bottle, wondering if Mom was exaggerating the whole environmental thing. I see an equal ratio of recycling and trash bins, so she may be onto something.

I scan the cafeteria for familiar faces—well, one in particular. Unfortunately, the only person I recognize is JoJo, and when our gazes catch, she purses her lips and shakes her head slightly in a clear message not to approach. *Don't worry, JoJo. As far as I'm concerned, you are the story cut due to lack of space.*

Nobody motions for me to join them or even sends me a welcoming smile, so I head to my old table and hope for the best. My friends and I always used to sit along the windows, taking advantage of any sun we could get. There's no one there when I sit down and unpack my food, but within a few minutes, I hear a throat clear.

"Are you new?" says an overly sweet voice. "Because this is our table."

Of course the table *belongs* to someone. I look up. A tall Asian girl with amazing long black hair is flanked by two white girls who just reach her shoulders. I can't immediately tell what group they may belong to or if their belted dresses are cool. Something else I should have studied—fashion trends. Though, half the girls are wearing leggings like JoJo was the day I went shopping with Angie, so maybe she's more normal than I thought. Apparently it *is* a thing to go out in your workout clothes.

In any case, I won't be the girl who's kicked out of her seat day one. I shrug. "Sorry. Didn't see a label on it."

"I'll get on that." The tall girl sets her own insulated bag on the table—points for Mom—and the others follow suit. "I know you," she adds.

I expect the news of my arrival has been passed around school like a game of telephone. "I'm Jenny Waters."

"Oooh, yes, you are." Her eyes widen in glee, the sort that makes my granola bar stick in my esophagus. "You're the most exciting news of the day. Well, except for the news about PATROL."

I swallow, sure she wants me to ask about this patrol thing, but I won't let her steamroll me. "And you are?"

Her lip curls, with respect or maybe impatience. "Ashling Chan." She gestures to the tanned blonde on her right—"Emily Weiss"—then to the olive-skinned brunette on her left—"Jasmine Marino. Sorry. We've never had a celebrity at school before."

I shift uncomfortably in my seat. "I'm not a celebrity. All I did was get on a plane. I'm a completely normal teenager."

Ashling unpacks her lunch, pulling out what appears to be a salad wrapped in a tortilla. It's a far cry from my PB and J.

She laughs. "Maybe you were, but not anymore. Everyone knows your name, especially since—"

"Jenny! There you are." Dylan pops up behind Ashling so suddenly I jump.

"Where did you come from?" I ask.

He throws his shoulders back so the *Star Wars* characters are front and center. "I apparated."

"You what now?"

Emily and Jasmine giggle. Ashling rolls her eyes. "Ha ha."

Oh. It's one of those references I knew would happen today.

Dylan scoots around to my side of the table and plops down beside me. "How's your day going?"

Maybe I'd be honest with him if Ashling and her silent followers weren't sitting there hanging on to every word. Besides, he abandoned me this morning. So I shrug. "Like any first day of school, I guess."

"Really?" He props his elbow on the table and gives me his full attention, which makes it impossible for me to take a bite of food. I can't have sticky peanut butter all over my teeth with him staring at my mouth, his brown eyes all big and wide. He smells clean, like soap. Did he just have PE and take a shower? His hair isn't wet, though . . .

"Everyone treating you nice?" he says.

I glance at Ashling and crew. "Sure. Ashling was about to tell me about some news that's bigger than me."

She dabs delicately at her lips with a napkin. "Actually, PATROL has to do with you. It might be easiest if I just show you on your phone."

My brow creases. "I don't have a phone yet."

All three girls gasp loudly enough to draw the attention of the next table.

"No phone?" Emily's voice is high-pitched. "But how do you

keep track of what everyone's doing? Or what *you're* supposed to be doing?"

"Or check the weather so you know what to wear?" Jasmine adds.

Um, ask people what they're up to? Write it in a planner? Watch the weather report?

"You basically don't have a life without a phone," Ashling concludes.

Dylan rolls his eyes toward the ceiling, tipping his chair backward for good measure. "That's a bit extreme. All sorts of people live without phones."

"Yeah." Ashling snorts. "*Old* people. And poor people. Whatever." She digs in her backpack. "I'll show you on mine."

"I don't think that's a good idea." Dylan plants his chair back on the floor, sending me a look I can't decipher. Concern mixed with, maybe, discomfort? Usually I'm good at reading people, but Dylan's like one of those classic novels they make us read in English—overly complex language masking a meaningful story. It's like he can't decide what signal to send me.

"What're you even doing over here, Dylan?" Ashling curls her pointer finger against her chin. "Isn't it awkward hanging out with your dad's old girlfriend?"

Dylan's cheeks redden. I feel mine heat up too. Angie warned me I was sort of famous, and Ashling just called me a celebrity a few minutes ago, but how much do people know about my situation? Apparently more than I'd like. I have got to track down a newspaper!

Dylan recovers more quickly than I do, flashing her an easy smile. "That's ancient history."

Ancient history. Or a few weeks ago, depending on your perspective.

Ashling presses her lips together. They curve into a cat-that-caught-the-canary smile. "Hmm." She taps on her phone and turns it to face me. "Here's the statement PATROL made this morning."

On her phone screen, a woman stands before a microphone. A strip across the bottom says her name is Dr. Indira Greaves, Theoretical Astrophysicist, Westing University.

It's loud in the cafeteria, so I have to hold the phone up to my ear to hear what she's saying. I miss the very beginning. ". . . and I've been elected to represent PATROL, People Assuring Time Relativity, Order, and Legitimacy, a group of concerned citizens formed to ensure the public gets the answers we deserve about Flight 237. The government thus far has done very little to uncover the facts of this case. We're not satisfied that the plane has been verified beyond a shadow of a doubt as the same plane that took off in 1995. And there are multiple possible explanations for the presence of the people aboard."

Like what? I want to ask her.

"We believe this is a hoax twenty-five years in the making and feel it's important to protect the sanctity of our concept of time. We posit that the blood tests performed by the FBI are unreliable. Has anyone actually seen them to verify their accuracy? Have they tested the passengers against family members to ensure they're a match? Take Jennifer Waters, for example." I gasp, shocked she singled me out, and she's still talking. "They can't possibly have compared her DNA to anything on record from 1995. She started school today. This girl is walking around with other teenagers without her identity being sufficiently veri-fied. It's a travesty! We request that all passengers on Flight 237 submit themselves for *public* testing, both against living family members and to verify their age. We also demand a more thor-ough investigation of the plane by an independent, nongovern-ment entity. We reject the belief that this plane full of people traveled through time, and we fully expect that these tests will verify our position that this is a hoax." She goes on to list a web-site where people can submit tips related to passengers. "If you have any information that will help us unveil this hoax, we encour-age you to post there. Thank you."

My nostrils flare, and it takes considerable control not to scream. *People Assuring Time Relativity, Order, and Legitimacy.* What a mouthful. The name sounds like something out of a science fiction novel, although so does our situation, so that's not saying much. And then there's the acronym—PATROL—like they're the neighborhood watch and we're endangering small children. Not to mention how they attacked me in particular, calling me out to the world. I slam the phone on the table. "When did this air?"

"Nine a.m.," Ashling says, the smug smile still on her face.

It explains the stares, why people were afraid to talk to me. A fair share of the Parkwood High population must believe this junk. And for these wackos to demand that I give them DNA . . . "Do they have any idea how my life has been turned upside down? I lost everything. And they're launching some . . . some witch hunt to try and prove I'm faking? What does some astro-physicist know about us anyway?"

"Jenny." Dylan's voice carries a warning, and when I look

across the table at the rapt expressions of Ashling, Emily, and Jasmine, I understand why. I'm having a meltdown in front of three strangers who'd probably like nothing more than an excuse to post on the PATROL website, or at the very least gossip about it at school. "Did Ashling tell you—"

"My sources say Dr. Greaves isn't the real leader of PATROL." Ashling dabs delicately at her lips. "She's just a figurehead. The organization's actually funded by a consortium of insurance companies who paid out death benefits on passengers and want to prove you all attempted fraud."

Her *sources*? Plus . . ."What?"

"Are you finished?" Dylan says.

I tear my eyes away from Ashling. Dylan is gesturing at my lunch, which I've barely touched, but I take the hint. I'd really like to know more about these sources of Ashling's, but there's a high probability I'll blurt out something I shouldn't if I stay at the table, so I gather my food and backpack and murmur goodbye to the girls. As we move through the lunchroom, it seems like everyone is watching the statement and peeking over their phones at me. JoJo wears a particularly satisfied smirk, probably hoping I'm about to be beamed back up to the mother ship.

Dylan leads me to the stairwell that heads up to the science wing, and we both sink onto the bottom step. "I'm sorry about that. Ashling's a—" He blows out a breath. "Well, when I saw her sitting with you, I figured she planned to cause trouble."

I shiver. "Would you have shown that to me if she hadn't?"

He hesitates. "I don't know. This morning I felt like I should give you some distance since, you know, being seen together could be awkward, and because I couldn't tell you . . ." He drags his hands through his hair, making it stand up. "But once I saw what was happening, I had to do something. You have *got* to work on your poker face."

I'm proving him right this very moment. I do let everything show, and sometimes I can't help saying it out loud either. The only exception is when I'm interviewing someone. I have, like, a reporter switch I'm able to turn on. I wish it worked all the time.

I wonder if that's the full truth, that he stayed away this morning for my sake. But it's not the most important thing now.

"What do these people think happened? That we were frozen for twenty-five years? That I'm a cyborg?"

Dylan tilts his head sideways and taps his finger on his lips, then reaches out to pinch my arm.

"Ouch!" I rub the sore spot. "Why'd you do that?"

He shrugs and smirks obnoxiously. "I didn't feel any metal parts."

I snort. "That's a relief."

But it does help.

The bell rings, echoing in the stairwell. The doors open, and students start streaming in. I jump to my feet. Dylan waves and is gone, our conversation left open. I shake my head. He's goofy, but I like it.

I know PATROL is full of crap, but nobody else will believe me unless I prove it. I could refuse to meet their demands, but I have nothing to hide. They want my blood or DNA or whatever? They can have it, because I'm exactly who I say I am.

CHAPTER TWENTY

An hour later, I've endured countless suspicious and averted glances thanks to PATROL's sucky timing, but it's okay. Because it's finally time for the class I'm most looking forward to—convergence journalism. When I asked Mom what that meant, she said it included the school paper plus other media. I don't care as long as I can get to work writing and editing.

The paper is the one place I feel confident. Or did, anyway. I understand how to get to the heart of a story, plan out an issue with a variety of topics, and lay out each page to draw the eye to the most important part. Plus, I really love editing to make a story better.

I enter the journalism classroom just before the bell rings, thanks to my AP environmental science class being on the completely opposite side of the school. (I am loving the new science options, though.) Several other students hover around a laptop at the end of an oval table. They don't notice me, but the teacher does.

"Jenny Waters!" She claps her hands from somewhere behind me, and I whirl at the familiar voice.

She's older, but it's my newspaper teacher from twenty-five years ago. "Miss Holmes!"

I rush to hug her, relieved to see a familiar, if a bit more lined, face. She must be getting close to retirement now.

She steps back, her gaze running over my face. "Astonishing." She holds up her left hand. "And it's actually Mrs. Vega now."

"Oh. Congratulations." I don't know why this surprises me. I realize I have no idea how old she is—or was.

Miss Holm—Mrs. Vega turns me to the class. "This is Jenny Waters."

The faces whip up from the laptop, including my new "friend" from lunch, Ashling. Of course. I should've known when she mentioned having sources. I wonder if that's what Dylan started to tell me about her. At least she wasn't taking any notes.

Mrs. Vega continues. "Jenny was assistant editor of the *Parkwood Press* her junior year, and the staff voted her in as editor in chief for her senior year. Which means we have an interesting situation."

Oh, no. I mean, I earned the editor in chief position, but this isn't my staff. I don't know how this paper works.

"We have two editors in chief," Mrs. Vega announces brightly.

"What?" Ashling rises from her chair, slapping her palms on the table. She was the one showing everyone something on the computer and, I suspect, my new co-chief. "You can't be serious. There's a real possibility she's a clone."

"A clone? Interesting theory, Ashling." I tap my chin with my pointer finger. "What are your sources for this hard-hitting investigative story?"

Because the insurance company theory sounded viable, but calling me a clone is sloppy and sensationalist.

Ashling flinches. "Go Google yourself," she mutters.

Out of the corner of my eye, I see Mrs. Vega suppress a smile. "Ashling, I assure you Jenny is not a clone. I know her. She's smart. She understands news, and I expect all of you to show her the ropes."

She gives me a gentle shove toward the table. I claim a spot near the front of the room.

"But how would two editors in chief even work?" Ashling asks.

"*That*"—Mrs. Vega points at her with a smile—"is a good question to ask, and I have a plan. Since Jenny is getting acclimated, I propose that you oversee production, along with news, sports, and multimedia. Jenny has a knack for advertising, so she can handle sales, features, opinion, and photos. How does that sound?"

It sounds complicated, and I'm also bummed I don't get news, but Mrs. Vega is beaming like this is the best idea she's ever had, and besides, she's the teacher, so I smile brightly. "Great! I'm on it!"

"Sure," Ashling grumbles.

"Excellent." Mrs. Vega claps. "I expect you two to work together."

I'm only half paying attention as Mrs. Vega has everyone introduce themselves and explain their roles, and that's a mistake because once she starts talking about our first issue, I'm already lost.

"Toby will update the site's code—"

"Mrs. Vega?" I say, hand raised.

"Yes, Jenny?" She's holding a tablet. It's so different from how she used to teach.

"Um . . ." I'm going to sound stupid, but I can't just continue sitting here lost. "Why does Toby have to code for the paper?"

We used computers to lay out issues in 1995, but the programs were all preloaded from disks. Our staff members didn't need coding experience.

"Oh, Jenny." An all-too-familiar mask of pity comes over her face. "I assumed your parents would have explained . . ."

I really wish they would have.

"They haven't told her *anything*," Ashling says gleefully.

Or not the most relevant things, apparently.

"That's enough." Mrs. Vega frowns firmly. "You're not behaving with the attitude of an editor in chief."

Ashling slumps in her chair, and I'm momentarily gratified, but my heart is still pumping. I'm afraid that whatever news Mrs. Vega is about to deliver will devastate me.

"The paper isn't printed, Jenny. It's online."

"Not printed?" I repeat dumbly.

Ashling's lips twitch. She clearly has more insults ready.

"It's been online for *years*," another girl says. "All that paper we were wasting just didn't make sense."

What else are my parents hiding? They could have made this easier for me so I wouldn't be caught off guard. Or maybe it didn't even occur to them. Because it's so obvious.

Mrs. Vega clears her throat and turns to the class, pretending I didn't make a complete fool of myself. "What ideas do you have for this year's *Press*?"

Should it even be called a press if it isn't printed? A hysterical giggle bubbles up in my chest. Somehow I don't think changing the name is what Mrs. Vega has in mind.

"We haven't done much with our Vimeo channel," one boy says. I think it's Toby, but I'm caught on the concept of the paper having a channel. A TV channel?

"What about a how-to segment?" he adds.

"Are you volunteering to produce it?" Mrs. Vega asks. "What about frequency?"

Others jump in, but I'm confused. I can't tell if we're still talking about the *Press* or if we've switched to a TV channel. All I know is it's suffocating in here. I feel my airways closing off, and I need to escape.

I raise my hand again.

"You have a suggestion, Jenny?" Mrs. Vega looks so pleased I hate to disappoint her, but I have to get out of here.

Warmth rushes up my neck. "No. Sorry. Can I use the bathroom?"

Ashling snorts.

Mrs. Vega ignores her. "Of course."

I rush from the room, escaping the one place I thought I'd really fit in.

CHAPTER TWENTY-ONE

For a moment I lean against the wall just outside the classroom, but Mrs. Vega *might* check on me, so I book it for the bathroom.

I *won't* cry in a stall.

It's such a cliché. Besides, I'm sick of crying.

I wish I had someone to talk to, someone who understands what it's like to be lost in this century. Art's number is safe in my desk at home, along with Mrs. Spring's. Mom and Dad keep trying to protect me, but they don't understand what I need to know to survive here. Plus, Captain McCoy may be satisfied letting the FBI handle things, but I'm not. Not when the conspiracy theorists have gone so far as to create a formal group to discredit us. I feel like Art will have some ideas about that.

"Jenny?"

I halt with my palm on the bathroom door, my eyes closed. Of course Dylan's here. I turn with a sigh and open my eyes. "How are you everywhere?"

He holds up a paper. "I have to bring this to the office."

"Oh." Still. He keeps popping up whenever I'm upset, like he's inherited Angie's knack for that.

"Are you okay?" His eyebrows are all crinkled up as he stares at me.

I must look like I'm about to cry. I lean against the bathroom doorjamb. "Not really. Journalism is the one thing I thought I understood, but apparently our paper is online and there's a channel involved and people"—what was that word Bradley used?—"toot?"

Dylan chokes on a laugh. I knew that wasn't right as soon as it came out.

"Of course I don't want to toot." Oh, no. That's worse. My cheeks warm.

"Keep going." Dylan makes a circular motion with his hand. "I can't wait to hear what comes out next."

I roll my eyes. "Never mind."

"You're talking about social media."

I stab my finger in the air. "Yes!" That's what Kelly called it. I should've asked more questions then. I didn't realize it would be so important. "Can you teach me about that so I don't look like an idiot?"

Surprise mixed with concern flashes across Dylan's face before he grins cockily. "I'm free tonight if you want to come by." He winks. "I can show you my book collection."

Is that supposed to be a line? "Intriguing, but"—I tap my finger on my lips and ignore the flutter in my stomach—"at the moment I'm more interested in the cyber world than paper and ink."

He nods slowly. "Well played, Jenny Waters."

I remember how weird he got before school, when he introduced me to Drew. "You're not going to Drew's big kegger?"

He rolls up the paper he's holding and slaps it against his other hand. "I told you. Those always get busted."

Exactly my point! "Well, thanks for giving me your night."

He shrugs. "It's no big deal. I'm finished with baseball practice by five thirty. I usually grab a bite with Jack after, but I'll tell him I got a better offer."

He grins in a way that makes it clear *I'm* the better offer, and my stomach flutters again.

"Who's Jack?" I ask, turning the conversation in a safer direction. I haven't seen him with anyone but Drew today, and that guy was sort of a jerk.

He waves a hand. "My best friend. He goes to another school. But we've played ball together since middle school. In the spring I play here and the rest of the year on a club team."

So when he said he was a baseball guy, he really meant it. I push away from the door.

He frowns. "Don't you need to . . . ?"

"Nope."

Now that I have a plan, I most definitely don't need to cry in a bathroom stall.

"Oh, wait." I grimace. "What does it mean to Google yourself?"

He tilts his head and lifts his left eyebrow. "You say that like you're afraid it's something dirty."

"Ashling made it sound that way, but Mrs. Vega didn't get after her, so . . ."

"Ah." Dylan slaps his rolled-up paper once again. "Google's an online search engine."

Huh. "I guess that makes sense. Apparently it's Ashling's source for calling me a clone. If that's the sort of information she relies on for news, I think I'll pass."

Dylan nods slowly, his grin gone. "Probably a good call."

The ride home from school is silent, since JoJo's there to prevent any real discussion. When I get home and open the front door, the aroma of chocolate chip cookies snaps me out of my funk. I bound upstairs and chuck my backpack.

"Is that you, Jenny?" Mom steps into the kitchen doorway, wiping her hands on her apron. She smiles. "Come have some warm cookies."

"I was planning on it." I grab a plate and snag three off the cooling rack, popping one into my mouth. The chocolate melts on my tongue. "Mmm. Best surprise ever."

Mom sighs. "I thought you might've had a tough day."

Of course she knows. This is the sort of thing they've been hiding from me. "You saw the PATROL statement."

She nods. "It's everywhere, and they're causing quite a stink. We've tried to keep you isolated from the media firestorm, but I'm afraid we won't be able to much longer. Your dad had to chase several reporters off the lawn today."

I lick chocolate off my fingers, swallowing what I want to say about how things would have been easier for me if they'd just told me about these people themselves. I'm not sure how much longer I'll be able to keep it in. "What's happening?"

"Well, there is something you should know about the FBI." Mom twists her apron ties around her fingers.

When it's clear she isn't going to say anything more, I tap my nails on my plate. "What, Mom?"

"Agent Klein's been in touch. They've requested another round of tests. Much more extensive than before. Actually, she called before the announcement of this PATROL group today."

I hold in an exasperated sigh. "Why didn't you tell me?"

She drops the apron string to grip my shoulders. "Because we want you to have a normal life. School and friends."

How is it possible she's so clueless about high school? I mean, she was a teenager once. "Mom, even before everyone started watching that statement today, they were looking at me like a weirdo. I want to do the tests—for the FBI, PATROL, whoever."

Mom purses her lips, her upper body tense, then relaxes. "Okay."

I'd better get all my demands out there now. "And I want a phone."

Mom frowns. "You were fine without one before."

"You're right. I was," I say. "And if I weren't living in a different century, I wouldn't ask for one. But I sat through a class today where I expected to understand every word, and it was like they were speaking a different language. Dylan's going to translate for me, but I need a phone. By seven tonight. And some sort of computer, too, because most of my teachers want assignments turned in via a 'virtual classroom.'" I make air quotes. "It was on the semester outlines they passed out."

Mom raises an eyebrow. "Dylan, huh?"

Maybe, a rebellious part of my brain answers, but I refuse to consider it. I point at her. "You're the one who set him up as my chauffeur."

Mom smiles. "He's a nice boy." She looks away to consider, then refocuses on me. "Fine. We'll get you a phone and a laptop. I'm sorry we didn't prepare you properly. There's just a part of me that would like to keep everything the way it was before."

I hug her, breathing in her rose-cinnamon-coffee scent. "I get it, Mom. But if I want to live in the now, I have to move forward."

Even if a part of me wishes I didn't.

CHAPTER TWENTY-TWO

By the time Mom pulls into the Grahams' driveway later, I have a brand-spanking-new phone. (Next step: fix this driver's license situation.) Mom added herself, Dad, Bradley (as "Brad"), Kelly, Grandma, and Angie as contacts, and then I added Art and Mrs. Spring. She also showed me how to use the camera and text people. Other than a few games, that's about the extent of her phone knowledge, anyway.

I grab my backpack with my trusty notebook, because I expect to take lots of notes on whatever Dylan teaches me about this new media stuff.

"So I'll get you around nine?" Mom says.

I hope two hours is enough time for a crash course. "Sure." I pat the front pocket of my backpack, where I stowed the phone. "I'll call you if anything changes."

I walk up to the front door and ring the bell. I wave at Mom driving away as the door opens behind me. I swing around and gasp.

"Steve!"

He looks good for his age. His eyes are still that bright blue, and his dark blond hair curls at the nape of his neck like it always has. I don't know what he does for a living—because I've avoided asking about him—but he's dressed casually, in a polo and khaki shorts.

"Nobody told me you were coming over—"

"Dylan didn't say you'd be home—"

We both stop abruptly, leaving us awkwardly staring. I should've anticipated this. But even planning to come over here, I didn't think, *Oh, Steve might be there.* I've compartmentalized him into a small part of my brain, like a secret that should never be spoken aloud.

"Jenny Waters." He steps onto the porch and wraps me up in a hug.

I tense for a moment, waiting to feel that old surge of anticipation, that zing in my gut that hopes for more. But his body doesn't feel the same. He's fuller. Not like he's gained a ton of weight, just like he's a man instead of a boy. And he smells different. I can't even explain what it is exactly. He just feels more like . . . well, more like Dylan's dad than my boyfriend.

He steps back and smiles. "It's really good to see you."

I'm so relieved that my pulse isn't racing, that I'm not reliving any of the butterfly feelings I used to experience with Steve. "It's good to see you too."

"Hi, Jenny," Angie says from behind him.

Steve and I jump. He drops his hands from my shoulders like we've misbehaved, even though our hug was completely innocent, like old friends greeting each other after a long absence.

"Hi, Ange," I say. I link my arm through Steve's and tug him inside. It's nice to tease her for a change. Besides, I deserve to have a little fun. Steve raises his eyebrow like, *What are you up to, young lady?* It's such a dad look I laugh.

I'm not like Tracey, whose fiancé waited twenty-five years for her. I don't want my boyfriend back when he's forty-two. It's so freeing to let go of the doubt that I'd lost the guy I was meant to be with.

I have to figure out how to live in this century instead of staying stuck in the old one. That's why I'm here tonight.

"Well, isn't this a fun reunion." JoJo walks in from the kitchen with a bowl of chips like she's watching a soap opera. She crunches loudly on a Dorito. "I hope you're gonna fight for him, Mom. I don't want to choose between you and step-Jenny."

I drop Steve's arm. JoJo has a special knack for sucking all the fun out of everything. She's pretty much the worst thing about Angie and Steve getting together.

It's unfair they named her after me, but that doesn't give her a pass to insult me every time we come in contact. "Step-Jenny? That's so clever. Maybe you could be the next David Letterman."

"JoJo, that was rude and unnecessary," Steve intervenes. He sounds just like my dad. "Jenny is our guest and friend. You will show her respect."

Yep. All gooey feelings definitely gone.

JoJo turns away without responding to either of us. "Dylan," she calls. "Your study *date* is here."

So much for taking back the upper hand.

Steve and Angie both flinch at the word "date." Even though this isn't a date, it's mortifying to even consider the prospect in their presence.

JoJo vanishes, leaving us in a tangle of awkwardness.

"So . . ." Angie adjusts her glasses. I can tell she has a million questions, but she knows she doesn't have the right anymore to ask them all. "What are you guys working on?"

Saving me from answering, Dylan skids into the room, breathless. "Sorry. Didn't hear the doorbell. What'd I miss?"

"Nothing. Can we get started?" I just want to leave this room. Especially since I can't one hundred percent deny there's a grain of truth in JoJo's insinuation.

"Sure." Dylan motions for me to follow him, completely clueless.

How can he not feel the tension in this room? But I guess if he can act like things are completely normal, I can too. I trail after Dylan, my steps lightening as we approach the hallway off the living room.

"Leave the door open," Steve calls.

Oh, no, he didn't.

"Dad." Dylan groans.

I don't think I could get any more embarrassed. "Seriously, Steve?"

He gives me a pointed look. "He's not me."

I was wrong; this *could* get more embarrassing. I feel like my entire body is on fire. I lock my head in place, refusing to let it swivel toward Dylan to see how he's reacting to all of this. When they had that father-son discussion at age eleven or whenever, did Steve say, "When I was seventeen, I couldn't get up the guts to kiss my girlfriend, Jenny, and it wasn't until I started dating your mother that—" No. I just can't go there.

"Steve, leave them alone." Angie tugs him into the kitchen with an affectionate smile. I stare after them.

"Um." Dylan pokes my arm. "I didn't know it was possible to turn into a tomato."

My eternal curse—showing every emotion on my face *and* embarrassment on every visible inch of skin. I finally unlock my neck muscles to face him. "I guess that's what happens when your friend's parents know your deepest secrets. At least the humiliation should stay within these walls."

For some reason, it's this statement that causes Dylan to turn red. "Let's go to my room before they return for act two."

CHAPTER TWENTY-THREE

Based on our previous conversations and Dylan's cheesy line about showing me his book collection, I anticipate wall-to-wall bookshelves. Instead I'm hit with baseball. World Series pennants, signed jerseys, and posters cover every available space. "Wow. You really love the Cardinals."

He's already at his desk, where he's pulled up two chairs. He twists around, face lit up. "Best team in the world."

"Agreed." His books, I see now, all with unfamiliar titles, are hidden behind trophies and baseballs. I peer closely at a ball in a plastic round case; it's signed. "Ozzie Smith?" I'm about to say he's my favorite player when I realize he's long retired by now.

When I turn, Dylan's standing behind me, his fingers woven through his hair. "Yep. Met him at an event a couple of years ago. Sorry, I'm not the best at keeping my stuff organized."

It's cute how self-conscious he is. "I bet that drives Angie crazy."

"Uh-huh. I tried to clean up before you came, though."

It's sweet. I like this insight into Dylan, how intensely he loves the Cardinals and those books he told me about. And that he was thinking about me before I came.

"Thanks." As I move toward his desk, I point at his *Star Wars* shirt. "Considering the theme in here, I'm surprised by your wardrobe choices."

He smiles with one side of his mouth. "I'm not so easy to read."

"Hmm." A challenge I should probably avoid. As much as I'd like to delve into more of what makes him tick, that's not why I'm here. I sit in one of the desk chairs, setting my backpack on the floor between us. "So where should we start?"

He toes my backpack. "What did you bring?"

I pull out my necessary supplies. "Notebook, pen, and phone."

Dylan smirks at the last part. "So you finally have a life."

I punch his shoulder. "I will once you show me how to use it. I never again want to feel like I did in class today."

The smile slips from his face. He clears his throat and turns to the laptop. "About that Google search Ashling suggested. Maybe—"

I wave a hand. "I'm not interested in whatever ridiculous stories people are putting out about me. I just want to understand how the paper works, and social media, so I don't look like an idiot."

"But there's something you should—"

"Snacks?"

We whirl around at Angie's voice. She's standing in the (open) doorway balancing two cans of Coke and a container of sour cream and onion Pringles.

Dylan rubs his fists over his eyes and blinks in an exaggerated way. "Soda *and* chips? Who are you and what have you done with my mom?"

I crinkle my nose. "What's so weird about soda and chips?"

Dylan jumps up from his seat like he's diving for a grounder instead of snacks. "Soda's usually forbidden in our house."

He passes me one of the sodas and the can of chips.

"Forbidden? Well now." I cock my head at Angie. "Interesting position."

She looks confused for a moment, then straightens. "I completely forgot about that."

Dylan settles back into his chair, already gulping his soda. "What?"

Angie huffs a laugh. "An old argument about vending machines in school from mock trial. Jenny was a witness for the team suing after a kid choked on a candy bar. I defended the school and the company that stocked the vending machine."

He looks between us. "So that means . . . what?"

I raise my Coke can in the air. "That she once argued passionately for teenagers' need for candy and sweets and is now denying them to you. Yet she has compromised her principles for me."

"It's your favorite." Angie grumbles. "I also forgot how you never let things go."

"Seriously? You were always relying on me *because* of my amazing memory." I put on my best Angie voice. "'Jenny, what was that English assignment again?' Or, 'Jenny, what did I wear to the basketball game last Friday, so I don't wear the same thing again?' I had, like, an Angie Rolodex in my head."

Angie smiles. "You sure did."

It feels good to joke with Angie. I still don't know how to be friends with a forty-year-old, but it's better than harboring this tight knot of resentment in my gut over decisions she made when she believed I was dead.

"Thanks for the snacks, Mom," Dylan says, a clear hint for her to leave.

She doesn't want to, I can tell, but I didn't come here to see her, so she walks out with a farewell tap on the door. I peel open the can of Pringles, breathing in the delicious, thankfully unchanged scent. "What were you about to tell me before Angie interrupted?"

Dylan glances at the doorway, shaking his head. "Never mind." He holds out his hand. "Let's start with Vimeo, since the *Parkwood Press* has a channel."

I hand him my phone, but his mention of a channel reminds me of something. "Actually, can you show me how to look up the PATROL website first?"

He leans back in his chair, cradling my phone. "Why? You just said you don't care what they're posting about you."

"I don't, but I want to know what this group is about so I'm prepared for whatever accusation gets thrown at me next."

"Fair enough." Dylan sits up, sets my phone aside, and touches a square space below the keys on his laptop. An arrow starts moving around the screen.

"Is that the *mouse?*"

He nods. "Yep. It's called a trackpad. I just used it to click on the internet browser."

"Where's the dial tone?"

Dylan moves the curser to the window at the top. "You don't have to dial; it's just connected all the time. Now I'm going to type in the website address."

He explains like it's perfectly natural for me not to know this. He never treats me like an oddity, which means more than I can express.

A second later, the PATROL page pops up. "Wow, that's so fast! Is it always like that?"

"Unless the router's slow or something, pretty much."

Bradley said things were faster online, but until this very moment, I didn't get it.

"It's so different from what we had before. It took forever to access each page, and it didn't look like *this*." I gesture at the PATROL page, which is downright fancy for having been created so quickly. "So the *Parkwood Press* is a page like that, where students can pull it up anytime?"

Dylan regards me steadily. "Jenny, *everything* on the internet is available anytime, almost as fast as you want it."

I feel like he's trying to tell me something more, but I decide not to push it. When I don't respond, he continues. "If you have a question, you ask it here. That's what Ashling meant earlier. Google is the biggest search engine, so if you Google something, you're just searching for it."

"Huh. And is it real information?" Because Ashling suggesting I was a clone definitely wasn't reliable, but if what Dylan is saying is true, it completely changes the way news works. How amazing is it to just ask your computer instead of spending hours making phone calls and reading through books and reference materials to track down information.

He bobbles his head back and forth. "Depends on the source, but I think once you play around with it you'll figure out what's real or not."

Speaking of questionable sources . . . He rolls his chair aside so I can look at the PATROL page. The group's name is written in a professional-looking font at the top, and the paragraph that follows is basically a repeat of the spokesperson's press statement. *Concerned citizens wanting answers*, blah, blah, blah.

"Who are these people?" I scan the page, but I can't figure out how to move it. "Do you think Ashling was right about insurance companies backing them?"

Dylan shows me how to scroll down. "If they are, I'm sure they won't put their logos on the website. Oh, here. 'Our Credentials.'" He clicks, and up pop the pictures of a dozen people who have apparently associated themselves with this group. Not only Dr. Greaves, the theoretical astrophysicist, but also a mathematician, a senator, a history professor, a researcher from the Smithsonian, a documentarian, an actor (what?), a CEO of a major local company, and the owner of a fast-food chain. "They're certainly trying to look official." I can't believe all these people have come together for the express purpose of proving we're fakes. "What is their *deal*?"

"I don't know, but look." He points at another section of the website: **PASSENGERS**.

I inhale, the taste of the sour chips bitter in my mouth, and take a drink of Coke to wash it away. "That had better not be what I think it is."

"I'm sure it is. After all, they put out a call for reports on everyone."

I click on the link, and familiar names jump out at me: Frank McCoy, Art Ross, Agnes and Ted Spring, Valerie Wen. And sure enough, there I am, Jennifer Waters. At least it only says St. Louis and doesn't list my home address. "Do you mind if I call someone?"

"Uh . . . no?"

"Sorry, I just . . . This is such an invasion of privacy!" I grab my phone from the desk and pull up Art's number. Dylan watches me dial with his eyebrows scrunched up.

"Who is this?" Art answers.

That is so him. "Nice greeting. It's Jenny Waters."

"Jenny! Wait. For real? Tell me what you were doing on the plane when we met."

"We need a code to have a conversation?"

Dylan sends a questioning glance my way, and I roll my eyes.

"I'm waiting, *Jenny*," Art says, like he still doesn't believe it's me. Maybe he has reason. Maybe people are calling him, pretending to be other passengers to get a story or information. Maybe even followers of PATROL, looking for stories to post on the website.

"Fine," I say. "I was writing an editorial about Columbia."

"Okay, Jenny, *I got your number.*"

I snort. "How long were you waiting to use that line?"

Dylan leans forward, frowning. "Who are you talking to, exactly? And why is he using a line on you?"

"Art Ross, from the plane."

"I already know who *I* am," Art says on his end.

Dylan's frown deepens. "That weird guy with the hand shirt?"

I shake my head at him, focusing back on the call. "Art, I called because I'm at a friend's and we're on the PATROL website, and have you *seen* this?"

"Yeah. You should see the reports 'concerned citizens' have sent in." I can hear the sarcasm in his voice. "More nuts than the people behind all of it. Total pseudo-science."

"I wonder if anyone has sent in reports about me yet," I say, moving the cursor back to the passenger section. I think about Ashling, or anyone else at school. *Jenny Waters doesn't fit in at Parkwood High. I hope you prove she's a hoax, because she definitely doesn't belong here!*

Dylan places a hand over mine. "Don't look. Seriously."

The back of my hand tingles at his touch. He's probably right. What will I gain from reading a bunch of lies?

"Yeah, you don't have to bother looking," Art chimes in on the phone, "but it's sort of fun to read people's whacked-out theories and then come up with actual facts to refute them."

I'm not so sure about that. "Wait. What do you think this group is *really* after?" Ashling could be right. There could be a silent party behind it all with a financial motive. "I mean, we're not a hoax. The initial tests prove it, and once we do more it won't be any different. And what's that name all about? *Assuring Time Relativity, Order, and Legitimacy.* For real?"

"It's interesting," Art says, "since time isn't a tangible object. How time passes is relative depending on the person, and obviously they have their undies in a twist about us messing up the expected sequence of things. I have some other theories about it, if you want to get together tomorrow."

Tomorrow is a Friday. "Don't you have school? Because I do."

He wants to meet you? Dylan mouths. He looks pretty irritated about it.

I shake my head.

"Nah, I'm taking a break," Art says. "Freshman year was a total buzzkill. Anyway, I'm busy Saturday before the meeting, so maybe we can just catch up there?"

"I guess." In the meantime, I can do some additional research, now that I understand how much faster and easier it is. "See you then."

He hangs up.

"So." Dylan raises an eyebrow. "I invite a girl to my room and she calls another guy . . . Talk about a confidence killer."

I snicker *"You're* threatened by *Art?"*

Dylan grins slowly, not his usual playful grin at all, and I realize I should have responded much more carefully. Instead, I zero in on the clock. "Hey, it's already seven forty-five. I definitely still need that crash course for class tomorrow, and Mom's coming back for me at nine. So . . . Vimeo, you said?"

He holds my gaze another moment. "Let's do this."

CHAPTER TWENTY-FOUR

Despite the nastiness yesterday, I feel confident going into my second day of school. I have an appointment at the hospital tomorrow. The doctors will do a complete battery of tests, including a CAT scan, MRI, and DNA tests against Mom, Dad, and Bradley. They won't be released publicly unless I say it's okay. I've decided I'll talk to Art and the rest of the Flight 237 support group and see what they think before I do anything.

But when Dylan and JoJo pick me up, JoJo's sly smile creates a minor ding in my armor.

She has never smiled at me.

"What's up with her?" I ask Dylan since JoJo is wearing earbuds again.

He frowns. "What do you mean?"

"She *smiled* at me."

Dylan side-eyes me. "She does do that occasionally."

Obviously he didn't see the *way* she smiled. Whatever. I won't let it bother me.

"Hey, did you do any more research on those PATROL people?" he asks.

"No. When I got home last night, I talked Mom and Dad into letting me open a few social media accounts, although they're all set to private. I'm supposed to let them *approve my friend and follower requests*," I repeat in Mom's voice.

He frowns. "Doesn't that bother you?"

The way he says it, I feel like it's supposed to. But as much as I value my privacy, it doesn't seem like an invasion in this case— probably because there's nothing there yet. "Maybe it would if I'd grown up with it like you. But considering there are people like Dr. Greaves out there . . . I don't want them cyberstalking me because I click Accept or Okay on the wrong person."

He flicks his fingers off the wheel. "Yeah, I don't really have that problem."

No, but there might be a few girls checking him out for other, not-so-nefarious reasons. I press my hands against my hot cheeks, afraid he'll ask why I'm blushing, but his eyes are on the road, so I'm safe either way.

"My only connections so far are family members. It's weird to see pictures of my cousins all older. Also how *much* of them I can learn online. It's like half their lives are out there for everyone to see." The thought of being so exposed makes me shiver. "I haven't actually posted anything myself yet, though."

For now I'm an observer, and I will be stalking those PATROL people at the earliest opportunity. Maybe after school today. Mom is supposed to pick up a laptop for me so I don't have to share theirs.

Dylan glances over his shoulder at me as he turns into the school. "Do you think they'll approve me?"

I purse my lips and twist my hand from side to side. "Iffy."

"At least I've been preapproved for your phone number," he says. We exchanged those last night. "So start studying up on those emojis."

Not really at the top of my review list. "Uh, okay."

When we get out of the car, JoJo casts me another suspicious smile before darting into school. This time Dylan sees it. "Huh," he says, throwing his backpack over his shoulder.

"She's up to something, right?"

He frowns as he watches her walk away. "You might be right."

We head toward the entrance. Today I am not invisible; instead, students are noticeably staring or even pointing at me. Drew jogs over and does the fist thingy to Dylan. "You missed a great party."

Dylan shrugs but avoids looking at me. "Had other stuff to do."

I wonder who he's trying to protect this time—me or himself.

"Your loss." Drew smirks at me before loping off.

Inside, Dylan and I pause. This is where we separate.

"I'll find you at lunch," he says.

I resist the urge to grab his backpack and plead with him not to leave me. Then I want to kick myself. I'm too reliant on Dylan, one. But it's more than that. I like being with him. I like his teasing comments that I can't quite interpret. And that's complicated for so many more reasons than just liking a boy.

As soon as I sit in calculus, the girl beside me leans in so close her long hair brushes my desk. "So. I got totally wasted at Drew's party last night. Jello shots. Sooo good. Ya know?"

"Um, not really." I've never had jello shots.

The girl (Lana, I think?) smiles knowingly. "Of course you don't. Well, anyway, so then this guy I've never seen before came up and kissed me, and I was like why not? He's hot. So we went into Drew's little sister's room and hooked up."

I don't understand why she's telling me this too-personal story. I barely met this girl yesterday; I'm not even sure she said hello. She must have actual friends she could confide in. If class weren't about to start, I'd get out of my seat and go sharpen a pencil or recycle scrap paper or *something* to prevent her from continuing to invade my personal space.

"Wow," she says. "You really are a prude."

I stiffen, unsure what to say when *she* was the one who over-shared without any invitation from me, but then the bell rings, and Mrs. Sims begins the lesson.

I have the strangest feeling maybe-Lana told me that story specifically to try to get a reaction out of me. It's still bothering me when I settle into my seat in English and someone taps my shoulder. When I twist around, the guy behind me says, "Didn't see you at Drew's party."

I groan. Not again. "I had other plans."

"You missed an epic blowout," the guy (Caleb?) says.

I hope he isn't the other half of the blind hookup story. "Sounds like it."

"Really." He scoots his desk closer to mine. "Drew comes up with the most epic party games."

"Uh-huh." I'm tempted to hand him a thesaurus so he can choose a new adjective in place of "epic."

Mistaking my "uh-huh" for encouragement, probably-Caleb continues. "Yep. Spider races."

I freeze. "What?"

"He had a shoebox full of them, and he painted different-colored dots on their backs." The guy cups his hand and pokes his palm with his pointer finger. "We each put a dollar in the pot, and whoever's spider reached the other side of the Ping-Pong table first won."

Cold twists through my veins. The spiders must have been *huge*. "Are you kidding me?"

This is about my worst nightmare. Once, when we were ten, Angie and I went exploring in the woods by her grandma's house and found an old cabin. We knew better than to go inside, but being fearless kids, we kicked in the door. There was a giant spider on the floor. I stomped on it, and it exploded into a hundred more spiders—turned out it was a mama spider with babies on its back. They started scurrying everywhere, including up our legs. Ever since, I've been terrified of them.

"How could you be sure they wouldn't escape and get all over his house?" I ask before I can stop myself. Even thinking about it, I feel hundreds of legs crawling all over me.

I swear there's an evil glint in his eye. "Some of them might have."

"Did someone win?" I can't help asking. Where'd Drew even get a box of spiders?

Probably-Caleb brightens. "Yeah. My spider ran straight across the Ping-Pong table!"

"And then what?" I scratch at my shin.

He shrugs. "I smashed it. The table was pretty nasty after that." He peers at me. "You don't like spiders, do you?"

I get the feeling he already knew that. But . . . how?

Considering that suspicious smile this morning, JoJo is my primary suspect. Clearly her parents told her stories about me, and now she's passing them along—as embarrassingly as possible.

The rest of the day, I watch for any sign of contact between her, Drew, maybe-Lana, or probably-Caleb, but I never see them together. She could have made an appearance at Drew's party and spread rumors about me there, though she was at home when I was over at her house. I don't blame Angie and Steve for telling JoJo about me. I was gone for twenty-five years. It makes sense they'd reminisce. They couldn't have anticipated these stories would come back to haunt me. I just don't understand why she hates me so much.

But.

These stories *are* coming back to haunt me.

I try not to think about it as I walk into journalism because at least today I'm on top of the new-media situation. I take a seat at the front of the table and pull out my notebook and newly loaded phone, ready to plan. Features, opinion, photos, advertising. I have pages with bulleted notes for each of them. I also made sections for news, sports, and multimedia so I can keep an eye on Ashling's half of the *Press*. Even if I'm not the full editor in chief, I still want to stay on top of how it all works together.

Speaking of Ashling, she sweeps into the room and sits across from me, folding her arms on the table. She smirks.

Oh, great. Her too? "Are you friends with JoJo?"

She raises her eyebrows. "JoJo Graham? No." She tosses her hair like the idea is beneath her. Which I guess I get. They don't appear to travel in the same circles, although admittedly I don't know much about JoJo's circle. I only asked because JoJo and Ashling have one key trait in common: they're card-carrying members of the Torture Jenny Waters Club.

A chair squeaks behind me.

"Good afternoon," Mrs. Vega says, moving around her desk. I hadn't noticed her when I walked in.

We murmur half-hearted replies.

"I hope you all came ready to work. I'd like our first issue to go live the week after next."

Go live. So weird. Even though I understand now, it seems wrong we're not saying "go to press."

Ashling raises her hand.

"Yes?"

"I have a story for the news section."

Mrs. Vega nods at her to continue. I flip to the news page in my notebook.

"An exposé," Ashling says. "I overheard some guys talking in band practice."

Definitely didn't picture her as a band geek. But I jot down "band guys."

"They said two boys—from another school—are selling pot out of the drive-through window at Coolie's."

I drop my pen, then quickly pick it up and write out what she just said. That *is* major. Even better than the cover story I wrote last year about who was hiding rats in the boys' locker room.

Mrs. Vega frowns. "If that's true, those boys need to report it to their supervisor."

Ashling nods earnestly. "Well, yeah. Of course. But can I pursue it?"

Mrs. Vega's lips remain pursed. "I'm concerned about your sources. Will they talk to you? Will they come forward?"

Ashling taps her manicured nails on the table. "If I write the story, they'll have to, right?"

"Not if you write it on hearsay," I jump in. I mean, she's talking about a conversation she overheard, not an actual interview.

Ashling turns on me. "Is that why you never did anything when it happened at that frozen custard place you worked at back in high school?"

I fumble my pen again. Is she implying someone was selling drugs through the Frosty's window? Plus, I'm still in high school! "You—I—you—"

"Ashling, that's enough," Mrs. Vega says.

"Is it, Mrs. Vega?" Ashling straightens in her seat, effecting a studious look. "Forget that. I think the other story our student body is all anxious to read about is our very own Jenny Waters. Is she for real? Or is she a hoax? Some sort of cyborg or an alien in a clone body?"

If I wouldn't get expelled for it, I'd jump across the table and tackle her. But I hold the anger tight at my core and respond calmly. "I'm not either of those. Do you need me to get a knife and cut open a vein to prove it?"

"No!" Mrs. Vega nearly shouts. "There will be no sharp objects. We believe you."

But a glance around the table shows the opposite. She might believe me, but Ashling, building on the PATROL statement yesterday, has placed seeds of doubt in the minds of everyone else.

Ashling leans toward me. "Maybe you've just studied Jenny

Waters so well you're able to imitate her. Maybe you just read the book?"

"Book? I don't know what you're talking about!"

Ashling's eyes widen in a look that's becoming all too familiar on her—satisfaction at my expense.

"You don't know?" She casts her smirk down the table. "She doesn't know." She looks back at me. "I told you to go Google yourself!"

"To read stories about me being a clone?" I burst out. "Why would I do that?"

"Jenny." Mrs. Vega crouches beside me, and somehow this makes everything much more serious. I turn my face toward hers. Her expression is full of concern. "No one's mentioned the book to you?"

I'm about ready to Hulk out and throw the table at the wall. "What. Book?"

She bites her lip. "The book Angie wrote about you."

CHAPTER TWENTY-FIVE

No.

Angie wouldn't write a *book* about me.

Mrs. Vega's saying something more, but it's muffled, like I'm inside a glass ball. I'm consumed by thoughts of all the things people have said that didn't make sense until this very moment.

Grandma mumbling, "Some truths aren't mine to tell."

Dad saying Angie would have something to share with me about being famous.

Dylan saying it was a "good call" not to search for myself on the internet.

"I did some writing." Angie's own words. "It made me feel closer to you."

She left out the part about writing a whole freaking book with *me* as the subject. And here I thought we could rebuild our friendship. "I can't think of anything else you need to know," she said.

"Jenny?"

Mrs. Vega's voice breaks through. I look down. I've shredded multiple sheets of notebook paper, creating a snowscape on the table.

I have to see this book *now*. I stand.

"Jenny," Mrs. Vega says again.

I'm getting sick of my name, the way people feel entitled to it. Like they know me. News flash, Jenny: *Angie* is the reason everyone knows your name.

But I need to find out how *much* they know about me. Besides, apparently, my fear of spiders and aversion to partying.

"I have to go." I pull what's left of my notebook out from under the shreds, flip it shut, and stuff it into my backpack.

"Go?" Mrs. Vega echoes. "It's the middle of the school day."

"I feel sick."

She looks at the rest of the class, like she's torn between her responsibility to them and to me. She leans close. "Okay. You can go to the nurse. But I'm here if you want to talk later. I have a free period at the end of the day."

I don't look at anyone else. I'm sure Ashling's mentally recording every reaction for her Jenny Waters exposé. Maybe she's even taking notes. Forget the school paper; she could write an article for the *New York Times*.

"Thanks, Mrs. Vega." My voice is strangled as I leave the room. I don't head for the nurse's office. I march for a side door near the band room that I know lets off beside a walking path. I stride into the trees, toward answers.

Leaving school without permission is the most rebellious thing I've ever done in my life. I laugh through my nose. I was so determined to get to the library for a newspaper, to figure out what everyone's been afraid to tell me about the world. Turns out what they've been hiding is a lot more personal. I'm sweating when I arrive, and I wish I'd chosen Keds instead of cute sandals this morning, as a blister's forming on the outside of my little toe.

But I'm here, and I will discover how royally Angie's screwed me over.

The automatic doors swish open, and I'm greeted by the familiar smell of books and musty carpet, which appears to be the same carpet the library had the last time I was here. I'm so grateful I'm tempted to get on my knees and kiss it.

To my right are the bathrooms and meeting rooms, just like before. I turn left instead, toward the main area where the stacks are. But I stop. Because right through the security sensors, beside the book return desk, there's a display: "Everything You Need to Know About Flight 237." *This* is why Mom and Dad didn't want to bring me here.

My first instinct is to grab every single book on that shelf and make a run for it, but I wouldn't make it to the street before somebody caught me. There are, like, twenty of them. I cover my mouth, and my feet carry me toward the display as if an invisible rope is tugging me forward. I scan the titles—*The Unsolved Mystery of Flight 237: Facts and Theories*, *A Timeline of Flight 237*, *Missing Mid-Flight*, *Left Grounded. Where's Walter?*—so I'm not the only one who has a whole book about me. Poor Walter. But I can't let it distract me. Right in the center, in prime position, is the book I came to see—*Jenny and Me*.

The cover features a picture of me and my former best friend, our cheeks pressed together, the camera close up. I don't remember this specific shot, but we look happy. It's my Angie, the one I left behind. I don't consciously tell my hands to reach for the book, even though that's why I came. I clutch it to my chest, hiding my face against my T-shirt as I search for a private place to read. It's pretty quiet, as I'd expect at this time of day.

The children's section is out; there are a couple of moms with small kids in there. I move away from the display, along the stacks. The book scent reassures me. I claim a padded armchair at the end of a row.

I smooth my hand over the book's cover and breathe deeply before opening it. I check the copyright: 2001. So this was published six years after I disappeared, when Angie was twenty-three and just out of college. When she should've been in her first year of law school. She's listed on the cover as Angela Russell Graham, so she and Steve must've gotten married during college or right after. And it's nineteen years ago, so before Dylan and JoJo.

I flip to the next page. *For Jenny. I will always miss you. If there are any typos in this book, I'm sure you'll catch them from heaven or space or wherever you're reading this.*

I sigh. It's just so Angie. But it's also devastating. Everyone really did believe I was dead. Years trudged by for Angie while hours passed for me in the air. It's inconceivable, and there's still no explanation. I hope some of Art's theories include a reason why this happened to us, how we lost twenty-five years of our lives—or maybe it's more like our families and friends lost twenty-five years of us. It's all so confusing, especially since I'm positive I wasn't anywhere but on that plane.

There's a table of contents, but I skip over it and go straight to the first chapter. And I read.

Angie starts at the beginning, when we met in second grade after she moved to town. We were in the same class, and I begged Mom to invite her over for a playdate. She wanted to play with Barbies, while I wanted to put on a show for my parents. We compromised with a play acted out by the Barbies. I wrote the script;

she figured out where they'd all stand and what they'd wear. I barely remember that, but I guess it made an impression on her.

I curl into the chair as I move through our childhood memories. She's included pictures of cards I made for her, snapshots of us together. It's like an Angie-and-Jenny scrapbook. And yes, the spider story is there. Based on how that guy in English approached me, I expected it to make me out as outrageously arachnophobic, but Angie actually tells the story more comically while still conveying that we were both scared.

These early chapters are actually pretty sweet.

It's when I get to the last couple of years that I want to throw the book across the aisle. I can't believe I was so wrong about Angie and our friendship. Like in chapter twelve, where she talks about the incident Ashling referenced earlier.

> *Jenny had more integrity than any seventeen-year-old you'd ever meet, and I loved that about her. But it sometimes meant I held certain things back. For example, the summer she disappeared, we had jobs at a frozen custard shop. Jenny had an amazing eye for detail and an unusually heightened sense for a story. But at the same time, she also saw the best in people. So it escaped her notice that two of our coworkers were selling pot to anyone who walked up to the window with a code word. If Jenny had known, she'd have probably felt obligated to turn them in to management.*

I thought Ashling was making that up just to get under my skin, but now it seems more like she only twisted the current story to get in a dig at me. I rub my temples, too weary to untangle it.

But it bugs me that Angie kept all that from me. Because she thought I would report them. Like some sanctimonious tattletale. Would I have? I honestly don't know. I don't think I could've just ignored Jeff and Cory selling drugs (of course it's obvious it was those two, now that I think about it). I mean, it could've shut down Frosty's if they'd gotten caught in a sting or something. Maybe I would've talked to them. Although, what kind of awkward conversation would that have been? *Hey, guys. Are you selling drugs? That's wrong. Just say no!* Yeah, that would've gone over real well.

But Angie *lied*. To me. I thought we told each other everything. Apparently that wasn't true for Angie twenty-five years ago *or* now.

But chapter thirteen is evidence that I, in fact, did tell Angie everything.

Jenny was an incurable romantic. She had a bookshelf full of romance novels, and she dreamed of being swept off her feet someday. She'd signed a pledge when she was fourteen to wait for sex until marriage, but in the meantime, she really craved a spectacular first kiss.

I can't believe she included my pledge! My friends knew about it, and I'm not embarrassed about the pledge itself, since it's my body and my decision, but I wouldn't have chosen to publish it in a *book*, for all potential boyfriends to read about before we can discuss it one-on-one. It explains maybe-Lana oversharing about her hookup and calling me a prude. I don't know why everyone always assumes I'm going to judge them based on what I've decided to do.

But the real kicker is a particular conversation Angie included next. I can't believe nobody has brought it up, because it's somehow even more embarrassing. It seems like exactly the sort of tidbit Drew or Ashling would delight in torturing me with.

Right before she left for New York, we were sitting in the food court at the mall, taking a shopping break, when Jenny said, "Do you think birds have sex?"

I sprayed Coke all over the table. "Whaaat?"

"Because if they do, it's really sad [my boyfriend] hasn't kissed me after two months."

I mopped up the Coke with a brown Sbarro's napkin. "Where did this come from?"

Jenny shrugged. "Some birds moved into our bathroom vent. I heard them making a racket this morning. I'm pretty sure they're having sex."

"Uh . . . no idea how to respond to that, but I'm pretty sure the problem with you and [your boyfriend] is that you're both too shy to make the first move."

"Maybe." She leaned forward, her eyes sparkling. "But since the birds aren't shy and we've all heard that spiel about the birds and the bees, stay tuned for baby news from our bathroom vent."

"Are you serious about the birds?" Because she was funny that way, saying whatever random thought was in her head

and turning it into some sort of extended metaphor. I always loved how she could relate the most random thing to her life or mine.

"I guess we'll see." She tapped two fingers against her lips. "I wonder if the baby birds will come before I get my kiss."

Unfortunately, they did.

She thought it was *funny* how I blurted out random thoughts? My cheeks are flaming. There's nobody around, but it doesn't matter. Countless people have read this passage. People I know. Oh my gosh. My *parents*. Why did they let Angie write this? And I notice how she doesn't list Steve by name, but people would've known. *Steve* would've known. She also left out the part where she dared me to kiss him first, sweetening the deal with an offer of free chocolate milkshakes on her for a month. Did she forget or leave it out for Steve's sake? I bet he would've found it *funny*.

I'm speeding through the rest to see what other embarrassing moments she's included when my name echoes through the library. "Jenny!"

CHAPTER TWENTY-SIX

I slap the book closed and register that the shouter is Bradley. "What?" I say sullenly.

His gaze lands on the book cover, but he doesn't soften. "It's four thirty. We've been looking for you for hours. Mom, Dad, Angie, Dylan. Everyone's panicked."

Wow. I guess I left school around one, so that sounds about right.

"Mom finally suggested I try here, since you kept asking to come to the library. Why didn't you answer your phone?" he demands.

It takes me a second to remember where I left it, under a mess of shredded paper in the journalism classroom. Hopefully it didn't get thrown away with the trash.

I stand and press the book into his chest. "Why didn't you tell me about this?"

"Angie asked us not to," he says, more quietly, casting a glance down the aisle as if he's just realized we're in a library.

I don't care where we are. "Bird sex!" I shout.

Bradley winces.

"She wrote about bird sex!"

"I know, Jenny. I'm sorry."

"You should've told me. You're my brother! That should count for something!"

"It does, Jenny." He's speaking in a calm voice, like he can influence me by osmosis. "I was trying to protect you."

As if he has a right to protect me. "You're my *little* brother. You're not supposed to protect *me*."

He gives me a look, and I know what he means by it. Maybe he was my little brother, but he isn't anymore.

"Young lady!" a voice says in a harsh whisper.

I whirl around to find a library employee addressing me.

"This is a public library. You need to take your extremely loud conversation about avian intercourse outside." He points behind him.

Laughter bubbles up, and I clap my hand over my mouth to stop it. I still want to strangle my brother and Angie and a few dozen other people, but here is this buttoned-up librarian scolding *me* for shouting about "avian intercourse" about fifty feet from the children's section. I've probably scarred some children for life, or at least created very interesting dinner table conversation for their parents.

"Sorry," I mutter, stifling a hysterical giggle, and bend down to gather my things.

"My sister's just had a shock," Bradley says, and I immediately sober.

I glare at him, resisting the urge to swing my backpack right into his solar plexus. "I want to finish that book."

The librarian clears his throat. "I think it's best if you just leave."

I can't believe I'm being kicked out of the library. Me. The girl least likely to cause a scene.

"Mom and Dad have a copy anyway," Bradley says.

Of course they do. Because they're on great terms with Angie. They probably gave her their blessing.

I whirl and march away, ignoring Bradley. I keep my eyes straight ahead, though I feel stares on me as I stride through the stacks toward the exit. So many questions run through my mind.

How long has that Flight 237 display been so prominently placed at the entrance? Just since we reappeared? Do they all recognize me, these strangers in the library? How many of them have read Angie's book and know all the intimate details of my life? How many of them have already laughed at me?

Bradley catches up to me at the curb outside. "Jenny, come on. I'll take you home."

I keep my back turned on him. "No, thanks. I'll walk."

"Like that's happening." He grabs my hand and tugs so I have no choice but to follow. "You're so mad at me you really want to walk three miles?"

Not really, but it sounded nice in theory. "Where have you been, anyway?"

He scrunches his eyebrows. "What do you mean?"

"I haven't seen you since Mom and Dad got back."

"Oh. Well . . ." He shrugs. "With my family."

My family. Like we're not his family anymore.

"And working," he adds as we reach his car.

This doesn't help. Because if my life had proceeded according to plan, I'd be working too. Probably in New York, far away, where I wouldn't care that he was focusing on his family and job, because I'd have my own.

Still, I've been gone for twenty-five years. He could make some time for me.

"Sorry," he says.

"For what exactly?" I lean against the car.

He tosses his keys back and forth. "Do you want me to make a list?"

I press my lips together to keep from smiling. Mom used to make him write out his apologies because they always sounded sarcastic out loud. "Maybe."

He catches the keys in his right hand. "I'm sorry that I don't know how to act around you. I may not have shown it when I was a kid, but I did love you, and losing you was like having an arm torn off. So when you returned, I didn't really know how to respond. A part of me has been afraid you'll disappear again."

I smirk. "An arm torn off?"

He punches my shoulder lightly. "I'm no good with words. Not like you."

There's a lump in my throat. "You're not so bad."

"As for the rest . . . you might think being an adult means I decide everything on my own, but figuring out what to say to you is tricky. From the moment you stepped into that room in the airport, I was afraid I'd blurt out the wrong thing. I didn't want to mess you up more. So I didn't tell you about our grandparents or about Angie and Steve, and I definitely wasn't mentioning this book. I was too afraid. You might think I was being a jerk, but really I was just being a coward. I'm sorry."

I really want to stay mad at him. But he's looking at me with these puppy-dog eyes, just like when he was five and asked me,

"Pretty please, Jenny, can I have the last cookie?" and it shouldn't work when he's a grown man, but somehow it does.

"Oh, fine."

He brightens, like I have indeed given him a treat. "Really?"

"But I want to know what else everyone's hiding from me."

He shakes his head vigorously. "Nothing. That's the last thing I can think of."

I narrow my eyes. "Mom and Dad didn't tell me the FBI wanted to do more tests. I had to offer to go in myself before Mom fessed up. And they kept the support group from me too."

"They're just trying to protect you."

Their *protection* is leaving me open to even more pain. "Take me home. This isn't over."

CHAPTER TWENTY-SEVEN

I may have let Bradley off the hook, but my parents are another story. Walking-on-eggshells time is over. I burst into the house with my shoulders back, my head high, and a long list of accusations. Bradley zooms off without coming in to say hi to them. He probably doesn't want to risk losing my tentative forgiveness.

I bound upstairs and toss my backpack on the top step.

"Jenny!" Mom rushes out of the kitchen, Dad on her heels. "We were so worried! You can't disappear like that!"

"You almost gave your mother a heart attack!" Dad says sternly.

My gaze whips toward Mom, because at her age this could be more than a figure of speech. "Are you okay?"

Mom waves a dismissal. "My heart is fine."

In that case, not fair. They don't get to play the you-aren't-allowed-to-disappear card after they've been lying to me. I refuse to feel guilty. They kept a vital piece of information from me that resulted in major embarrassment.

I point at them. "How could you let Angie write a book about me?"

Mom flinches, her focus shifting to Dad. "Is that what this is about?"

Maybe I was right to trust Bradley, at least a little. He didn't tell them why I was at the library, just that he'd found me. Although, I'm surprised it wasn't obvious.

"I found out at school today. Which was a sucky way to discover your best friend wrote a tell-all about you."

Mom holds out her hand. "It isn't a tell-all. It's a touching tribute."

I can't bring myself to mention the bird sex conversation, but surely they read it. In what universe does that qualify as a "touching tribute"? And there are other stories in there too. Angie doesn't flat out write me as a stick-in-the-mud prude, but it's clear that's how she saw me. My parents probably did read it and think it sounded like a touching tribute, but anyone my age would laugh their heads off—they already have.

"Mom, I don't think you read the same book."

Mom's eyes soften. "Every word. All those wonderful anecdotes about how you always made everyone around you feel so noticed, because you paid attention if they did something great in class or got a new haircut. How you were always up for an adventure, like visiting five ice cream shops in one night to figure out which one was best."

I drop my chin. "I got sick after eating all that ice cream." It was worth it, though.

"Angie's book is no excuse for you to skip school," Dad says.

I cross my arms. "Sorry."

Though, I'm not. I deserved to find out how much everyone betrayed me.

"Yes, I can see how sorry you are," Dad says dryly.

I step forward, my voice low. "I want to know what else you're hiding from me."

"It's not hiding, it's—" Mom looks at Dad, her eyes broadcasting a distress signal. "Listen, Jenny. We didn't tell you about the book because Angie asked us not to. She asked for time while you were adjusting. She thought the book was old enough the kids at your school wouldn't know about it."

I grunt in disbelief, but then I consider yesterday. The leering looks and targeted stories didn't start until today. "I don't think they did at first. I'm guessing someone clued them in."

Mom bites her lip. "Well, the media have brought it up . . ."

I laugh derisively. "The truth finally comes out! Why you won't let me watch the news or read a paper."

Dad presses his lips together and exhales through his nose. "Part of it. But also what we told you before. It's not healthy to read what everyone's saying."

Apparently I've been going about that all wrong, too—if the *Parkwood Press* is online, so is every other news outlet. It seems so obvious now. If my brain wasn't so scrambled from everything I've been dealing with, I would have made the connection sooner. "You put off getting me a phone or a laptop because you didn't want me to figure out how easy it is to find all this information on the internet now."

Mom looks to the side. "We were sort of hoping you wouldn't figure that out yet."

It seems everyone was hoping I'd stay ignorant. Even Dylan steered me away from searching about myself—actually, I think he *was* going to tell me something, before Angie came in with snacks. I wonder if she was eavesdropping and interrupted intentionally? Whatever. Now that I'm properly informed, I will Google everything I want to know.

"Maybe the other students Googled you and found the book online," Dad suggests.

I tap my foot. "Oh, no. I think it's closer than that. JoJo."

Mom frowns. "Why would JoJo do that?"

"Because she hates me."

"That's a very serious charge," Dad says.

"It's true." And it explains her nasty smile, if she told everyone about her mom's book and got them to read up on me or even just shared the juiciest passages. Screwed Angie too, which seems like another check mark on JoJo's to-do list.

"I can't believe that of JoJo," Mom says. "She—"

The house phone rings. She glances toward the kitchen, torn.

"Go ahead," I say.

She leaves and returns a moment later. "It's Angie."

"Of course it is." Because Angie has a Jenny's-pissed-and-I-have-to-smooth-it-over radar. She always has. Except our arguments were never this monumental before. "I don't want to talk to her. Ever."

"Jenny . . ." Mom holds out the phone with her hand over the mouthpiece. "Please let her explain."

Explain? First Angie married my boyfriend. Then she wrote a book about me. Writing is *my* thing. It's like I disappeared and she tried to become me. I don't see how she can argue her way out of this, and I'm not interested in hearing her try.

"No." I push past Dad and run for my room, slamming the door.

I used to trust a lot of people. My parents. Angie. Steve. Bradley (at least, for we-have-to-keep-this-in-the-family stuff, if not Jenny-padded-her-bra-in-middle-school sort of details . . . he was, after all, an annoying little brother). I'm not sure who's left now. Maybe my Flight 237 support group. At least they aren't conspiring against me. If I hadn't left my phone at school, I might call Art again, or maybe Mrs. Spring, just to confirm it. I could use the house phone, but I'm afraid Mom and Dad might pick up another line and listen in. There has to be someone who's on my side.

I wonder where Dylan falls in all of this. Bradley says he was out looking for me this afternoon too. I bet he has a ton of excuses to give me, just like Angie.

Several hours later, after Mom and Dad finally go to bed, I sneak down to the bookshelf and search until I find Angie's book. It's not even hidden, so I guess it wasn't such a secret.

After the bird sex chapter, there's a chapter on my dedication to the *Parkwood Press* and a few others on activities we did together, but I don't bother reading them. I can't focus on those memories anymore. It's all overshadowed by the impression she's left of me for the world. All this time, I thought we were having fun, but behind my back, she saw me as a righteous, holier-than-thou girl whose life was stunted by rules and who got her romance from novels. No wonder JoJo resents being named after me.

What I don't get is why Angie didn't have the guts to tell me about the book herself. Is she ashamed of what she wrote? Does she regret it now that I'm back? I'm not sure it matters. We're done.

CHAPTER TWENTY-EIGHT

Thank goodness I don't have to face Dylan or anyone else at school for a couple of days. I'm almost relieved my Saturday is filled with doctors and nurses poking and prodding me. I'm injected with fluids for the CAT scan, then forced to remain completely still with my unpleasant thoughts in a tube for the MRI, and I have enough blood drawn I'm dizzy when I stand. Mom, Dad, and Bradley only participate in the blood test, which they'll use to compare our DNA, but Bradley stays all day, living up to his promise to be around more. He shows me videos of Kira and Eli (so cute!) and brings me a copy of the first book he illustrated to read while I'm waiting. My anger at Angie continues to simmer, but it's not so bad a day, considering the circumstances. Unfortunately it doesn't leave time for my research into the PATROL members.

Walking into the group that evening is like breathing in a huge gulp of air after swimming underwater. I grab a brownie and cup of water and make my way to the circle, securing a spot beside Mrs. Spring. Art isn't here yet.

Captain McCoy calls the meeting to order. "I'm sure everyone saw the announcement about this PATROL group."

A chorus of murmurs runs around the circle.

He sighs heavily. "I've been in contact with the FBI. There's some concern PATROL will whip the public into a frenzy, so the FBI has contracted an outside group to reexamine the plane and release the results. I understand most of you are cooperating with their request for additional tests?"

"Request?" Walter, the copilot whose mom died, sneers. "More like a demand. And I don't even have anyone for them to test my DNA against."

Interesting; Mom and Dad didn't give me the impression the FBI was pressuring me to do the testing. But then, they've omitted a lot.

Captain McCoy pats his knee. "It's okay, Walter."

"None of this is okay," Walter grumbles.

I grimace, remembering that somebody wrote a book about him too. I wonder if he knows. Was it his mom? I think I remember Angie saying she founded the support group for the crew and passengers' families.

Captain McCoy smiles grimly. "How do you all feel about making our results public? If you're on board, I'd like to give a press conference putting PATROL's allegations completely to rest. Agent Klein has given me the okay."

"Really?" Excitement nudges aside my outrage over the book, because this could change everything. "She's going to let us start talking to the media?"

Captain McCoy puts up a hand. "She'd still like us to wait until the final tests are completed before granting interviews, but she's agreed to work with me on this press conference to deal with PATROL."

"Does it have to be all of us?" Jobless Miss Klaffke tangles her fingers in her long skirt. "I'm not sure how I feel about putting my personal information out in public."

Art slinks into the room and sits beside me, much less animated than usual.

"If we don't," Valerie says, "they might never stop. Look at how they attacked Jenny the other day."

I nod vigorously. "I'm all for letting them see whatever results they want so they'll leave me alone."

Captain McCoy sits back in his chair. "Why don't we all think on it while we share?"

I open my mouth to spit out my story, but Tracey shoots forward on her seat, bubbling with excitement. "I'm getting married!" She holds up her left hand, her ring finger sparkling more than before. Looks like she got upgraded.

"Holy moly, Tracey!" Mr. Spring whistles.

"Are you sure?" Valerie asks.

Tracey beams. "One hundred percent. Since our last meeting, Keith and I have been reconnecting, doing all the things we used to do together, getting to know one another all over again, and I don't care that he's older. He's still the same Keith. I'm not wasting any more time waiting. We're eloping."

I have immediate visions of Hawaii or the Bahamas. "To where?"

She waves her be-ringed hand. "Oh, don't worry. We're not flying. Just going to the courthouse with some friends and family."

I exhale. Until this moment, I hadn't considered flying again. If I do, it certainly won't be soon.

"Well, congratulations," says Miss Klaffke. "It's nice to hear some happy news."

I wish Tracey could send some of that my way.

"Yeah. Good for you," Art says sulkily.

I perk up. Art has been so pro–time travel from the beginning. He practically popped off the plane waving an "in your face, 1995" flag. Just two days ago, he said it was "fun" to read through PATROL's hoax theories and come up with arguments against them.

"What's wrong, Art, honey?" Mrs. Spring is every bit as sympathetic with Art as she is with me.

He slumps into his chair with his arms crossed over his stomach. "All my friends are *old*, like in their *forties*."

I elbow him. I mean, does he realize who just asked him the question? Mrs. Spring is in her eighties. Sometimes Art acts like he's in middle school instead of being, technically, an adult.

He shrugs at me and continues, oblivious. "They got *married* and had, like, *kids*." He says this with the same disgust I reserve for someone who puts pineapple on pizza.

Mrs. Spring has the patience of a saint, because instead of marching around me and kicking Art with her Naturalizers, she asks calmly, "And what about your parents, Art?"

He raises his eyebrows. "Them? Oh. Dead."

He says it so casually several people around the circle gasp. He sits up and holds his palms out. "Whoa. Hold on. They were dead *before* we disappeared."

Mr. Spring frowns. "But at the airport when I asked about your family, you said you weren't close."

Art lets his hands fall and shrugs. "Yeah. My family. The uncle who raised me 'cause the state made him. All he wants is cash from the tabloids for his nephew who returned from space." He curls his lip. "I don't want anything to do with *him*."

Okay, I'm starting to get a better picture here. He said he had plans today, so maybe they were with some of these friends with kids? Considering my mess with my friends, I can understand why Art might not be handling his own so well. I vow to check in on him more often. This group is great, but we could support one another outside it too.

Miss Klaffke, who's sitting on his other side, squeezes his hand. "I'm so sorry for what you're going through, Art. We're here for you."

"Yeah," I say, hoping to distract him, "and you came in late, but we were talking about PATROL. I think you had some theories about their whole let's-protect-the-order-and-legitimacy-of-time mission statement?"

Art perks up. "I did discover something funky about those PATROL people. I tried to call you yesterday"—he nods at me before turning back to the group and scooting forward on his chair—"but this is huge! The two founders of PATROL, Dr. Greaves and Dr. Rozanov, coauthored a paper on time travel when they were in college. They're total believers!"

"Believers?" Captain McCoy says.

"Yes!" Art pumps his fist in the air. "So it's shady they're trying to prove we're a hoax."

People who believe in time travel, riling up a bunch of people who don't. What could their motives be? Now I'm sorry I didn't call Art yesterday. Talking to him would've distracted me from all the book drama. "You'd think they'd be more like the FBI, trying to determine *how* we did it."

"The ever-present question," Valerie says. "Although I'd frame it more as *who*. I'm more inclined to go with a higher power than aliens, unless anyone believes there *was* a mad scientist back in 1995 who turned our plane into a time machine."

People around the circle chuckle, though nobody takes up the conversation further. I'm more interested in Art's intel.

"What should we do with this information?" I say. "It seems like a big deal, like we could use it to discredit the whole group."

Captain McCoy rubs his chin. "I think we should look into it more before we do anything with it. I'm really hoping the FBI comes up with conclusive results that will shut our detractors down regardless."

Art and I share a skeptical look. I'm not so sure they're going to believe anything the FBI releases. "I heard something else."

Art leans forward eagerly. "What was it?"

I hate to mention it, since *Ashling* is my source. "That maybe PATROL is funded by insurance companies trying to discredit us to get their death payouts back. That might explain why the science Dr. Greaves and her partner follow doesn't line up."

Captain McCoy frowns. "I, for one, have definitely gotten calls from the insurance company, as a claim was made against my death. I'm sure others have too." There are nods around the circle.

"They've called me," Walter says grumpily, "even though when Ma died she left everything to cancer research."

"I still say we should let the FBI handle it and hold off on attacking PATROL," Captain McCoy says. "I don't think it will help our case at the moment."

I'm not happy with Captain McCoy's decision, but he's our leader. Plus, I did just argue yesterday that we couldn't put out a story in the *Parkwood Press* based on hearsay. We do need to verify all the information.

"Any luck on the job front?" Captain McCoy asks Miss Klaffke, tabling the PATROL discussion.

Miss Klaffke straightens, startled by the abrupt subject change, then folds her hands in her lap. "Not yet. I'm exploring some options. Thinking about pursuing a new degree." She turns so her knees point to her left. "I'm more interested in an update from Valerie. Did you go on the date?"

Color fills Valerie's creamy cheeks, but she also appears sad. "Not yet. First, my husband and I have decided to move forward with an official divorce. He moved on, and I . . . I understand."

What a difference between Tracey and Valerie. One whose fiancé waited twenty-five years, the other whose husband found someone new.

The lady beside Valerie puts an arm around her. "Are you okay?"

Valerie smiles tremulously. "I will be. It's the right choice for him. We can't go back. I still love him, but, you know, he is sort of old."

She smiles at Tracey, who shrugs to show she's not offended.

"And your former student?" Miss Klaffke says.

Valerie smooths her skirt. "I'm keeping an open mind."

So despite Tracey's happy story, we're all still pretty messed up. Art distracted me with his PATROL research, but now that we're back to sharing time, I think I'm going to explode if I can't have my turn. And, really, they should know about the other books too. It's their right. Without waiting for Captain McCoy to call on me, I blurt, "My best friend wrote a book about me!"

I wait for the gasps of outrage, the offers to run out and hold her down while I pummel her in the ribs (not that I'd really do that), the follow-up questions for more details.

But nope. What I get are a circle full of mildly guilty and sympathetic expressions, except for one: Art, who stares at me like I'm the most foolish girl on the planet. "Did you just figure that out?"

"You knew?" My head swivels left, to Mrs. Spring. "You all knew?"

She reaches for me. "Jenny, I—"

"No!" I jump to my feet, causing the metal chair to squeal against the linoleum floor. "You're supposed to be my support group. The ones who understand what it's like to get dropped in a world that doesn't make any sense. But you knew and you didn't tell me?"

I shove the chair away and run from the room, pounding up the stairs toward the exit and open air.

The people from Flight 237 don't see me as an equal; they're just like everyone else, treating me like a child to be "protected" from the truth. It's ridiculous and I'm tired of it.

I push through the glass door into the parking lot. The humidity hits me immediately, but I drink it in. The sun set while I was inside, so I march toward the lone light in the lot.

I can't escape completely. I'm stuck here, thanks to my parents' continued refusal to let me drive.

"Jenny!"

It's Mrs. Spring. I can't believe she followed me—and pretty quickly too. I don't want to turn around, but I'm not that rude. With a sigh, I pivot, and my eyes widen. It's not just Mrs. Spring; it's the whole group. Art slouches at the front with his hands in the pockets of his baggy jeans. It occurs to me that, while blunt, Art's reaction was the most honest. I think he might have even tried to tell me at the first meeting, when Mr. Spring interrupted him.

Captain McCoy spreads his arms. "Hear us out. Please."

I cross my arms over my chest and wait.

He nods at Valerie, and she steps forward. "I didn't share this part of the story because it just made it sound so much worse, but when we first got back, my husband didn't tell me about his new wife. He acted really happy to see me—and I'm sure he genuinely was." She stares up at the barely visible stars. "He said my parents were beside themselves, and we should go there instead of to our house, so that's what we did. After all, my parents are in their late eighties now. I was just as anxious to see them. He said he wanted to give me space, so we shouldn't share a room. And he was different—older—so I thought he was being considerate." She refocuses on me, her gaze direct. "But it took them four days to tell me he was happily married with children, and that was devastating. Because I spent four days mentally trying to adjust to how my life would be with him, imagining having children with a husband who might not be around to see his grandchildren. I wish he'd just told me right away."

Wow. Valerie had so much more at stake than me, being *married*. And for her husband, a man she'd vowed to spend her life with, to not have the guts to tell her the truth. I mean, it's not as public as what Angie did, but in other ways it's a lot worse. I don't really know what I'm supposed to say. "I'm . . . sorry?"

She moves closer. "My point is that we've all had people we love lie to us out of some misguided sense that they're sparing us. Take Frank, for example."

She gestures behind her, and I realize she means Captain McCoy.

He wipes his brow, either due to discomfort or the heat radiating off the parking lot. Brown and gray strands of hair cling to his forehead. "Yes. Well. My sister, who inherited everything after my 'death'"—he uses air quotes—"sold my house and car—which was a classic, mind you—and used the money to start a meth lab, which later exploded and killed two of her workers. She called when I reappeared and fed me a very long sob story, then asked me to testify at her parole hearing."

Thank goodness Bradley didn't turn into a meth head while I was gone! "Um, that doesn't sound like someone sparing you," I say. "I'm sorry, but your sister sounds whacked."

Valerie shakes her head. "Frank, you left out the part where your friends kept avoiding any mention of your sister, so the first you heard about her conviction was her phone call."

Captain McCoy sighs and scratches his neck. "In their defense, they're mostly a bunch of old gossips now, sitting around at the coffee shop talking about missions they flew in the Korean War."

I tug on my hair. "I get your point about people protecting you. But I thought we were in this together. So why didn't *you* tell me about the book?"

Mrs. Spring walks toward me with her hand outstretched like she's approaching a skittish wild animal. "Because you're a unique case. I know you don't want to hear it, but you're a teenager."

She's right. I don't want to hear it.

"And your parents have a say." She gently touches my shoulder. "They asked us not to mention it until you brought it up, and tonight you did."

When did my parents even talk to them about this? It dawns on me that before that first meeting, they probably called Captain McCoy or the Springs and asked them to spread the word. They went to a lot of effort to make sure no one would tell me. "Parents suck."

Mrs. Spring chuckles. "Sometimes we do."

I turn to the copilot. "What do *you* think about having a book written about you?"

He stares at the pavement, toeing a loose piece of asphalt. "It's weird. A private investigator my ma hired wrote it, exploring different crazy theories. It's not so much about me, really."

"Oh." I assumed it was another life story like mine. I actually might like to read that, if it includes theories about where our plane went. "Have any of you read the book about me?"

They all either murmur no or shake their heads.

"We're interested in knowing the Jenny you are now, not whoever you were before." Mrs. Spring rubs my arm. "Will you give us a chance to do that?"

After hearing Valerie and Captain McCoy's stories, it seems petty to blame them for what really goes back to Angie and my parents. They're stumbling through like me, and as much as I resent being singled out because of my age, it doesn't surprise me. Besides, it's time for the Jenny in the pages of Angie's book to stay in the past where she belongs. For me to become new Jenny. A confident Jenny whose goals don't stay in list form in her notebook. That's the Jenny they can all get to know.

I nod. "All right."

"Great," Art says, flapping his T-shirt away from his body. "Can we do it inside? Because I'm roasting out here."

I roll my eyes and follow the group back into the church. After another hour of discussion with Mrs. Spring's comforting lily-scented perfume wafting over me and intermittent pats on my knee, I feel much calmer.

CHAPTER TWENTY-NINE

Art is full of theories about time, and as we head up the stairs to leave the support group, I let him talk.

"Since they haven't found any sort of device on the plane, I think we're dealing with—" As he pushes open the door to the parking lot, we're blinded by a bright light.

A woman sticks a microphone in my face. "Miss Waters, how are you holding up in this new century? Do you appreciate the support from your fellow passengers?"

I blink at her, too stunned to answer.

Art puts an arm across me. "Dude. What are you doing here? This is a private meeting, and you know we're not supposed to talk to you."

"It's a public space," the reporter says.

She turns her high-wattage smile on me, along with the high-wattage light on the camera behind her. She's wearing capris, a sleeveless shirt, and heeled sandals. Man, broadcast news sure has gotten more casual since 1995.

"Miss Waters," she says, "how do you feel being the poster child for Flight 237?"

I frown, picturing a poster of myself with the flight number across it in cursive script. "I'm no more special than anyone else. We're all in this together."

The light catches on her gleaming hazel eyes, and I realize I've done exactly what they've told us not to do: I've engaged.

Her dark hair swishes over her pale shoulders as she shakes her head. "You're a star, Jenny Waters. Your best friend, Angela Russell Graham"—she leans in and drops her voice like she's telling me a secret—"married your boyfriend *and* wrote a book about you!"

Internally I'm screaming that this is none of her business and I have no comment. But as a journalist myself, I know that if I walk away now, after I've already answered one question instead of saying "no comment," it will only make things worse. Plus, at the moment, she's asking about my personal life, so maybe I'm not actually violating the FBI's gag order.

"And now you're going to school with the Grahams' children, Dylan and Jennifer. She's named after you, right?"

It's surprising to realize that while I don't mind digging into other people's business as a reporter, I'm uncomfortable being on the receiving end. Also how much it hurts to hear her mention Dylan. I've been so focused on how Angie burned me I haven't really processed Dylan's betrayal. But I won't give her the satisfaction of seeing my reaction.

I tilt my head to the side and smile. "Who did you say you work for? The *National Enquirer*?"

The insult hits its mark. She flinches, and I hear someone behind me stifle a laugh. Art. Of course. We're trapped at the top of the steps, blocking the rest of the group from coming up into the parking lot. They're standing behind me—and not just physically. I am strong. I will not let this century tear me down.

The reporter purses her lips. "Are you refusing to comment on the book?"

So that's how it's gonna be. "Are you refusing to tell me who you work for?"

She hooks her thumb at the camera on the guy's shoulder, where the station's call sign is clearly listed. Crap. I'm not helping myself by antagonizing the reporter. I realize this, but I really don't want to talk about Angie on TV. It's too new.

Captain McCoy pushes up beside me. "Miss Barren, how did you find out about our meeting tonight?"

I'm impressed by his tone. He doesn't sound upset at all, more like he ran into her in the grocery store and is asking her if the plums look ripe today.

Miss Barren flicks her eyes to the side before meeting Captain McCoy's gaze. (She never told me her name either, which was rude. I introduce myself to interview subjects first thing.) "A lucky coincidence," she says.

"Hmm." Captain McCoy is unconvinced, and so am I. Somebody tipped her off. A family member? Because who else knows we're meeting? I guess someone, even her, could have followed one of us, although I'd expect her to have ambushed me earlier, when I was alone in the parking lot, if that had been the case.

She turns on me again. "About the book, Jenny?"

She won't give up, and while I haven't forgiven Angie, not even close, it's not the public's business. So I smile tightly and go with Mom's line. "Angie Russ—Graham wrote *Jenny and Me* to show how much she loved and missed me. She told me writing it made her feel closer to me." Technically we haven't discussed the book yet, but clearly that's what she meant by that statement. "She believed I was gone and wrote it as a tribute. She couldn't have known I'd return and be faced with it."

I nearly choke on the words. They may be true, but they're not what I feel. Just because she thought I was dead, she didn't have the right to air all those intimate details. I hate this reporter for making me say it out loud.

But I must sell it well enough, because she nods. "I see. And have you answered PATROL's call to be tested yet, Jenny?"

"Yes!" I blurt. Behind me, Captain McCoy clears his throat, a warning I should shut up now, but my mouth has a mind of its own. Besides, I've never agreed with this policy to keep the passengers silent, even though I didn't expect to be the spokesperson. "And for your information, the FBI already planned more extensive tests before there was any PATROL, *Miss Barren*." I put special emphasis on her name just to show her how rude I think she is. I don't care if it's juvenile. They want to emphasize how young I am? Fine. "I'm confident the tests will confirm my parents and I are one hundred percent DNA matches."

I resist the urge to add, *And that I don't have any alien DNA.*

Miss Barren nods thoughtfully. "But will they be able to verify conclusively that you aren't cloned from the preserved DNA of Jennifer Waters?"

For a moment I'm shocked into silence, and I'm sure it shows on my face, ruining everything I've accomplished in this interview so far, but then I laugh and gesture behind her. "Did you paint that logo on your camera?"

My implication is clear, and from the way she narrows her eyes, I see I've made an enemy.

"Jenny has a point," Art jumps in. "Let's run with your cloning theory for a moment. Say some *mad scientist*"—he exaggerates the title to make it sound extra ridiculous—"or perhaps a *master illusionist* figured out how to make the plane disappear. A real David Copperfield."

Miss Barren looks blank. Seriously? David Copperfield made the Great Wall of China disappear! I mean, they should've at least asked him how it might've been done.

Art appears equally exasperated with Miss Barren. "Anyway, once the scientist-slash-illusionist has the plane, they have access to the DNA of all the people, so they clone them and make them *the same ages* they were when they got on the plane, right?"

Miss Barren opens her mouth to answer and then closes it like she realizes the flaw in her own logic now. I try not to smile smugly because the camera is still running. I think it's pointing mainly at Art, but I really don't want that image captured on TV.

"*Bzzz!*" Art says like he's pushing a buzzer on a game show. "Wrong!" He turns to point at Mr. Spring behind him. "Because even if cloning has been perfected in the twenty-first century— and I don't think it has been—that's some extra-advanced science to speed up Mr. Spring here's development so he could age eighty-something years in the twenty-five years we were missing. Unless you're suggesting this alleged conspiracy began like a hundred years ago, *way* before our plane disappeared, the scientist-slash-illusionist somehow knew everyone who would be on it, and stole our DNA at just the right times in our lives so they could incubate our clones to be the right age today."

Wow. Just wow. I'm so impressed by that explanation I want to tackle-hug Art right now. Unsure if he's the hugging type, I hold up my hand for a high five, which he indulges. I don't even care if high fives aren't cool anymore.

Miss Barren opens and closes her mouth like a fish, then clears her throat. "That's a compelling argument, Mr. Ross." She lifts her chin. "I'm only asking what viewers want to know."

Art's face screws up in disgust, clearly about to go off on the "viewers" in a way that would completely negate his well-articulated argument against cloning, so I quickly jump in. "Maybe viewers should be asking about PATROL. Why are they so bent on proving we aren't who we say we are? What's their motive? I hope they own up to their mistake once we all prove we did nothing but get on a plane."

I'm itching to throw out the information Art gave us about the two PATROL founders writing a paper supporting time travel, or even Ashling's tip about the insurance backers, but I will abide by Captain McCoy's wishes to hold off; it's wise to check our sources.

Captain McCoy steps in again. "We understand viewers are trying to come up with explanations. We are too." He raises his eyebrows and lowers his chin. "We'd be happy to discuss it further when we've been officially cleared to do so."

Whereas Miss Barren treated me and even Art like easy-to-manipulate kids, she's clearly intimidated by Captain McCoy. She signals the cameraman, and he clicks off the light.

Miss Barren wiggles the microphone in my direction. "I'll be in touch." She whirls, her heels clicking as she strides away.

"Do you think they'll air what Art said?" I ask Captain

McCoy as we step out onto the parking lot to make room for the rest of the group to file out.

Art puffs out his chest. "They'd better. I sounded good."

I twist my mouth. "Yeah, but she could edit it so you don't."

"If she does, I'll have one of my great-grandkids take care of it," Mr. Spring says.

"Considering it was the first passenger interview, I'm sure Greta Barren will air all of it." Captain McCoy turns to Mr. Spring. "But I'm curious. How exactly would you do that?"

Mr. Spring holds up a phone. "With the video I took of the whole thing."

Even if I had my phone, it wouldn't have occurred to me to record that incident. Mr. Spring is closer to being a modern teen than me.

"Good thinking, Ted. It's smart to have a backup," Captain McCoy says. He turns to me and Art. "But I think our bigger concern at this point is what the FBI will have to say about your interview."

Forget the FBI, though. I have to report to a higher power: my parents.

CHAPTER THIRTY

I've discovered hiding things from Mom and Dad never turns out well, so I confess as soon as I get home. After a long talk about ignoring pushy reporters and following the guidelines set up by the FBI for my protection, they make me call Agent Klein, who gives me *another* excruciating lecture before finally telling me Captain McCoy already alerted her anyway. Lucky me: scolded by my parents *and* the government. We watch the ten o'clock news, anxious to see Greta Barren's piece, but it doesn't happen. She's not rushing it, I guess.

On Sunday, I call Art so we can finish our conversation about his time travel theories, and he can give me more details about Dr. Greaves and Dr. Rozanov's time travel paper. Art was studying physics before he dropped out of college, so most of what he says goes over my head, but it's okay. As much as I'd like to understand why we're in a different century, at the moment I'm more concerned about what the PATROL people are up to. I sense more of a story there.

During the five o'clock news, Greta Barren's piece finally airs, and I give her points for not sensationalizing it. Interestingly, she followed up on my PATROL question—framing it like she'd already been investigating them. It turns out Dr. Greaves's husband is the president of a major life insurance company that paid out policies on twenty-two passengers. He's not an official member of PATROL, but it's a definite connection. The story proves Greta Barren isn't a total hack of a journalist, but I still don't trust her. I *am* worried she'll scoop me now that she's investigating PATROL too. Her story runs again at six and ten.

The atmosphere at school is different the moment I step inside the next day.

"Hey, Jenny!" says a girl I've never spoken to before. "Saw you on TV yesterday!"

"I knew you weren't a clone," says Caleb (now confirmed) when I enter English.

"I'm so relieved. I bet your spidey senses told you, huh?" I manage to conceal my smirk until I'm facing the front of the room.

By the time I get to lunch, more people have slapped my back and held out their fists for me to (awkwardly) bump than in the whole time I've attended Parkwood. It's better than last week, but I really prefer my life before, when I was an above-average student who achieved notice sometimes for my *Parkwood Press* articles instead of for being accosted by a reporter at what should have been a private meeting.

I aim for a table in the corner. I still like the windows, but I don't sit at my old table, since it "belongs" to Ashling's crew. Although Mom drove me to school, I'm not deliberately avoiding Dylan, but I haven't seen him yet. I spot JoJo across the room and return her glower. I'm positive she made sure everyone at school knew about the book.

Whatever. I'm not wasting time on her.

The chairs around me fill up as soon as I sit. They introduce themselves, and I nod, but I don't internalize their names. They're not really interested in being my friends.

"Jenny, what was it like meeting Greta Barren?" a brown-skinned girl with blue-framed glasses asks. Actually, I recognize her. She's in my journalism class, so her question probably goes beyond you-met-a-locally-famous-person-and-I-want-to-hear-all-about-it. "Was she nice?"

I swallow my bite of ham-and-cheese sandwich and consider how to answer, especially in light of how my classmates view me. I decide to be New Jenny. I might be physically sitting in a corner, but that doesn't mean I'm hiding.

"She insinuated I was a clone and pried into my personal business, so not particularly, no." I wipe my hands on a napkin. "I'm all for someone getting their story"—I eye the girl in my journalism class, like *you know what I mean*—"but there's a point where it veers into sensationalism. I mean, a clone?"

I shrug to show how ridiculous this idea is, and the people at the table laugh around me. Okay, new plan to go with New Jenny: embrace notoriety. "And have you heard the one about me being a cyborg?"

The pale boy with the unfortunate acne issue next to me chuckles nervously.

I tip my face toward the ceiling. "Gosh, I wish!"

Blue glasses girl smiles. "Why?"

I lean forward. "Think about it. I could store everything in my computer brain"—I tap my temple—"and never study again."

I collapse back in my chair. Everyone's nodding along with me like I'm brilliant. New Jenny is working!

"What's that Art guy like?" The redheaded girl across the table lasers me with startling green eyes. "He seems pretty cool. Are you guys, like, together?"

"Me? With Art?" I squeak. I know he's not that much older than us, but it's weird to think about us as a potential couple. Even though we share the Flight 237 experience, I just can't imagine him as anything other than a friend. He's just too . . . Art. "Definitely not."

"Jenny!"

As one, my new friends turn their attention to a spot over my shoulder.

Dylan bends down between me and the pale boy. "I need to talk to you."

Old Jenny returns, unprepared to confront Dylan. "No."

Dylan glances around the table at my new fans. He nods as if he's made an important decision. "I can just say it here . . ."

I push back, bumping him with my chair. "Oof!"

I scoop the remains of my lunch into my sack and smile at the table. "I'll see you guys later."

They stare at us with wide eyes. "'Bye, Jenny," says blue glasses girl.

I really should've paid attention to names when they all introduced themselves. Bad call on my part when they first sat down. Even worse call on blue glasses girl. She's on my staff, so I should already know.

I follow Dylan through the cafeteria, not surprised he accosted me here. I retrieved my phone from the office this morning, and I had a ton of texts from him, starting Friday after school and continuing all through Saturday. Messages asking if I was okay. Messages saying he was sorry. Messages pleading with me to let him come over so we could talk. Followed by silence yesterday. Either he figured out I didn't have my phone or someone told him to give up.

With each step, heat builds under my skin. Because, yes, Angie wrote the book about me, and I'm still sure JoJo ensured my classmates went out and read it. But Dylan, he's been my only . . . friend here. And he didn't tell me. He let me find out from *Ashling*.

By the time we reach the same stairwell we chatted in before, all my senses are tingling. If I were violent, I might even punch him. I really wish I knew how to punch someone, but I'd probably break my knuckles. Instead I shove the stairwell door, but it has some sort of automatic thing on it that prevents slamming it, and it whooshes shut slowly, completely ruining my moment. I glare at it for good measure.

When I turn to face Dylan, he's smirking, and that's just too much. I march forward and shove *him*. "You think that's funny?"

He raises his hands in surrender, his mouth a serious line. "What are you so angry about?"

"What am I so—are you kidding me? After all those text messages you sent me?" I'm in his face, my nostrils flared. I'm sure every freckle on my nose is standing out in sharp relief.

He backs away. "Um . . . no?"

"You've been lying to me from the moment I met you!"

He waves the hands he still has up, like he wants to make sure I can see them. What?

I point at him. "What are you so worried about? I'm not some karate expert. If I were, you would know about it. You and the rest of the world. Thanks to *your mom*."

I spit the last two words out like a curse.

He lets his hands fall to his sides, like this is now a sign of peace. "Okay, yeah. You're right. I could have told you about the book. But can you try to see it from my side? Like you said, she's my mom. She didn't just ask me not to tell you; she pretty much commanded it."

I cross my arms over my chest. My heartbeat is slowing down, and I don't feel so flushed anymore. "So you were just following her orders?"

Dylan huffs. "This is so messed up. I can't believe she let it go on this long. I tried to come by on Saturday, to explain the whole thing, but you weren't home."

He did? Huh.

"Messed up is an understatement. Do you know how I found out?" I recap Friday's journalism class. "It was horrible! And then I got ambushed by that reporter."

"Hey," Dylan says. "On the bright side, at least you found out *before* you were on camera."

My jaw drops. "I can't believe you just made a joke about it."

He runs a hand through his hair. "Sorry. Can't help it sometimes."

I've noticed that, how joking is his default mode. It's why I can't get a solid read on his signals.

"You're right, though." If I had found out from Greta Barren . . . I shudder. I would've made a complete fool of myself on TV. I wouldn't have had the presence of mind to make a decent statement.

Dylan steps forward, his expression earnest. "But, Jenny, did you mean what you said on TV?"

I stiffen. I see where he's going with this, and I won't be pushed. News flash, Dylan: you can't believe everything you see on TV.

"About my mom?" he continues. "That you know she wrote it as a tribute and she loves you? Because that's all true," he rushes to add.

I lower my chin. "Do I look like I'm all, 'Hey, Angie, let's put this misunderstanding behind us and skip happily through a daisy meadow. So what that you aired all my personal business to the entire world, including these brand-new classmates who can now giggle behind my back about bird sex? No big deal!'?"

"Uh . . . no." Dylan looks as if I just socked him, and I realize that I do, in fact, know how to punch. It's just with words instead of my fist.

"Did you read the book?" I tighten my arms and tap my foot.

"Yes." A flush creeps up his neck. "I mean"—he tugs the collar of his T-shirt, which today has a huge Snoopy on it—"my mom wrote it, and I like to read, so sure I read it a couple of years ago, before I knew you."

He's read it. I've read it. We could have a *Jenny and Me* book club.

Oh my gosh, there probably already was one.

I'll think about that later. For now, I need to wrap this up with Dylan before the lunch crowd takes over the stairwell. "So you know she shared private conversations. How would you feel if your best friend put your private conversations in a book for the whole world to read?"

He opens his mouth like he's about to argue, then deflates. "I'd be pissed."

I start nodding, and he adds, "Did you know as soon as she found out you were alive, she called her publisher and said all future royalties should be sent to you for your college fund?"

I recoil. "I don't want money from that book." But this explains her comment that day we went shopping, about me being fine financially. It had nothing to do with my parents.

"She doesn't either. But it's started climbing up the bestseller list again."

Ouch. So even more people are reading it.

"I understand where you're coming from," he says, almost pleading, "but you have to admit these circumstances are unique, and you should give Mom a chance to explain."

Argh! Every time. "I can't get away from those 'unique circumstances,' like the fact I disappeared and was presumed dead gives her a screw-Jenny-over-for-free card."

Dylan bites his lip. "It's a pretty good excuse."

"What?" Crap. I didn't mean to say the second thing out loud. At least I managed to control my tongue last night, when it really mattered.

Dylan steps up so he's in front of me again and gently takes hold of my wrist. "Whatever happens with my mom, I care most about you and me. Because I know you're real, not some memory written in the pages of a book or an alien planted in our midst to spy for an invasion or whatever else people say. You're the girl who argues Shakespeare's the best writer of all time even when you know it's lame. The girl who comes into my room asking about my Ozzie Smith ball even when you're freaking out because you have no idea what's going on in the part of the world that's most important to you. You think the way my mom wrote about you makes you sound weak, but you're strong because you stand up for what you believe in, even when it isn't popular. I know who you are, Jenny Waters, and I hope you'll forgive me for letting you down."

My pulse is jumping beneath his thumb; I resist the urge to jerk my arm back before he notices how he affects me. "That was . . . maybe the best speech anyone's ever given me. But you had all weekend to practice it. How am I supposed to trust you?"

He keeps his eyes on mine, not even a flicker left or right. "Because even though you're right—I did practice—it was because I didn't want to mess it up. There were so many moments I wanted to tell you about that stupid book, from the very first day I met you. I asked Mom more than once to tell you, but it wasn't my call. From now on, I don't have anyone else's secrets to keep. So you *can* count on me."

I look up into his brown eyes, and I want to. Why am I such a sucker? Probably because in many ways, he's as much a victim in this situation as I am.

"Please, Jenny."

The bell rings, and a stampede begins outside the doors, the perfect excuse to pull away. As I start upstairs, I call back, "I'll think about it."

CHAPTER THIRTY-ONE

I should be doing my calculus homework, but every time I try, the numbers blur. So instead I pick up the notebook I had with me on the plane. I started this notebook junior year. It includes stories I wrote for the paper—back when it was an actual paper— but also the other stories I've written since. Nobody's writing the story *I* want to read about Angie, so I start it myself.

ST. LOUIS, Aug. 24—Jennifer Waters recently discovered that during her absence, her former best friend, Angela Russell Graham, had not only stolen her boyfriend and produced twin children—one evil, one annoyingly irresistible—but also published a book giving her distorted version of Waters's life story.

Yeah, this is veering into Greta Barren territory. The difference is, I don't plan to publish it.

Perhaps Waters could have forgiven Graham, if she had stuck to tales of childhood jaunts to the ice cream shop or nostalgic games of Life in which they named the baby blue and pink stick children in their cars Jake, Blake, and Lake. But no, she had to dig into the secrets we told each other—

Oops! Slipped into first person. Who am I kidding anyway? It's not a news story. It's a ranty journal entry.

A short rap on my door is followed by Mom sticking her head in. She holds out the house phone. "Grandma wants to talk to you."

"Oh." I snap the notebook closed. At least Grandma will distract me from my, er, calculus. I hop up to retrieve the phone and wave Mom off. "Hey, Grandma."

"So you know everything now."

"*Do* I?" I scoot back on my bed and lean against the wall. It doesn't seem outside the realm of possibility that my family will drop some other life-changing revelation in my lap. Like Bradley was switched at birth in the hospital and some other man-boy out there is actually my biological brother. My life is already a sci-fi soap opera, so why not?

"Stop sulking, Jenny."

"Sulking?" I avoid looking at the notebook.

"I don't believe a word of that statement you made on TV," she continues.

Smart Grandma.

"But that doesn't mean you shouldn't try to."

I mentally walk through her logic. "You want me to buy into my own press statement?"

"You'll be much happier if you let this go."

"I'll be much happier if I build a huge bonfire out of every copy of *Jenny and Me* and the fumes travel around the world, magically erasing everyone's memories of it."

"If I thought that'd work, I'd go gather the kindling right now," a voice says from the doorway.

Angie. Mom is such a traitor.

"Sounds like you have company," Grandma says in a much-too-satisfied tone.

They're all traitors.

"Yeah. I'll talk to you later." I hang up and cross my arms. A death stare is the only greeting Angie deserves.

Angie moves into the room and tosses a movie theater–size bag of Skittles between us. My fingers itch to grab it and start popping candy into my mouth. She knows my weaknesses way too well. Which is the root of the problem.

Angie perches on the edge of the bed. "Dylan and Steve may be optimistic about what you said on TV, but I know you better than that. Your reporter instincts kicked in. You recognized what Greta Barren was doing and weren't about to let her air your business on TV. It always amazes me how you can turn that mask on when you go into reporter mode, but when you're in front of someone you know, it's totally clear what you're thinking."

I shrug, wishing I could channel that reporter mojo right now. I wonder if Angie suspects JoJo outed her.

Angie glances around the room. "I can't believe how much this still looks the same. Minus the posters. I wish . . ." Her gaze lands on the notebook. "Ah. I bet there are a few choice words about me in there."

Heat creeps up my neck, but I still refuse to speak. The silent treatment may be the tactic of a ten-year-old, but I don't care. She craves words. I will not give them.

"If you want to publish something about me," Angie says, "I wouldn't blame you. It'd only be fair."

She also knows I won't do that. For the very same reason I didn't give Greta Barren her sensational story. A list of Angie's offenses bubble up, trying to escape. I clap a hand over my mouth to contain them. She turns away; I'm pretty sure she's hiding a smile. I grab a pillow and throw it at her. She's perched so close to the edge she topples onto the floor. I scramble forward to look over the side at her.

Angie rubs her hip. Her shirt's hanging off her shoulder, her glasses askew. "Guess I deserved that."

"And more." Crap. I spoke.

To her credit, Angie doesn't react to my slip. She fixes her shirt, adjusts her glasses, and sits cross-legged on the floor. It's a position she often chose in my room, and I can almost picture the old Angie in her place, wearing a tie-dyed T-shirt and cutoff shorts, her bleached hair pulled back in a ponytail, her bangs brushing her eyebrows. Except this Angie sits with her back super straight, and her button-down shirt is tucked into her khaki shorts. Did the royalties from *Jenny and Me* help pay for her outfit? Dylan said it was climbing the bestseller list *again*.

"I brought a movie," Angie says. "And two giant Cokes that are probably turning to Coke water on the kitchen table as we speak."

"You *brought* a movie? An actual, physical movie? I thought people didn't do that anymore."

She shrugs. "I've had this one a while."

Not cool, acting like we can just move on without addressing her *latest* betrayal. "That's it? You're not gonna apologize or give me a bunch of excuses?"

Angie stares back at me steadily. "I could. But you know me as well as I know you. Even though you weren't here when I decided to write the memoir, you could script my apology and everything I'd say. That statement you made, well, it's what I feel."

I reach for another pillow.

She holds out her arms in a T. "Go ahead."

"Oh my gosh, Angie, that is so you! You expose me to the world, and I'm supposed to draft your apology?"

Instead of launching the pillow, I hug it to my chest.

She drops her arms. "We always did say when I started winning big cases you'd write my media statements so I didn't sound like an idiot."

I shake my head. "This is so not the same."

She shifts up on her knees and plants her elbows on the bed. "Jenny . . . I was grieving. I used that book as a way to work through it. Looking back, there are some passages I probably should've excluded—"

"Ya think?" I whack her lightly with the pillow.

"I was young, and my editor said I needed to dig deeper, and, well, that's where some of those stories came from. But I'm sorry, because now that you're back, I realize they may create some uncomfortable moments."

I poke her shoulder. "Bird sex, Angie."

She winces. "Yeah, that . . . came up in a conversation with my editor. She loved it and said it would make you look sweet.

That line about the birds and the bees was hilarious! And then when your parents read it, they wanted me to add the part about your pledge, just to make sure no one took it the wrong way."

I cover my cheeks. "You had a whole discussion with my parents about that passage?"

"I talked to your parents about everything. Even tried to give them some of the proceeds once the book started doing so well, but since I was pregnant by then, they insisted we keep it." She lifts her shoulders and scrunches up her face. "As for that passage, it made them smile, because they also remembered the birds in the vent."

I don't want to talk about the money because it just reminds me how *many* people have read the book.

"Well, my classmates think I'm like"—I try to think of a comparison but come up blank—"some boring tattletale goody-goody."

Angie cocks her head. "Why do you care? You never did before. That's what I've always loved about you. That you're you and you own it."

Huh. And yet . . ."Everyone couldn't read all about it before."

She rubs the spot between her eyebrows. "You're right, of course."

I hesitate, but there's something I still really want to know. "Why didn't he ever kiss me, Angie?" I rush to add, "And this is not because I still want him or anything. Because he's *old* now."

She looks disgruntled for a moment, and I think it's because of the question, but then I realize I just called her old too. Oops. But I don't care. Because one careless comment is nothing compared to what I'm experiencing.

She shakes it off. "It was like I told you all along. He was too shy." She studies me as if determining whether I can handle something and then tilts her head like she's made a decision. "He never made the first move with me either. I had to kiss him."

"Oh." I actually don't mind hearing this. I mean, I don't need details on whether he slipped her the tongue or anything, but it's okay. School, PATROL, the book—it's all pushed my hurt over Angie and Steve to the back page. I care more about me and Angie than Angie and Steve.

Besides, after seeing them together, it doesn't seem so strange. They looked so . . . comfortable with each other. And the way Steve teased Dylan—as embarrassing as it was—makes me think Angie brings out a lighter side of him.

"He really did care about you, Jenny." She reaches out like she's going to touch me and thinks better of it. "He still does . . . just differently, of course."

Yeah, differently. And Angie too. Because there are twenty-five years separating us. Twenty-five years, a husband, two kids, a book, and countless memories I'm not a part of.

"I just . . ." She flutters her hand. "I know you're angry, and you have every right to be, but I'm so happy you're here. Losing you was like losing half of myself. I never quite got back on track."

She wipes a finger under her eye. Angie isn't vulnerable. This isn't right.

"Angie . . ."

"What about that movie?" she asks, brushing her fingers through her hair as if that will distract me from the tears.

The urge to pound Angie with pillows has dwindled. I think back over our conversation. I could ask her why she didn't tell me about the book right away, like I've asked everyone else, but because I know Angie as well as she knows me—even with all that distance between us—I already know the answer. She thought our friendship could survive Steve, but she knew the book would change everything. So she's not asking me to forgive her. Instead she's just asking me to go sit next to her for a while.

I set the pillow aside and get off the bed. "What movie is it?"

Angie stands beside me and pushes her glasses up her nose. "It's a Sandra Bullock movie from about five years after you disappeared. About an FBI agent who goes undercover at a beauty pageant. It's hilarious, and I thought you could use a laugh."

I don't want to forgive her. But I'm also a stranger in this time, and Angie knows me better than anyone else, even my parents. She's different, but she still calls me on my idiosyncrasies and knows what I'm thinking. It comes from years of friendship, and I can't replace that with a new friend in days or weeks. Obviously we can't go back, and we can't have the same close bond with her being so much older, but I can't quite cut her off either.

"Mocking the FBI, huh?" I grab the Skittles. "Show me to the Cokes."

CHAPTER THIRTY-TWO

When Angie leaves, she offers to come back to watch the sequel sometime soon. I'm open to it. We don't chat further, but her movie choice is evidence of how well she knows me. The scene with the main character using her self-defense skills as her talent in the Miss United States pageant—solar plexus, instep, nose, groin—priceless.

Maybe I should give those last chapters in her book another chance, but I find myself actually wanting to take Bradley's original advice and not read any more about myself.

As I lie in bed, it hits me how much I've missed over the past twenty-five years. Angie was so casual about the movie, about it being a part of her history. There's so much else that's just part of her past, of Mom and Dad and Bradley's past. I stopped watching the miniseries about the 2000s because it hurt too much, but I can't dismiss whole decades if I want to relate to my family. I need to understand what they experienced while I was gone, even if it's secondhand. If I have any hope of fitting in here, I need to figure out how the world came to be what it is today. I also need to get a grip on how my family and friends became who they are. When I went downstairs to search out Angie's book, I noticed several newer photo albums, including a wedding album for Bradley and

Kelly. I'll ask Mom and Dad to go through them with me, to tell me the stories behind them. It might be painful to talk about the time while I was missing, but I think it will be a start toward healing too.

On a more fun note, I can start catching up on the movies and books I've missed. Maybe I could write a column for the *Parkwood Press*. Like reviews. I'd be discovering them for the first time, and maybe some of my classmates would, too, or maybe it'd just bring back happy memories of something they love—or don't. If they hate the movie or book and I love it, we can have discussion. I've been studying up on the archives of the *Press*, and this new format allows for significantly more reader interaction. It's easier for readers to tell us what they think than when they had to write a physical letter to the editor.

I'm about to snap on my light and grab my notebook to jot down some ideas when my phone buzzes on my nightstand.

Dylan's name lights up the screen, but the message fades too quickly for me to read it. I wonder what he wants so late. My heartbeat accelerates, a smile blooming as I reach for the phone.

I pause, my hand hovering over it.

Because I recognize this sensation. I've felt it before. Like freshman year, when Mom called from the kitchen that Mike Harlowe was on the phone, and he asked me to the homecoming dance. Except it's amplified now.

I've been trying to deny it since the first day of school, when Dylan picked me up and I felt that first kick. I wanted to turn it into something simpler, but I can't anymore.

I like Dylan.

And not in a *hey, we're pals* sort of way. I'm totally crushing on him.

I snatch my hand back and bury my face in my pillow, groaning. I can't get involved with Dylan that way.

I squeeze my eyes tight, debating whether or not to pick up the phone.

On the yes side: what I'm feeling has nothing to do with his text, so answering him isn't declaring my interest.

On the no side: I've been relying too much on Dylan, and I should just cut things off before I get in any deeper. My life is already such a mess without adding the complication of a boy.

On the yes side: that speech!

I lunge for the phone, my body apparently deciding independently of me, and unlock it.

Dylan: Hey. Thanks for forgiving my mom.

Okay, his text has nothing to do with a potential *us*. My heart slows as I focus on his message. I didn't forgive Angie. I'm sure she knows that. But I'm not getting into the Jenny-and-Angie-emotional-roller-coaster saga with Dylan. I don't have words to adequately respond to this statement, so I search for an emoji, which Dylan himself taught me is today's universal language.

Ohmygosh there are so many. The smiley faces aren't right. Kissy faces would definitely be way too much. And though the confused emoji is most appropriate, that would defeat the purpose of allowing Dylan to think Angie and I are cool.

Me: 👍

This seems noncommittal enough, not agreeing exactly but acknowledging his statement. I'm also hoping it shuts down further conversation about me and Angie.

Dylan: . . .

I flop back onto my pillow, my pulse kicking up again. I scrunch my nose. This is not good. More-than-friends feelings for Dylan are so complicated.

One thing's for sure: I have forgiven *him*. After what he said today, how could I not? He said he knows I'm real and not a memory. Or an alien. Ha.

The phone buzzes in my hand, and I nearly drop it.

Dylan: What are you up to?

I smile.

Me: Well, I should've been sleeping, but I had this idea . . .

I forget my reservations, and for the next hour, neither of us sleep.

CHAPTER THIRTY-THREE

After my late-night texting session with Dylan, I'm jittery at the prospect of seeing him again. It's different now. I'm not sure exactly where he falls on the Jenny-and-Dylan-may-be-a-thing spectrum, but now that I've acknowledged how *I* feel . . . well, I just don't know how to act around him. Probably like an idiot, my cheeks flaming so that my freckles form a connect-the-dots picture across my nose.

Whatever. I have a purpose today. I'm the co–editor in chief of the *Parkwood Press*, and I have an idea to pitch. I'm actually grateful Mrs. Vega put me in charge of features and opinions because this will fit in perfectly. I spend lunch in the library, Googling popular movies and books from the past twenty-five years. I love the internet! It's so much easier than dragging out a bunch of reference books.

At least this research was. I'm having a harder time tracking down clues about PATROL's true motives. Short of trying to disguise myself and interviewing them directly—which Angie's book has probably made impossible—I'm not sure about my next steps. Maybe a phone interview? I might be able to get away with that. With his science background, Art has a better chance of speaking intelligently with them, although I'm not so sure about his interviewing skills. Maybe I could go Clark Kent with some glasses and a suit, and show up at Dr. Greaves's husband's company for an intern interview or something. I *might* get away with it.

But first I need to get on a better footing here at school, and I feel like I have this. I stride into class with a confidence I've been lacking since I got thrown into this whole new version of the *Press*.

I spy the girl with the blue glasses at the far end of the table and move to sit beside her. I dump my backpack on the floor. "I'm so sorry. I know this is horrible, but I'm totally blanking on your name."

Thankfully, she doesn't appear offended as she says, "It's Chloe."

"Chloe. Nice to meet you. Officially." I snap my fingers. "You emailed me about writing a feature on three of our orchestra members who made it into the youth symphony."

"That's me." She smiles. "You've had a lot going on."

"Yeah." But I need to stop focusing on myself and pay attention to the rest of the world or I'll never find my place in it. I point at a sticker on her notebook. "You thinking about NYU?"

She strokes the sticker with a wistful expression. "Yeah. But my parents are against it. They say Mizzou has one of the best programs in the country and it would cost so much less."

I nod sympathetically. "I love New York." The words pop out before I realize what sort of questions they might lead to, but Chloe doesn't pry, and that makes me want to say more. "I used to want to go to Columbia, but that was when my grandparents lived there." I swallow around a lump in my throat. "They . . . passed away a while ago."

Chloe bites her lip. "I'm sorry." She looks back at her notebook. "You know, the top-rated journalism school these days is Emerson College in Boston."

I manage a smile. "Boston, huh? I've never been there."

But I should consider it, since my original plan no longer makes sense. It's more than the hole Grandma and Grandpa have left in New York. *Maybe* I'll fly again someday—although I'm leaning more toward a train or driving to school—but I'm not sure I'll ever take that New York to St. Louis flight. No matter how often people tell me that multiple planes have flown that route with no incident, I will remember that *my* plane took that path and I lost what equated to a quarter of a life.

Mrs. Vega sweeps into the room, Ashling sneaking in behind her as the teacher sets her messenger bag on her desk. She turns and strides over to me, leaning down. "Okay, Jenny?"

She let me spend yesterday's class period in an empty classroom, calling advertisers, so this is the first time I've seen her since I left Friday. I search myself and find that I am, if not okay, getting there. "I will be."

Mrs. Vega holds my gaze another second. "Good. But just in case, I sent you an email with my cell number. If you need to talk, anytime, you call me."

It means a lot to have her looking out for me. "I got it. Thanks."

Mrs. Vega nods, then moves back to her desk and leans against it with her ankles crossed. "Tell me how things are coming along for our first issue. We go live next Wednesday."

Despite my learning curve, I feel like my sections are shaping up nicely. I report that most of the advertisers have signed on again, and I'll be seeking out some additional opportunities. As I list the article ideas for features and opinion, I let the staff members who'll be writing them explain what they're about. Everyone's supposed to turn in their drafts by Thursday so I can edit them and turn in final copy by Monday.

Ashling has a similar style for her half of the paper. Noticeably absent: her drug bust story.

Mrs. Vega claps. "Fantastic. What else do we have in the works after this first issue goes live? I want to keep a number of ideas in the pipeline."

I raise my hand. "I'd like to do a column."

She nods. "What're you thinking?"

I explain my idea for a weekly "Blast from the Past" column as I catch up on what I missed.

Ashling opens her mouth in an exaggerated yawn. "Bo-ring."

Mrs. Vega frowns. "Ashling." She turns to the rest of the class. "Do you think our readers will be interested in Jenny's column?"

"Well . . . ," Chloe begins, and I can already tell from her apologetic expression that she's not about to cheer me on. "I mean, it's fun for you to discover all those things, but it's not new to us. So where's the news value?"

Ouch. Not on the part about it not being new to them. I get that. But on the part about me not recognizing what's news. I've always had a great sense for that. Apparently that's something else I lost on the plane.

Chloe continues, "I'd be more interested in hearing what it's like for you and the other people from Flight 237, coming back after missing so much. If they'd be willing to talk to you and we put it in the *Press*, you could use those stories for college applications or something."

My breath hitches. She's right, but it hits so close to home. "Technically we're not supposed to give interviews."

Although Agent Klein might be lifting that restriction soon, if the latest round of results confirms we're exactly who we say we are.

"*You* gave an interview," Ashling says with an annoying smirk.

I rub my neck. "Yeah, that was . . . unplanned." Maybe I could get permission for these stories, especially if they aren't focused on the plane. Some of the other passengers might be open to it, if I'm the one writing them. "What if it's not just the people on the plane but their family and friends?"

Mrs. Vega nods. "You could build our readership beyond the school, maybe get us some new advertisers. Plus, if the stories are strong enough, I have a friend at the *Post-Dispatch* who might take a look."

"Wow, that would be amazing." To have a byline not only in the *Parkwood Press* but also a mention in the *St. Louis Post-Dispatch*—any college journalism program would love that on my application!

Others around the table murmur agreements and give me smiles and a thumbs-up. For the first time since I joined this class, I feel like more than Mrs. Vega's nostalgia project.

I sit up straighter in my chair and smile at Chloe. I mean, I won't do it unless Agent Klein gives the okay and the other passengers agree, but I think some of them will. Maybe I'll start with myself to show them what the column can be. Ideas start scrolling through my mind.

"I have a tip for next week," Ashling says, interrupting my brainstorm. I hope it's not another imaginary drug deal.

"Yes, Ashling?" Mrs. Vega pushes off the desk.

"Since Jenny plans to explore the passenger side of the Flight 237 story, I think we should pursue the PATROL view as well. My godmother, Greta Barren, has an inside source there. She's willing to let me tag along on her interview."

I stiffen. "Greta Barren is your godmother?"

How has that not come up? Did everyone else already know that? I'm dying to try to signal Chloe to see if *she* knew, but it would be totally obvious.

Ashling smiles sweetly. "She was my mom's little in Kappa Delta, and she's my inspiration for becoming a journalist. How do you think I knew about the insurance companies being behind PATROL?"

"It hasn't been positively confirmed yet," I say. "And now that Greta's put the allegation out there, I doubt her source is going to admit anything."

Ashling cocks her head. "That's exactly why they want to talk to us. To set the record straight. But you don't know Greta. She always gets her story."

I just bet she does. By any means necessary.

Mrs. Vega leans over the table. "Ashling, exactly what sort of story are you proposing? An investigation into whether insurance companies are backing PATROL or a human-interest piece finding out what the group is all about?"

I can understand Mrs. Vega's confusion, considering how Ashling framed her initial comment. She made it sound like we'd be on opposite sides—passengers versus PATROL.

Ashling looks up at the ceiling. "I'm not completely sure. I want to go talk to them and really dig into the story, like any decent reporter would do. It wouldn't be right for us—as an impartial news outlet—to only cover Jenny's side."

For a long moment, Mrs. Vega stares at Ashling, as if she can see into her brain and ferret out her true intentions.

"I'll allow it," she finally says, and I can't hold in my gasp. Mrs. Vega turns to me, her expression calm. "Ashling can go interview PATROL. It's good experience, and she has a point about exploring all sides of a story. However"—she holds up a hand in Ashling's direction—"a journalist must also remain objective. And I expect both of you to remember that as you write your stories."

Ouch again. And yet, it's not an entirely unfounded reminder, considering it will be near impossible for me to be objective collecting stories from the other passengers. I want to portray them in a positive light. To tell the world what they're going through. But it's also not exactly the same sort of thing as what Ashling's pursuing, trying to find a way to discredit me personally. Because I'm sure that's what she's after.

Especially when she smiles smugly at me after Mrs. Vega turns her back.

I wish I had the results of the FBI's more extensive medical tests to throw in her face, but it wouldn't be enough. We both know the damage is done. Ashling has been undermining me from the moment I stepped inside Parkwood High School, and she's just declared outright war. Just when I started to fit in, Ash-ling pointed out that I'm a puzzle piece from an ocean scene when we're working on a wildflower field. Now I have to prove all over again that I belong in their picture.

CHAPTER THIRTY-FOUR

As I wait outside school for Mom to pick me up, grateful for the unseasonably cool breeze that whispers across my neck, I resolve not to let the Ashlings of the world derail me. No matter what sort of story she comes up with after talking with PATROL, I'll write a better researched, more well-rounded story readers will identify with.

A text comes through from Mom saying she'll be a few minutes late, so I pull out my notebook to start a new plan. Because talking with Chloe about colleges made me realize I need to figure out my priorities there.

Phase I: Decide where I'm willing to travel.
Phase 2: Choose new college.

It feels good to make a real plan. Aside from schoolwork, I haven't done it since the plane landed. Maybe that's why I've been so lost, drifting along like a reader gasping at a dozen shocking plot points piling up. I'm tired of editing my life when I should be drafting it. I pause to chew on my pen, because it may be the end of August, but I'm now behind on item two. I would have been submitting an early decision application to Columbia this fall, but now I have to come up with a completely new list. Chloe said Emerson is the top journalism school, and it wasn't even on my radar. I need to make an appointment with the school counselor. What if the process for college applications is completely different?

I adjust Phase Two and add sub-points.

Phase 2: ~~Choose new college.~~ Research college options.
    Step 1: Look up top journalism schools on the internet.
    Step 2: Schedule a meeting with the school counselor.
Phase 3: Convince Mom and Dad

A hand on my shoulder startles me into tossing my pen. "Ow!"

I twist around. "Dylan!" I cover my mouth. "I'm so sorry."

He rubs his forehead. "Me too. I just learned two important lessons. You're more absorbed in your notebook than JoJo with her earbuds in."

He bends down to pick up my pen and presents it to me. "Also, the pen really is mightier than the sword."

A small dot marks the spot where the pen hit him. "Sorry."

Dylan shuffles back and forth and then squats beside me. "It's weird hulking over you like that."

His new position makes him super close. I can see tiny gold flecks in his brown eyes.

"So," he says.

My traitorous heart kicks up again. "So . . ."

He stares at me, his two front teeth working the corner of his bottom lip. He's never been this hesitant with me. It must be our texting last night. Between that and what he said yesterday, he's rethinking everything and wants to take things back a step. It makes sense.

"I get it," I start. "You—"

At the same time, he says, "Would you—"

We both stop. I motion for him to go first.

He inhales. "Would you like to go out with me this weekend?"

His question is perfectly clear, no hint of a joke.

"Go out?" I echo. "Like on a date?"

My voice has this awful horrified tone to it, which isn't how I'm feeling at all. My heart is thumping *yes, yes, yes,* while my brain says *no, no, no, you can't, you can't, you can't.*

He rocks back and runs his hand through his hair. "I guess that's a no."

"No . . ." I say it quickly, but the way I trail off leaves a question in the air. A question I need out in the open before we go anywhere. "It's just . . . your parents."

He smiles ruefully. "Yeah. Complicated."

"So complicated." I nod vigorously.

"But they're history." His eyes are like lasers on mine, super focused. "Right?"

I think Dylan means *he's* history, not *they're.* That's why I should break eye contact, run for the school entrance, and hide in the girls' bathroom where he can't follow. But some hidden Jenny inside me, a Jenny who doesn't care as much about complications, answers Dylan's unspoken question about whether Steve is history. "Definitely."

It's the rest of the drama that's still hanging over us—Angie and the book and whether JoJo was involved in spreading it around the school.

Dylan rocks forward again. "Then will you go out with me Friday night?"

Yes, yes, yes!

No, no, no.

YES!

I hope I don't regret this. "I will."

CHAPTER THIRTY-FIVE

I haven't told Mom and Dad about my date. I know I'll have to, but it'll bring up all sorts of questions I don't want to answer yet.

Instead, I focus on my new college plans and the more immediate issues I need to deal with.

On the let's-do-cartwheels-and-hire-a-skywriter side, Agent Klein sent a copy of my test results via private messenger today (along with a link to log in to an electronic account for all my medical files—crazy!), just in time for our special pre-press conference support group meeting. I am one hundred percent confirmed to be Jennifer Ann Waters, born January 15, 1978, DNA match for Carol, Mark, and Bradley Waters, no traces of alien or foreign elements anywhere in my body.

I walk into our meeting with my head high, ready to pitch my new and improved idea—well, Chloe's idea—for the *Parkwood Press*. We're at a new location to avoid any Greta Barren incidents. (I still can't believe she's Ashling's *godmother*! After class, I asked Chloe if she knew, since it seemed like the sort of thing Ashling would have bragged about. Chloe said maybe Ashling mentioned it at some point, but she moved to Parkwood halfway through junior year, and the connection hadn't come up since then.)

"You're in a good mood," Mrs. Spring says.

I guess I am. "I'm starting to figure things out."

She pats my knee. "Good for you, honey."

I bite into my brownie—excellent as usual—and wait for everyone else to get settled. Valerie sits on my other side. I hold out my half-eaten snack. "Who makes these, anyway?"

Valerie glances down. "I think Frank does."

"Huh." I eye Captain McCoy with renewed interest.

"Good evening, everyone!" Captain McCoy says, and we all respond in kind. "Did everyone who's willing to share their results publicly bring them?"

There's a general shuffling as we pull papers out of our bags and pass them to Captain McCoy. It looks like Walter is the only one not participating; even Miss Klaffke hands hers in. Once Captain McCoy has them all, he exhales and pats the stack. "I've scheduled a joint press conference with the FBI for Saturday. These results will go a long way to putting PATROL's arguments to rest. They can prattle all they want about our flight being impossible, but they can't refute the science of us being who we say we are." He scans the circle, his gaze landing briefly on Walter. "And if you aren't participating, that's perfectly fine. We have enough to prove our case."

Captain McCoy places the papers in a briefcase beside his chair. I notice Walter eyeing them, which is weird since he didn't participate.

I'm eager to explain that my column can also be used to support our cause, but I feel like I should ease into it. "Now that they have these results, does that mean we can start talking to the media?"

Captain McCoy nods. "After the press conference, you can

answer those calls we've all been getting from *Good Morning America* and the *New York Times*. Agent Klein will be sending you an official notice. I think there might be some remaining restrictions about discussing the testing, but I assume nobody's going to tell *Dateline* they actually had a time hopper concealed in their pocket and spoil the FBI's investigation findings."

A few people around the circle laugh, but most look as confused as me. Art leans around Valerie. "It's a *Doctor Who* thing."

I frown. "Doctor who?"

"Exactly!" Art says as if he's explained anything at all. This is why Art belongs firmly in the friend zone. Dylan is so patient with me, taking the time to make sure I understand what people are talking about.

Captain McCoy leans forward with his elbows on his knees. "Now that we have a plan for the results, how's everyone doing?"

Wait! I wasn't finished with the media discussion, but Miss Klaffke has already raised her hand.

"I'll start. I've been studying up on possible jobs. I worked in an office my entire life, and I'm sure I could learn how to use all the new programs, but I'd rather take care of people. So I'm getting certified as a home health aide. It doesn't pay a lot, but I live with my daughter, who's more like a sister now, so we'll get along fine."

"Good for you, Sarah," says the woman next to her. She's not much older than Tracey, with sun-bronzed skin and multiple piercings up her left ear. I really need to learn the rest of these names, especially if I want to include them in my column, but some of the people just come and listen. Either they don't have anything to share or, more likely, they're holding it close.

"Keith and I set a date!" Tracey beams at the group. "Two weeks from Friday."

Tracey and Keith would make a great story—a positive outcome after all the turmoil. This is my opportunity. "Hey, Tracey, would you be willing to let me write about you and Keith? For my school paper?"

Tracey's expression shifts from excited to wary. "Um. I'd have to ask Keith. Just about the wedding? Or more about us?"

"We-ell." Here's my chance to explain what I want to do. "I've been trying to figure out how I fit into this new century, and before this all happened, I planned on journalism school. I still want to do that, and this week in my journalism class, someone suggested I could do a column about what it's like figuring out a new normal after a twenty-five-year gap."

Dead silence around the group for one beat. Two.

Oh, crap.

"You're a *reporter*?" Walter spits, jumping up from his seat. "Like that Greta Barren? Have you been spying on us, gathering all our stories so you could write about us and sell them for your college applications? I'm out of here."

He swoops down and suddenly grabs Captain McCoy's briefcase with the papers full of DNA tests. "And I'm taking these with me."

He storms from the church fellowship hall, the doors slapping shut behind him.

For a moment everyone's too stunned to do anything; then Captain McCoy leaps from his chair, sending it screeching across the floor, and chases after him.

Half of us rise from our seats as well, swiveling toward the doors to the parking lot. We hear a car start and peel out. The door opens, and Captain McCoy trudges back in, shaking his head.

"What just happened?" Art says. "I thought *I* was the designated conspiracy theorist."

His statement breaks the tension with a few chuckles.

I throw up my hands. "I would never write anything about anyone without permission! Especially after what Angie did to me. You guys know that, right?"

"Yes," Miss Klaffke says.

"Of course, Jenny." Valerie nods.

Mrs. Spring pats my hand. "We trust you."

The support pours out, and I'm so grateful tears prick my eyes. "I didn't mean to upset Mr. . . . . Walter," I finish awkwardly, my face hot. "And the DNA tests . . ." That's our proof to get PATROL to stop chipping away at us publicly, since the FBI won't release the results.

Captain McCoy sighs as he pulls his chair back into the circle. "He's going through a lot he doesn't want to talk about here." He looks toward the door. "Unfortunately he might not come back now."

I hide my face. "I'm so sorry!"

Captain McCoy holds up a hand. "It's not your fault. I've known Walter for years. As for the tests, if I've learned nothing else about this century, it's that there's a backup of everything. I'm not sure what he hoped to accomplish by stealing those papers, but they're easily replaced, just a bit delayed."

"We could've sent them electronically, you know," Mr. Spring says.

Captain McCoy smiles self-consciously. "I'm probably being paranoid, but I just don't quite trust it all yet." He glances toward the door. "But considering Walter just ran off with the hard copies, it might have been safer that way, so go ahead and send them to my email for the press conference."

Of course. The electronic copies. Mr. Spring has a better handle on the twenty-first century than me. This is not okay.

I wonder what Walter plans to do with the hard copies.

"With this new development, it's probably a good idea for us to meet again Monday and regroup after the press conference," Captain McCoy says.

There's a murmur of agreement around the circle.

Mrs. Spring rubs my back. "Why don't you tell us more about this project for your school paper, and then we can decide if we want to participate?"

I smile gratefully at her. "Sort of like releasing the test results, it's only if you want to do it. I figured if it came from me, you'd trust it more than some national reporter or even a local news station. I'd interview you privately, along with your family—or fiancé"—I gesture at Tracey—"then write the story for my school paper. I want you guys to be completely comfortable with anything that's out there, especially because of how PATROL has attacked us in the media." I wince again, thinking of how Walter's left us open until we can regather the results. "If you'd rather, we have a Vimeo channel—I just learned what that is—so we could even make them like broadcast interviews. Then it would really be in your own words."

Tracey nods, her expression more receptive. "I'll talk it over with Keith and let you know."

Miss Klaffke raises her hand. "I don't know how interesting my story is, but I'm sure my daughter will be on board."

Thank goodness this isn't a complete disaster. "Awesome!"

Mrs. Spring looks to Mr. Spring, who nods. "I believe we're open to it. We'll just have to check with our family first."

My heart swells.

Captain McCoy tilts his head. "I'm not so sure about what I shared concerning my sister. It's already out there if you look—any arrest records are—but I'll think about speaking to my job and readjusting to life in general."

Valerie bumps my shoulder. "Same here. I sincerely doubt my soon-to-be ex wants to be featured in an article, and I don't blame him. His teenagers don't deserve that."

For the first time, I consider Valerie's . . . stepchildren? I'm not really sure what their relationship is. Talk about some messed-up family dynamics, your dad having a long-lost wife reappear. I have no idea what his new wife looks like, but Valerie's really pretty, so that must've caused some anxiety that their dad might go back to her. Considering what people at school have said to me, I'm sure their classmates have come up with some creative comments. "I totally get that."

"But," she adds, "perhaps you can hold me in reserve down the line."

"Count me in for the broadcast interview," Art says. "I already nailed that ambush from Greta Barren. The camera loves me."

He frames his pockmarked face with his hands.

"Oh, yes. It sure does." He *did* come across as smart and articulate.

"Thank you, everyone." It occurs to me there's another

reassurance I could add. "Just so you know, my first article will be about me. I don't expect any of you to jump in without seeing that I'm in this too."

The meeting continues with further updates, and I'm relieved no one seems afraid to share with me in the room. Walter's reaction didn't poison anyone into thinking I'm writing a secret exposé. I don't know what I would do if I lost the support of this group.

CHAPTER THIRTY-SIX

I can't write, I can't concentrate in my classes, and I have no one to talk to about it. All thanks to my looming date with Dylan. The last time I had a date, I talked to Angie, and that's obviously out of the question.

Plus, even though my anger is more like a simmer than a boil, the issue is so much bigger than the book. I'm seventeen. I care about graduating from high school and figuring out whether to go away to college and leave my family again. She's forty-two. I don't even know what her concerns are. Probably whether her *kids* will go away to college. Even if I put aside my hurt over everything she's done, we're at completely different stages of life. I don't mind sitting next to her, watching a movie, but I can never again confide my secrets to this Angie, and that's as painful as anything. She's physically here, but she's passed me by.

Chloe is super nice, and we've been eating lunch together every day, along with her other friends. But she already has a best friend, the redheaded girl who asked me about Art. Her name is Madison. She plays the viola and wears so many charm bracelets I'm curious whether the constant jingling adds another layer to the orchestral harmony. I'm hesitant to confide in them about my date because of all the complicated dynamics. I mean, I like

Chloe and Madison, but what if one of them says something to someone else about it? Or, worse, posts it online? My classmates are constantly taking pictures and videos to post online, of the most random things. I'd really rather keep whatever's happening between me and Dylan low-key until we figure out if it has any potential.

I've gotten close to my Flight 237 group, but I can't imagine talking to any of them about a boy. Like, "Hey, Art, what should I wear for my date?" Yeah, right. He'd laugh his head off. I guess I could call Kelly, but I haven't talked to her since those first few days I arrived. I'm definitely not calling Bradley. Despite his age, he'd probably laugh at me too. Which leaves the only other person I've gotten close to since I arrived—Dylan himself.

When I see Dylan at school on Friday, he's all easygoing and arranges to pick me up at six. So when Mom gets me from school, I finally have to suck it up and tell her about it.

"Ihaveadatetonight," I mumble.

She nearly slams into the car in front of us. "What? Did you say you have a date?"

We're now causing a traffic jam. The minivan behind us honks. "Mom!"

She shakes her head and moves forward. "A date," she repeats like I've announced I'm trying out for the Radio City Rockettes. "With whom?"

I really hope she doesn't actually hit someone now. "Dylan."

"Wha-at?" The car swerves with her arms as she turns to face me, and the wheels bump up on the curb. She quickly rights it. At least we didn't take out any trees or other vehicles.

I bury my head in my hands. "I should've waited until we got home to tell you this."

"Noo," she drags out. "I'm just surprised." She schools the shock off her face and focuses on the road as we turn out of the parking lot. "I like Dylan. Where's he taking you?"

"Um . . . he didn't actually tell me." I should've asked, because I have no idea what to wear. This is part of why I'm so twisted up about it. But I assume it will be casual. He wouldn't take me somewhere fancy for a first date.

Would he?

Mom casts me a rueful glance. "They never get it, do they? How we worry about the details."

Wow. I smile in return. "No, they don't."

By six, with Mom's help, I'm ready in a casual sundress with my hair loose and a light application of makeup. I have on sandals, so I'm good for about anything except bowling.

Oh, no, we're totally going bowling. I need to change into socks and tennis shoes and—

The doorbell rings. "I'll get it," Dad booms.

"Uh-uh, you won't." I rush past him down the stairs, narrowing my eyes to ensure he doesn't follow.

I open the door, not sure what I expect, but it's definitely not for Dylan to be standing there in the same T-shirt he was wearing at school today. The image of a golden bird and arrow surrounded by a flaming circle isn't what I'd call romantic.

"Hi," Dylan says.

"Hi." I bite my lip and peer up at Dad, wondering if he finds this as weird as I do, but Dad's focused on walking down the steps.

"Where are y'all headed tonight?" Dad asks when he reaches the bottom, crowding me on the landing. It's really not big enough for three of us.

I press my elbow in Dad's side and give him a stern back-off look.

Oblivious, Dylan's face lights up. "Art Hill. It's movie night. I figured we'd pick up food for a picnic. It starts at eight thirty, so with traffic afterward, I should have her home by midnight if that's okay."

Dad grins. "I read about that in the paper." Yes, the newspaper has returned to our house. Dad turns to me. "You're about to catch up on some of that stuff you missed."

I don't love that Dad and Dylan are in some secret club that excludes me. But I'm more concerned that I'm inappropriately dressed for an outdoor movie at Art Hill, a large grassy area in front of the Saint Louis Art Museum.

"Do I need to change?" I indicate my dress.

Dylan shrugs. "You look great to me. I have chairs and a blanket, so it's up to you."

I put significant effort into this look, and I'd be fine in a chair, but if I decide to sit on a blanket, I'll be constantly wondering if I'm flashing my pink cotton underwear.

"Give me a minute." I run upstairs. Mom intercepts my panicked look and follows me to my room. We dig through my closet for a few minutes, deciding on a sleeveless V-neck shirt and capris.

I rush back down the stairs. "Ready."

In the car, Dylan explains we can either pick up food on the way or get it from the food trucks at Art Hill. "I pulled up a list of the options on my phone. Why don't you see if any of those interest you?"

I skim through the food truck options. "They make all of this food right in these trucks?"

"Sure," Dylan says, acting like it's normal for me not to know such a thing exists. "They drive around the city and set up shop at different events."

They do look yummy, but they also look expensive. As much time as I've spent with Dylan, we've mostly focused on my issues. I don't know if he has a job or how he's paying for this date.

"What if we just pick up some sandwiches on the way?" I throw out.

Dylan nods. "Sounds good. But I wanna hit the cupcake truck for dessert."

I breathe an internal sigh of relief, feeling like I've passed an initial test. Although it seems like first dates are always a series of tests to see if you fit together.

After we pick up our food, Dylan runs a hand through his hair and casts me a rueful smile. "I thought since we have this weird awkwardness where I already know things about you I shouldn't, it might be fun if we play a little game."

Way to bring up the elephant in the car, although I admire him for it. I twist so my back is toward the passenger door. "What sort of game?"

"A getting-to-know-you game. I found these questions online, but if you think it's too lame . . ."

Oh, I'm not letting him back off now. "By all means, fire away."

His shoulders relax. "Okay. I figured I'll ask you and then you ask me."

I motion for him to proceed, then realize he's watching the road. "Carry on."

"What's the last show you got addicted to?"

"TV show?"

"Yeah."

I'm not sure this game is such a good idea. "Um . . . *Beverly Hills, 90210.*"

Dylan snaps. "I know that show! My mom named me after one of the characters. She cried for, like, a whole day when the actor who played him died."

And suddenly I want to open my door, jump into oncoming traffic, and let a semi pummel my body until it appears the age I should be. "Ohmygosh, can you just let me out at Brentwood?"

We're only halfway to Art Hill. I'm sure Dad would pick me up.

"What?" Dylan turns, and his face falls. "Jenny, no. Okay, forget the TV question, although I'm sorry for mentioning my mom."

He doesn't get it. It's not just the mention of Angie. It's the fact he wasn't even *alive* when my favorite show was on. Plus, Luke Perry's *dead*? He wasn't that much older than me. Like, maybe ten years? Mom didn't mention that when I watched the rest of the show—probably more of her protecting me. I don't know how Dylan and I can possibly have anything in common.

"Want to hear something funny?"

After that? He'd have to be a miracle worker to rescue this conversation. "Not if it's going to make me feel like an antique again."

He sends me a pleading glance. "Once when I was twelve, my best friend called and told me to get over to the park because this girl I liked was there."

He pauses. I lean away from the door. "And? It's not funny yet."

His mouth quirks up. "Well, the thing is, I was half asleep when he called, and I ran straight out to the garage for my bike. I didn't notice until I got to the park and Jack was standing there with his eyes bugging out that I forgot to put on shorts."

My lips twitch. "Seriously? It wasn't, uh, uncomfortable while you were riding your bike?"

He shifts in his seat, as if he can feel it now. "I guess I was more focused on seeing the girl."

I get what he's doing here, sharing his own embarrassing story to lessen mine. "Did she see *you*?"

He nods. "And all her friends. I was famous for a few days—hashtag boxerboy."

"The girl put it *online*?" Now that's not funny; it's mean.

"I rolled with it."

Considering his usual attitude, I bet he did—on the outside anyway.

He wiggles his eyebrows. "I made boxer biking sexy."

I picture a scrawny, twelve-year-old Dylan riding around in *Star Wars* or Cardinals boxers, and I can't help giggling. "I'm sure all the girls wanted you after that."

"You're lucky I'm still available." He winks at me in a totally corny way. "New question. What do you usually do on the weekends?"

I cross my arms. "Read."

"Me too!" he exclaims exaggeratedly. "What kind of books do you read?"

Heat rushes into my cheeks. "Lots of different stuff. But, I guess romances are some of my favorites," I mumble. Angie totally mentioned that in *Jenny and Me*. We used to trade books.

He bites his lip. "Have you started *The Hunger Games* yet?"

"Not yet." I haven't read a nonschool book since I landed in the twenty-first century. Every time I start to relax, new drama pops up.

The traffic slows as we reach the exit for Forest Park, where Art Hill is located. I haven't been here since I returned. It's really different.

"Well, you're about to get a taste."

I swivel away from my examination of the zoo, which we're passing. "What do you mean?"

"That's the movie tonight. *The Hunger Games*."

"Does that have something to do with your shirt?" I remember him talking before about a girl on fire—although nothing about a bird.

He looks down. "Yeah."

In that case, I guess he *did* dress up for our date.

We're silent as Dylan parks and we gather the chairs, blanket, and food for the trek up to the hill. It's weird. As far as years he's been alive, Dylan is technically older than me. He's eighteen, whereas I won't be for a few more months. But I feel older, or maybe just like I'm supposed to be.

"Next question," he says as we spread out our blanket and food. "What do you want to be when you grow up?"

I frown. "You already know."

He tilts his head like he's disappointed in me. "I want you to tell me. Besides, you're not the same girl you were when you got on that plane. You might have changed your mind."

"Fine." I sit cross-legged on the blanket. It's only seven. We have an hour and a half until the movie starts, but the viewing area is already packed. Around us, families with children of varying ages toss balls and frisbees. Young couples, old couples, groups of friends gather on blankets and chairs, talking and eating. It's loud and beautiful, and at the same time overstimulating and the perfect place to form our own little cocoon.

Dylan has a point. I have changed because of the plane. Adapting to this new century hasn't been easy, and I'm still figuring out a lot of things, but my overall objective remains the same.

"I want to be a reporter for a major paper like the *New York Times*," I finally answer.

He props his chin on his fist. "And how are you working toward this goal?"

I laugh. "Now you sound like a reporter."

He raises his eyebrows. "Are you going to answer me?"

"Well . . . my original plan was Columbia. I'm looking into different schools now. And I'm working on some articles about Flight 237 for the *Parkwood Press*, starting with one about my own experiences."

He sits up, alert. "Will *I* be part of these articles?"

I think this is why I've had trouble starting the stories, because I'm not sure how personal I want to get. "Do you want to be?"

He rubs his chin. "I'm not sure."

I nod and tell him about the meeting. "That's the thing. I promised the rest of the people from the flight this was a way to tell the story our way. That's really important to me, that we get to share our stories, but in a way we can control."

Dylan starts passing me food. "That's hard, what with social media. Sometimes things get posted that you don't want out there."

"As boxer boy learned," I say.

"Ouch." He mimics a knife to the heart, and I begin to feel more like it's been with Dylan from the start. This playful, my-embarrassing-moment-is-worse-than-yours boy is the one who's jumbled my usually organized mind.

Time to turn the focus back on him. "So what do *you* want to be when you grow up?"

Dylan smiles. "No idea. I'll be one of those undecided majors."

I fumble my sandwich. "You don't have any idea at all? There's nothing you really love?"

His smile widens. "I see I've shocked you. It also bothers my—well, anyway."

He totally just stopped himself from saying it would bother Angie, and I get it.

"The problem is that I love too many things," he says. "I like to read, but I'm not sure what I'd do with that. I really like math too. And science isn't bad. I love baseball, and I'll definitely play college ball, but I'm not good enough to go pro. I figure I'll sample a variety and see what sticks."

"What about—" I stop, because it probably won't end well if I start mapping it out for him. But I can't imagine entering college without a clear plan. I mean, I have a phased plan just to get there.

"That just drives you crazy, doesn't it?" He taps my nose with his bread crust, then pops it into his mouth. "I've seen you making lists, figuring out all the angles. But you could do with a little more spontaneity in your life, Jenny Waters. And I am just the guy to provide it."

I'm not opposed to this plan.

"I guess you'd better tell me more about your girl Katniss," I say, hoping I remembered her name right this time.

Dylan's face lights up as only a true fan's can. I'm a little skeptical about this whole dystopian thing, but I'll give it a try.

Twenty minutes later he stops. "I've spoiled a lot. Although I guess the movie will do that too. Didn't think that through so well."

I wipe my lips with a napkin. "No, you've convinced me to read it. And I love this."

"Your turn. Tell me about your favorite book series."

I tilt my head forward and look up at him. "You really want to hear about my romance novels?"

He spreads his arms to indicate the picnic. "I love romance."

"Hmm." I purse my lips, hoping any blushes will be attributed to the heat. "There's this one I love about a girl who doesn't know she's a princess . . ."

He nods solemnly. "That sounds familiar."

I throw an apple, and it hits him solidly in the solar plexus. He retrieves it and rubs his "wound," then throws up his arms in surrender. "Sorry. I'll listen."

I wag a finger at him. "You'd better."

And he does. Before I know it, another half hour has passed, with us laughing over the admittedly cliché plot.

Dylan glances at his watch. "Let's get our cupcakes before the movie starts."

He jumps up and holds out his hand. I hesitate but then give him mine, and he doesn't let go after he helps me up. We walk hand in hand toward the food trucks, and my hand's a bit sweaty, but it still feels nice to hang on to Dylan. He has to release me to pay for the cupcakes and waters. We chat easily as we stroll back to our blanket.

I chose a red velvet cupcake, and it's divine. Dylan holds out a forkful of his turtle cupcake. "Wanna bite of mine?"

Are we there already? Sharing food? It does look tempting. "Okay."

He slips the fork in my mouth. The chocolate and caramel mixes with the cream cheese icing already on my tongue. I imagine I can taste a bit of Dylan. "Mmmm."

Dylan's eyes soften, and he leans forward.

He's going to kiss me.

"I've never kissed anyone before. I don't know what to do."

"I know," Dylan says.

"You know?" I sit back.

"You said . . ." Dylan trails off.

I said it out loud. *I've never kissed anyone before. I don't know what to do.*

My cheeks flame. They're probably darker than the cake I'm holding. And unfortunately the sun is barely starting to set. "And you said, 'I know.'"

"I did. I—" He runs a hand down the side of his face, until his mouth is cupped in his palm.

Dylan knows because of the book. Because he read the book and Angie wrote that I "really craved a spectacular first kiss," then went on to say that I never got it before I left. The words are burned in my brain.

"How messed up is it that you know I've never kissed anyone because you basically got a Jenny handbook in advance of this date?"

He drops his hand to his side and scrunches his nose. "It is a dilemma. And it puts a lot of pressure on me, honestly."

I snort-laugh, a little hysterical. "What?"

"Think about it. Any other guy might go in for a kiss, thinking he only has to live up to some other random teenage guys. Whereas *I*"—he pats his chest—"know potential comparisons are those overly muscled men on the covers of romance novels who probably create sparks with their lips."

A giggle bubbles up from the vicinity of my chest as I picture two people kissing, fireworks exploding from their lips. "Are you ever serious?"

I collapse onto the blanket, staring up at him.

"I'm serious about *you*." Dylan leans over me, propped on his elbow, grinning almost . . . tenderly. The sun is setting spectacularly behind him, forming bursts of red and gold behind his dark blond head. My laughter subsides.

"You worry too much, Jenny." He's so close, and he says it like he's sure kissing me is the right thing, but he still doesn't move in.

I do worry a lot. It's why I like to have plans. A part of me still wonders whether he's learned this on his own or from reading about me. Another part doesn't care. I've waited a long time for a first kiss.

He leans in close enough his face blots out the setting sun but waits for a signal from me. I give a slight nod to indicate that, yes, I want him to kiss me, and then his lips are on mine.

I feel a jolt at the first touch of his lips, and I briefly think maybe we've just broken the space–time continuum with our kiss. His lips are soft and sweet with the lingering taste of buttercream icing and chocolate cake. He tangles his fingers through my hair, pressing our mouths more firmly together, and I open my lips slightly, eager to experience more. His tongue slips inside, and I shiver at the contact, wrapping my arms around his neck.

Someone whistles, and suddenly all the sounds of the surrounding festivities return—the kids playing, the "Over here!" shouts as people attempt to find their friends, vendors selling their wares. I break away from Dylan, self-conscious. I look up, and there's a small boy, probably four or five, staring down at us, strawberry ice cream dripping down his arm from the cone in his hand. "Nathan, come here!" a woman calls, and the boy runs off.

I scramble to sitting and bury my head in my hands. "Oh my gosh. I can't believe we just did that in front of all these people."

Dylan rubs my shoulder. "I wouldn't change it for anything. Best first kiss ever."

I peek out from my knees. "Really?"

He twists so he's eye level with me. "You can quote me on it."

I'd choose Dylan over a romance novel hero any day.

People start cheering around us, and I emerge from my cocoon. "The movie's about to start."

Dylan settles me against his side. "You're gonna love it."

I cuddle into him. "I can't wait."

CHAPTER THIRTY-SEVEN

I can't keep a silly grin off my face. I enjoyed the movie, but what I loved most about our date was how Dylan shared something with me that was important to him. The atmosphere at Art Hill was perfect. It gave us time to get to know each other—maybe more than we should have in a public place. I touch my lips, remembering that first kiss.

And the second when he dropped me off at home, a goodnight kiss that lingered on my lips as I snuggled into my pillow and dreamed of our next date. He may not have put all my worries to rest, but he definitely left me with pleasant dreams.

I'm anxious to start drafting my first article for the *Parkwood Press*, but I'm also due for a visit with Grandma Elaine, so Mom and Dad drop me off Saturday morning. Grandma has the TV on when I come in, and this is more how I remember Grandma's house. It's *Wheel of Fortune*. I glance at the clock on the wall. "Since when do they show *Wheel of Fortune* at eleven thirty in the morning?"

Grandma tries to rise from her chair, the tension visible on her face as her arm muscles strain with the effort.

I rush forward and kiss her cheek. "Don't get up."

She relaxes against the seat. "My legs just don't work the way they used to."

I noticed. I mean, she uses a walker. But still. Grandma used to walk five miles every morning, and now it takes her thirty seconds just to stand up.

"Game Show Network," she says.

"What?"

"Game shows all day long. That's why *Wheel of Fortune*'s on."

I smirk. "Sounds like cheating. Haven't you already seen, like, every episode?"

Grandma reaches for a crochet project on the end table beside her and begins weaving the needle in and out. She looks at me over the top of her glasses. "You think I have a photographic memory?"

"It doesn't seem to be suffering too much."

She smiles and taps her temple with the pointer finger of the hand not holding the crochet needle. "I'm sharp enough."

Thank goodness for that. As much as I hate seeing her diminished physical state, if I had to choose, I'd definitely prefer alert and all-there Grandma over spry Grandma. I wonder if she feels the same, but it doesn't seem like an appropriate question to ask.

"Can we switch to the news at noon, though? 'Cause Agent Klein and Captain McCoy are holding the press conference about our test results."

Grandma crochets several stitches, as if she's unsure. "I suppose."

Crocheting is silent work, so for a few moments the only sound is the background of the wheel spinning, contestants calling out consonants and buying vowels, and dings as Vanna White reveals letters. I wonder how much plastic surgery Pat Sajak and

Vanna White have had to still look basically the same after twenty-five years, unless this is a really old episode. I'm trying to figure out the solution to a food and beverage puzzle when Grandma speaks again.

"Tell me what's new in your life."

Based on the teasing glint in her eye, I'm sure Mom told her about Dylan, but it's fun to make her wait for the information she really wants. "Well. I have an appointment with the school counselor Monday to talk about college."

"And?" Grandma sets her crocheting down and focuses her entire attention on me.

"There are a lot of options out there. I don't think I want to go to Columbia anymore."

She smiles gently. "Because of your grandparents?"

"Partly. It's not the same without them there, but I'm also just not sure I could do that flight to New York again."

Grandma nods. "That's understandable."

"And then there's you and my parents, not to mention Bradley and his family."

Grandma Elaine is in her nineties. I have so little time left with her. My parents are in their sixties and showing it. Bradley doesn't need me, but I'd like to get to know my adult brother, as well as Kelly, and to be around for Kira and Eli.

"Those are some big considerations," she says, and I know she gets it. "Do you still want to write for the *New York Times?*"

I sniff. "It might be the only paper left by the time I finish college."

"Don't give up hope, Jenny. You never know when your hand might come up all aces and kings."

Sure this is another bridge reference, I just nod.

Grandma raises an eyebrow. "Anything else you want to tell me about?"

So much for distracting her. I shake my head. "I went on a date with Dylan last night."

"You like him."

I can't hide my grin. "I do, Grandma. Is it too weird?"

Her own smile isn't judgmental or hesitant. "Carol says he's a nice boy."

"He is . . ." I glance at the clock. "Hey, it's twelve oh five. Time for the news!"

Grandma tilts her head. "Hmm."

"Grandma! I really want to see the statement." And avoid discussing Dylan with Grandma. Forever. I'm glad it's dim in the apartment because I'm sure my cheeks are bright red. It's like everyone's on a mission to embarrass me.

"If that's more important to you, dear."

Grandma changes the channel. It's a weather report, which is pretty pointless at this time of year (it's hovering in the nineties and so humid you shouldn't bother styling your hair in any way), followed by a report about a house fire downtown and a police chase. Finally it switches to the airport. Agent Klein stands at a podium in another black pantsuit, Captain McCoy off to the side in his pilot uniform. Microphones from all the major news stations are attached to the podium, including from national outlets like CNN and MSNBC. Grandma and I both lean toward the TV.

"Thank you for coming today," Agent Klein says. "Our team

of medical professionals and scientists have analyzed the results of all seventy-two passengers and crew from Flight 237."

I pull out my phone and open a text message to Art: Did you know they were testing all 72?

Art: They can't rule out a hoax without including every single person on the plane, Einstein.

Me:

I don't know why I assumed it was just the people in St. Louis, but it makes sense—

"Look at you on your phone," Grandma says. "Just like Brad when he comes over!"

I look up and notice Grandma has paused the news. "Sorry, Grandma."

"It's okay. Are you ready for me to start this up again?"

"Sure." But I hold on to the phone.

She hits Play, and Agent Klein begins speaking again.

"We appreciate their cooperation. After CAT scans, MRIs, DNA comparisons with family members, blood tests to determine their ages, and other proprietary tests—"

Me: Proprietary tests? What does that mean?

"—we've determined the passengers and crew of Flight 237 are the same seventy-two people who boarded the plane on August 2, 1995. There is no evidence their bodies underwent any biological manipulations or engineering."

Art: Things they did with our blood and DNA that you *don't* want to know about.

"Regarding the plane, we're also satisfied that it was not tampered with in any way. However, in order to put all public questions to rest, we will allow outside access to an independent testing company."

Me: Maybe I do.

"We continue to search for answers regarding why Flight 237 leaped forward in time, but we've concluded those answers do not lie with the plane itself or the people who were on it."

Art: Learn to live with disappointment.

Me: Talk to the hand.

Art: 😆

"At this time, Captain Frank McCoy would like to speak on behalf of the crew and passengers of Flight 237."

Captain McCoy nods at Agent Klein and moves into position. "Thank you," he says. "As Agent Klein stated, I speak for the crew and passengers of Mid-States Airways Flight 237. We understand that the world wants answers, that some of you are scared or concerned about our presence in this century. We're scared and concerned too, and we're just as baffled by what happened on August second. We all boarded a plane, followed our flight plan, and somewhere over St. Louis airspace, our plane jumped ahead twenty-five years. We did not encounter any turbulence, only a flicker of lights."

Me: I forgot about the lights!

"We did not notice anything out of the ordinary on our equipment. No flux capacitor next to the altitude indicator." Captain McCoy smiles, and Grandma and I chuckle along with the reporters at the *Back to the Future* reference. It's nice to be in on a joke again.

Art: Frank's been watching more than the Syfy channel . . .

"The FBI won't release our private information, but many of

my fellow crew and passengers have agreed to make their medical results public to further reassure you. Because we have nothing to hide."

Art: Except Walter . . .

Me: Good point. What do you think he did with those results he took?

Captain McCoy spreads his arms wide, then lets them fall and leans toward the microphones. "But those who don't? It's because they're hurting. They've lost loved ones, had their lives turned upside down, and are just trying to figure out where they fit into this new world we landed in."

Art: Probably shredded them.

Me: Made a bonfire.

Art: Ritual sacrifice to the cloud gods who dumped us here.

Okay, that one's just bizarre.

"So please don't harass them. I understand you're curious and you want to know what it's like adapting to life in a new century, but we appreciate you giving us time. I'll take a few questions now."

He points toward a reporter, who asks, "PATROL has been receiving tips on its website. One suggests the plane was stored and preserved on a property in rural Kansas for the past twenty-five years. What's your response?"

Art: Hilarious!

Me: Ridiculous!

"I just told you I was flying that plane without interruption. Unless this person has an explanation for how my memory could be altered—and the memories of every person on that plane—to believe that I was on a continuous flight from New York to

St. Louis . . ." Captain McCoy shakes his head. "Furthermore, I reject the notion that you could 'preserve'"—he makes air quotes—"a plane for twenty-five years without it showing any rust or wear and send it up into the air at the exact spot where it disappeared. That's some magic trick. But if the person with the tip can produce some sort of evidence . . ."

Me: Nailed it!

"Next question?" he says, signaling to another reporter.

"Will you fly again?"

Art: Yep!

Me: Really?

Captain McCoy sighs. "Well, MSA doesn't exist anymore. But I'm looking into what's changed and what I need to do to get back in the air. I love flying. So it's not out of the question."

"Brave man," Grandma says.

"Yeah," I say, thinking about Art too. Captain McCoy's determination to return to work reminds me about some news he called me with this morning.

Me: By the way, good news! Agent Klein cleared my articles for the school paper.

Art: 👍

Captain McCoy calls for another question.

"We understand you've formed a support group. What can you tell us about how people are doing? Like the Springs or Jenny Waters?"

The TV clicks off abruptly.

I whirl on Grandma. "Why'd you do that?"

"It's not good to watch things about yourself in the media."

My phone buzzes with another message from Art, but I focus

on Grandma. She starts crocheting again, avoiding my eyes. I'm tempted to go over there and stick my face in hers so she can't escape my death stare. I thought we were done with this hiding-the-news-from-Jenny crap.

"I can just find it online later. I know better now." Although I'm not sure I will. I doubt Captain McCoy said anything other than "Buzz off," except in a nice way.

"Just because you can, doesn't mean you should," Grandma says.

"Why are you so stubborn?" I ask.

Grandma laughs. "It's what keeps me alive. I'm too stubborn to die yet."

I stiffen. "Don't say things like that."

"Jenny, if you can't joke about death when you're my age, you might as well give up."

"But you're not supposed to be this age," I whisper.

"Let's go for a walk." Grandma sets her yarn aside and begins pushing herself up toward her walker.

I jump to my feet. "No, Grandma! It's okay."

She stares at me sternly. "I may not be power walking every morning, but I still need my exercise. So you get the door. I'll introduce you to some of my neighbors."

Grandma's right. I can't keep dwelling on how old she is. Instead I should focus on where we are now.

That press conference was a step in the right direction. Captain McCoy handled it like a pro. PATROL has to back off now that our test results are out in the open.

CHAPTER THIRTY-EIGHT

Fueled by positive energy from Captain McCoy's press conference, later that afternoon I write my first article for the *Parkwood Press*, and I think it's pretty good. Admittedly, the first draft, written in my notebook, is peppered with hearts in the margins, but once I transcribe it into the new laptop Mom and Dad got me, I keep it serious (although I might continue to emojify internally).

My article is a firsthand account from the plane. I headline it "They Don't Have Our Squawk." It won't make any sense to readers at first, and that's why I expect it to catch their attention. It's a good thing I wrote everything down right away that day, but I'm also loving Google for fact verification; it really is so much easier than the library. (I did cave and watch the rest of the press conference. Art's last text was about Captain McCoy having my back, and he did, refusing to answer any questions about me or the Springs.)

My door opens, and I just register the small bundle of energy before she jumps on my bed and tackles me. "Auntie Jenny!"

I barely rescue my laptop from Kira's attack. "Hey. I didn't know you guys were coming over."

She hangs on my neck. "Daddy told Mama he got in trouble for being a bad brother."

"Oh." I curl my lips in, trying not to laugh. Kira really does hear everything, although Bradley already earned a ton of points back sitting at the hospital with me. "Well, I'm glad you're here."

Except I'm not so glad Bradley's here once Mom and Dad tell him about my date with Dylan, as he teases me mercilessly. It's so much more embarrassing than twenty-five years ago, maybe because back then Bradley hadn't dated himself and didn't understand it. Now he knows exactly what's involved, and he's relentless, even when Kelly orders him to stop in a voice she usually reserves for the kids. News flash, Bradley: if I smack you upside the head now, Mom and Dad probably won't even blink. But the evening is still fun, catching up with my niece and nephew and getting to know Kelly now that the awkwardness of returning from the dead has passed. I grab the photo albums in the living room, and we spend an hour paging through them; then Dad pulls out his laptop and streams even more photos and videos on the TV. This is my family now, and it feels like things are finally falling into place.

Before bed I receive a text from Art: PATROL is suspiciously silent . . .

He's right. They haven't responded at all to the press conference, and that is strange, but I refuse to let them ruin my good mood, so my response is brief: Let's take the win for today.

On Sunday, we attend church, and the pastor preaches on Jesus raising Lazarus from the dead. Mom keeps patting my hand, like *I* returned from the dead. I resist the urge to lean over and remind her I was alive all along. In the afternoon I start reading *The Hunger Games*, so of course I have to text Dylan about it.

Me: I'm getting a totally different view of Gale and Peeta in the book.

Dylan: Yeah. The casting seemed odd at first but grew on me. BTW, sorry I didn't call yesterday. Had to work.

Huh. What with Grandma and the press conference and everything else, I didn't stress about the fact he didn't call me, even though he was on my mind much of the day. I have to go look up "BTW." Oh. But also, he has a job?

Me: Where do you work?

Dylan: Gap. At West County Mall.

I nearly choke. I'm sure my eyes are bulging, so I'm super relieved he can't see me right now. Although, it's also nice to know at least one mall I remember survived.

Me: You work at the Gap? You? Of the least uniform T-shirts ever?

Dylan: Yep.

I search for an emoji with an empty speech bubble. Whatever. Can't find it.

Me: Speechless.

We continue texting off and on throughout the day as I read. Like the other night, I fall asleep texting. When I wake up Monday morning, my phone is dead. Oh, well. Dylan offered to pick me up for school, but I still don't want anything to do with JoJo. I realize I can't avoid her forever, but I can certainly do my best for as long as possible. Besides, there's no reason for her to burst my happiness bubble first thing on a Monday morning.

But as soon as I hop out of Mom's car, it's evident I don't need JoJo to bother me. Drew, who's ignored me since I shot down his kegger invitation, is lounging on a bench in the circular drive.

I try to skirt past him, but he uncurls himself and moves into step beside me.

"Hey, Jenny." His gaze sweeps over me like I'm wearing a string bikini instead of a round-necked shirt that covers my collarbone and shorts that didn't even cause my dad to blink.

"Drew." I speed up, pretending I don't notice his leer. I'm sure he's just trying to rattle me again.

Lana and another girl from my calculus class are standing by the doors, huddled over a phone. When I approach, they step away and giggle. As I walk inside, I'm sure I hear them say Dylan's name, and I draw up short, but when I turn, they've skittered off.

My shoulders tense. Caleb walks by. "Hi, Jenny." He winks. "Fun weekend, huh?" He waves his phone at me.

"What are you talking about?" I ask, but he keeps walking, acting like he didn't hear me.

I shake it off, moving farther into the atrium.

"Jenny!"

Chloe and Madison rush toward me, their expressions shell-shocked like a nuclear warhead's approaching the school.

"What's going on?" I clutch my backpack straps.

"I've been texting you all morning!" Chloe says.

I shift, noticing that everyone coming in the doors is watching me. Again. It's like we've hit rewind on last week. "My phone's dead."

Chloe sighs. "You've got to charge it!"

"I don't need a technology lesson," I whisper-shout. "I need you to tell me why Drew's feeling me up with his eyes."

She grimaces and looks to Madison.

"Just tell her," Madison says. "It was in the texts anyway."

Helpful.

Chloe inhales like she's about to tell me my grandparents died. Good news, Chloe. Already handled.

"There's a picture online of you kissing Dylan, and it went viral," she blurts.

I shake my head, sure she's wrong.

"There's a story too," she adds. "The headline says, 'Jenny Waters Finally Gets Her Kiss! Finds Romance with Boyfriend's Lookalike Son.'"

CHAPTER THIRTY-NINE

I step back like Chloe's slapped me.

And at that moment, over her shoulder, I spy Dylan racing through the school's front doors.

"Jenny!" he bellows from the opposite side of the atrium, and for a split second everything around us stops, even the dust in the air. I note at least twenty phones out, ready to document whatever goes down.

Then everything speeds up, and I make a quick decision. I turn to Chloe. "Do you have a car?"

She does a double take. "Madison does."

I focus on Madison. "Will you drive me somewhere?"

"But . . . school . . ." The panic on my face must overcome her sense of academic responsibility. Madison grips my wrist, her bracelets jangling as she tugs me in the opposite direction of Dylan. "Let's go."

"Jenny!" Dylan calls again behind us, but when I twist to see if he's catching up, he's not. There are too many people in the way, holding up phones and asking him questions.

I haven't even processed this yet, and he's making it so much worse. I don't know who took that picture at Art Hill, but Dylan should know better. He even mentioned it on our date, how social media takes the story away from you. He'll probably try to play it off like it's no big deal, but a news story is so much bigger than a few girls posting pictures of him riding his bike in his boxers.

I thought I could control the story. I was so naive. I don't know what this article says—or who wrote it—but I know it's not what I want out in the world. It's ruined whatever Dylan and I might have had.

Chloe skips to keep up with me and Madison. "Jenny Waters, ditching school. Who'd've thought?"

"I just can't talk to him." Tears spill out. I swipe them away.

Chloe holds open the door beside the theater.

"I knew this wouldn't work." I rush through the door. "He knows what I've been through. He never should've kissed me in public."

Madison checks for teachers before dashing across the street to the parking lot. "Um, not to be obnoxious, but it didn't look like you were exactly pushing him away."

I tug my hair over my cheeks. I hate that she's right. I knew we were surrounded by people. Thousands of people. I let him kiss me. More than that, I encouraged him to kiss me.

We climb into Madison's car, and she backs out of the parking space, scanning the area like she's afraid the principal's going to jump on her hood and start pounding on the windshield. But we leave the grounds without anyone stopping us, probably because school hasn't started yet; people are still pulling in, trying to make it before the late bell.

Madison glances at me in the rearview mirror. "Where to?"

I can't go home. Unlike everyone else's parents, who are at work, Mom and Dad are retired and thus sitting in their chairs this very moment. At least that's what I assume they do all day. I don't really know. Soon they'll be getting a call from the school. Again.

"Steak 'n Shake?" It's open twenty-four hours.

Chloe nods. "Sounds good to me."

I lean between the seats. "Can I see the story?"

Chloe wrinkles her nose. "You're not gonna like it."

I hold out my hand. "It can't get any worse than my best friend writing about that bird sex conversation."

Madison snorts. "Have you *been* on social media?"

"I mean, Dylan"—I stumble over his name—"showed me all the different sites. I have profiles, but I'm only friends with family members. I haven't really gone on any of them since I set them up."

"Is that why you haven't accepted my follow requests?" Chloe asks.

Honestly, I haven't paid any attention to all those notifications. It's all so overwhelming. "Sorry."

Chloe waves a hand. "The thing is"—she shares a loaded glance with Madison—"people can be really vicious, and this story has gone viral. Like, it's been shared with scientists studying seals in Antarctica, and people are making all sorts of comments, so it's not just the story itself."

A knot forms in my stomach. I was so smug, thinking I understood how media worked in this century, but I don't. I hold my hand forward. "I still want to see it."

Chloe sighs. "Okay." She taps on her phone. "Here's what started it."

The picture catches my attention first, and I gasp. It fills the phone screen, a side view of Dylan hovering over me on the blanket, his arm wrapped around me but my face fully visible. Our lips are locked together, my eyes closed, and yet it's clearly me and clearly him. My knee is hitched up so it looks like we're in a much more passionate embrace than we actually were. And the kid with the ice cream is standing in the background. I mean, Dylan wasn't actually lying on top of me. He was more leaning over me, but it looks like we're rolling around on the blanket, about to have sex with a kindergarten audience.

"Oh my gosh." If I'd fit, I'd crawl under the seats and hide until some other scandal replaced the Kiss Seen Round the World.

"Yeah," Chloe says, "whoever took that photo really worked for the most sordid angle."

Thank goodness I changed out of the dress, but— "My parents will see this!"

Chloe winces. "Oh. Yikes."

"And Angie and Steve."

Madison bites her lip. "Well, they'll probably give you a pass, considering . . ."

Like that's reassuring. I use my fingers to enlarge the photo—a trick I *have* mastered—but the telltale line under it is missing. "There's no photo credit."

"I noticed that too." Chloe nods. "The photographer must want to remain anonymous."

"We're here," Madison announces.

I look up, dazed. Chloe's phone goes dark as we exit the car. "I was wrong. This is worse than Angie's book. Because there's a *photo*."

I haven't even read the article itself. Or the comments Chloe warned me about.

We march inside and slide into a booth, Madison beside me and Chloe across from us. By the time the waitress asks for our order, I'm ready. "A chocolate milkshake."

She raises her eyebrows but writes it on the pad.

Chloe pats my hand. "I'll take strawberry."

"Cookies and cream," Madison says. "I've never had a milkshake at eight a.m., but I'm all for solidarity." She pumps her fist like we're at a pep rally.

Chloe motions at the phone I'm still holding. "You'd better read fast because any minute I'm sure my parents will be activating the app to find my phone and we'll be busted."

"They can track you with your phone?" Dylan didn't tell me about *that*.

Madison drums the table. "You can turn it off, but what's the point? They'd know."

My parents probably love that feature, considering they lost me for so long. No wonder they were so upset that day I went off to the library without it. Although it may complicate things when I forget to plug in the phone and it dies.

I hand the phone to Chloe to reactivate the screen and return to the story. Like she already warned me, the headline says, "Jenny Waters Finally Gets Her Kiss! Finds Romance with Boyfriend's Lookalike Son."

Jennifer Waters is no longer a kissing virgin—

"A kissing virgin? Seriously? Who wrote this?" I skim for the byline. "Greta Barren! I should've known."

Chloe leans across the table. "I think you pissed her off that night outside your meeting. And it probably doesn't help if Ashling's complaining about you too."

I exhale noisily and keep reading.

On Friday night, Waters enjoyed an evening out with none
other than the son of her former boyfriend, Steven Graham,
and best friend, Angela Russell Graham. The two were
spotted at Art Hill setting up a picnic and chatting while they
ate. They then walked hand in hand to the food trucks, where
they purchased cupcakes from vendor Lulu's Cupcakes.
Graham shared a bite of his turtle cupcake with Waters, who
audibly groaned in pleasure.

I shift on the red plastic seat. "Is she kidding? This isn't
journalism!"

"Are you at the cupcake part?" Madison bends over to try to
see what I'm reading.

"I didn't groan." Did I?

"Maybe you had a cupcakegasm and couldn't help yourself,"
Madison says.

"Either way, this is disturbingly detailed, like she was right
next to me the whole time." How did Greta get this information?
I was super focused on Dylan, but it's creepy I might've missed
her spying on us.

After lengthy discussion about favorite books, Graham
leaned in for a kiss, only to be rebuffed when Waters
hesitated. However, he turned the situation around with a
witty comment that had her rolling onto the blanket, and he

quickly took advantage of her prone position, swooping in to steal her long-awaited first kiss. (A kiss twenty-five years in the making!) She responded eagerly, returning his kiss for several moments. The kiss ended when a nearby father whistled, reminding the couple they had an audience of impressionable young children.

Now I do groan. "I can't believe this is a legitimate news site. 'Swooping in to steal her long-awaited first kiss'? I mean, as an editor, I wouldn't allow that, and we're a high school paper!"

The waitress brings our milkshakes, momentarily interrupting my tirade. She studies me so long I'm sure she's picturing me on a blanket with Dylan.

"Thanks," I say, pulling the drink toward me, and she finally leaves.

Chloe takes a long suck on her milkshake. "Maybe she has a secret dream to write romance novels. But also, the station probably just wants hits on its website."

The chocolate sours in my mouth. "What did I do to deserve this?"

"I guess . . ." Madison pushes her glass around the table. "You got on a plane?"

"Note to self: stay off planes." Not that I need that reminder.

"Darn!" Chloe adopts an exaggerated frown. "I really wanted to visit Paris someday."

"Then here's my advice." I point my straw at her. "Take a boat."

"Ha ha." Chloe resumes drinking her shake.

"So what do the comments say?" I stir my whipped cream into the chocolate. "That I'm a slut?"

"Whoa!" Madison shakes her finger at me. "Now who's using nasty words?"

I shrug. I'm afraid they're using much nastier words.

Chloe screws up her face like she's gotten a brain freeze from the ice cream. "More along the kinky lines. What with dating Dylan's dad first."

I spread my hands. "Which is why I wanted to keep things to ourselves."

"PATROL says it's a 'travesty against the space–time continuum.'" Madison deepens her voice like she's mimicking a stuffy scientist.

I choke, even though a similar thought crossed my mind. Madison pounds on my back.

I swirl my straw in my shake, which isn't providing the solace I anticipated. "They're suspicious, don't you think? With Dr. Greaves's husband working for an insurance company? Also, Art discovered she cowrote a paper on time travel being possible, but they've spent all this time trying to prove we *didn't* time travel instead of trying to figure out how we did." The fact that Captain McCoy's press conference didn't put a stop to PATROL makes me even more curious about them. "The timing of this story is weird too. Why'd Greta Barren wait until today? Dylan and I went out Friday night."

"All of that is strange, although they aren't necessarily connected." Chloe frowns at the phone, as if Greta might pop out of the byline and explain her motives for sitting on a juicy story for two days. Her mouth opens slightly, and she looks up at me. "I could go undercover for you, infiltrate PATROL—"

The bell over the door jingles; I twist toward the entrance, praying it's a random customer popping in for breakfast.

A brown-skinned woman with round cheeks similar to Chloe's marches in, her footsteps so heavy I'm surprised the glasses stacked on the bar counter aren't shaking.

"Uh-oh," Madison murmurs.

Chloe straightens, pushes her empty milkshake glass to the center of the table, and folds her hands on the table edge. "Hi, Mom."

"*Hi*, Mom? You skip school to grab a milkshake, and that's all you have to say?"

Chloe smiles weakly. "Do you wanna give me a ride back?"

Wow. She's brave.

Chloe's mom whirls on us. "Madison, I told your dad I'd make sure you returned to school. Jenny"—her expression softens, and this doesn't bode well for me—"I got in touch with your parents too. They're on the way."

I gulp. "Thanks."

"We'll wait with you until they get here," she says as she slides into the booth.

Great. So much for planning a PATROL sting operation. I bet Art would have some interesting ideas for how Chloe could approach them. But I obviously have more immediate issues to deal with. We wait in silence. I take a long slurp of my milkshake and get brain freeze for real for my efforts.

CHAPTER FORTY

Mom and Dad are silent on the ride home, but I can tell they're disappointed. I'm just relieved they aren't asking me a million questions about Dylan and the kiss. I can't even wrap my mind around how huge this is. The kiss and the article and *everyone in the world who's seen it.* It's so much worse than Angie's book. I was starting to think the internet was a helpful tool, but it's a disguise. In reality, the internet is a game of telephone on steroids.

As soon as we pull into the garage, I hop out of the car and then rush inside, up the stairs to my room, and slam the door. A couple of minutes later, Mom knocks. "Jenny, we need to talk."

I bury my face in my comforter. "I don't want to talk about it."

She opens my door. "Not optional," she says firmly.

I was afraid of that.

She moves into my room and sits beside me, folding her hands in her lap. "That picture . . ."

I shoot to sitting. "It wasn't what it looked like. I swear! It was only a kiss. Whoever took it made it look so—"

Mom holds up her hand. "I believe you."

"You do?" I had a detailed explanation ready. I slump onto the bed. "Why are so many people out to get me in this century? Why do I have so many *enemies*?"

She strokes my cheek. "When did you become so melodramatic?"

"Um, you saw that picture, right? Every time I think things can't get worse, they do. I hate it here!"

Mom crawls onto the bed and hugs me. "Sometimes I do too, Jenny. It's not what any of us planned for. But it's where we are."

She sounds like Grandma, which makes sense, I guess. Not that it makes me feel any better.

"And perhaps there are some people who seek to exploit you, but you also have friends here. Like those girls at Steak 'n Shake. And your group. And Dylan."

I grunt.

"Jenny." She tips my chin up with her knuckle. "You're not alone."

I want to believe her. The problem is, she tells me I'm not alone, but I stare at the deep lines around her eyes and the gray roots along her scalp, and I'm reminded that I'm so much closer to being completely without my parents than I should be. I don't want to think this way, to focus on what I have to lose instead of what I have now, but it's hard to be a half-full girl when this world keeps emptying out my glass.

But Mom endured twenty-five years of sorrow. To her, I'm a miracle—like Lazarus. Maybe that's why she can look at this viral news story and imagine it's a minor bump. It probably is to her. So I must put on a brave face. "I know, Mom. But can I just have some time to process?"

She cups my cheek, her eyes full of love. "Of course, sweetheart." She kisses my forehead and heads for the door, where she pauses and turns back. "You might want to charge your phone."

Ha! Like I want anything to do with that evil device. "Sure."

She leaves, and I scan my room. Now what?

My notebook beckons me from my desk. I will record everything so I don't forget how I've been abused and so I have the true story down. And then I have some decisions to make about the people in my life.

Mom and Dad leave me alone for most of the day, except around twelve thirty when Mom brings me a grilled cheese and a Coke.

"Why don't I charge your phone for you?" Mom asks.

I set my notebook aside. "Why do you care so much about it?"

Mom hands me the food. "Because we can always get ahold of you that way."

I pop open the soda. "Are you tracking me like Chloe's mom?"

Mom shrugs helplessly. "Can you blame me?"

"I guess not. Although, you used to trust me."

She purses her lips. "You used to stay where you said you'd be."

Ouch. Better not go there. "I'm not sure it would've worked on the plane."

I wonder what the app would have said during those twenty-five years. If the same thing happened today, would we know what had happened to us instead of sitting here with a million unanswered questions? Maybe the people left behind would be able to see seventy-two phone signals, levitating at the latitude and longitude where the FBI calculates we jumped from 1995 to today. Or maybe the conspiracy theorists are right and aliens abducted and returned us. Maybe with an app, scientists here on Earth could have followed the signal to find our plane, with our bodies hibernating in a UFO cleverly cloaked behind the moon. I don't buy into that theory, but I do wish Siri had an answer to the question, "How did our plane jump ahead twenty-five years?" I guess there isn't quite an app for everything.

"I suppose you're right," Mom says. "The plane tracking never showed anything, but I still feel safer knowing where you are."

I point my sandwich at her. "You're lucky I'm not one of those teenagers who sneaks off in the middle of the night. I'm sure there are ways around that app. But the phone's on my nightstand. I didn't take it this morning since it was dead."

Mom walks over and retrieves it. "I'll take care of it."

"No rush," I say around a bite of cheesy goodness.

Mom tucks the phone in her pocket. "I guess your dad and I won't be using the removal of phone privileges as a punishment."

I laugh. "Probably not."

Once I finish my lunch, I return to my writing. This one will *not* be transcribed onto my laptop.

An hour later, there's another knock on my door. I'm about to tell Mom I'm busy and ask if we can just talk about it all later when Angie comes in.

I groan. "Oh, great. Just who I wanted to see."

"I'm sure." Angie closes the door behind her. "So. You and Dylan."

I cross my arms. "I cannot have this conversation with you."

She moves closer and perches on the edge of the bed. "I suppose you can't, but I convinced him to stay home and let me talk to you first. Because I feel like a lot of this is my fault."

Ding, ding, ding! Give the lady a prize!

"If it weren't for the book, Greta Barren wouldn't be so

317

focused on you. But Dylan . . ." She swallows and presses a hand over her heart. "Dylan is the very best of me and Steve, and I'm sorry you're once again exposed in a way you'd rather not be. Won't you at least talk to him?"

Her stare is so direct I feel like I'm back in 1995 on the opposing mock trial team. "Cut it out, Angie. I'm not some witness you're cross-examining."

She laughs through her nose and breaks eye contact. "I know. It's just"—she rubs the spot between her eyebrows—"this is weird. Right? You're dating my son. Never in a million years could I have imagined such a thing."

I scoot to the wall. "I said I can't have this conversation."

"Well, that's too bad, Jenny Waters!" Her voice raises, and for a moment she sounds more like my Angie. "Because I had to pick up my son at school today for hitting another student."

Okay, we're back to adult Angie. "Dylan hit someone? Who?" I think back over my morning. "Was it Drew? Because I sure wanted to smack him."

Angie wrinkles her nose. "I've never liked that boy. But thankfully, no, because his parents are extremely litigious."

"As if you can't handle that."

Her answering smile is tinged with sadness. "It's nice you still see that part of me."

"So who was it then?" I can't imagine Dylan resorting to physical violence with anyone else.

She clucks her tongue against the top of her mouth. "See, that's why I'm here. As an emissary."

She never used to meander so much getting to the point. "For

Dylan?" I say. "Because I can't talk to him. It will never work between us."

The headline shouts in my head as if an on-air anchor is reading it: *Jenny Waters Finally Gets Her Kiss! Finds Romance with Boyfriend's Lookalike Son.* If we stay together, people will always harp on that connection. I thought it didn't matter, but it does—not just for me, but for Dylan too. How can he bear that comparison?

She sighs. "Partly. His only blame is trusting someone he should be able to. His sister."

"JoJo?" I'm not sure what she has to do with any of it, unless— "Did Dylan hit JoJo?"

Angie presses her lips together. "That's what the witness who ran to the principal reported. Although, Dylan said it was a shove, and JoJo grudgingly agreed, but the school has a no-tolerance policy, so Dylan was sent home. I took JoJo out of school too because I wanted to get to the bottom of this mess."

My mind races as I connect the dots. "Is it because JoJo told everyone at school about the book?"

Angie shakes her head. "JoJo didn't do that."

"Oh, yes, she did." I'm positive. That smug I-have-something-awful-in-store-for-you smile she sent me the morning I found out was proof enough for me.

"JoJo and I have our issues, but she'd never do something that harmful. However . . ." Angie's shoulders droop. "She is indirectly responsible for the article."

I figured that's where this was going. My hands curl into fists. "How?"

"Dylan told her about your date. He thought she'd be happy

for him. But she told him it was a . . . an unwise . . . idea to date you, and they got into an argument." She fidgets with a button on her shirt. I'm positive Angie substituted whatever word JoJo actually used to describe the thought of me and Dylan dating. "So after he left, she called Ashling Chan and told her where you'd be."

"That snake!"

Angie's head whips up, her eyes fierce behind her glasses. "I'm going to assume you're talking about Ashling Chan."

Her too. But JoJo is the worst sort of dirt-slithering reptile, and I won't apologize for saying it.

Angie purses her lips but doesn't press me for clarification. "It seems JoJo thought Ashling would use the information in the *Parkwood Press*, which is obviously not much better, but—"

"Of course it's not better! That's *my* paper!"

It explains so much, why there wasn't a photo credit, even the language in the story. If Angie's right about JoJo not being the one to spill about the book, Ashling's the next logical choice. She even tipped me off, telling me to Google myself. I picture her and the others huddled around the laptop that first day in convergence journalism, probably researching *me*. I'm such an idiot. Ashling's the one who told me about the book. Probably couldn't stand holding it in any longer. And Greta Barren is Ashling's godmother, so that also explains how she'd get her to hold off on running the story until Monday morning, when it would cause the most drama at school. I definitely didn't handle that well, running off. I'll have to explain to Mrs. Vega.

It doesn't matter concerning the Grahams, though. JoJo still told Ashling about my date with Dylan, and it's all ruined.

"You know what, Angie? You can't fix this for JoJo or Dylan.

I don't want anything to do with your family." I scramble off the bed and point at the door. "I want you to leave, and I never want to see you again."

Angie stands slowly. "You don't mean that. You're just upset."

"Wrong on the first point." I hold up my pointer finger, then my middle. "Right on the second. Which doesn't preclude me being serious about the first."

"Jenny, please don't throw away years of friendship because of a"—she gulps—"jealous girl's mistake. She's sorry now that she's seen the damage. Dylan is a wreck. And I still love you, no matter how different things are."

Tears clog my throat, but I refuse to let them out. Angie keeps stubbornly clinging to this ideal of us the way we used to be, but we're not those same two girls anymore. She's an adult; she's left the girl I loved behind. I'm not the same either, not after everything I've been through in this new century. "News flash, Angie: we can't go back. Don't you get that? We used to be the same. We had goals. But you gave yours up. You're a mom, and even now you're standing here talking about your kids as much as about us. We're not the same anymore."

I know I can't take back these words, but they feel true. Flight 237 robbed me of so much more than a change in century. My best friend passed me by, and she might be standing right in front of me, but she's not my best friend anymore. She can't be. She had to grow up.

Angie doesn't brush away the tears that flow down her cheeks. "I'm sorry, Jenny." She moves past me to the door, raises her hand and then drops it. "You're right. I can't be who you need me to be anymore, but Dylan's his own person. I realize he's connected to me and JoJo, but has he given you any other reason to push him away?"

Those are pretty strong reasons. Just because she says JoJo's sorry doesn't mean she won't go around chronicling our relationship for the world, and I can't deal with that. I can't imagine why Dylan would want to either.

I stare at the wall. "Goodbye, Angie."

She exhales. *"A bientôt,* Jenny."

She walks away before I can respond, but I know what she's doing, giving me the French version of "see you soon" instead. It's another reminder of when we were teenagers *together,* but also a sneaky way to avoid saying goodbye herself.

Mom's standing in the hallway, her mouth open. I hold up a hand. "Not today."

"All right," she says evenly.

"Where's my phone?" I ask.

Mom brightens like I've offered to clean the bathroom. Probably because asking for my phone demonstrates I'm a normal twenty-first-century teenager. "In the kitchen."

I retrieve the phone and return to my room. I dread looking at it, but I at least want to see if Chloe or Madison checked in.

As soon as I open my messages, I regret it. There are texts from people I don't even know. How did they get my number?

If you need a partner for your next sexy photo shoot, I volunteer as tribute.

Ew!!!

You should be ashamed, corrupting that boy after dating his father. Go back to 1995!

If only that were an option . . .

Then there are the people I *do* know.

Hey, girl, call me and I'll make you groan more than a cupcake. Dylan's got nothing on me. Drew

It's followed by some sort of obscene emoji that shouldn't exist. Delete, delete, delete.

There are texts from Chloe this morning, trying to warn me, with a link to the article. DON'T READ THE COMMENTS, it says. There aren't any after that. I wonder if her mom confiscated her phone after she ditched school with me.

Art texted me too: Need me to open a can of whoop-ass on Greta Barren?

And then there are the texts from Dylan.

Early this morning: Call me!

There's a picture out there of us.

I don't know how they got it.

Still before school: Jenny, please call me!!

While I was on my way to school: Where are you?

Are you ok?

After I left with Chloe and Madison: Why did you run away?

And on and on. I scroll down to the last one, not even bothering to read it. I have to push him away completely, because there's a whole world out there judging me, and dating Dylan in particular is the worst sort of mistake. It will only hurt both of us in the end. It's better to cut things off now, before we get in any further.

Me: I can't be with you. It was a mistake to give you my first kiss. Please don't text me again.

I realize there's a way to make sure he can't, a trick he taught me that day at his house. I block him from my contacts. I feel a sharp pain in my heart when I do it, but it's necessary. For both our sakes.

There are also notifications on my few social media accounts. I can't bear to read those. In fact, I never want to see this phone again. It's just another symbol of this horrible century. I power it down and stuff it under my mattress. Mom and Dad will just have to trust me when I go out, like they used to. I'm done with anything that spreads gossip about my life.

CHAPTER FORTY-ONE

Shockingly, Mom and Dad allow me to drive myself to the support group. I rub my forehead as I turn into the parking lot, thankful I made it without having to navigate a work zone or getting pulled over for something random, like a taillight going out mid-drive.

Mrs. Spring sidles up to me as I push the button to lock the car with a *beep.* "Jenny, honey, walk with me."

Her eyes are full of an emotion with which I've become all too familiar—pity. Because I'm now the most pitiful girl in the world, despite the fact there are many more deserving people. Like starving children in Africa. Or even children closer to home, stuck in an endless loop of foster care. Yet everyone continues to focus their pity on me.

"You saw that awful picture." If she hadn't grabbed hold of my arm, I'd turn away and hide my face. Mrs. Spring seeing that photo is almost worse than my parents—or Grandma. I hadn't even thought about Grandma, but surely she saw it too. I groan. The ramifications just keep coming, like I'm holed up in a shelter and the world is battering at me with a huge log like the townspeople in *Beauty and the Beast* trying to storm the castle.

"At least it wasn't a video," Mr. Spring says.

Ohmygosh, I hadn't even considered a video, despite the fact

Greta is a broadcast journalist. I laugh helplessly. I guess there's one reason to be thankful Ashling probably wrote the story herself instead of passing the tip on to Greta. "Thanks for the perspective, Mr. Spring."

So I walk into the meeting with the Springs flanking me, and despite my thoroughly craptastic day, I feel better. That's what this group is about, supporting one another through the ups and downs of being thrust into an unknown century. I square my shoulders. Ashling and Greta Barren may have stolen my story, but that doesn't mean I can't move forward with my plans and ensure it doesn't happen to anyone else.

It's business as usual when we arrive—the refreshment table, a circle of chairs, people chatting in small groups, some already seated. Art coasts in right before Captain McCoy calls the meeting to order and casts me an uncharacteristically serious look before sitting on the other side of Mr. Spring.

Captain McCoy immediately turns to me. "Jenny, I'm just going to start off by saying we all saw the news, and we're so sorry that happened. Greta Barren is a menace, and you don't deserve that."

Mrs. Spring and Valerie reach for my hands. I swallow the last bite of brownie; it's hard around the lump in my throat, and I don't even try to stop the tears that streak down my cheeks. "Thank you. I—I don't know what I would do without you guys. I'm so tired of this century. There's no privacy. I couldn't even go on a date without someone taking a photo and turning it into something . . . something disgusting." I swallow. "And what's worse is that I used to love the news. But if this is what news is now, I just . . . I don't know if I want to do it anymore."

Valerie squeezes my hand. "That's exactly why you should. There are still a lot of good reporters out there, and you can be one of them. The world needs you."

I want to wipe my eyes, but I don't want to let go of her or Mrs. Spring. Valerie seems to understand, as she reaches for a tissue with her other hand and gently wipes my cheeks. Must be her teacher training.

I hear her, but how can I make a difference? There are so many reporters out there like Greta, publishing people's private business. It's one thing if they're doing something unsavory or illegal that the public has a right to know, but the world has no right to my love life. Dylan and I weren't hurting anyone by going on a date. I feel a sudden affinity with pop stars plagued by paparazzi. That's not the sort of journalist I'd ever want to be, harassing people who want to be left alone.

On the other hand, there are stories I want to tell. Stories like ours. But I'm just not sure I have it in me anymore. If I can figure my way through everything that's new in the world to survive here. Every time I think I understand how media works now, I get broadsided all over again with another you're-clueless reminder.

"I say we egg her house." Art pumps a fist in the air.

I choke on a laugh. "How old are you anyway?"

He shrugs. "According to my license I'm forty-five. But if you mean how many years have I lived, I turned twenty last week."

"Huh." I cock my head. "Because right then, you sounded about twelve."

Everyone laughs, breaking the tension.

"Although I appreciate the support, I don't think retaliating— at least with eggs—will help." My luck, Greta Barren has cameras set up around her house, and there'll be a whole new story: *Jenny Waters Explores Juvenile Delinquent Tendencies.*

"Did you start without me?"

There's a general squeak of chairs as we turn at Walter's question, shocked to find he's returned at all. But more surprising, he's holding the briefcase he ran off with in the middle of our last meeting and wearing a suit like he's headed to a board meeting instead of our support group.

"Walter!" Captain McCoy stands.

"I brought back your briefcase." Walter moves into the middle of the circle and drops the case at Captain McCoy's feet, ignoring everyone's stunned stares.

"Why did you run out last week?" Mrs. Spring is the only one who appears concerned instead of ready to pounce on him.

Walter stands there calmly, his hands hanging at his sides. He always has been rather quiet, and I suddenly wonder if that makes him dangerous. He hasn't leaked our stories—that I know of—but he's been sitting here listening all along, and he could. "Why are you guys all staring at me?"

Captain McCoy steps forward. "Walter, would you please explain why you ran off with our"—he gestures at the briefcase—"private information, refused to answer my calls for days, and then walked in here like you're about to give a presentation?"

Captain McCoy's mention of our private information brings up another question: Did *Walter* tip Greta Barren off to the location of our other meeting?

Walter lifts his chin. "Because I am."

At first I'm not sure which question he's answering. Wait. He's going to give us a presentation? With what? Now that he gave back the briefcase, his hands are empty. He didn't bring in a projector or anything.

"About what?" I ask.

Walter spins in a slow circle. "Why don't you all relax, and I'll explain everything?"

"Everything?" Art mutters as he sits back. "Have you discovered the secrets of the universe? Why we're here?"

"Yes!" Walter's not facing me when he says this, but I can tell from the excited tone of his voice that he's jumped on some sort of crazy bandwagon.

"What does that mean, Walter?" Mrs. Spring asks calmly, and since she's sitting beside me, he swings toward us.

Oh, wow. Definitely drunk on something, but I don't think it's alcohol. His eyes are feverish. He tugs on his tie. "You've been ignoring the truth all this time, about how we got here, how we jumped ahead twenty-five years. Ignoring the people who have answers." He pauses, sweeps around in a circle again, studying each of us with his glistening eyes, and before the words come out of his mouth, I already know what he's about to say. "PATROL. People Assuring Time Relativity, Order, and Legitimacy. They're the ones who understand what's going on, and you won't listen."

"Are you kidding right now, Walter? You took our test results to PATROL?" Captain McCoy tilts his chin down and frowns, as if Walter is a small child who stole candy from the box in front of the cash register and he just can't believe it.

Walter moves toward him eagerly, an almost manic energy in his steps. "Yes, to give Dr. Greaves and Dr. Rozanov the proof they needed to redirect PATROL. The press conference was taking too long. But, Jenny"—he turns to me—"I'm sorry I used you as my excuse to run out. I didn't mean what I said the other day. I'm sure you'd never expose us like that snitch Greta Barren. I'm sorry for what she did to you."

So that was an act? If it was, how are we supposed to believe anything he says now? "It's funny you should mention that, considering this group you're supporting doesn't seem so sorry about Greta's story. Just this morning they commented that my relationship with Dylan Graham is a 'travesty against the space–time continuum.'"

Walter raises his hands in a universal call for peace. "That wasn't PATROL. It was someone claiming to be part of our organization. If you check, you'll see PATROL hasn't made any official statements since I brought them the test results. PATROL no longer believes our flight was a hoax, and we have an entirely new focus."

Hmm. Since I listened to Chloe and Madison's advice and didn't read the comments myself, I don't know what names were attached to them. Art did point out they didn't make a statement on Saturday after the press conference.

"*Our* organization?" Valerie leans forward with her elbows on her knees. "You've joined them?"

Walter nods vigorously. "I have. They believe us now, thanks to all the inspections on the plane, plus the physical tests we all went through. They agree the tests confirm we're the same people who got on MSA Flight 237 in 1995."

"So are you here to apologize on their behalf?" Art asks. "Because if so, it's a pretty weak effort so far."

Agreed. Walter's not the best emissary. But if he'd brought

actual PATROL people into the room, there would've been a revolt. Art might have produced those eggs he threatened.

"Absolutely. They wanted me to come." Walter glances toward the door.

"They regret how things went down," he continues. "I'm sure you heard Greta Barren's story about Dr. Greaves's husband, and yeah, he did want her to prove it was false so his insurance company could recoup some money."

I knew it! But it's also pretty stupid to admit. Again, not so bright to send Walter as their representative.

"But Dr. Greaves also didn't believe the science part of it," Walter continues. "Until now. You can trust them."

Valerie picks up her purse. "I'm going home."

"Me too," Miss Klaffke says.

"But PATROL wants to help us." Walter follows after them like an eager puppy. "They have a plan. It will change everything!"

Captain McCoy crosses his arms. "I don't need any more change, Walter. And whatever you've gotten into with these PATROL people, I think you'd be better off staying away from them too."

Mr. Spring grips Mrs. Spring's hand. "Agreed. We've had more change already than two people should in their twilight years."

I eye Valerie and Miss Klaffke sneaking away from the circle while Walter is focused on Captain McCoy and the Springs. I guess our meeting isn't happening, and I'd been looking forward to updates from everyone. As strange as it may be, these people are as much my friends as Chloe and Madison.

"We'll see you next week, honey." Mrs. Spring pats my arm as they leave.

"Come on!" Walter says. "They really want to help. If just one or two of you will go with me, you'll see!"

As there's a mass exodus for the doors, Art scoots over into the seat Mrs. Spring vacated. "Go with him? To the mothership? What do you think they've done to him? Brainwashing?"

I study Walter, who's staring at the exit, his shoulders slumped. He's been so lost since we landed. No family, no job. "I think they gave him a new purpose somehow. I want to find out what it is."

"What do you have in mind, Nancy Drew?"

I purse my lips. Not Nancy Drew. I sense Walter holds the key to the PATROL story. We already know Dr. Greaves and Dr. Rozanov believe in time travel. This whole thing about PATROL having a plan that will change everything—does it have something to do with that? Whatever it is, they've convinced Walter to join them despite the awful accusations they've made against us from nearly the moment we landed. "I'm thinking more Nellie Bly, pursuing my story whatever it takes."

Art shrugs. "Okay, Nellie. What's the plan?"

He doesn't even ask me who Nellie Bly is. She feigned insanity to infiltrate an asylum and expose its cruelties to effect change, then traveled around the world in seventy-two days, chronicling her journey in the *New York World*. Legendary!

I'm not quite ready to go all the way undercover, but I am prepared to commit to this story. Valerie said the world needs more reporters like me, and I can start by exposing PATROL. "We're going to find out what Walter's new friends are really up to."

Art nods. "I like it, ferreting out the true agenda of PATROL."

As Walter pushes through the door with a last dejected look at Captain McCoy, I grab my purse and stand. "Let's catch him before he leaves."

I wave goodbye at Captain McCoy. He turns. "Good night, Jenny."

I hope he doesn't come outside too quickly and cause Walter to bolt.

Art waves too and we leave the fellowship hall. I scan the parking lot. Walter's headed for the compact car parked beside mine. "Walter, wait up!"

He turns, and when he spots us trailing him, he stands up straighter. "Are you coming with me?"

There's so much hope in his voice I hate to crush it. I choose my response carefully. "I'd like to believe in PATROL, Walter."

The words taste like dirt in my mouth. I'm such an awful liar. He's going to see through me.

"Yeah, me too," Art says more convincingly. "But, we need more information before we just go off to meet these people. They haven't exactly done anything to make us trust them."

Walter steps forward, his palms out. "I understand where you're coming from. But you don't know them the way I do."

I glance at Art and shift closer to the streetlamp, leaning against the trunk of my car. "How *did* you get to know them, though?"

Walter shuffles along in my wake, moving into the light. Perfect. I can see his facial expressions now.

"Dr. Greaves is a really nice lady," he says earnestly. "It turns out we have the same favorite bar. She came in several nights in a row, and then one night she asked if she could sit with me."

Yeah, that's not suspicious. "Your favorite bar? By any chance was this bar around before we leaped forward? And mentioned in that *Where's Walter* book?"

"Sure, it's been around forever." Walter frowns. "Are you implying it *isn't* her favorite bar?"

Art raises an eyebrow at me, like, *How gullible is this guy?* I sort of agree, but I also think Walter suffers as much from extreme vulnerability as naiveté.

I motion for Art to keep his mouth shut and let me take the lead. "I don't know, Walter, but it seems like a big coincidence."

He scrunches his brows, taking a moment, then shakes his head. "So what if she did seek me out? I'm really grateful, because she's changed my whole perspective on everything."

I so want to record this conversation, but I also don't want Walter accusing me of sneaking stories like he did before.

"Are you all okay over there?"

Walter jumps and twists toward Captain McCoy, who has just exited the church.

"Yep. All good, Captain!" Art calls.

Captain McCoy stands there for a moment, considering us. *Go home, Captain McCoy!* A few tense moments later, he turns toward an older Mustang parked near the door. He pauses half inside the car and looks back at us. "You'd better get home soon, Jenny. It's a school night."

The underlying warning is clear, and the last thing I want is for him to call my parents out of misplaced concern. "We're just wrapping up!"

But, right. School.

Once Captain McCoy is safely inside his car, I sigh dramatically. "Unfortunately, Walter, Captain McCoy brings up a good point. I can't go anywhere with you tonight since I have school tomorrow."

Walter grips my wrist. "But tomorrow will be too late!"

I feel the first tingle of unease, the tiniest bit of fear that this is more than gullibility, that Walter might do something truly crazy. I glance toward the Mustang, but Captain McCoy isn't watching us anymore. He's leaning over, retrieving something from his glove box.

Art steps forward. "Hey, man, let her go."

But instead of releasing me, Walter tugs me roughly off-balance as he twists toward Art. "You have to come *tonight*. It's your only chance to erase everything."

"To do *what*?"

The extent of my incredulity is lost in the roar of Captain McCoy's Mustang. The sound startles Walter enough to drop my arm. I rub it as I scoot closer to Art and whisper, "Can you record this?" I'm past caring whether Walter thinks I'm like Greta Barren. I don't want to forget a word of this conversation, and it's not like I can whip out my notebook. Besides, Mrs. Vega just taught us our state follows the one-party consent rule for recording conversations, which means I can still use this tape even if I don't have Walter's permission. Art nods, making it two out of three consenting anyway.

Once Captain McCoy's taillights disappear, Walter turns back to us. "PATROL can take back everything. No best friend married to your boyfriend. No tell-all book about your life. No viral story about your first kiss." So Walter *has* been paying attention. "No friends who only care about their kids," he adds with a nod to Art. "What would you say to that?"

Wait, what? I realize Walter's still half watching Art, which means he can't start the phone recording. I step toward him so he'll focus on me, clasping my hands behind my back, although he doesn't *look* dangerous anymore. More . . . excited, with a side of indoctrinated fervor. "I'd say that sounds impossible. PATROL can't change the past, so the only other way they might be able to 'erase' those things is to screw with my brain, and I'm not entrusting my brain to a bunch of people who have been slandering me for weeks."

Walter fidgets with a button on his suit sleeve. "They're sorry about that."

I don't care if they're *sorry*. I care about what they're up to now and how it will further screw with my life. All of our lives. "Walter, *why* will tomorrow be too late?"

"I'm not actually supposed to tell you."

Art steps up beside me, signaling toward his pocket, I assume to confirm he's taping now. "I thought PATROL sent you here to get us."

"Not exactly. That was more my idea . . ." Walter's twisted the button so much the thread is about to snap.

"Then what exactly, Walter?" I say. "I don't have all night." I soften my voice to tone down my exasperation. "And it sounds like you don't either."

He rubs his neck. "No, I don't. And if you come with me, school won't matter anyway."

I blink. "Why? Has PATROL figured out how to unvanish

336

the years I missed? Like, *Snap, here are the degrees you already earned. No more high school needed!*"

"No, Jenny, even better." He leans closer, his eyes fevered again. "We can all go back to 1995, and you can live those years the way you were supposed to."

CHAPTER FORTY-TWO

"I . . . you . . . what?" I feel like I'm back in the airport conference room, when Mr. Fernandez first told us we'd jumped ahead. I couldn't process that information, and I can't fathom what Walter's saying now either.

I turn to Art for help. He looks equally astonished.

Walter nods so forcefully I'm afraid he'll snap a tendon in his neck. "That's what I've been trying to tell you. PATROL knows how to get us back home, where we belong."

"Back home," Art echoes, his voice a strange mixture of disbelief and awe.

Mostly disbelief, but that hint of awe lets me consider it.

Home.

1995.

What if PATROL *has* figured out a way to return? Could I really go back?

Do I . . . want to go back?

I know if Walter had approached me with the offer to leap back into my old life three weeks ago, I'd have signed up without a second thought.

Mom and Dad the appropriate ages. Angie, younger Angie,

always there to talk with for hours on end about anything from our favorite show to our biggest dreams. The Steve I knew, our sweet dates, and that feeling of anticipation that there might be more down the line. My grandparents all alive and well. The absolute certainty about my path in life. Even Bradley leaving stink bugs under my pillow and being a general pest.

Then there's now. An uncertain path forward for so many reasons. My parents, the same people they always have been, but older. Angie here, but our relationship all broken. Grandma Elaine, as quirky and wise as ever but with limited time left. Bradley all grown up, but with a wife and two adorable kids I'm already in love with.

And also, Dylan. Funny, earnest Dylan, who will talk to me for hours about books and knows when to be serious and when to tease me out of being too serious and makes my heart trip with his gentle kisses and considerate nature. A boy who wasn't even a possibility in 1995.

Then.

Now.

Then.

Now.

Now.

Now.

I choose now.

A lot of this new life sucks right now, but I find I don't want to erase it. I'm stronger for going through this, enriched by knowing the Springs and Valerie and Captain McCoy and Art. Information is so much easier to access versus twenty-five years ago, which has its negative points, for sure, but will really help in my future career. Kira and Eli are the best, and I wouldn't want to risk my presence in 1995 affecting Bradley meeting Kelly and them not being born. I especially can't imagine a world without Dylan, which means, I realize, that I believe Angie and Steve were meant to be together.

So, regardless of whether PATROL has found some way to go back, I'm gonna pass. I am finally ready to join the twenty-first century.

But Walter clearly isn't, and he's buying this back-to-the-past story PATROL is selling. He's obviously desperate. I need to find out more before they do something dangerous.

"Walter." I relax my expression, hoping I achieve a sense of wonder. "How? It just seems so impossible."

Art jerks in surprise. Based on his pressed lips, during those moments I was thinking through whether I'd want to go back, he was already formulating his arguments against PATROL.

"When I met Dr. Greaves, she explained she and Dr. Rozanov formed PATROL because the science didn't line up with their studies on the possibilities of time travel," Walter says. "At first, all they wanted was to make sure the right tests got performed, to figure out what actually happened."

I really wish he'd get to the how, but since he's backing up, I might as well get all the details for my story. "I thought you said her husband wanted her to check into it for his insurance company."

"Oh, that." Walter waves a hand. "Yes, he was pressuring her at first, but it turned out the statute of limitations on those insurance payouts is long past."

"Of course it is," Art mutters.

Ignoring him, Walter continues, "Once the politicians and others joined PATROL, things got out of control, and she got swept up in the media side of it. She had really thought we were a hoax, but when the tests came back, she wanted to believe it was real."

"Why would anyone even *attempt* a hoax like that?" It's a question that's bothered me all along.

"Fame. Money." He ticks them off on his fingers. "Lots of reasons."

"I haven't seen any money, and the fame sucks."

Art snorts in agreement, as Walter nods earnestly. "So I decided to help her redirect PATROL and figure out the real secret to our time jump. And it worked!"

I have so many issues with what Walter just said I'm not sure where to start. Best to begin with the most unlikely claim. "You figured out why our plane traveled through time?"

"Not *me*." He presses his hands to his chest. "But I helped. By proving absolutely that we had done it and providing the coordinates where it happened. So now, all we have to do is fly through the same portal and we'll be back in 1995."

"Is that what you're doing tonight? Flying through the portal?"

"Yes! I have a plane ready."

I blink. I didn't actually expect him to say that. "Haven't thousands of planes flown through the same place since 1995?"

"They *have*," Art says. "And once we landed here, the FAA sent multiple drones along the exact same flight plan as Flight 237 to ensure there wasn't anything like a portal before they let any commercial airlines fly it."

I elbow Art and raise my eyebrows in a clear *chill out* signal. He's thrumming with so much energy I half expect him to let out a sonic boom, and I'm afraid he'll shut Walter down before I get the rest of the story.

"That's what's so brilliant about Dr. Greaves and Dr. Rozanov's discovery. The portal *moves*," Walter says triumphantly. "That's why no other planes have jumped through it for the past twenty-five years!"

I'm about to ask why they're so sure this portal will automatically send us back to 1995, since a moving portal seems just as likely to change destinations, but Walter isn't finished.

"Dr. Rozanov—he's the math and physics genius—has carefully calculated its location for tonight. It will open at Lambert Field for two hours, and he believes it's our last opportunity for two *years*, so we have to go for it."

"What kind of plane?" Art asks suspiciously, although toned down quite a bit. "Because I know you haven't been recertified for commercial airlines, so I'm sure you're not taking *off* from Lambert, and you can't just fly any plane over the main airport without IFR clearance."

Welcome back, plane groupie.

"I'll be careful. Although"—Walter's mouth twists—"the current coordinates are a bit tricky."

"You'll be *careful*?" Art bounces on his toes, gesturing wildly with his arms. He just can't help himself. "You'll be caught is what will happen. And then you'll never fly again. They'll take away all of your certificates and possibly send you to jail for falsifying your flight plan—assuming you plan to make one."

Art's so fixated on aviation details he seems to have completely missed Walter's final, disturbing words. I have to get clarification. "Tricky how?"

"The portal's at a low altitude, very close to a control tower. But it was built in 1997, so it won't be there once we go through. It'll be fine."

Art and I exchange a look of dawning horror. I take the lead. "Are you saying you'll be flying *at* the control tower?"

Walter shrugs. "Like I said, it won't matter because the plane will go through the portal before the tower, which didn't exist in 1995. It'll disappear."

"But what if it doesn't?" It's really hard to keep my voice calm, but I don't want to spook him. "What if the portal isn't there and you hit the tower? There are people in there. It'll kill them. And you!"

I just thought PATROL was made up of a bunch of conspiracy theorists, but maybe now that they can't discredit us any other way, they've decided Walter is the perfect Flight 237 scapegoat.

"Don't worry, Jenny." Walter pats my arm. "It's going to be fine."

"It's not, Walter. And you wanted us to come with you?" Art looks genuinely freaked. "Don't do this."

"I have to. I need to set things right." Walter starts turning toward his car, but looks back. "It only seemed right to invite you. The other passengers deserve the chance to go back too. Not just me." He places his palm earnestly against his heart. "Or the doctors."

Art stills, his energy finally channeled. "They're going with you?"

I'm equally astonished. At the very least, they aren't sending Walter on a suicide mission.

"Of course they're coming," Walter says. "We'll prove their theory about the portal, and then we'll come back for everyone."

Is it possible Dr. Greaves and Dr. Rozanov truly believe they've found a portal to the past? It's hard to wrap my mind around it, considering how they called our whole reappearance into question. But then, that group has been a mess of contradictions from the moment they formed. Even if they have bought into their own delusions, they're putting other people at risk, and they're going about it the wrong way.

I'm not sure reason will get through to Walter, but I have to try. "Is this the safest way to test the portal? What about a . . . drone or something? Then—*just in case they've miscalculated*—you won't endanger yourself or anyone else."

Walter backs away. "My life is already ruined. And I have no reason to stay here anyway."

I don't want to let Walter go, but if we don't, will Dr. Greaves and Dr. Rozanov come up with some other dangerous scheme? I think we have to see this through. I realize what I need to do.

He's half inside his car when I wedge myself into the door. "Walter, please. Where are you meeting them? I know Art doesn't believe you"—I glance back at Art and gulp—"but *I* want a chance to fix everything."

It's due to the fact my definition of *fixing things* is different from Walter's that I'm able to come across as sincere. He studies me for several moments before nodding. "Spirit of St. Louis Airport, twenty-two hundred hours."

I back away from the car and watch him drive off.

Art joins me. He has his phone open to the voice memo app. "I got everything. Now what?"

"Now you call Agent Klein and tell her to get over to Spirit of St. Louis Airport by ten o'clock. She has a plane to stop."

CHAPTER FORTY-THREE

Agent Klein promises to call both me and Art once she confirms our information and orders us not to go anywhere near there ourselves so we don't get caught in the fallout. As much as I really want to see her stop them, if I don't go home, I'll be grounded indefinitely. I already disappeared once today; I don't need to worry my parents again.

When I get home, it's only eight thirty—ninety minutes until the plane is scheduled to take off. I wonder how long I'll have to wait. They're sure to arrive at the airport early for pre-flight stuff, right? It can't take that long for the FBI to apprehend them.

I call a quick hello to my parents and run up to my room. That's when the what-ifs start to bombard me. What if Walter lied to me about where they were meeting? What if they take off from somewhere else? What if the FBI or the FAA or whoever else gets involved can't stop them in time and they crash into that tower and kill everyone inside? Did we make the wrong choice letting Walter go? Should I have followed him?

To distract myself from the worry, I retrieve my phone from where I stuffed it under the mattress and power it up. It seems so long ago that I put it there, so angry over the pain it caused me. But now I realize it isn't the phone's fault. It was Ashling and Greta who treated my personal life like it was open for public consumption. Yes, a phone was likely used to take the picture, and online news outlets spread the story to a wide audience and allowed people to comment on it. But I'm just as much to blame in the whole situation, kissing Dylan in a public place. I knew better. I knew Greta was out there, even if I didn't anticipate she'd have eyes on me that night. I should've been more careful, and I shouldn't have put so much of it on Dylan. After facing the possibility of a world without Dylan, I can't believe I shut him out. Who cares what people say about us? It's rare to find someone who really gets you the way he gets me.

I unblock his number. I wonder if he could tell? My last text to him is still sitting there, telling him we can't be together. Even worse, that it was a mistake to give him my first kiss. News flash, Jenny: don't hit Send in the middle of a meltdown. I open a new text window, but my thumbs hover over the keypad, unmoving. I don't know what to say to him, how to apologize. I don't think I *can* apologize in a text. That's how I messed things up in the first place. I have to fix it in person.

My phone dings with an incoming message. I switch over. It's from Art—the audio file. Yes! Wait, that's not audio. It's an image. I zoom in. It's Agent Klein guiding Dr. Greaves into the back of a dark sedan. Thank God they got there in time! Also, so much for keeping *Art* away from the airport. He must have been just as worried as me and decided to go anyway, just to be sure they didn't take off. The picture is solid gold.

Me: How did you get this??!! I owe you! 😘

Oops. That was supposed to be a smiley emoji. I start typing a retraction, but Art's reply comes before I can send it.

Art: Whoa, Nellie. Thought you were into that Dylan guy?

At least it's obvious he didn't think I meant anything by the emoji. I clearly can't be trusted with texting.

Me: Don't worry, I am. Thumb slip. Gotta go write!

I grab my laptop and start the audio file playing, typing and listening as I go. Shortly after I start, Agent Klein calls to confirm what Art's picture already told me—that she's taken Walter, Dr. Rozanov, and Dr. Greaves in for questioning. She doesn't have time to answer any clarifying questions; she just wanted to reassure me she'd taken care of it. But it's enough. An hour later, I have a solid story. The first issue of the *Parkwood Press* goes live Wednesday. I think there's still time to get this in there. But I have to clear it with Mrs. Vega, and I don't want to wait until school tomorrow.

I scroll through my contacts and find her number, then hit Call. She answers after three rings. "Hello?" she says in a groggy voice.

Only then do I realize it's ten o'clock. Oops. Guess she's one of those early-to-bed kind of people.

"Um, hi, Mrs. Vega, it's Jenny Waters."

"Jenny?" She clears her throat. "What's going on? Are you okay?"

I guess that's the logical question when a student calls late at night.

"I'm better than okay. I just uncovered the most amazing

story." And I spill it all to her. "So can we get it in this week's issue of the *Parkwood Press*?"

There's a long pause on the other end of the phone. "Hold on, Jenny. I'm going to get my laptop, but go ahead and email it to me."

"Okay." Was that a *yes*? Or an *I need to read it and make sure it's good enough before I say yes*?

I won't know if I continue to sit here, staring at *my* laptop. I log into my email and send the file to Mrs. Vega, switching the phone to speaker so I'll hear her when she comes back on.

"I'm back," she says. "Just give me a minute to read through this."

I sit there, biting my thumbnail, *listening* to her reading it, humming and saying "oh my" and "wow."

"You can back this all up?"

"I have an audio file of the conversation," I confirm.

"Good." There's an interminable silence while she continues reading, then finally, "This is fantastic, Jenny!"

"Really?" I mean, I felt like it was good, but the affirmation from Mrs. Vega means everything.

"Yes, but I don't think it belongs in the *Parkwood Press*."

My heart drops all the way down into my stomach. "What? Why not?"

"Because this is breaking news. Do you mind if I send this to my friend at the *Post-Dispatch*?"

"Do I *mind*?"

Mrs. Vega's laughter bubbles out of the phone. "I assume that means I can forward it on."

"Yes! Now! Yesterday!"

"I'll let you know what he says. I don't know that he'll just run your story verbatim, but I could see him using parts of it. Try to get some sleep, all right?"

Sleep? Like that's happening, when my words could be in the *Post-Dispatch*! But, sure, whatever. "Okay, Mrs. Vega."

I hang up the phone and stare from my laptop to my phone, these magical pieces of technology that allowed me to write and file a story so quickly. And now it's winging its way to an editor at the *Post-Dispatch* via email, where he could be reading it, right now.

Um, no, I'm not sleeping anytime soon.

I run out and tell Mom and Dad about the possible *Post-Dispatch* story, forgetting that in my eagerness to get to work, I didn't fill them in on Walter and PATROL when I came home. They're a bit stunned Walter tried to get me to join him on the plane, and I can tell they're worried about me wanting to do anything to go back to the past. It takes a few minutes to calm them down, along with many reminders I didn't join his ill-fated mission. Once we get past all that, they're appropriately excited and give me the same advice as Mrs. Vega—go to bed and see what happens in the morning. How am I supposed to sleep? This is the biggest story of my life!

Well, actually, I guess the biggest story of my life was skipping twenty-five years, but that just happened *to* me. This is a story I'm breaking.

I return to my room and stare at my email window, willing a new message to pop up from Mrs. Vega, letting me know whether her friend plans to use my story, but nothing comes at ten thirty, or ten forty-five, or eleven. Maybe *she* went to sleep. After all, I woke her up.

I want to talk to someone about this whole thing. Dylan immediately pops into my mind. He'd be excited for me, but I can't exactly call him up and be like, "Hey, sorry I was such a jerk earlier, but here's some good news on my end!" I've already been way too selfish in this barely off-the-ground relationship.

Chloe would be all over it, but what if it doesn't happen? That would be embarrassing, to tell her I'm getting a story in the *Post-Dispatch* and have it not pan out.

I flop onto my bed, the laptop open beside me. I guess I could tell Art, but I actually am sort of exhausted.

After checking my email one last time, I close the laptop and curl onto my side, willing sleep to find me. Surprisingly, it does.

CHAPTER FORTY-FOUR

As soon as I wake up the next morning, I reach for my laptop. There's an email from Mrs. Vega from five thirty a.m.

Good news, Jenny!

It turns out the *Post-Dispatch* had already been investigating PATROL, and were concerned by their silence since the Flight 237 news conference. My friend had interviewed several dissatisfied PATROL members about the group's disbandment but hadn't been able to obtain comments from Dr. Greaves or Dr. Rozanov or figure out their next step. You provided the missing piece. He fact-checked the information from your story and included it in his, with your account of last night as a sidebar. Here's the link.

There's a good chance the wires will pick it up too.

Congratulations!
Marianne Vega

I click on the link. My breath sticks. There it is.

ON PATROL: THE TRUE HOAX OF FLIGHT 237

The byline says, "By Kevin Zugman, St. Louis Post-Dispatch." Obviously that's Mrs. Vega's friend.

Directly underneath is the photo Art took of Agent Klein and Dr. Greaves. I laugh at the fact he got a newspaper credit before me.

The story is fantastic. Like Mrs. Vega said, Mr. Zugman had clearly already been working on this. He has quotes from the senator and school board member who were part of PATROL. Apparently they received a vague email from Dr. Greaves yesterday saying PATROL would be pursuing a new mission following the passengers' conclusive test results, but Mr. Zugman couldn't reach Dr. Greaves for comment. Then, right there in the paper, it says this:

> Thanks to the assistance of Flight 237 passenger and
> *Parkwood Press* co–editor in chief Jennifer Waters, the
> *Post-Dispatch* discovered the new, diverging mission of
> the founding scientists. Here is Waters's account, with fact
> corroboration by *Post-Dispatch* staff.

And there it is—my story! In an actual, daily newspaper. I squeal and bounce on my bed. I wrap my arms around the laptop, which is totally awkward, but who cares?

I skim the rest of the story. It's all there, everything Walter told us about Dr. Greaves and Dr. Rozanov, confirmed by Agent Klein. They had a copy of their real, unfiled flight plan with them, the path heading straight for the Lambert control tower, but they also weren't shy about confessing once they were in custody. They actually requested that the FBI send a drone through the portal "before it closed and moved again," because, they insisted, they'd solved the mystery of Flight 237 and the government had a duty to validate it. This appears to confirm Dr. Greaves and Dr. Rozanov *did* believe there was a portal and planned to go through it with Walter. However, because they went rogue and were willing to endanger the lives of everyone in the control tower to test their theory, there will still be charges brought against them and, unfortunately, poor, deceived Walter.

I pull out my phone and find the article there. Because now that it's real, I'm sharing it. I send it to Art, Chloe, and Madison, then Bradley and Kelly, and post it on my social media accounts (even though they reach mostly the same people). I really want to share it with Dylan, too, but I still feel it'll be better to see him in person.

I can't believe people all over the city and probably beyond, perhaps even in New York, are reading my story.

"I love technology!" I flop backward.

Mom rushes into my room. "Jenny?"

I sit up, brandishing the phone. "It's here! My story! Did you read it?"

Mom drops the spatula she's carrying to her side. "I did. It's wonderful. We've actually been getting calls all morning."

My heart thumps. "Calls?"

She nods. "TV. Radio. They all want to talk to you about

uncovering the truth behind PATROL. Agent Klein has already made a statement. So have members of PATROL who want to distance themselves."

I set down the phone and grimace. It's buzzing with notifications, probably from the texts I just sent, but also maybe from Greta Barren or other reporters like her. "I'm not ready for that. What if they still want to talk about"—I don't want to discuss Dylan with Mom—"stuff besides PATROL?"

Mom taps the spatula against her apron. "You don't have to talk to them. Let Agent Klein deal with them. Or Art."

"Good idea." I pull up a text to Art—he did reply, saying he'd already seen the story and has been getting calls. I tell him I've done my part and now he's the spokesperson. "I hope he doesn't tell someone off on live TV." I focus on Mom. "I'm also not looking forward to everything else I have to deal with at school, though. Yesterday it was like I was some Disney princess who flashed the crowd at Mardi Gras." Mom gives me a watch-yourself look. Yeah, that probably wasn't the best analogy to use with her. "Sorry."

Mom shakes her head. "No. It's a different world than when you were in high school before. But you've made friends, right?"

Dylan's face flashes immediately to mind, even before Chloe and Madison, and I wonder if I've made the right call, waiting to talk to him in person.

"What is it?" Mom asks.

If I bring up Dylan, Mom will oversimplify it all, tell me he'll forgive me with a straightforward apology. So I wimp out and go with the other topic we've discussed ad nauseam. "Angie. I told her we couldn't be friends anymore."

Mom purses her lips and raises one eyebrow, like she knows I was thinking about someone else. Then she sinks onto my bed. "I believe we already had this conversation. You and Angie have been friends for years. No matter what you said, she'll forgive you. Just like I knew you would forgive her."

Despite the fact I brought up Angie to avoid the Dylan topic, Mom's words release some of my tension. There was a bit of me worried about Angie, even after everything we've been through, but Mom's right. Angie will forgive me. We won't be what we were before, but we can be *something*.

"And as for your *other* friend"—I appreciate how Mom's respecting my choice not to discuss Dylan—"I'm sure the circumstances will merit some grace. Now." Mom stands. "I was just starting some French toast. So how about you eat some breakfast, and I bet things will look better."

Because why wouldn't things look better after goodness smothered in butter and syrup?

I spot the boy in question ahead of me after my second class, and I run to catch up. "Dylan!"

He turns toward me, his eyebrows raised. "Oh. You're talking to me?"

Now that he's in front of me, I realize I should have planned out what to say during that time I was deliberating over whether to text him or not. I'll have to wing it. "I'm so sorry. I was really messed up yesterday. I shouldn't have blamed you for what JoJo did."

He stiffens. "I'm not responsible for my sister's actions. That picture hurt me too, you know."

I wince. "I know," I say quietly.

"Not only that, but apparently you went on some adventure with Art last night and didn't even feel the need to call me after Walter invited you onto his hijacked airplane. As far as I know, you were ready to zip on back to 1995, so I think you're right."

It takes me a moment to process everything he just said. Yesterday flashes through my mind from Dylan's point of view. He woke up to that awful picture, tried to tell me about it. I ran away from him, refused to answer his calls or texts, and then sent him that awful message:

I can't be with you. It was a mistake to give you my first kiss. Please don't text me again.

Oh!

No! No, I'm not right! The text was the mistake! I want to scream, but it's like the words are strangled in my throat. They refuse to come out of my mouth.

He studies me with an inscrutable expression. "It's not a good idea for us to be together."

He walks away, and I want to grab his T-shirt and hang on until he listens to a thousand more *I'm sorry*s, but I'm not even sure how to say them. I've never seen Dylan so somber. I intended to hurt him with those words, to push him away, but I never imagined how my actions the rest of the day would compound them. I forgot that he feels threatened by Art, even though I know it's completely unfounded. He obviously saw the story, with my words and Art's picture, and put a completely different interpretation on it. I was so convinced I needed to apologize in person, and I screwed it all up even more.

I move on to class, where the stares I get are more respectful today, but they only tangentially have to do with my story. They're all clamoring to talk about the crazy PATROL people who could have crashed into the Lambert control tower last night, although a few wish the FBI *had* sent up a drone just to see if they were right about the portal. (I'd also feel better if the FBI had closed that loop.) It's bigger than the kiss, which is what I hoped for, but it no longer matters now that Dylan wants nothing to do with me.

Chloe catches up to me before journalism and nudges my shoulder. "That article was amazing! How on earth did you snag it?"

For the first time since I arrived at school, the glow from this morning returns, overtaking my heartbreak over Dylan. "Mrs. Vega arranged it, with her friend who works there."

"Ashling's gonna die!"

I set my jaw. "Oh, she so is."

Chloe tilts her head at my fierceness. With everything that happened yesterday, I didn't have a chance to fill her in on Ashling's role in the kiss story.

As soon as we enter class, Mrs. Vega pushes away from her desk and applauds. "Jenny. In all my years, I've never had a student take that sort of initiative. You saw the opportunity for a story, you went after it, and you followed it up with excellent writing. Well done."

I duck my head, smiling at my chest. "Thank you, Mrs. Vega. So much. I couldn't have done it without your support."

She smiles. "All I did was pass along a well-researched, well-written piece to a contact. He was grateful for the scoop."

Ashling glares from her seat at the table, and my lips strain from the effort not to smirk triumphantly.

"And I'm so looking forward to your series on your friends from the support group," Mrs. Vega says.

"*I'd* rather read about Jenny and Dylan Graham," Ashling says. "They appeared to be getting on so well, making out at a public movie."

News flash, Ashling: if you dish it out, you'd better be ready to choke it down yourself. "You should know, Ashling, since you took the photo and wrote that inventive piece your godmother slapped her name on."

Ashling inhales, her cheeks going white.

Mrs. Vega's smile droops into a thin line. "Is that true, Ashling?"

Ashling looks wildly around the table, avoiding Mrs. Vega. "I—I—Jenny has no idea what she's talking about."

Mrs. Vega frowns. "It's a very serious allegation, Jenny."

I meet her gaze. "I wouldn't make it if I didn't believe it, but let's consider the evidence. First, Ashling's been trying to discredit me from the moment I arrived, with constant digs about how clueless I am in this century." I hold up fingers as I list each point. "Second, the person who told Ashling about my date with Dylan already confessed. And third, Greta Barren is Ashling's godmother, so that solves the mystery as to why Greta would be willing to hold the story until Monday morning, when it could do the most damage to me. I bet if you check Ashling's phone the picture's on there."

Ashling dives for her backpack, but Chloe beats her to it.

"You have no right to confiscate my phone!" Ashling says.

"That remains to be seen." Mrs. Vega takes the backpack from Chloe and starts toward the door. "Come on, Ashling. We'll go see what the principal has to say. Because if one of my editors in chief violated our school's honor code, that's definitely my business. The rest of you, please continue working on the next issue."

I suddenly realize there's another way I can get through to Dylan.

"Mrs. Vega," I call after her. "If I have a story for you later today, can we still get it approved for the issue tomorrow?"

"Sure," she says as she nudges Ashling out the door.

Chloe leans in. "What are you up to?"

"I messed things up with Dylan. I need to fix it."

"With a story in the *Press*?"

I nod. "With *my* story."

CHAPTER FORTY-FIVE

After Mom drops me off at the curb the next morning, I park myself at the bench where Dylan asked me out barely a week ago and wait. For the third day in a row, I am the main topic of conversation, and this time, it's my own fault. I've already received texts from several classmates who've read my article, which went live early this morning, but there isn't one from Dylan. Either he hasn't read my story yet, or he's still angry.

I don't blame him if he is, but I had to try. Because I failed at knowing how to fix things two nights ago, when I should have picked up the phone and called to apologize for disparaging our kiss even more than Greta Barren already had. Then I failed at expressing myself when he was standing right in front of me. Which was really sucky of me, considering when he apologized to me, he gave me the most amazing speech ever. I practically have it memorized.

So putting my apology out there, where the entire population of Parkwood High School—and anyone else who cares to—can read it, seemed like my only hope of reaching him. To avoid engaging with the students passing me by, I pull it up to read once again.

SIDETRACK
TO THE FUTURE

By Jenny Waters

As co–editor in chief of the Parkwood Press, it's my
prerogative to occasionally take over the opinion column.

Today's opinion: viral media sucks.

Counter-opinion: unless you control the story.

I would propose, however, that it's very difficult to
control the story in today's news environment, a lesson I've
learned rather quickly in the past two days.

Ever since I landed in the twenty-first century, people
have been clamoring for my story, and you, Parkwood
students, will be the first to read it.

One of my favorite movies is *Back to the Future.* It came
out in 1985, when I was seven. For the unfamiliar, the film
takes the main character back thirty years in a time machine,
where he meets his parents as teenagers and his mother
awkwardly pursues him. As much as I love this movie, it was
never my dream to jump into a time machine and explore the
lives of my family members at different ages.

Fast-forward to Aug. 2, 1995. I boarded a plane and–
bam–three hours later I landed in a completely different
century. Time travel achieved! Cool, right?

Not cool. You want to know what it was like for the
passengers and crew of Flight 237? In the coming weeks,
with the permission of my fellow passengers, I will be telling
some of those stories, but for now I will share mine.

I stepped off the plane to a world full of baffling

technology and terminology I didn't understand. Everyone in my family was twenty-five years older—or dead. All my friends were adults, many with kids my age. Bonus: my best friend had written a bestselling book about me.

Cue PATROL: People Assuring Time Relativity, Order, and Legitimacy. Honestly, it's hard enough trying to adjust to all these life changes without a conspiracy group shouting to the world that you're an alien pod person or clone. So it's no wonder I had some issues with my relationships.

I would really prefer to keep my love life private, but considering the circumstances, the whole world already knows about my involvement with Dylan Graham. Yes, he's the son of my best friend and former boyfriend. Yes, we kissed. Yes, it was my first kiss.

No, I don't regret it. Not even after Greta Barren published it for the world to see.

The other night I was offered the implausible choice to return to 1995 or stay here, today. Even though I knew I couldn't play any part in PATROL's dangerous plan, which put lives at risk, I'll admit I considered the question of going back. But while I could regain so much that I've lost by returning, I'd lose a lot too.

I can't imagine a world without Dylan Graham. I don't want to, and I don't care what the world has to say about it. He's the best thing that's happened to me in a long time. So while I never dreamed of traveling to the future, I'm grateful it happened.

Will we ever know how or why we left the lives we knew behind? I'm hopeful, although I've accepted the fact it might remain a mystery. I do not presume to have control over this developing story, but I grant permission to share it wherever anyone wishes. As a result, I suspect it will stay confined to the *Parkwood Press*.

Stay tuned for more Flight 237 passenger and crew stories. We're taking our stories back.

"Jenny?" I look up from my phone, surprised to find JoJo standing before me. Her hair is somehow duller, perhaps because she has the purple strands pulled back in a low ponytail, the ends straggling over her shoulder. She shifts in front of my bench, her eyes cast at the pavement.

I straighten. "JoJo."

She tugs on her pony. "Listen. I just wanted to say I'm really sorry about calling Ashling. It was a jerk move. I didn't think through what she would do with the information, and I'm just . . . I'm sorry, and I hope things work out with you and Dylan."

"You do?" I've never seen her so subdued.

She nods. "I really do." She twirls a ring around her pointer finger. "It was really hard, growing up with them reminding me all the time that I'd been named after this perfect girl"—I wince—"and then you rose from the dead like the freaking Chosen One, and there was this part of me that was afraid you'd take your rightful place as the Jennifer in our family."

Wow. That's just . . . a lot. "I'm glad you told me that."

She sighs. "But what you wrote about Dylan—"

"Are you apologizing?" Dylan comes up beside JoJo.

My heart thumps as I hop to my feet, missing JoJo's response. She murmurs something unintelligible and scurries away. I watch her go with mixed feelings. I'd like to hear what else she has to say, but then there's Dylan, definitely the most important Graham.

"I'm ready to listen to you now." Dylan crosses his arms over his T-shirt, which crumples but not before I glimpse it.

Without considering what I'm doing, I grab his forearm and try to pry his arms open. "Is that a *Back to the Future* T-shirt?"

"Yeah, Dylan! She's all over you!" Drew punches Dylan's shoulder as he passes.

Dylan rolls his eyes. "Shut it, Drew." With his arms still firmly in place, he nods toward an alcove by the library door. "Let's go somewhere more private."

We're getting close to the bell, but I skipped out on school Monday and came late yesterday, so what's the difference? New Jenny has already set a precedent for delinquent behavior.

I give up on trying to see his T-shirt, but I can see Michael J. Fox peeking over his arms, and it gives me hope that my article worked.

"So?" he says.

I'm prepared this time. "I'm sorry. For bailing on you when you really are the best thing that's happened to me in this century. For saying our kiss was a mistake when it was better than any kiss from an overly muscled model on a romance novel cover."

He tries not to smile, but I can totally see it about to burst free.

Encouraged, I continue, "For not considering your feelings when that story hit or calling to talk to you about everything else that was going on with me that day. Before anyone else, you cared enough to get to know me outside of Flight 237 and that stupid book, and I screwed things up. When Walter suggested

I could go back to 1995, all I could think was that if PATROL's crackpot theory was even a possibility, that might screw up the whole space–time continuum so you wouldn't exist, and that would be the worst outcome ever. I just want to be here, with you. And I don't care what anyone says about it."

He considers me, fully straight-faced now, his arms still crossed over his shirt. "And you're not going to freak out if someone follows us and posts a picture online again?"

They found the photo on Ashling's phone, and she confessed everything after that. Mrs. Vega said Ashling seemed genuinely sorry, that she got caught up in her frustration over sharing the editor in chief position she'd worked so hard to achieve, as well as her eagerness to please Greta. Either way, it's one less person to follow us. But his question is so much more loaded than that. He wants to know if I'm willing to accept life here and now, where people might continue to document our lives—and not just reporters. I'm a semi-public figure thanks to the unexpected turn my life took. I don't like it, but it's how things are.

"No. In fact . . ." I step forward, ready to lay one on him right now. I'm sure there are several phones trained on us.

Dylan throws up his arms and retreats. "What, here?"

I point at his shirt, where Michael J. Fox stands beside a DeLorean. "You *are* wearing a *Back to the Future* shirt!"

He shrugs, grinning. "It was the least I could do. Since you basically wrote me a love letter. And I already had it. I'm a fan of time travel, you know."

I purse my lips, pondering the odds of him actually having an eighties-themed T-shirt lying around. His shirts do tend toward movies, so I guess it's possible.

"It wasn't a love letter," I mutter.

"Hey, now. Don't belittle my love letter. 'No, I don't regret it' are the most romantic words I've ever read." He eyes me meaningfully. "I'm going to print it out and press it between the pages of a book."

I almost believe him. "*The Hunger Games?*"

He presses his lips together and shrugs. "It would be appropriate."

The bell rings, warning us class starts in six minutes.

Dylan holds out his hand. "Shall we?"

I raise an eyebrow. "You really aren't going to kiss me and make this official?"

He glances up at the school entrance, where several classmates and even a couple of teachers are watching us. "Naw." He leans down and brushes his lips against my temple. "The best things are worth waiting for. Like you."

I tug him closer as we walk toward the curious onlookers. "You're right. But for me, it was just a short delay."

A NOTE FROM THE AUTHOR

When I wrote *Your Life Has Been Delayed*, I couldn't possibly imagine the pandemic that would upend all of our lives. I decided to move forward with my original vision of Jenny's arrival in present day—a world in which the most unbelievable thing to happen was a plane landing from a different century! I hope the read provided an enjoyable and thought-provoking escape.

—Michelle I. Mason

ACKNOWLEDGMENTS

You just read my book! That is so amazing. Whether you loved it or hated it, I'm incredibly grateful you picked up my story. My journey to publication has been a long one, but so worth every rejection and shelved manuscript that led to this point.

Thank you, God, for giving me all the words and for granting me patience over the past ten years. Many times along the way your answers were "no" and "wait," and I know now that's because the timing wasn't yet right. It's finally here!

So many wonderful people made this book possible. Thank you to:

Elizabeth Bewley, fabulous agent and career counselor. I slogged for seven years in the query trenches to find the right partner for my publishing career, and you have been the perfect fit. You immediately understood my characters and knew where to find the best home for them, and you never tire of answering my endless questions. You're a bona fide dream maker! Thank you also to everyone else at Sterling Lord Literistic.

Allison Moore, editor extraordinaire, for loving Jenny and challenging me to make this book so much stronger, from questioning my more creative metaphors to helping me finally nail down that ending. This book would not be what it is without you, and I am forever grateful!

The rest of the Bloomsbury team: Donna Mark, Diane Aronson, Nicholas Church, Lex Higbee, Ksenia Winnicki, Phoebe Dyer, Faye Bi, Erica Barmash, Beth Eller, Jasmine Miranda, Cindy Loh, Mary Kate Castellani, and the amazing sales team! For my gorgeous physical book, cover designer Danielle Ceccolini and artist Rosemary Valero-O'Connell and interior designer Yelena Safronova. I wish it were Jenny's version of the world so I could give you all a great big hug (unless you aren't huggers and then a nice handshake).

Legendary commercial pilot Jeff Steig, who patiently educated me in plane and airport terminology, explaining how things worked in both 1995 and 2018 (when I first drafted the book). My conversations and emails with Jeff framed the idea for how the first chapter of this book would play out and guided my subsequent research. Any mistakes or misrepresentation of aviation facts are my own.

My critique partners and readers!!! Kip Wilson, you read basically everything I write, and our monthly email check-ins keep me sane. Amy Trueblood, Carla Cullen, and Richelle Morgan, you not only read this book, but have read multiple other manuscripts and been an encouragement to me for many years along this journey. Kristin Smith and Beth Ellyn Summer, aka Most Amazing Pitch Wars Mentors Ever, thank you for turning around and providing feedback on this book so soon after overhauling my 2017 Pitch Wars book and becoming such wonderful friends since. And thank you to Julie Christensen, Shelly Steig,

Kyrie McCauley, and KC Karr for reading this book at various stages.

Krista Van Dolzer, my original mentor from The Writer's Voice: your advice and friendship over the years have been invaluable. #teamkristaforever

My local writer friends/lunch buddies, Jamie Krakover and Julia Maranan: thank you for talking through querying and plot bunnies and everything else. Hey, you two should probably meet at some point.

The entire Pitch Wars 2017 class: thanks for talking me down when that TV show was announced and encouraging me to hurry up and query this book. Best advice ever! Also for reading my query and helping me get it ready. I'm also privileged to be part of an amazing debut group of middle grade and young adult authors, #the21ders. I would have no idea what to do this debut year without all of you. I'm so grateful to be on this fantastic ride with you!

Every single nonwriter friend who has asked about my writing, prayed for my book to be published, squealed along with me, and otherwise supported me on this journey: I can't thank you all personally, so have some amazing homemade virtual brownies. I love each and every one of you. But a special shout-out to my own best friend since forever, Chrissy Stricker: you give entirely new meaning to the word "perseverance." Love you, my friend!

My family! To my dad, Ladd, for modeling what it means to do work that you love and my mom, Karen, who inspired my love of reading. To my brother, Christopher, for always coming when I call and being the coolest uncle ever. To my in-laws, Chuck and

Barb Mason, for all of your love and support. To my aunts, Mendi Baker and Robin Faszold, for encouraging and promoting me to everyone you know. To all of the Faszolds, Masons, Bakers, Hunters, Justices, Berrys, Ralls, Kelleys, and Rays. You're all the absolute best!

Luke and Anna: Your love for reading makes all of this worth it. I can't wait to share this book with you and am kind of glad it was delayed so that you're both pretty much old enough to read it now. Just, I'm sorry for the bird sex part.

Finally, Greg: I already dedicated this book to you, and what I said there was the truth. All the best moments in this century have happened with you, since we met in 2001. Thank you for always believing in my writing and encouraging me to follow my dream of publication. Now, as for that theme park, keep dreaming, honey . . .